The Constant Mistress

ANGELA LAMBERT

The Constant Mistress

HAMISH HAMILTON · LONDON

HAMISH HAMILTON LTD

Published by the Penguin Group
Penguin Books Ltd, 27 Wrights Lane, London w8 5tz, England
Penguin Books USA Inc., 375 Hudson Street, New York, New York 10014, USA
Penguin Books Australia Ltd, Ringwood, Victoria, Australia
Penguin Books Canada Ltd, 10 Alcorn Avenue, Toronto, Ontario, Canada m4v 3b2
Penguin Books (NZ) Ltd, 182–190 Wairau Road, Auckland 10, New Zealand

Penguin Books Ltd, Registered Offices: Harmondsworth, Middlesex, England

First published 1994

1 3 5 7 9 10 8 6 4 2

Filmset in Monophoto Garamond
Printed in England by Clays Ltd, St Ives plc

A CIP catalogue record for this book is available from the British Library
ISBN 0-241-13452-8

To Jenny Towdrow
my dear friend and 'almost-twin',
and in memory of Jill Tweedie

O Rose, thou art sick!
  The invisible worm
That flies in the night,
  In the howling storm,

Has found out thy bed
  Of crimson joy:
And his dark secret love
  Doth thy life destroy.

William Blake, *The Sick Rose*

Contents

Dramatis Personae

The ages are those of the characters in early 1992, when the book opens.

LAURA KING, aged 44

CONSTANCE LIDDELL née KING Laura's only sister, 50

GORDON SHUTTLEWORTH ('THE POSSLEQUE'), Constance's live-in lover, 55

PAUL LIDDELL, Constance's ex-husband, Laura's ex-brother-in-law, 52

MAX, Laura's nephew, aged 31, married to DANI, a Polish girl, with a two-year-old son KASPAR

CORDELIA (CORDY), 29, and KATIE LIDDELL, 21, Laura's nieces

PAULA ELPHINSTONE, formerly KING, Laura's mother, 74

LEONARD ELPHINSTONE ('UNCLE LEONARD'), her second husband, 80

MRS RIPA, Laura's consultant in the liver department of a London hospital

CARMEN, Laura's Spanish cleaner

MARTHA, an American friend of Laura's

JENNY, Laura's friend

MADELEINE, Laura's friend, married with five children, 46

MICK (MIKEY) CHARLES, Constance's first boyfriend, 47

BETH CHARLES, Mick's second wife, 44

HUGO HAMMOND, Laura's first lover at university, 46

CONRAD PARSONS, Constance's first employer, later her lover, 68

I

Mrs Ripa

Laura King was forty-four when she was told that she had only about a year to live: two at the most. Until then she had taken for granted that half her adult life still lay ahead. Once she got past her fortieth birthday – the Big Four-O as people called it – she had come to terms with early middle age. She had achieved a certain confidence, holding herself in a way that suggested outer reserve and inner flamboyance, walking like a woman in the prime of life: not young any more, but not vulnerable either. The discovery that she was going to die so soon made her feel cheated. She flailed and struggled against the idea that the rest of her life had to be compressed into so short a space of time.

Her existence had provided lavish opportunities for love and work, and although she knew she was privileged, she had never felt particularly lucky, let alone humble. Laura took charge of her own future at an early age. When she was fifteen, for instance, she had suddenly insisted that everyone should stop calling her by her first name, which was Stella, and use her third one instead: Laura. Such was her determination that the new name was quickly adopted – not only by her friends but also her parents, her teachers and her sister Constance.

Constance was six years older and about to get married at the time, to a man she had met at Oxford, which meant changing her name to Mrs Paul Liddell. Her younger sister thought that sounded like a very good idea. Furthermore the Paul who was soon to become her brother-in-law also happened to have a

sister called Stella (a round-faced, pious girl with t
so it was easy to claim that being called Laura w
confusion. 'Two Stellas in one family is too many,
everyone firmly.

Few people care to dwell much on death, and it had
seriously crossed Laura's mind that – unless she were killed
car or plane crash – she would not live to reach three-score year
and ten. The idea of dying before she was fifty, and from an
illness she hadn't even heard of, seemed both unjust and
unlikely.

Her condition had first made itself known before Christmas. For
a few days she had felt extreme weakness and exhaustion; her face
looked pale and her pulse bounced faintly but very fast. This (which
Laura put down to stress and overwork) culminated in her fainting
twice in one day during a conference in New York at which she was
interpreting. Fortunately she was staying with her current lover
rather than in a hotel. Rafe's doctor had been summoned. He sped
to her side, lifted her eyelids, felt her pulse, took her blood pressure,
tested her haemoglobin level, and had her admitted to a private
hospital, where it was quickly discovered that she was suffering
from slow but severe internal bleeding. Laura was transfused with
two litres of blood through a vein in the crook of her arm. The
colour came back into her cheeks, her lassitude vanished, and she
had time to wonder why, aged fourty-four and impeccably
contracepted, she should have had a major haemorrhage.

She lay in bed for three days looking at the *New Yorker* and
the extravagant flowers which arrived daily from Rafe. (He
himself had been called away on business and could not visit
her.) When eventually she got home she had been referred to the
best liver unit in London.

'Could there be a mistake?' she asked her consultant, a sinewy,
bright-eyed Italian woman called Mrs Ripa. 'Perhaps you've
mixed up something milder with whatever it is you say I have –
hepatitis C – or even mistaken me for someone else? Could the
samples have been swapped accidentally?'

'Believe me, Miss King, I would not be telling you unless I were sure,' Mrs Ripa answered. 'I have discussed your case with my colleagues, and – as you know – we analysed two separate batches of blood samples as well as a PCR, a liver biopsy and antibody tests. I am afraid you definitely have cirrhosis due to hepatitis C. Because it is fairly rare, I sent the second sample to a senior colleague at another hospital; a world expert. He confirmed my diagnosis. I can't imagine how it had gone so far without your being seen earlier. You must be very stoical.'

'No, but I'm very busy,' Laura said. 'When I felt tired or unwell, I assumed it was due to the stress of work. And, anyway, I couldn't afford to take time off before Christmas.'

Mrs Ripa had convinced her that there was no possibility of a mistake in the diagnosis. She could have been incubating the virus for years – many people did, apparently, in a benign form. Invited to recall any childhood accidents, Laura remembered that at the age of nine or ten she had fallen into a ditch in Africa and swallowed a lot of brackish water. She'd developed jaundice but once it had cleared up nobody gave it another thought. She had needed blood transfusions twice in her life, apart from the recent incident in New York. Once, when she'd had a tonsillectomy at the age of about fourteen, and once – Laura hesitated – after an abortion.

'When was that?'

'Just over twelve years ago.'

Mrs Ripa noted the facts in her folder.

Laura wanted to say, Talk to me as an equal, as an intelligent professional woman like yourself. Treat me like a grown-up. She fell back on her fluency in Italian to cut through the patient–consultant formalities.

'*Voglio la verità*,' she urged. 'The *whole* truth.'

Mrs Ripa, practised at evaluating such requests, saw that she meant it. Normally she broke bad news to patients with a relative present to cushion the blow. Laura had insisted that she was capable of grasping the information by herself, and wanted to be told if she would probably live or probably die, and if the latter, *when*. Mrs Ripa generally gave people time to get used to the idea of their own imminent death, allowing the truth to sink in gradually. But she recognized in Laura a brave and kindred spirit, able to bear life's realities head-on. So drew a long breath, squared her shoulders and looked directly into the set face on the other side of her desk.

'Hepatitis C has invaded your liver,' she said. 'It is a virus which grows in liver cells, but it's much less infectious than Aids unless your blood enters someone else's blood stream. At worst, you have about a year to live. At best, two or even three, unless we arrange a liver transplant – which is something you should start considering now. You say you don't drink a lot of alcohol, and, frankly, I'm surprised that in your condition you have been able to tolerate it at all. From now on you must cut it out completely. You might have another haemorrhage at any moment, which could be fatal. On the plus side, one of the benign aspects of liver disease is that some patients feel well, sometimes exuberantly well, until almost the very end. You can carry on working, if you feel up to it, and lead a normal life. Try to limit contact sports.'

Laura flashed an unexpected smile. 'Does sex count as a contact sport?' she asked.

Mrs Ripa smiled back. 'Probably not. Unless you are *very* adventurous.'

She reflected that, as the disease took its course, Laura's libido was unlikely to prompt the desire for sex.

Laura declared with unexpected firmness, 'I *definitely* don't want a transplant. Out of the question. Nor will I change my mind.' To herself she thought, for the first of many times, *Because I deserve to die*.

The information Laura had been given was not as gloomy as the notes in her confidential file.

Diagnosis: cirrhosis due to hepatitis C. Source: ?blood transfusions aet.

4

14 and 32?? Patient is single woman with multiple sexual partners. Prognosis: v. poor. Refuses option of liver transplant and, given lack of dependants, is not a priority case. Action: monitor closely; offer counselling. Next appt: 1/12. Treatment: consult Prof MacI.

Laura's conscious mind – controlled, rational, considerate – had responded bravely and even humorously to the news. Good manners carry people through every crisis. She said please and thank-you to the laboratory technicians, smiled at the taxi driver and inquired about the children whose school photographs grinned from the dashboard of his cab.

When she got home, she was not ready to talk to anyone. Her finger did hover on the point of telephoning Desmond, her former neighbour. Desmond was gay; his partner had died of Aids not long ago. Desmond would understand. Then she thought, I can't burden him with me as well. She went down to the kitchen and was, as she thought, calmly making coffee when she leaned over the sink and threw up. There was a pain in her stomach as though she were about to walk into some crucial exam for which she was unprepared. Her heart was beating not only fast but oddly, and her breathing was rapid. She dried her mouth on a kitchen towel, went upstairs to the bathroom, and vomited again.

She ran a deep warm bath scented with oil taken from some luxury hotel and soaked away the smell of sick and fear. It was still only seven o'clock. She sat unseeing through the first hour of the evening's television, then took two sleeping pills and went to bed.

That night she dreamed of pursuit, as her unconscious mind howled its protest and disbelief; heard her own frantically pattering footsteps, and could neither turn aside to avoid what lay ahead, nor run fast enough to escape whatever it was that hastened stealthily behind. She kept waking with a thundering heart, the fear of death engulfing her.

The following morning she got up early and prepared breakfast. Later, lying in the bath again, she examined her long, naked body. It had darkened to deep apricot. She often sunbathed on the edge of hotel swimming pools or beside the sea and had assumed that, like the sleek, bronzed men among whom she spent her working life, she had a year-round tan. Now she understood that this discolouration, like the nosebleeds, was another symptom.

Thick blue veins threaded down the centre of her chest and branched out across her abdomen. They looked startlingly prominent. Her belly rose in a hard high curve above the surface of the water. A flat stomach had been one of the bonuses of childlessness. Over the course of the last year hers had swollen until now she might easily be in the fourth month of pregnancy. Some of the women waiting in the clinic had worn maternity dresses and looked heavily pregnant. Laura had simply assumed they *were* pregnant. Soon she would look pregnant, too. She frowned at the irony and unfairness of it.

After breakfast, while her cleaner hoovered and ironed, Laura sat in the double drawing-room at her desk beside the back window. It overlooked a tiny garden upon which cold January rain dripped and splattered. In order of priority, she must ring her sister and, she supposed, her mother in Miami. Next, the business calls. She was due to interpret at a conference in Rome starting on Monday; then she would telephone Brussels and Paris, to cancel her February bookings. She need not work again. She had collected all the rugs she was ever going to collect, bought all the clothes and make-up she was ever likely to need. She had enough money to see her through a year without income. Time to make a will: to dispose, not to acquire.

'Carmen!' she called. 'Will you bring me a coffee, and then go and work upstairs? I have to make some calls.'

Although Carmen's English was rudimentary, it was good enough to understand bad news. Carmen was morbidly enthralled by sickness, pain and grief.

Laura dialled her sister's number in Tunbridge Wells.

'Constance,' she said, her voice reed-thin. 'It's me.'

'Laura! Darling, what's happened? You sound dreadful!'

Laura had planned to break the news unemotionally but at the sound of her sister's instant, intuitive concern she broke down.

'I'm going to die,' she said. 'Oh, Constance, you know I had those tests repeated? Well, it's bad news. I went back yesterday.' Her voice shook and her breath came in gasps. 'I'm going to die – *soon* – oh, Coco, heavens, I can't believe it – I'm going to *die*.'

'Laura, *no*! Hold on, let me sit down. No, look, I'll come up right away. I was just about to go to the library – lucky you caught me – I'll cancel and drive up. Be with you in an hour. Bit more. Hang on for me. Oh Stell', sweetheart, this is awful!'

'Coco,' said Laura, reverting to her babyhood name for her big sister. 'Coco, don't come. *Don't*. I've got masses of calls to make: work and everything. People. Should I ring Mother?'

'Do you want me to? Oh *let* me come and be with you.'

No, Laura thought, my sister doesn't deserve this and I have no right to impose on her. She will try to look on the bright side, suggest a second opinion. Or she'll insist I move in with her to be looked after. She'll summon Mother from Miami. I don't want any of that. With an effort she spoke calmly and lucidly.

'*No*, Constance. *Listen*, dammit! It's not that bad. I've got another couple of years. I can go on working, if I want to. I can *even* make love, so long as it's not too vigorous.'

'Shouldn't you be in hospital?'

'Not yet. Eventually, I suppose.'

There was a pause.

'Laura. I do love you.'

A silence, a longer silence. Then Laura said, 'I've been a lousy sister to you – a really appalling sister – but I suppose I must love you too. I mean, sorry, you *know* I do. I always have, in spite of being so prickly. But I won't come and stay and I'd rather leave it a few days before I see you. While I get used to the idea. It takes time to sink in.'

7

Her voice dwindled. Constance's voice grew strong to compensate, and, very much the older sister, she said briskly, 'All right. Now can you explain to me *exactly* what it is you've got?'

Constance, Laura's only sibling, was fifty. She had three grown-up children and a partner whom she called the Possleque. The word meant something absurd like 'person of the opposite sex sharing living quarters equally'. It wasn't even true; their relationship was patently unequal, with Constance fetching and carrying and making much of the square-faced, dependable computer buff whom she had met a dozen years after her divorce. Laura didn't see why she couldn't call him her lover and be done with it, like the French with their admirably direct word *concubin*.

Women of Laura's generation were unique, the first women in history who could make love without needing the inducement of money or marriage. For Constance – a mere six years older – love and commitment were still essential. Constance had grown up in the Fifties, too early to avoid the ancestral burden of terror and guilt. She was among the last of the medievals; her sister was one of the first of the free.

Laura King had never been married, never had children, and only once been pregnant. That had ended in an enforced abortion just as she was getting used, even looking forward, to the idea of motherhood. The circumstances of the abortion had been so implacable that they precluded any second thoughts. The lost foetus had been perfect, they told her. She knew she *could* conceive a normal child; and although she had never again wanted to do so, the knowledge was obscurely comforting in the face of other women's dumb and triumphant fecundity. She and the man who had produced this child-who-was-not-to-be parted for ever. After an interval of grieving for them both, Laura put the past adamantly behind her.

Now, for the first time in years, she wished her father

8

had been around. She could have flung her news and herself against his rock-like, imperturbable figure. But he had died twelve years ago, and although his death had been violent, sudden and unnecessary, it had put an end to his lifelong disapproval of her 'moral laxity', as he uncompromisingly described it.

Her mother had married again. 'Uncle Leonard' had been a family friend for as long as Laura could remember. When his wife ('Auntie Janet') died at about the same time as Laura's father, the two couples contracted conveniently into one couple and Mrs King soon became Mrs Elphinstone. Her new husband had suggested that they should live in Miami, a paradise for senior citizens like themselves. So it must have turned out. Laura's mother rang every few weeks with news of her triumph in some bridge tournament or her improved golf handicap. She sounded exuberantly, indecently happy.

Yet Laura missed both her parents. When they were children, Constance had been Mummy's Little Helper and Laura had been Daddy's Girl. Who, now that he was dead, would give her advice? After her father's death she had changed, becoming colder and more calculating. As a result she was more successful but less lovable.

At six o'clock in the evening Laura telephoned her friend Martha, making an effort to keep her voice steady and light.

'Martha, hello, sweetheart! How are you? Am I interrupting? What sort of a week have you had?'

A shitty week. Thank God for the weekend.

'Any plans? What are you doing tonight?'

Martha planned to get pissed and watch a lousy movie on TV.

'Don't do that. Come over to me, we'll have a bite to eat and go out and see a good one instead.'

Great idea. Martha would pay for supper. On expenses – no problem.

'I'd actually rather eat at home. If I made something quick and simple like smoked salmon and scrambled eggs, would that suit you?'

Martha was on her way. She'd bring *Time Out* and a bottle of wine – hang on, she'd go take a look in the fridge.

'No wine for me, darling. I'm not allowed alcohol.' Laura's voice threatened to give way. She took a deep breath and went on, 'I'll explain when you get here.'

Not allowed *alcohol*? Why on earth?

'Tell you when I see you,' Laura said hastily. 'Bye!'

Over supper she gave Martha a modified version of the diagnosis, not wanting to lose control again, aware that each time she repeated the verdict it became more real, more of a death sentence. Martha urged her to try another specialist, a bigger hospital. There were people in the States who . . .

'The trouble with Americans is they don't believe in death,' Laura interrupted. 'You think all it takes is a different medic, bigger hospital, better research – the cure has to be somewhere. But what I've got is on the far side of science. I may have had the virus inside me, biding its time, ever since I was a kid of ten. It won't go away now.'

'OK. So if you can't deal with the virus, get rid of the rotten, stinking liver. Have yourself a new one. Get a transplant.'

'No,' Laura said flatly. 'I won't do that.'

'Why not? Tell me, you madwoman, why the hell *not*?'

'Because I don't deserve it. There aren't a lot of spare livers around, or surgeons that good. It should go to a better person than me. Someone whose children need them. I don't deserve it.'

'Are you *crazy*?' Martha asked. She leaned across and took Laura's hand. 'Listen . . .' she began.

Laura broke in before she could start again. 'We're going to be late for the film.'

They came back afterwards and sat opposite each other in deep wing chairs, each cradling a cup of hot chocolate.

'This is a first, anyway: no alcohol,' said Martha. 'At least you'll die sober. Oh, Laura, you're my *friend*. What am I going to do without you? I'm such a selfish bitch, darling. I'm sorry.'

'*Don't cry*, whatever you do,' said Laura.

'Don't be so bloody *British*. I'll cry if I want to. I need to cry. I'm crying.'

It was nearly midnight before they summoned a taxi. When the doorbell rang, they embraced. Martha lifted a tendril from Laura's cheek and brushed it back.

'I could always stay the night, if you need company.'

'No, I'm fine.' They hugged each other again.

When the sound of Martha's taxi had faded, Laura steeled herself to speak to her mother. It would be early evening, Happy Hour, in Miami. Best to reach her before she'd had too many cocktails.

Uncle Leonard answered the phone, all beamy transatlantic informality. It had not taken him long to assume the protective colouring. 'Hi Laura! How ya doing? Good, good! I'll go fetch your mother.'

She heard him call out, 'Honeybunch? It's your younger daughter!'

Her mother's voice came breathlessly down the phone: 'Sorry, dear, I was on the patio, fixing drinks. How are you?'

Laura's courage failed her. She had intended to give her mother the full diagnosis but the voice on the telephone was so distant, so absorbed in other people, strangers to Laura, that she merely said, 'Not too bad. Had some tests in hospital this week: looks as though I may have a liver problem. I've got to cut out drinking for a start.'

'Darling!' Her mother's voice was shocked. She lowered it to an appropriately confidential level. 'Laura, honey, you're not getting to be an *alcoholic*, are you?'

'Certainly *not*. Look, don't worry about me. I dare say I'll be fine.' There was a plea in the 'dare say', but her mother had never been a subtle woman.

'Do you want to come out *here* for a week? The weather's glorious. Miami's really something in January. It would be a tonic for you. Do you good to get away from the beastly English winter.'

'No, honestly Mother – I'm fine. Back to your guests! And don't worry about me, whatever Constance may tell you.'

Another plea. What Constance will tell you is that I'm dying, Mummy, long before my time, and I'm frightened. I need you to hold me, enfold me, make me safe, kiss it better.

'What do you mean, dear? You *are* drinking too much, aren't you?'

'No, Mother. Not now, not ever. Are you sure you can say the same?' Her mother giggled flirtatiously.

'Sometimes I'm a *bit* of a naughty girl, Leonard says! But at my age, you might as well enjoy yourself.'

Laura replaced the phone feeling like a child rejected in favour of the grown-ups. Yet what could that stranger Mrs Elphinstone, who no longer even shared her name, offer from three thousand miles away? What comfort could she have given, even if Laura had told her the truth?

Repeating her news half a dozen times had been like hammering in a stake. Now her heart hammered against her ribs, her breath hammered up through her throat. She was reminded of the time when her brother-in-law Paul had left Constance. Laura had been no use at all just when her sister, pitiful with anguish and helplessness, most needed support. Now, as then, her throat was so locked that she could scarcely eat. Her voice sounded strangled and breathless and it took all her will-power to control it. She had controlled it for her mother, who had noticed nothing. Constance had noticed.

Martha had noticed. Not her mother, busy having geriatric fun in Miami.

Laura prepared for bed. She could resist sleeping pills because she was schooled in self-discipline, but she wished she had a man to hold her. Not Rafe, not Jürgen and certainly not Bruno his predecessor, for she felt sure they would all shrink from illness and death. Who, then? There was only, had only ever been, one. Thinking of men, she eventually surrendered to sleep.

Laura made one all-embracing decision straight away: she would stop work rather than face pity or the knowledge that allowances were being made for her illness. But she had never spent much time on her own and could not imagine eking out her final months drifting through London's art galleries and museums, or watching three films a day in the company of others like herself, superfluous to life's requirements. Company was what she craved – the company of men.

Laura had hoped for a partnership that began with physical passion but went beyond it, something that would console her and endure. She had found it once and lost it again. There was no one man to ask, so she would have to ask them all. It would have to be done subtly, gradually. She would start by giving a dinner. She would invite the men who had shaped her life and ask them to take care of her in the time – however long it was – she had left.

For more than fifteen years Laura had basked, gloried, revelled in the knowledge that she was equal to the demands of the world in which she lived out her strenuous professional life. It was a world of airport terminals and international hotels; of conference centres where rows of interpreters like Laura sat before their microphones listening, judging, watching, concentrating. Her skills had commanded a high salary and her proficiency had earned respect. Now she must learn to inhabit a new world of hospitals, learn a new hierarchy of consultants, doctors, nurses – she would know their order of precedence soon enough – and groom herself for the cold formalities of death.

Laura had a simple, medieval image of death: a skeletal man in a black cloak, bent over a scythe. It was Dürer's death, Bergman's death – death as portrayed in old church frescos and devotional prayer books. She had dispensed with her notion of God long ago, but you had to believe in death. You had no choice.

The morning after Martha's visit, Laura drew up an invitation list of twelve men, the significant dozen out of the many she had known. With the help of the London telephone directory, *Who's Who* and her own international contacts book she tracked down current addresses for nearly all of them, but in case an invitation went astray she added an extra name, making thirteen. There was of course another man, the one unthinkable man. That secret had corroded and corrupted Laura, but it would die with her. He could not be invited or appealed to. Luckily, there were plenty who could.

The date for the dinner was five weeks hence; not too long – she could not afford to be profligate with time – but far enough ahead to be reasonably sure her guests would be free. February was not a social month. The fifteenth was a Saturday, the day after Valentine's Day. The invitations said:

Laura King

At Home
67 Markham Street, SW3
on 15 February 1992
at 8pm

Dinner 8.30
Dress: Informal   RSVP

In the top right-hand corner of each card she wrote a Christian name, and on the back of several she scribbled: 'Darling, do me a special favour – just this once could you *possibly* come on your own?'

Curiosity, she hoped, would persuade these men to decline a weekend shooting in the country or staying with friends, to invent some excuse as to why they could not be with their wives that evening. They would arrive from Paris, New York or Monte Carlo to find out why Laura King expected them to travel hundreds, even thousands of miles to dine with her. Curiosity would deliver them to her door. None would expect to find himself one of a dozen round her dinner table, with Laura herself the only woman present. She smiled at the prospect.

Wrapping up warmly against the dark January night, she walked to the pillar box. Television screens pulsed and flickered, turquoise behind drawn curtains. As she approached the King's Road, the growl of traffic grew louder. The crisp envelopes slipped from between her gloved fingers and she felt the old exhilaration of posting a love letter written against one's better judgement ... No going back on it now! She hurried back to the warmth. As she double-locked the front door the constriction in her throat returned.

The short February days seemed to cheat Laura of one of her months. She no longer allowed herself to hope that there was any chance of a misdiagnosis, nor did she console herself with belief in an after-life. A terminal illness meant just that. The end.

Eleven of her invited guests accepted. A few telephoned, unable to contain their curiosity.

'Laura, my dear, what's all this about? Don't tell me you're getting married? No? Can I bring anything? Champagne?'

One or two pressed her on the subject of wives.

'Absolutely not,' insisted Laura.

Those from abroad inquired discreetly whether they could spend the night with her. No, she said again.

'You'll make me jealous,' they bantered, secretly annoyed. 'All this is to introduce some new chap, isn't it?'

'No,' Laura assured them. 'But I can't put you up for the night. I'll book you into a hotel.'

'Don't worry, I'll fix something up myself,' they demurred, so that she knew there was more than one Laura in their lives. None inquired if she had developed cancer, heart disease or any of the illnesses *they* feared. No one associated Laura – clever, pliant, laughing Laura – with mortality.

Laura asked Mrs Ripa about the throat when she returned for a second appointment. 'I can manage without the sleeping pills and the tranquillizers,' she reported, 'but I might need something soon for my throat.'

'Let me have a look.'

A light was shone into Laura's wide pink yawn. Her lipstick left a tiny mouth-print on its stainless-steel edge.

'Nothing there that I can see,' said Mrs Ripa. 'Does it hurt?'

'Not exactly, but it feels sort of blocked all the time.'

'Engorged.'

'The very word.'

Mrs Ripa reached across the desk to hold Laura's hand. Her brown wrist, emerging from the white jacket, was slender. 'That's to be expected,' she said. 'It's fear. You are afraid. Of course you are. No one wants to fall ill – especially not in their mid-forties. Tranquillizers would relax your throat, but in time the tightness will pass by itself. It's a psychosomatic reaction with no physical origin. There's nothing wrong with your throat. And you will find you can even learn to live with fear.'

*

Two more envelopes dropped through Laura's letter box in the final week before the dinner. One said RETURN TO SENDER – ADDRESS UNKNOWN. This was the invitation to Larry Goldstein, the young American who had picked her up in a bookshop when she was sixteen and still at school. He had been the first man to put his tongue in her mouth (she found it slimy and revolting at the time) and the first to touch her breasts, which made her swoon with pleasure. He had been a law student at Columbia University – class of '63 – so she had easily traced his address through the Law Faculty. Well, he had moved or forgotten. Her breasts remained as highly tuned as ever.

The second envelope was from Edouard. She recognized his handwriting on the envelope at once, with its Greek e's and short loops. It had become cramped and quavery. His brief note said, 'You knew of course that curiosity would compel me to accept your charming invitation. Do not forget that love is an even stronger motive. *Je t'embrasse.* Edouard.'

She had met Edouard de Trifort at her first major conference as an interpreter and after that they had seen each other often in the next few years. He had persistently asked her to marry him, despite the thirty-year difference in their ages, but because of it she had not accepted. Yet he was the most subtle and civilized of all her suitors. Laura hoped he would tell her about a retirement spent browsing in libraries and celestial evenings at the Opéra.

By the Tuesday before her dinner her guests had reached the full complement of a dozen, if she included herself as the twelfth. She had arranged for someone to come in and cook and a waitress to serve the meal. She had agreed the menu; ordered the wine and flowers. Carmen had waxed the furniture and polished the silver.

Laura bought a dress of gossamer wool in a shade that flattered her rusty complexion. It folded back from her bosom and was cut high at the waist so as to minimize the awkward curve of her belly. The skirt fell in deep folds almost to her ankles. With it she would wear dark-red suede slippers: jesters' shoes with a pointed embroidered toe and flat heel. No jewellery, not even her gold watch. She would not show off any man's gift. She wanted them all to see that she was not poor. She had no mortgage, no debts and now (since even a terminal illness has its merits) no pension to worry about. She was turning to these men, not because she could not afford to look after herself, but because she *chose* not to. She wanted them to take responsibility for the time left to her, and since there was no one man – a father, a brother, a husband – whose obvious duty it was, she would ask them all to share it.

The men whom Laura had loved – many of whom were the international bankers, diplomats and businessmen at whose conferences she had interpreted for fifteen years – had fought for success in a remorseless world. They valued her beauty but also her professional skill. As an interpreter she was an equal, yet not a rival, an insider who posed no threat. Men had always been grateful for the pleasures which Laura offered – not always the pleasures of the bed. A civilized conversation over dinner, a stroll round the city together for an hour or two next morning, a taxi shared on the way to the airport – sometimes that was enough. All these men craved pleasure for, despite the power and money which most of them could command, they had very little pleasure in their lives, and none that was not paid for. *Pleasure* had been what Laura offered.

Laura knew that in turning to them now she risked a rebuff. Some might recoil from the thought of her as a sick woman – men were often squeamish. She pictured them catching one another's eye over the dinner table, signalling: what an impossible request! They might tell her that the plan was quite impractical, hospital was the only place for her. Maybe they were right. She would hold the dinner and see what happened next.

2

Laura King's Dinner Party

By half past seven house and hostess were burnished to perfection. Laura sat on the sofa, which had been pushed back against the front window in her double drawing-room to make space for the table. Heavily freighted with a cargo of silver, glass and damask, the table gleamed in the soft glow of side lights and table lamps. The candles were not yet lit, but stood tall and white as lilies. Laura held a glass of tonic water to which she had added apple juice so that it looked like champagne. The waitress had been briefed to replenish her glass with this throughout the evening.

At ten to eight the doorbell rang. The hired butler ushered in Conrad, looking formal and wary. His eyebrows rose as he entered the room and saw the table.

'So, my dear Laura, we are not to be alone,' he said.

You have grown old, she thought. Your witticisms were more polished once.

He inclined his elegant, sculpted skull and kissed her on both cheeks. '*Salute, bellissima!* You're looking well.'

Five minutes later Kit Mallinson arrived, a caricature of the impecunious don. He wore a green corduroy suit with faded, threadbare patches. He wove awkwardly past the chairs, shook her hand, pushed a bunch of daffodils at her and said, 'Sorry I'm early.' He glanced at Conrad, debonair in a fine-spun jacket and highly polished shoes. 'Oh God! I took "informal" literally! I see I shouldn't have done. How do you do? I'm Kit.'

'Kit Mallinson,' Laura told Conrad, 'a very old friend of my sister and her husband – and mine, naturally. Kit, this is my first boss, Conrad Parsons.'

'Sir,' said Kit, turning thankfully to the proffered tray of champagne.

At eight o'clock Jürgen Neuhaft arrived. Laura had hesitated before inviting him. On the surface he was austere and meticulous, but just below simmered on excruciating sensitivity and a boiling temper. Jürgen was the one man to whom she had considered giving a prior explanation, lest he should erupt in rage when it dawned upon him what she had organized.

But Jürgen too had grown older. Ten years and greater affluence had evidently calmed him. His eyes swept the room and he bent over her hand with a parody of the Prussian heel-click.

'Meine Königin!' he said, tweaking at her affection with their old joke.

'Herrschaften!' she replied, to show that she remembered too.

Jürgen was dressed exactly right for the occasion, neither too formal nor too casual. Like most prosperous Germans he had taken on the safe neutrality of European Man. 'Let us not talk now,' he murmured. 'Later. Call me. It is too long since we . . . met.'

Next came Edouard, punctilious and dapper. Her heart contracted when she saw him. He had grown old. His manners were eighteenth century, guarded and exquisite. He did not look well. His face was drawn as if tugged downwards by the great ropes in his neck but his eyes lit up at the sight of her.

'Ma chère petite Laure!' he said. He (and only he) had brought her a present, and before taking a glass he handed her a tiny tissue-wrapped box. 'Do not refuse!' he said, and Laura smiled.

'Or you'll take it back.'

After that they came in a cluster, her past flashing before her eyes. Mick, her first love, his face hideously scarred since they had last met; Nicholas Hope, who had loved her hopelessly; and

Joe Watson, who had never loved her at all. For a moment, as each man entered, she saw the face she had once known beneath the pattern of age.

They circled one another warily, wondering when some women would arrive to ease the atmosphere, wondering what they were doing here, what Laura was playing at, why they had agreed to come. One or two had evidently turned up for the dinner preening themselves, imagining that Laura's latest lover had left her and that now she was toying with the notion of warming up an old flame. They had been wrong. Pity.

They drank champagne as fast as it was offered, needing intoxication to smooth over their sense of unease.

At twenty past eight, with a diplomat's timing, Hugo Hammond arrived. He alone was wearing a dinner jacket.

'Hugo!' Laura said in momentary dismay. 'Did I put "Black Tie" on your invitation by mistake?'

'No, you wrote "Informal". In the circles in which I move nowadays, my dear Laura,' he purred, 'a dinner jacket *is* informal.'

'Oh, Hugo, you're showing off!' she cried, and saw, by the tiniest crease between his eyebrows, that she had overstepped the mark. Hugo was an important man, not to be teased.

Who on earth should she steer Hugo towards? Joe and Mick were talking too loudly, both ostentatiously Northern, darting hostile glances at Conrad and Edouard who stood near by, immaculate and urbane. She led Hugo over to them. They'll fox him, she thought.

By half past eight Rafe and Desmond had arrived, and were engrossed in auction house gossip. They had met each other through Laura in the last two or three years, and were thus among the very few of her guests who were acquainted. Laura led Edouard across to join them and he slipped between them like a silver sardine between two gleaming trout.

Bruno was the last to arrive, but as effusive as ever. The helicopter from Monte Carlo – bad weather – then the security at Heathrow – London taxi drivers . . . He cradled her elbow in a confiding palm.

'Who *are* all these men,' he asked, 'when I want to be alone with you?'

At nine o'clock Laura rescued Kit, who was standing alone with his back to the company, examining her books.

'Where's Paul?' he asked. 'I thought Paul would be here.'

'Oh, I couldn't ask *Paul*,' she said. 'I haven't seen him for . . . oh, must be twelve years.'

'I gather there are plenty of people here you haven't seen for years. Me, for one.'

'Paul's different,' she said. 'He's my brother-in-law. Was. Have *you* see him?'

'Not lately. He lives abroad nowadays.'

'Oh, really?'

She handed Kit a box of matches. 'Do me a favour: light the candles on the table, could you?'

The men drifted towards their place cards, examined them (Hugo swapped his around so as to sit, Laura noted, beside Jürgen rather than Conrad – how odd) and settled themselves. The butler slid chairs smoothly into place behind Edouard, on Laura's right, as his seniority deserved, and then Conrad, on her left. She had placed Desmond at the head of the other end of the table. I need an ally there, she thought, someone to wink at me through the candlesticks.

The food and wines were perfection. Laura was not surprised: this was what she had paid for. The waitress was deft, curving her rump adroitly out of reach of Bruno's predatory hand. Conversation, after a slow start as the guests waited for Laura to preface the meal with some announcement, grew into a muttering crescendo of male voices. From time to time someone would lean down the table towards her with a question – 'What year did we meet, Laura?' or 'This man here says he knew you when you were twenty! I'm jealous!' – and she would smile and tip her glass at him.

This is the climax of my life, she thought. The last twenty-five years have been a wave rising slowly towards the crest of this moment.

The butler placed a decanter of port on the table. As the last plates were cleared, Hugo caught her eye and raised an eyebrow. 'May I say a few words?' he mouthed.

God forbid! Laura thought, but she smiled, stood up and went round the table to where he sat. She whispered in his ear, 'Bless you, Hugo. No, but *I* should like to. Can you try and make them be quiet?'

He waited for her to resume her place, then tapped his fork against his crystal glass. The chatter faded. 'Pray silence for Laura.'

Trembling slightly, Laura rose to her feet. 'Gentlemen, you may smoke,' she announced. 'And I promise you, that's the last pompous thing I have to say.' There was an encouraging ripple of laughter.

'What, no loyal toast?' someone muttered facetiously. Hugo frowned.

She began by thanking them for their generosity in coming and for waiting so patiently to find out why they had been asked. They adorned her table, she said, by their intellect and achievements. They made a remarkable gathering and – here the obstruction returned to her throat and she had to swallow – she was proud of having loved them all, not only long ago, but still, here, this evening.

She alluded to the wordly success of some and the former glories of others. 'Down there sits my old friend Mick, who taught me to dance, thereby making himself irresistible; and Conrad, who gave me my first job, and much else besides . . . There is Joe, who tried to teach me things I did not, at the time, know I needed to learn, and taught them better than he knew.' Laura caught the eye, briefly, of each one as she named him. 'Seeing you all gathered around my dinner table tonight proves how well I chose, or how lucky I was to have been chosen, whether I was nineteen or . . . or thirty-nine.' She paused to let them chuckle indulgently.

She moved towards her darker purpose, waiting as they composed themselves and grew serious. Soon they would find out why they had all been summoned here tonight.

'Five weeks ago, with no possibility of a mistake, I was diagnosed as having a terminal illness: an obscure liver disease. For anyone who knows about such things, my condition is called hepatitis C. I know you will believe me when I say that I do *not* have Aids, but any doubting Thomas among you will find a note from my consultant in the small bathroom on this floor.'

She gestured behind her, drew a deep breath, and resumed. 'I have a year, at most two, left to live. I would like to shake off all care and business by spending that time in your company.

'As you all know, I have never married or had children. I realize that these are supposed to give women fulfilment in their lives, and I want to assure you truthfully that I have not missed them. All of you here tonight, in your various ways, have shaped my life. To whom else should I turn? My father is dead. My mother lives in Miami. My only sister, Constance, has her own concerns, and so do her children. I long ago disclaimed their care, the closeness and the duty owed to blood. I have no desire to take what I see as the cowardly way out, creeping back into the bosom of my much-neglected family.'

Laura looked round the table and tried to gauge their responses. Hugo was busying himself in an elaborate ritual of cigar-cutting and lighting. Kit returned her gaze fondly, sadly. Bruno tipped his head sideways and crinkled his eyes in a parody of sympathy. Jürgen looked away. Mick sank his scarred head in his hands. Joe drained his glass and reached for the port. He's drunk, she thought. He isn't listening.

She resumed. 'I should like, month by month, to be sustained by you. I'm asking you to take me in, to let me come and be with you in turn. It's not – how could it be? – a demand, but a request.

'What form that care takes is up to you. Some of you may be able to take me into your homes. Others may like us to enjoy a last holiday together. I don't know how quickly my health will deteriorate, and it may reach the point where you would prefer to pay for a nursing home.

'I have nearly finished what I have to say. My end – the word I prefer is "death" but I have already discovered that few people are comfortable with it – will not be sudden or unexpected. I will not embarrass you. But my health will inevitably decline. During the final months and weeks – whenever they are, and I am as curious as you to know how long this process will take – I shall be – what do they say? – *frail*. You may have noticed that already I have the dropsical stomach characteristic of this condition. Its medical name is ascites, and it will get worse.

'I am not in pain. I am not infectious. I shall not become incontinent. But it is in your power to enable me to approach my death unburdened . . .' – her voice wavered – 'because, you see, I have been very *fond* of you all.'

She had not meant to stop so abruptly, but she could go no further without breaking down. She resumed her seat. Unexpectedly, raggedly, they clapped. She looked down the table. Their faces were refracted through her tears. Edouard covered her hand with the dry, brittle bones of his own. There was a pause, during which half a dozen wondered whether to speak, feeling for the mood of the moment lest they got it wrong. Then, slowly, Edouard relinquished her hand and rose to his feet.

'I speak,' he began, 'not with the authority of love, let alone worldly success, but because I can safely say I am the oldest here. While Laura was giving us her heavy news, I thought of words by Pascal, in his great work *Pensées*. They may be translated roughly like this, though Laura would do it better: "We are fools to depend upon the society of our fellow men. Wretched as we are, powerless as we are, they will not help us; we shall die alone." I can only speak for myself, but I want to say to Laura' – he turned towards her – 'you may depend upon me. If what you say is true and you must die, you will not die alone. I am honoured by your trust.'

One or two others added their assurances, and then Laura moved round the table, encouraging some to change places; 'I have often wanted you to meet Nick . . .' Or Conrad, or Hugo.

The pretty waitress distributed coffee.

It was after midnight when Laura ushered the last man out. She returned to sit at the window, drawing back the curtains and looking at the street lights, their illumination softened to a haze by lingering fog. Behind her the table was cleared, to reveal beneath the heavy cloth a plain deal top set on strong splayed legs. That too was folded up and taken away and her own furniture replaced in its usual positions. The butler hovered behind her. Laura stood up and removed a bundle of notes from their hiding place behind the clock.

'It was a great success,' she said. 'Thank you all so much.'

'The kitchen is cleared and tidy,' the butler informed her.

She handed over the notes, adding an extra ten each for him and the cook, a fiver for the waitress, who, she suspected, had been generously tipped already by some of her guests.

'Goodnight.'

She closed the door behind the three of them and turned back into her silent house, wishing that someone – anyone, it would not have mattered who – had, after all, insisted on staying. Carefully she unfolded the tissue paper round Edouard's box.

3

Mick Charles

'How will you get here? Car or train? I can't meet you at the station but Beth could. Shit, you won't recognize each other.'

'Mick . . . For heaven's sake. I'll take a taxi.'

'A *taxi*?' he said, and she heard the Northern horror of extravagance in his voice. Taxis were luxuries. She remembered that after leaving her dinner Mick had headed up to Sloane Square to catch a tube to his friends in Finsbury Park, even though it was eleven-thirty at night. He would take taxis only if the ambulance failed to arrive.

'Yes, Mick, a *taxi*,' she repeated, adding 'dear' so as not to get off to a bad start.

'Bloody hell!' he said. 'Don't go calling me that in front of Beth.'

'What, not even "dear"?'

'Just call me Mick,' he said firmly. 'Or' – the shadow of a hesitation – 'Mikey.'

Laura strangled a hysterical giggle of disbelief. 'Mm-hmm. Mikey. Right. While I'm about it, in case I embarrass you, what should I wear?

'Nothing too – come on Laura, *you* know – nothing posh. That dinner of yours last Saturday – it was great, sure, but we're not in that league. We're simple folk, oop Nor'.'

'Don't you bloody patronize me,' she flashed, and heard his grin.

'Thought you were supposed to be ill.'

'It doesn't make me different,' she said. 'I'm Laura King who has hepatitis C. I am *not* a walking terminal disease with a martyred expression and a sugared tongue.'

'Good. Because *I'm* Mikey Charles whose face was smashed in a motor bike accident more than twenty years ago. I am *not* a walking disfigurement. Don't forget, we're in the same boat now.'

I could hardly have got off to a worse start, thought Laura irritably as she put the telephone down. She surveyed her drawing-room, its bloom dulled by a thin February sun. This whole idea is crazy. I want to call it off. I don't want to go anywhere, cope with wives, be a good guest. I want to stay here. And then what do I do? *Rot?*

The telephone rang. He's changed his mind, she thought. Thank God for that!

'Hello?'

'Darling, it's me. Constance. How *are* you?'

Laura suppressed the invariable jump of anxiety she felt at the sound of her sister's voice. 'Coco, this was a crazy idea of mine – this farewell tour of Those I Have Loved.'

'I told you, Laura, you should come to me. Kate's bedroom is spare these days. I could make it really comfortable and welcoming for you. I'd bring you books from the library – two a day, think! – and tapes. The library even lends videos. I'd honestly love to look after you.'

No, thought Laura, I have repudiated all that. No, no, no, no. 'What a *good* sister you are,' she said aloud. 'But no.'

Her dinner party had already been transformed by repetition into a series of anecdotes, with which she settled down to amuse her sister. She had always thought Constance didn't laugh enough.

The following morning Laura packed some loosely cut sweaters and trousers. She had bought the latest winner of the Prix Goncourt to read on the train, a gloomy family saga about the aftermath of World War I. It was important for morale to keep up her French. But as it turned out, the train had hardly got beyond Luton when she fell asleep, the book splayed across her bulbous lap. She awoke just in time to make herself up before arriving. She powdered her nose, stroking extra powder over the dark shadows under the eyes. She swept rouge across her sallow cheekbones and renewed her lipstick. I refuse to look dowdy for the benefit of Mick's unknown wife, she thought, but scent? No, perhaps not scent.

When she and Mick first met in 1965, she had still used Yardley's lavender water or eau-de-Cologne 4711. Anything else, her mother had said, would be absurdly sophisticated at her age, or (much worse) vulgar. I spent half my adolescence worrying about being vulgar, Laura reflected. Or rather, 'common' – the thing my parents most dreaded. Everything they said and did and wore was designed to fade invisibly into the protective colouring of middle-class taste and manners. Call vulgarity by any other name – ethnic, colourful, eccentric – and there's nothing wrong with it.

My mother in Miami is, by the sound of her, joyously vulgar these days and I have weightier worries that no one can dispel. Before I die I must find someone to shelter me, and unburden my conscience so that I can get on with this tiring, bloody business of facing up to death.

Laura opened her black and gold compact and smoothed her expression for the mirror's approval. Her skin was erupting in tiny red veins. Must be nerves, she thought, how silly.

A woman in a light raincoat stood at the barrier holding a cardboard placard bearing her name. Laura was touched. She walked towards her.

'Are you my taxi?' she asked. 'I'm Laura King.'

'I'm Michael's wife, Elizabeth, but everyone calls me Beth, like they call him Mikey. Here, give me that case.'

'I'm sorry,' said Laura. 'I *told* him I'd get a taxi.'

'Can't have you doing that. Waste of money. House is ready.

I'd nothing to do, so I thought I'd fetch you myself. Car's over there.' She slung the case into the back seat.

'I would have bought you flowers . . .' Laura said. 'I was going to buy some at the station.'

'No need for that. We've got plenty out back. Daffodils are early, seeing it's been such a mild winter.'

Beth straightened up. 'Let's have a look at you. Did Mikey tell you I was a nurse? Your abdomen's quite distended. That's ascites. I expect they told you. Is it uncomfortable? They give you anything for it?'

'*Is* there anything?'

'Diuretics. Never mind. Let's get you out of the cold and back home. We can chat before Mikey comes in and starts demanding food.'

The house was in a terrace set on a hillside. Four storeys tall, one entered at street level. From the hall one could descend the narrow stairs to the kitchen, whose back door opened on to a sloping garden, or go up to the bedrooms, their floors covered with vinyl and cheap shaggy rugs. Each room had vividly painted walls: deep turquoise, like an Indian sari, ochre-yellow, or paprika-red. Laura's bedroom on the top floor was a spring-like viridian green.

'Fantastic colours!' she exclaimed.

'Glad you like them,' said Beth. 'We need something to cheer us up during the long dark days. I've put you in Tom's room. He's away at college. You mind a duvet? I can find some blankets if you'd rather.'

Laura hated duvets, the smothering sweatiness of them, but already she liked Beth enough not to want to give her extra trouble. 'A duvet is fine,' she said.

Mick seemed surprised and ill at ease on seeing her. She wondered what account he'd given Beth of last Saturday. Had he ridiculed her extravagance or her friends, or pretended to have been the star of the occasion?

'You two met up OK, then?' he said. He ignored Laura's

gesture as she rose to kiss him on the cheek and headed straight for the fridge. He jerked open a can of beer and put it to his lips.

'I brought you something,' Laura said. She had spent a long time choosing books for him: a couple of well-reviewed novels, a recent heavyweight biography and a new collection of verse. She handed him the dark red package. He scarcely glanced inside.

'Shouldn't have bothered. I never get time to read, what with student essays and trying to keep up to date with lit-crit. Bloody Americans are so long-winded. Thanks, anyway.'

They ate lunch in the basement kitchen at a long, plastic-covered table. Beth pushed newspapers, sewing patterns, envelopes, a vase of daffodils, an ashtray and a sleepy ginger cat up to the far end and handed a fistful of cutlery to Mick. This was evidently a gesture for Laura's benefit since Mick looked surprised, but he laid three places and reached over to the dresser for willow-patterned side plates.

'Dave in for lunch?' he asked.

'Not today. He's on a job over at Sheffield.'

'What does Dave do?' Laura asked.

'He mostly lives with his girlfriend these days,' Beth said.

'Doesn't grace *us* with his presence.' Mick scowled.

'No, I meant, does he study, or have a job, or . . . ?'

'He's a plumber . . .'

'Heating engineer,' said Beth and Mikey simultaneously.

Laura noted that Mikey's battered face could still blush. He had placed her on his left, to give her the benefit of his good profile. It was still impressive: the cheekbone high, almost Magyar, the bold jutting chin deeply cleft below a fine straight nose. His eyes remained that extraordinary dark blue, like a thunderstorm sky, and the iron-grey hair was thick and springy. The left side of this face was that of a handsome, sensual man; the right, a smashed-in pit whose skin gleamed bluish-purple, striated with taut skeins of paler scar tissue. His forehead dipped above the right eye, giving him a permanent scowl. Only his beautiful curved mouth was intact.

Mick jammed a cigarette between his lips, lit up and inhaled hard.

'Coffee?' asked Beth.

'Yeah, I'll have a cup,' he said before Laura could answer.

She stood up. 'Let me make it. That much I *can* do. I'm not entirely helpless.'

'Nescafé's on the dresser, under the Superman mugs,' said Beth. 'Sugar next to it. Milk – do you take milk? We both do – in the fridge behind you.'

When they each had a mug of coffee, Laura said, to break the silence, 'How did you two meet?'

'How the hell do you think an accident victim meets a bloody nurse?' asked Mick. 'In hospital.'

Beth swung round. 'Michael, *fuck* off, will you? It's a perfectly normal, civil question to ask. And take that foul expression off your face. It didn't stop me marrying you and the boys won't inherit it, so shut up. Count your blessings and mind your manners.'

Mick smashed his cigarette into the ashtray, banged his mug on to the table and stamped upstairs. The front door slammed.

'I'm ever so sorry,' said Beth.

'No, I'm the one who should say sorry,' Laura replied. 'It was a crass thing to ask.'

'He dreaded you seeing him again,' Beth continued. 'Ridiculous, isn't it? Twenty-three years on, and he's still as vain as a peacock. He nearly didn't come to that dinner of yours because of his face, although he was dead curious to know what it was all about.'

'I'm not surprised,' said Laura. 'When I first saw him, I thought he was the most beautiful man I'd ever laid eyes on.'

'He probably was. Any other reason why you fancied him?'

Laura cast her mind back to the Mick she had met in 1965. He

33

had been a year ahead of her at university. She was instantly attracted by his dramatic good looks and even more by the way he danced. She had never in her life seen a man dance as well as Mick. At boarding school they had learned Scottish reels, the Dashing White Sergeant and the quickstep. Laura had jived a few times at teenage parties, spinning out and ducking under acrid armpits, clutched briefly to sweaty male chests, but she couldn't do the twist. Mick was expert at it.

She'd first spotted him at the Freshers' Fair: flat hips jutting forwards, torso leaning back, his bent knees and elbows pumping like pistons in time to the Stones' raucous rhythm. Sometimes he would anchor one foot on the floor and let the other swivel on its pointed toe as elegantly as Nureyev; or he would stamp hard on the beat with both heels, chin tilted upwards and eyes half closed, as if his body were beyond all conscious control. He seemed totally absorbed, unaware of his partner, let alone Laura watching him mesmerized from the edge of the floor.

'He danced well,' she told Beth. 'And – to me, anyway – he seemed so confident and sure of himself in his jeans and black leather jacket. I came from a different world. When I got to know him a bit, I realized how much he'd read, not just the A-level set books like most people. But he had also seen German expressionist cinema and French films, which were all new to me. He'd even *met* one of the Beatles backstage after a concert! Me with my passion for Barbra Streisand and Cleo Laine and – oh, I don't know, even Tom Courtenay, Albert Finney and the new working-class heroes – suddenly they all seemed terribly old hat, as we'd have said then: square.'

'Yeah,' said Beth flatly. 'He's still keen on foreign films. Runs the university film society. I go along sometimes.'

Beth stood up to make some more coffee and, with her back to Laura, she said with clenched vehemence, '*Christ*, I envy you!'

'Why envy *me*? I never got anything from Mick except pain

34

and misery and unrequited love. All my own fault, sure, but nothing to *envy*.'

'No. But you knew him – saw him – remember him as he was when he was young and beautiful. I've seen photos of course, and I could tell how gorgeous he must have been from the expressions of people who came to see him in hospital. Their faces just crumpled in shock and a sort of awful disappointment. I knew something wonderful was gone for ever. Yeah, I love him as he is, always did, difficult bugger and all that, but I'd give anything to have seen him as he was.'

'Why did he let me come here?' asked Laura. 'Why did *you* let me?'

'*I* was curious to meet someone who'd known him then, and I think *Mikey* honestly wanted to be kind, for once. We both work bloody hard for the local Labour party, but apart from that he knows he isn't very nice to people these days. When he heard your after-dinner speech (he was dead impressed, by the way) he saw a chance to make up.'

'Thanks!' said Laura bitterly.

'Don't be like that. If you're going to face up to dying, you'd better get used to pity.'

Right, Laura thought: a good, straight-talking woman. She grinned.

'I was curious, too,' Beth continued. 'About him *and* you.'

In a few days' time, Laura thought to herself, I can ask her about their marriage, but not yet. Aloud she said, 'Tell me about the accident.'

Riding his motor bike late at night, not entirely sober, Mick had skidded round a wet corner at speed and come off. The bike went spinning on its side across the road, harmlessly. Mick went under the wheels of an oncoming car as it swerved to avoid the bike. No crash helmet. He could have died.

Surgeons had miraculously saved his life and stitched his shattered face together, but the bones on the right side were smashed to splinters. The reconstructed face bore witness to how near death he had come. Ever since then Mick had thought himself hideous, deformed, a grotesque monster.

'But he's got guts,' Beth said. 'Every year he has to stand up and lecture to a new student intake, and every year he doesn't sleep for several nights beforehand. But he does it.'

'Has it made him bitter?'

'It has, and unfortunately he takes it out on the boys. They're both good-looking and he envies them. Better if you don't comment – he'd be ever so jealous if you praised them.'

'I'll bear it in mind,' Laura said. 'Now, could I possibly go and lie down for half an hour? Can we leave the washing-up?'

'Oh, Lord! Yes, of course – you must be . . . Sorry.'

Beth stood up and smoothed the long white shirt down over her leggings. 'Some other time, if you like, if it would help, we must have a talk about *you*. Your illness. I've nursed in a liver ward. If there's anything you want to ask, I'd tell you the truth. Unless you'd rather not know.'

'I'd like that. I *do* want to know. Thank you.'

The two women smiled complicitly at each other.

How many times, thought Laura as she lay under the duvet, did I offer God ten, *twenty* years of my life if He would make Mick Charles ask me to marry him!

Mick had noticed her watching him dance that long-ago evening, and without ceasing to gyrate had tipped his hand to his lips and mimed a drink. Laura squeezed to the front of the crowded bar.

'A small shandy and . . . um . . . a whisky, maybe.'

'Single or double?' asked the glistening barman.

'I suppose . . . a double,' said Laura.

Mick abandoned his partner with a nod when the music ended and went across to Laura. He sniffed the glass she handed him.

'Christ! What's this? Neat Scotch?'

'Would you have liked some water in it?' she asked anxiously.

'Long as you don't hold me responsible for the consequences. I'm Mick Charles, by the way.'

'How do you do?' she said, holding out her hand. 'I'm Laura King. First year.'

He leaned close to hear her above the din. 'Reading?'

'Modern languages. French and Italian with supplementary Russian.' She would have gone on to explain that she spoke Swahili, having lived in Africa for several years as a child, and had also started to learn Mandarin when her father was posted to Hong Kong, but the music started again.

He took her untouched shandy from her, drained it and said, 'Dance?'

'I'm not awfully good at the twist.'

'Just relax and follow Mick. He'll show you.'

She did what he said and it worked. His body moved mesmerizingly before her eyes and she made herself into its mirror image, copying his pumping arms and thumping legs, leaning towards him and bending her body to synchronize with his. The other people on the floor receded to a dark circle, like spectators round a bonfire. His limbs moved like flame, hers flickered sweetly in unison, and she lost all awkwardness and all sense of time.

At one point he pulled her close and buried his mouth against her ear. 'Thought you said you couldn't twist!' he yelled.

She grinned back. 'I can't! Never done it before!'

He shook his head and up-ended both palms. His hair clung to his skull as though he had been swimming, or in the rain. They danced on.

Afterwards he wanted to walk her back to her room but Laura dared not risk further contact, which would almost certainly lead to a necking session. Her mother had told her it was the girl's responsibility not to allow a man to become too excited. Even Constance – married by now to charming, sexy Paul and already with a second baby on the way – said there was a moment when 'they just can't control themselves any longer, so look out!' Laura felt that she herself was dangerously out of control. Heaven only knew what might follow, and she was still a virgin.

37

She found the first-year girl with whom she had arrived. Mick, standing by the door as she left, merely said, 'Cheers, then! Might see you around. You never know your luck.'

Laura had been staying with them for a week when Beth was called to work an emergency night shift at the hospital. Mikey sat at the kitchen table pretending to read student essays while Laura cleared the supper, washed and dried the dishes, put them away, and wiped the table.

He looked up. '*Now* what are you going to do?'

'Make coffee. Watch television. Read a book. Write a letter. Any number of things.'

'Write to who? Your bloke?'

'I haven't got a "bloke".'

'Funny. I could have sworn I met a dozen at your place only recently. Like *Twelve Angry Men* – all sorts and conditions.'

'They're not "my bloke". They're ex-blokes. I'm not with anyone.'

'Ex-lovers?'

'Some of them. Not all. You're not.'

'More's the pity. Why didn't I ravish you and try that long-preserv'd virginity?'

'I often wondered. Why didn't you?'

'Virgins always scared me. Who deflowered you in the end?'

She flashed a wicked look at him. 'Hugo.'

'Hugo! Christ! Not that pompous ass in the penguin suit?'

'Afraid so. I'd much rather it had been you, but you had that fat girlfriend who smoked too much.'

'Pat. Everyone smoked in those days. Anyhow, she wasn't fat. She just had big tits.'

'Not like me.'

'*You* had breasts like little apples. I remember your breasts. My hands can feel them now. Come here.'

'No,' Laura said. A chill seeped through her veins.

'Why not? This illness put you off sex? Or is it me . . . ?'

She seized on the excuse he had offered. 'Not you, Mikey. I take these pills and — this great stomach makes me feel hideous.'

'I know the feeling. Come here. I won't hurt you. I just want to cradle your little breasts once more.'

As soon as she could persuade her mother to buy her a brassière, Laura had fastened the hooks around the back of her flat rib-cage each morning, a badge of female adolescence, a promise of things to come. In due course nice round breasts sprouted, a matching pair. They never quite filled the last half inch of the white cotton cups shaped to receive them, and it was not until she was old enough to shop for herself that she discovered the joys of an A cup and a bra that fitted properly.

Later, when loose, flowing dresses and cheesecloth shirts were fashionable, breasts became softer and less constricted. Soon Laura relinquished bras altogether for the new badge of feminism, the uncorseted bosom. The day she ventured out with unsupported breasts for the first time since the age of thirteen, she felt light and airy. It was ten years before she wore a bra again. On her thirty-fifth birthday Laura stood in front of the brightly lit mirror in her bathroom and inspected her breasts like criminals, full face and in profile. They didn't droop, but nor did they jut any longer. Laura decided they must be returned to the custody of a bra.

By then bras had blossomed into an erotic art form. Lace and satin, the matt and the shiny, were engineered into tiny fabric bridges, designed to display her breasts like trophies. Even to her own eyes they looked enticing. For the first time, Laura understood lingerie fetishists. She bought matching sets of bra, pants and slip, colour co-ordinated in soft golden-browns or shadowy blues. Men were often appreciative enough to buy lingerie for her. It seldom fitted.

Now, however, not even the most cunningly engineered bra could alter the fact that Laura's breasts were not what they had been when Mick's fingers had last cradled them. She moved uncertainly towards him, her heart thumping a muffled beat. He extended both hands, palms upward as though in supplication, and closed them gently over her breasts.

'They're softer than they used to be,' he said.

'No wonder. They're a quarter of a century older, poor things!' she answered, trying to lighten the atmosphere between them.

'Give me a kiss.'

'No, Mikey.'

'Give me a kiss.'

She leaned away from him. 'No.'

'Give me a kiss for Mick, then.'

Her eyes misted over. She clenched her hands, drew a deep breath and tightened her elbows against her sides. Saliva flowed into her mouth, moisture gathered behind her eyelids. She stepped back a pace and looked him in the face.

'Oh, Mick. Do you *know* what you once were to me? I used to think about you night and day. I looked for you everywhere. For a whole year I searched the streets, people's rooms, all the pubs and coffee bars. I don't know how I got any work done. I used to go to English lectures in case you might be there. You were the first person I looked for when I turned up at a party. I sat in cinemas studying the people silhouetted against the screen, not the film, trying to spot you. Oh, Mick! I thought of nothing else. I used to sit in my room at night copying your handwriting or trying to draw you. *God*, I loved you!'

Never before had she confessed her love to him.

'And now you won't even kiss me,' Mick said.

'It isn't because of your face. Believe me. It has nothing to do with that.'

'Why, then?'

'Beth. Time. Years. Men. Everything.'

She had been freighted with melancholy. Only now did she realize how much she must have bored him, carrying her burden of impossible hopes, fixated upon a man who had taken her out twice, found her too young and earnest, and dropped her. The pages of her diary for that year were filled with obsessional fantasies about him. Bad poems; diminishing hopes; wild surmise; a long depression; and, in the end, resignation. Unrequited love had drained the year of all joy.

Her unconscious mind must have retained vestiges of the religion that her reason had long ago abandoned, for her inner ear often resounded to hymn tunes. Now, like an unseen choir, the opening bars of 'Love Divine, All Loves Excelling' crashed out. Laura raised her voice. 'I'm tired. I'm going to bed.'

When she had been with the Charleses for two weeks Laura began to realize how poor they were. Beth cut Mikey's hair for him, Dave's and Tom's too whenever they would allow it, and her own as well. She often mended in the evenings, darning her tights or Mikey's socks. She turned sheets 'sides to middle'. She even reversed the collar and cuffs on one of his good shirts to the inside, so that their frayed ends were invisible. It was an evening's work unpicking and resewing the microscopic stitches, merely to postpone spending £25 on a new best shirt for another year. Beth concentrated in silence on the brightly lit rectangle of worn cotton while Laura and Mikey talked or watched television across her bent head. Laura, who paid her cleaner forty pounds a week and would spend more than sixty pounds to get her hair cut and coloured every six weeks, felt mutely reproached by these economies.

One evening *News at Ten* reported that the Prime Minister had named the date for the General Election. It had been long-expected, but Mikey and Beth were jubilant.

'Thirteen years is a long time,' said Laura noncommittally. She had always been professionally neutral about politics. Having interpreted all over the world for the last fifteen years, attending international finance conferences, sitting in on defence negotiations and civil rights talks, she had lost faith in political ideology. Power and money, military uniforms and big shiny limousines motivated politicians, rather than a desire to improve humanity's lot.

Mikey was about to ask if she was a Labour supporter, but Beth, sensing trouble, said, 'Have you ever met Neil?'

'A couple of times,' said Laura. 'I haven't actually interpreted for him, but I've met him at the socializing afterwards.'

'Isn't he impressive?' asked Mikey. 'He came and talked to party workers here last year. Great speaker, great guy. He's got it all worked out. The corrupt fat cats in the City and on Tory councils are in for a shock! The media are going to have to eat their words!'

His eyes were shining. He was infused with energy and passion. Beth watched fondly as he dialled a number and talked ardently to someone whom – Laura noted – he addressed without irony as 'comrade'.

He was ebullient as he put the phone down. He's riding for a fall, Laura thought.

'Do you think people are prepared to pay higher taxes?' she asked.

'To get kids off the streets into homes of their own, people into hospitals without a three-year wait –'

'Mikey,' Beth interrupted. 'Steady on. Keep it for the doorsteps.'

'Yes,' he went on. 'Yes, I do. *I'd* pay higher taxes. Wouldn't you?'

No, thought Laura. 'Yes,' she said.

After this the Charleses both moved urgently into action. Bundles of posters piled up in the front room; leaflets for canvassers; pictures of their local candidate with his young family. One afternoon Laura took advantage of their increased commitments to shop for them. Taking a taxi to a supermarket outside the town, she let it wait while she filled up a trolley. She bought a whole leg of lamb, remembering the spiny rolled breast of lamb they had eaten for lunch last Sunday; and fresh fish rather than tinned tuna. She ransacked the shelves for treats, finding to her surprise that she could get many of the same luxury items as were on offer in the King's Road Waitrose: wild rice, dried mushrooms, single-property olive oils, virgin and cold-pressed; intense balsamic vinegar from Modena, the finest dried apricots and plump, moist prunes from Agen. Filled with happy gratitude for Mikey's and Beth's kindness, she piled her trolley high.

When she came back, the house was empty. Laura packed away her purchases in the fridge and at the back of cupboards. She went out again and, on impulse, selected a case of wine from Oddbins. She pondered what it should be. Mikey drank beer; Beth, tea or Nescafé. Laura decided Côtes du Rhône was the right compromise between raw plonk and a château bottle.

'Can you get me a taxi?' she asked the youth behind the counter. He gave her a long look, then dialled a number. Moments later the cab arrived.

As Laura climbed into the back seat and gave the address, the Asian driver glanced at her in the rear-view mirror and said, 'Lady in your condition, Madam, it is very bad to take alcoholic beverages.' He rocked his head with the ambiguous Indian wobble used to deflect hostility.

'I am not pregnant,' she said, smiling to show she was not offended.

'Oh, Madam, I am very sorry. Please forgive me. It is my foolish mistake.' His head rocked again. He turned up the car radio. It was the news: famine in Mogadishu, killing and torture in Serbia.

The car stopped outside the Charleses' house and Laura paid the fare. She walked up the front path, the driver following with the case of wine in his arms. As she opened the door with the key she had been given, Mikey came storming up the stairs from the kitchen.

'What the *fuck* do you think you're . . . ?' he began.

Laura halted, and the Indian driver bumped up against her, backed away and mumbled an apology.

'Now what? What the hell is *that*?'

'Nothing is too good for the workers,' said Laura smoothly and, pointing to the foot of the stairs, she gestured to the driver. He put down the case of wine, gave her a look in which fear, support and pity were mixed, accepted the note she pressed into his hand and hurried through the front door. Mikey kicked it shut with his foot.

'Look here, you patronizing bloody cow, don't waste your charity on us.' His twisted face was further distorted by fury. 'If you have money to give away, give it to the Party. Or the poor. Or Ethiopia. But don't you fucking put food in *my* fridge.'

'Very well, then,' said Laura. 'Take it back. Or distribute it to the beggars in the streets. Do whatever will salve your social conscience. But don't stand there abusing me.'

Trembling with rage and fear, she walked past him and up the stairs to her bedroom on the top floor. She sat down on the bed stupefied by the violence of her emotions. I want a drink! she thought. Or a man to put his arms round me. Or Martha, or Constance, or anyone. I want to go home. Her mind began to reverberate with the ominous thunder of 'Eternal Father, strong to save . . .' She stood up and began to pack. 'For those in peril . . . on the sea . . .'

'Later that same evening . . .' said Mikey. 'It is dark. Rain beats against the windows. An empty wine bottle stands on the table, amid the débris of a meal.'

Beth laughed, a loose meandering giggle filled with the promise of sex. '*Two* wine bottles,' she said. 'One empty and one still half full. Shut your nonsense, Mikey, and come to bed!' She turned to Laura. 'He always talks in film scripts when he's pissed.'

'Just you wait. One of these days it'll be finished – the *Ulysses* of the cinema. A day in the life of a Northern city, its mean streets, its lost loves, its youthful hopes and –'

'Course it will, my darling.' Beth tugged the white polo-neck sweater down over her fine breasts. 'Well, I'm for bed. Anyone else?'

'I'll be up in a minute,' said Mikey.

Beth bent down and pushed her lips against his ear.

Laura stood up. 'My bedtime too, I think . . .'

'No. Stay and keep him company for a bit,' said Beth. 'Honestly' – she put her arms round Laura – 'that dinner was fucking marvellous. Haven't eaten so well since Mikey took me out for our twentieth wedding anniversary!' She laughed. 'And whatever that wine was . . . brilliant!'

'Ten bottles left,' said Laura. 'Night, Beth. See you in the morning. I won't keep him up long.'

It was 1967, the end of Laura's second summer term. Mick, she knew, had sat his final exams and would soon be going down and lost to her for ever. Laura had decided, after weeks of earnest thought, that he was the ideal person to take her virginity. She had not fallen in love with anyone else and in the dreamy mid-Sixties when everyone swayed to the gentle, mystical rhythms of pot and pleasure she felt isolated by the fact that at almost twenty, the troublesome membrane was still intact. She had necked with strangers in the darkness of parties, but Mick was the only man for whom she felt *passion*. The fact that it was a purely cerebral passion did not disturb her since at this stage she did not know the difference.

She had continued to see him around from time to time, though much less often in her second year. Presumably the imminence of Finals had driven him into libraries, forcing him to renounce parties and film-going in favour of all-night sessions over books and lecture notes, with strong coffee or benzedrine to keep him awake.

She got his address from the college. 'It's important,' she said. Seeing her taut expression, the bursar decided to waive the rules. This Pill, he thought, and this so-called sexual freedom are all very well for my chaps, but they've created a lot of problems for their young women. He smiled. 'I can see it is! Here you are, then. Don't say I gave it to you.'

Laura picked a Monday evening just before term ended: not a favourite night for parties. She bought a packet of condoms, in case Mick had run out. At seven o'clock, when everyone else was in Hall for supper, she had a bath, washed her hair, shaved her legs and armpits, and put on clean pants and a lacy bra. She stroked her nipples through the bra and felt ripples of pleasure. She was pretty sure she wasn't frigid, but her face reflected in the mirror was blank, sexless, not even flushed.

It was a muggy evening. She had decided not to cycle in case it hurt too much afterwards or she bled a lot, so she joined the queue at the bus stop. She waited for more than twenty minutes and was about to abandon the whole idea when a bus arrived. Mick lived well outside town in a dreary semi-detached house. Laura had not told him in advance that she was coming in case he tried to put her off. She had brought a bottle of wine and one of whisky. She would pretend it was a surprise, to celebrate the end of his exams. Her high heels clattered up the uneven path. She pressed the doorbell.

His head emerged from an upstairs window. He saw her and looked astonished for a moment. 'I'll come down!' he called.

The front door opened, and Laura, as she had planned, held the two bottles gaily towards him. 'Congratulations!' she said. 'All over! Time to celebrate!'

'You are a strange bird,' he said. 'I don't see you for months and now suddenly – this.'

'Can I come in?' she asked.

'I'll have a word with Pat. She's trying to get the baby to sleep.'

'*Baby?*' Laura said. 'What baby?'

'Oh Laura, didn't you know? I thought someone would have told you. Pat got pregnant. We were married six months ago. In a register office. The baby's eight weeks old now.'

His words should have been hammer blows to her heart, but instead a sense of guilty relief suffused her. Her arms dropped to her sides.

'Is it a boy or a girl?'

'It's a boy. He's called Justin. Do you want to come up and have a look at him?'

No, I don't, thought Laura. 'Yes, I'd love to,' she said aloud.

He led the way up a narrow staircase with a smelly, peeling carpet. Halfway up a plywood door had been installed. Mick pushed it open and called out, 'Here's a surprise! Laura's come to see us, and she's brought us something to celebrate the baby and the end of my exams.'

'Who?'

'You know. Laura King. Are you fit to come down, love?'

'Never mind. I'll just tiptoe in and peep at him and go away,' said Laura.

Pat wore no make-up, her hair needed washing, and her breasts seemed bigger than ever. The baby was lying on her lap, naked, across a towelling nappy. His penis was very plump and pointed. It looked much too big for the rest of him. His testicles were prematurely wrinkled. Laura, who had never seen a naked male before, though she had expected to do so this very evening, felt awkward and childish. This, then, was adult life. She gazed down at the baby. His eyes were half closed, his limbs slack.

'He's beautiful,' she whispered. 'I've never seen a new baby before. Isn't he *small?*'

'Eight pounds six ounces,' said Pat. 'Eats like a pig.'

'He looks exactly like Mick, doesn't he?'

'Hope so,' said Pat. 'I'm in trouble otherwise.'

'Do you want to stay and have a glass of wine?' asked Mick.

'No – honestly and truly – I must be going now. But thanks for letting me see him.'

There was an unmade double bed against one wall of the room and, as she emerged, she glimpsed a leaky bathroom on the landing. Mick took her down to the front door. She stepped out and turned back. He looked handsome – he always would, he couldn't help it – but the aura of glamour had vanished. He looked like a tired young husband. His T-shirt had a hole in it and his bare feet were grubby. You are my love, her mind assured him, you are my dear and only love.

'The baby's terrific,' she said.

He smiled. 'Glad you think so. We're pretty knocked out by him too. Well, thanks for coming. And for all the booze.'

'Thanks for having me,' she said politely. She gazed for the last time at his face, his great carved splendid face. 'Bye, then. Good luck.' A bus was coming. 'I'd better run and catch that. Bye, Mick . . .'

'Sound of footsteps climbing stairs. A silence, broken by the ticking of the clock. The two remaining figures do not meet one another's eyes.'

Laura laughed. 'Is it true you're writing a film script?'

'True I'm writing one. Not true it's *Ulysses*. But it's not bad.'

There was a pause. Laura filled his glass. He lit another cigarette.

'Do you have to go tomorrow?' he asked. 'I'm sorry about – I lost my rag. Fucking stupid pride.'

'Don't worry. But yes, I think I will go. You have lots to do, election and everything, and Tom's back soon, isn't he?'

'Tom can doss down on the settee.'

'No.'

There was a longer silence.

'Mick . . . What happened to your older son?'

'Told you. He lives with his girlfriend. Stick around and you'll meet him.'

'Not him. The other one.'

Mick looked at her. 'I didn't think you would have remembered.'

'You still don't understand, do you? I remember everything.'

'Do you remember his name?'

'Justin.'

'Justin. That's right. Yeah. Justin. Typical trendy Sixties name, wasn't it, Justin? Poor sod's stuck with it for life. Or maybe not.'

'What happened to him? And his mother, Pat?'

'Pat gave me the push after the accident. My face was a real mess for months. It isn't a picture now, but it was a fucking nightmare then. *Texas Chainsaw Massacre* time for Mikey. They wouldn't let me have a mirror. It was Beth who brought me one in the end. She said it couldn't be as bad as I was imagining. It was, though – she'd had time to get used to it. And she didn't know what it had been like before.'

He sighed.

'Pat stopped coming to visit me in hospital after a couple of months. Then she moved out of our flat and went back to her mother. Took Justin with her. He was just a toddler, hadn't even started school. No chance I could have looked after him. When the divorce laws changed, she divorced me.'

'Where is she now?'

'No idea. She remarried, wrote and said I needn't pay maintenance. I wasn't ever going to see the boy again, so it didn't seem right.'

'Did you mind?'

He stared at her. 'Course I fucking *minded*. I still do. He's my son, my oldest son. He might be anywhere – America, Australia, London. He might be famous by now – he'll be twenty-six in three weeks' time. Might be a film actor. Looked just like his dad, didn't he? Handsome bugger. All I can do is hope he'll get in touch one day. Star in the film I'm writing for him. Myself when young.'

The clock on the kitchen mantelpiece struck, and she counted its chimes. Midnight. The cat woke with a start, scratched its ear, turned round irritably until it found a new position and buried its nose back into its soft haunches.

Laura reached a hand across the table. He clenched his fist around it. His head was down, she couldn't see his face.

'Maybe I shouldn't have brought the whole business up again.'

'You're the only person left, apart from Beth and my mother, who knows about Justin. You make me feel he really exists. It's good to talk about him. When I'm in London, I look for him. I go into pubs and look for him. I sit on the Underground looking into the faces of any bloke under thirty, trying to recognize myself. I even started ringing up J. Charleses from the London telephone book once, but when I did get through to people I felt such a dick-head that I stopped. "Are you called Justin Charles?" "No, mate. Jack." Or Jim. Or for that matter Jane or Jill. Justin's lost and gone for ever. I don't give a damn about Pat. But *him* . . .'

Laura said, 'Beth's great.'

'Yeah. Second time lucky.'

'You did well. Look, do you mind if I go to bed now? Is that OK?'

'I'll sit here and finish the bottle.'

He stood up and put his arms round her. She leaned her head into his shoulder and inhaled. Wine. Wool. Sweat. Cigarette smoke. He said, 'Will you let me know when . . . I mean, if . . . ? I'd like to see you again.'

'No,' Laura said. That was one thing she'd decided. Definitely no deathbed farewells. 'No, Mikey. This is it. This is goodbye. Or tomorrow morning will be.'

'Tonight we have looked into each other's souls,' he said. To cover his embarrassment he added, 'How you bring my youth flooding back.'

'Mine too.'

'I never meant to be cruel. You were so young, so intense, and so frightfully middle-class. I was scared of you, in a way. And you always seemed so *gloomy*.'

'It was love, Mikey, just love. Let me go, sweetheart.'

'Of course. Go on, then. Go. Goodnight. Thanks for all the booze. Sleep well. Don't mind me. Wish you'd kiss me. But you won't. Never mind. Too late. Night, Laura.'

'"Goodnight, my love, goodnight, sweet love, goodnight, goodnight."'

Heavily, wearily, she climbed the long flights of stairs to bed.

4

Conrad Parsons

Laura returned with relief to the soft and golden comfort of her own house. A pile of post awaited her, from which she picked up first the letter addressed in her mother's rounded handwriting. The airmail sheet was printed with an airy sketch of a seagull in flight.

'Oh, my poor darling,' Mrs Elphinstone wrote,

We are both shattered to hear the news! Constance tells me it really could be quite serious. I had no *idea* it was that bad when you first called me, and I've been worrying about you ever since. I guess you're still my baby, no matter how old you are!!

Laura, dear, please listen to me and don't frown in your usual impatient way. Leonard and I live in a really beautiful apartment block right next to the sea. It has its own private beach, residents only, no one bothers us. We have breakfast on our own balcony every morning looking out across the ocean, and the weather is just *fabulous*!!!

It would be an ideal place for you to convalesce. We have a nice big guest room. I would make it all *so* nice for you!

I quite understand that you don't feel you can go and stay with Connie, and I think you're right. But won't you let us fly you over here and come stay with us? I would look after you with real care, my darling, and if you *did* need a doctor the hospitals here are *marvellous*! Don't worry about the money, we could work something out between us, or you could use up the last of Daddy's little nest-egg.

The letter ended with effusive assurances of love and anxiety, and a manly scribble. Laura was comforted by her mother's concern, but not for a moment did she consider accepting the invitation. She could think of nothing worse than dying in Miami amid a gaggle of quacking, bronzed geriatrics. She turned to the computer beside her desk and composed a gently worded refusal.

Next, she picked out another airmail-flagged envelope, this one postmarked Amalfi. It was from Conrad.

What an entertaining and original evening you prepared for us! I felt like a character in a play. And the little waitress was enchanting.

It is distressing to hear about your illness, though I salute the bravado with which you propose to throw yourself on the mercy of old friends and former lovers (I hope I count as both).

I enclose an open first-class return ticket to Naples and something to cover incidental expenses en route. I urge you to come before Easter if possible, for after that the world's necromaniacs descend upon Pompeii.

The letter was signed in his tiny, clever handwriting. The cheque, drawn on Coutts, was for a hundred pounds. Without reading the rest of her post, lest anything in it should make her change her mind, Laura dialled his number.

'Providing I can get on a flight, I hope to be with you in three days' time,' she said.

Conrad Parsons had been her first employer. When she came down after university in the turbulent summer of 1968, uncertain what to do with her degree, Laura had ignored offers from several companies who had been impressed by her languages. Russian was nearly as exotic then as Mandarin Chinese, and she was proficient in both. Instead, attracted by its premises in Soho and the promise of intellectual glamour, she had chosen to work for a small publishing house called Lively and Parsons (known in the trade as the Quick and the Dead). Her job was to check and proof-read foreign dictionaries. Constance had told her that at this stage of her career the money wasn't important. What mattered was that the job had interesting prospects (and, she did not add, marriageable colleagues).

Laura and two other girls, friends from college, had found an attic flat in Hampstead. From this top-floor eyrie Laura travelled by tube every day to climb sixty-five stairs to another top-floor eyrie, whose grimy windows overlooked the roofs and treetops of Soho. She soon learned the geography of fire-escapes and flat roofs, some with secret unexpected gardens. Directly below her office window was a rose-covered pergola, whose owner climbed through a skylight with watering cans in dry weather to gloat over his treasured blooms. Sunbathers would emerge from other skylights to lie spreadeagled across towels on the soft asphalt, turning their naked bodies towards the London sun until they looked as though they had just returned from the Mediterranean. If it occurred to them that they could be overlooked from a higher floor, they evidently did not care.

Leaning out of the window one hot day, Laura was describing what she could see to the secretary with whom she shared an office when a male voice remarked drily, 'With such powers of observation, young lady, you should be writing books, not editing them.' She turned to see Conrad Parsons, the firm's co-founder, standing in the doorway. 'I'm sorry,' she said. 'It's my coffee break, honestly.'

'My dear child, you are allowed to look out of the window. Besides, it shows off your pretty brown legs.'

Laura pulled her mini-skirt ineffectually over the tops of her thighs and blushed.

'I was looking for Cameron,' Conrad Parsons said, naming her boss.

Several days after this encounter Laura hurtled down the five flights of stairs one evening to find Conrad pushing through the swing doors at the bottom leading to the street. She pulled up just in time to stop herself cannoning into him.

'Gosh, nearly! Sorry!' she said.

'You again. Not at all. I was on my way to the Colony for a drink. Would you care to join me?'

'Oh! Goodness. Well, yes, thank you. I'd love to. Do I look all right?'

'You have evidently not been to the Colony Room Club before. No one will object to the way you are dressed. Quite the reverse.'

'Are you sure?'

He stopped and looked at her. '*Why* do girls always say, "Are you sure?" If I weren't sure, I would not have said it. But if you need praise to boost your self-esteem, then let me assure you, you look perfectly acceptable as you are.'

'I *wasn't* fishing for compliments,' she said. 'But my father's in the Colonial Office, and if it were the sort of place *he* goes to for a drink, I wouldn't be at all acceptable looking like this.'

Conrad laughed. 'I don't think you'll find it's like your father's club.'

The small, crowded room was full of cigarette smoke and sweaty middle-aged men, most of whom gave her an appraising glance and then ignored her. Several greeted Conrad.

'What will you have to drink?' he asked Laura.

'Oh, I don't know – anything. A shandy.'

'Muriel does not serve *shandy*,' he said. 'Don't you drink anything else?'

'Is a glass of wine all right, then?'

He raised his eyebrows. 'I had been told that today's young were more decadent than my generation, but you prove this theory wrong. Such innocence must be cherished. Certainly you may have a glass of wine. White?'

Laura, piqued, said, 'A Chablis would be perfect.'

'Would it?' he said mockingly. 'How about champagne?'

'I don't like champagne. It goes with weddings and twenty-first birthdays and stuck-up public schoolboys showing off.'

'It goes with a great deal more than that. Stop looking petulant and I'll bring you a glass of Chablis.'

The moment he left her to make his way over to the bar, a short, stout man with thinning hair appeared beside her and said, 'So *you're* Conrad's latest bit of skirt. Literally! I wondered why we hadn't seen him recently.'

'I am *not* his bit of skirt!' Laura objected. 'I bumped into him just now when I was leaving the office and he invited me for a drink.'

'That's how all office affairs start, my dear,' said the man. 'And you must admit, he's *most* attractive . . . ?'

'He's old enough to be my father,' she said defensively.

'Don't tell *him* that, will you? He'd be most upset. Don't you care for older men? You should, you know. They can be very generous. I hope you will allow me to prove as much over dinner sometime?'

'Leave her alone, Peter,' said Conrad, handing her a glass of wine. 'She's one of our proof-readers and I won't have the poor girl frightened by an old goat like you.'

'We *are* touchy about our latest protégée!'

Laura turned away, and caught sight of her boss coming through the door. Were it not for Peter's remarks, she would have thought nothing of it; now, she found herself ill at ease.

'Look!' she whispered to Conrad. 'It's Cameron!'

'So it is.' He held up his arm and called out, 'Over here, dear boy!'

The two men started talking shop. After ten minutes she said to Conrad, 'Thank you very much for my drink. I think I'll make my way to the tube now.'

He made no attempt to dissuade her, but merely said, 'Off you go, then!'

She felt irrationally disappointed. Peter had led her to assume that Conrad would make a pass at her. His failure to do so seemed almost insulting. 'Goodbye,' she said. 'See you tomorrow, Cameron.'

Peter was right, however. She and Conrad would have an affair, which long outlasted her job as a proof-reader and continued, on and off, for several years.

*

Laura packed two suitcases with loose shirts in brilliant colours that flattered by concealing her expanding abdomen. She dug out sandals and espadrilles, and bought a pair of sunglasses. She wondered what to bring Conrad and ended up in Hatchards hesitating between a book of Japanese erotic prints and a much-praised history of the decline of the aristocracy. In the end she bought both.

Before her departure she rang Constance to talk about her mother's invitation to Miami. The loving anxious letter had jabbed her conscience.

'Coco! It's me, Laura.'

'Darling, I'm so glad you've rung. I do *worry* about you, but I don't want to overload your answering machine, and I assume everyone leaves messages all the time. How are you feeling? How's the Great Plan going? Are your chaps coming up trumps?'

'Looks like it. I've just spent three weeks with Mikey Charles and his wife. Do you remember Mick – the one I was hopelessly in love with in my first year?'

'Which year was that?'

'1965.'

'I was pretty swamped with babies round about then. No, I don't remember him.'

'Anyway, I couldn't quite last the whole month. The North makes me feel guilty. So *dour*. So *direct*.'

'Never mind. How *was* your first love? What's become of him?'

Constance admitted that she had given their mother a full account of Laura's illness and its implications, and tried to persuade her sister to spend a few days in Miami.

'You ought to do *that* much – it would give her such pleasure. Any longer and you'd drive one another crackers. But if hepatitis C is as bad as you say it is, she needs to – well, you know what I mean . . .'

'Say goodbye?'

'All right, yes. Spend some time with you, and say goodbye.'

'She can say goodbye on the phone.'

'Laura! Don't be such a bitch! She's your *mother*.'

'And you're my *sister*, and I'm not coming to stay with you *either*.'

'Crikey! Being ill hasn't changed you, has it?'

'That's what I keep trying to tell people. I'm not heavenly choir material yet. If anything I'm worse-tempered than usual.'

'I dare say that's just one of the symptoms.'

'*Must* you be sweetness and light?'

'Must you be quite so rude? Listen, I wondered if you wanted me to get in touch with Paul and tell *him*? He lives abroad now, but he contacts the children occasionally. Do you think he ought to know?'

'I haven't seen him for years. I should think a dying ex-sister-in-law is the last thing he needs. Oh, hell! Listen, Constance, you do what you like. I must go. Talk to you when I get back from Naples.'

'Where?'

'Naples. Send you a postcard. Bye . . .'

Laura used some of Conrad's hundred pounds to buy a guidebook to the Bay of Naples and ordered a taxi to the airport.

The bright blue air, when she descended the aircraft steps at Naples, was warm and scented with ozone and kerosene, and – as the passengers filed across the tarmac – the cloyingly sweet smell of duty-free perfume. She retrieved her luggage and telephoned Conrad to announce her safe landing.

'Good,' he said. 'You know the address. It's quite a long taxi ride, but the views are famous. Don't let those bandits cheat you. If the meter registers more than fifty thousand lire, it's been fixed. Never mind: I'll deal with it when you get here.'

The car wove through the narrow streets of Naples. Donkeys and men with handcarts trundled alongside Alfas, suicidal Fiats and trolley-buses. Laura asked to be taken along the coast road to see the great sweep of the bay. *Vedi Napoli e po' mori*, she remembered. Now she had seen it. Time to die. As the taxi thundered down the *autostrada* skirting the slopes of Vesuvius and the charnel-house of Pompeii, Laura was almost blinded by the brilliant southern light. She leaned back and closed her eyes.

Conrad's house at Amalfi could not have been more different from Mikey's, where she had been less than a week ago. Built down the side of a rock face that fell straight to the sea, its entrance and reception rooms were at street level. From here an elegant spiral staircase descended to the bedrooms and bathrooms, continued down to Conrad's study, and ended beside two changing rooms that led out on to a terrace with a turquoise-blue swimming pool. The side of the house facing the sea was made almost entirely of glass, reinforced and strengthened by stainless-steel struts. The sea, a deeper blue than the swimming pool, danced and sparkled to the horizon.

'Don't be deceived,' warned Conrad. 'It's heavily polluted. Only the local street urchins swim in the sea. And tourists, of course. Let's go back upstairs. You must be dying for a drink.'

'You forget, I'm not allowed to touch alcohol,' Laura answered.

'Not even champagne?'

'Nothing. My liver and its consultant forbid.'

'Ah. That is a pity. I shall have to drink the champagne alone; and you will have . . . ?'

'Mineral water.'

After his white-aproned maid had deposited their drinks and withdrawn they scrutinized each other in the harsh glare of the sunlight. The dry skin around Conrad's eyes was wrinkled and fell into pouches. Deep lines ran from nose to chin and into the sinewy strings of his neck. His thinning hair revealed a polished scalp. He must be in his late sixties, Laura thought, but – to use Mother's approving phrase – he's still a fine figure of a man. In his black T-shirt and cotton trousers he was still a viable sexual proposition. Just as well, since Conrad had never been seriously interested in anything else.

That evening, over a dinner of baby artichokes in olive oil and seafood risotto, Conrad was unusually garrulous. Laura wondered whether he was lonely. She asked if he had many visitors.

'A few. The odd friend. Very occasionally one of my daughters. By and large, those who invite themselves I seldom want to see, and those whom I ask seem not to want to come.'

'But why are you down here at all?'

'In the mid-Eighties – perhaps you weren't aware of it – most of the small gentlemanly publishing houses were bought up by large American conglomerates. They kept their names but everything else changed. I had just turned sixty, Lively was pushing eighty. He still tottered in from time to time to check the odd contract before taking our oldest authors off for lunch. Not much life in him any more.'

'Never was much.'

'He was the ballast of the firm; I was the – what shall I say – the wind-filled sheets.'

'My dear Conrad! How poetic!'

'In due course an American publisher approached us as well. Soft words and a wide-open cheque-book are hard to argue with. Lively soon overcame his scruples. He had no children; my daughters weren't interested. With no one to take over, why hang on?'

'So you came down here?'

'Oh, there was a period of transition. We both had consultative status – Lively's dead now – and I tried to see that the long-serving employees were either kept on or paid off handsomely. In the end the Yanks were pretty ruthless. They kept the few they wanted and turfed out the rest. The Eighties ended in carnage. I took the money and got an architect friend to design this house for me.'

'Lucky Conrad. You always were a hedonist.'

He smiled his beguiling, conspiratorial smile. 'You should know. You always were a very apt pupil.'

After dinner they sat in white armchairs overlooking the darkening sea.

'Where do you keep all your books?' Laura asked.

'I got rid of them. I rationed myself to fifty and sold the rest. I knew I'd never open most of them again, but I thought if I brought fifty I might actually *read* those fifty.'

'What are they?'

'Old favourites. *Tom Jones. Life of Casanova. War and Peace.* Oh, and *The Leopard* . . . Lampedusa's absolutely right about the feudal nature of Italian society. The Mafia has replaced the old aristocracy as the source of pity and terror, that's all . . . Well, you can see the books for yourself in the morning . . .' – he gestured towards his bedroom – 'or, of course, now.'

'I'll look at them tomorrow. *I've* brought you a couple. Shall I go and get them?'

As she stood up, Laura felt in her muscles and her heavy body the ache of tiredness, but she went into her bedroom to find the books. Turning to the flyleaf of each, she wrote, 'To Conrad, with love from Laura, March 1992'. Love from Laura . . . Was that all they came down to in the end, those ten years? Was it ever love?

Conrad Parsons had been her first 'older man'. Before him she had known only the hard, clumsy limbs of men her own age, whose breath and skin smelled fresh, who woke clear-eyed and yawned shamelessly at the morning before rolling towards her to ease their strenuous erections. The third time Conrad asked her to join him for a drink, she became aware of the live wires of desire that thrummed between them, and recognized with a shock that the desire was mutual.

He had taken her one autumn evening to the French Pub, frequented by a Bohemian crowd as well as a handful of girls her own age. Laura felt awkward under the regulars' sophisticated appraisal.

'I ought to be getting back,' she said after twenty minutes. 'It's my turn to cook supper tonight. We have a rota.'

'Do you?' he mocked. 'Your turn next to do the spag bol?'

This was so accurate that Laura winced. Afterwards she wondered how he came to be so familiar with the routines of bachelor-girl life.

'Actually,' she said coolly, 'not spag bol. *Dio loso qua* tonight.'

'Do tell me, what is that, dear girl?'

She grinned. 'It's supposed to be Sicilian for "God knows what", since what goes into this dish is everything left in the fridge at the end of the week.'

'Allow me to save you from this fate by taking you out to dinner.'

'But what about Ruth and Judy?'

'They can come along as well. Would you like that?'

Laura's first conscious step towards love was the realization that she did not want to share Conrad with her flatmates.

'Is there a phone here? The least I can do is let them know I won't be back.'

Conrad gestured towards a black public telephone fixed against a wall. A fat man, very drunk, was using it. His other hand held a cigarette, which he was waving in a languid self-justifying circle.

'I'll ring from the restaurant,' she said.

They walked back to Conrad's car. Laura was acutely conscious of his height, the length of his stride, the silence between them. He handed her into the front, slid into place beside her and headed north. They stopped at a set of traffic lights. Laura stared rigidly ahead, counting the seconds. The silence mounted. She turned towards him to say something. Conrad leaned across and kissed her on the mouth. The lights turned green and the car behind hooted impatiently. Conrad sat forward, changed gear, and as the car moved on he glanced at her and said, 'Don't look so astonished. You must have been kissed before.'

'Yes,' said Laura breathlessly, 'but never by anyone as old as you.'

He threw his head back and roared with laughter, and at the

next traffic lights they kissed again. I would have been just twenty-one then, she thought, and Conrad in his mid-forties — about the same age, in fact, as I am now.

After Conrad had admired the books she had brought him, Laura said goodnight and retired to bed. Her room was cool. Muslin curtains billowed in the balmy night air. The sheets had been turned back and a cotton nightdress lay limply across the bed like the heroine of a Victorian melodrama. Laura scooped it up and went into a marble bathroom.

She woke to a dazzling morning. Dropping her creased clothes into the laundry basket, she showered, dressed and, frowning in the sunlight, walked out on to the terrace to find Conrad.

'Today,' he said, 'I shall take you to the Villa Cimbrone. Pompeii can wait.'

His car banked on the curves of the coastal road like a great bird. The vast bowl of the sky seemed to palpitate and shimmer with the noon heat. Skirting the cliffs far below, the sea lapped and twinkled. Villages bordered by olive groves and terraced vineyards clung to the plunging hillsides.

He parked the car under the shade of a tree in the centre of Ravello and they walked to the villa. Its sub-tropical garden of dark green umbrella pines and palms was interspersed with marble statues. There was a bower of English roses beyond which, overlooking the edge of the cliff, ran a semi-circular belvedere with more classical busts.

Laura and Conrad leaned on the balustrade and gazed across the gulf of Salerno. He pointed to the furthest tip of the bay. 'Over there is Paestum, which has classical ruins — very remarkable — I'll take you to visit that, too. Used to be Greek before it became Roman. You know what destroyed it?'

'Volcano?' asked Laura.

'Malaria. Vesuvius and Pompeii are behind us, on the other side of these mountains.'

He moved away to stroll down a small path leading back into

the pine-scented grove. Laura took off her sunglasses, but the light reflected from the sea was so blinding that it brought tears to her eyes. She rubbed them, and the tears began to flow in earnest. She laid her arms on the warm white marble of the balustrade, buried her face against her warm skin and wept. Heat bore down on her shoulders and the backs of her legs. The mundane and the sublime jostled in her mind. The world is so full of things I haven't seen, she thought, and I must put some suncream on my shoulders or they'll burn, and in a year or so I shall be dead! Footsteps scrunched towards her across the gravel.

'Oh, Conrad!' said Laura, her teeth and fists clenched, 'I don't want to *die*.'

'Let's go and find some lunch, then.'

In the ebbing heat of late afternoon Conrad swam several leisurely lengths. Laura, wearing a long sleeveless shift, lay in a deckchair under a sunshade, too self-conscious to expose herself to his gaze. He came to the side of the pool, rested both elbows along the tiles that edged it and, looking up at her, said, 'So you're obsessed with death, are you? No wonder. I'm obsessed with sex, and the increasing difficulty of obtaining it. Shall we talk about it?'

'No,' Laura said, rejecting the implied deal.

She folded her hands behind her head, noticing that Conrad glanced at her armpits. They were, as always, clean-shaven. The springy black tufts escaping under the arms and between the legs of Mediterranean women had always struck her as coarse and animal.

Shaving legs and underarms had been part of the Saturday evening boarding-school ritual. Some girls, the more hirsute or squeamish, had used a foul-smelling depilatory called Veet. They would lie on their beds in the dormitory, arms akimbo, while the thick white paste did its work. Afterwards it would be swirled away down the plughole, and with it the dark strands of underarm hair. This process disgusted Laura. She preferred shaving, although her taut skin goose-pimpled and shrank from the rasping strokes of the razor-blade. Nowadays there was only a fine, pale fuzz to be attended to once a month. She knew by heart the contours of her uplifted armpit, the concave valley between taut sinews and swelling arm muscles, and no longer needed to use a mirror. Serenely hairless, she closed her eyes beneath Conrad's gaze.

Conrad had bided his time before making a move. He bought her dinner, listened to her and drew his own conclusions: she was no virgin. Conrad did not seduce virgins. Laura had long ago stopped seeing Hugo and had broken up with her previous boyfriend, the serious and spindly Christopher Rumbold. By November, after several months without a lover, she was getting frustrated. Too young to feel sexual desire in the abstract, she needed a man upon whom to project it.

Conrad moved gradually from kisses to potent embraces that left her outside her flat at the end of an evening trembling with confusion. In public he would not hold her hand in case they were spotted. At work he greeted her with an impersonal nod or smile. She wanted to ask Cameron if he knew about her and Conrad, but asking would give the game away. Then she would think: what game? Couple of drinks, couple of dinners, a few kisses – does that amount to anything? Yet she knew it did, if only because she could no longer behave in the same carefree manner as 'before' – before Conrad had noticed her. Now when he passed her in the corridor or came in to her office, she was wooden with self-consciousness.

Conrad waited until she was bewildered by his restraint and ardent for more, yet when he did eventually make a pass it took her by surprise. One lunch hour they had gone to Primrose Hill. They had eaten in a small Greek taverna and were strolling along paths littered with fallen leaves when she checked her watch and said with a heavy heart, 'Cameron will be wondering where I am. I ought to get back.'

Conrad looked at her. 'A friend of mine has a flat very near here. He is away. He has given me the key.'

A statement, not a question or an invitation. She stopped in her tracks and felt her mouth go dry. Her heart was pounding so hard that her legs trembled. He took her arm, quite formally, and they set off.

It was a second-floor flat in one of the big stucco houses bordering Regent's Park. The bed in a corner of the drawing-room, behind a screen, was unmade, as though someone had got out of it in a hurry. Laura wondered if anyone else used it for trysts. Conrad drew the heavy lined curtains across the window, which softened the late autumn sunlight into muted diffuse shades. Even the sound of the traffic was muffled. Laura stood by the bed, her passive, boneless stance disguising her racing heart. She wondered whether she was expected to make the bed and if so, where she might find clean sheets. Conrad kissed her and began, methodically, to undress her.

Laura leaned back in her chair after dinner, her breasts cradled by the soft curve of her top. A tray of coffee stood between them. 'It is *good* to have you here,' he said, and his face began to take on the granite expression she remembered. Lust had always hardened his features.

'I ought to have warned you,' she said quickly, 'I'm *hors de combat* these days.'

'In that case,' he said with sudden ruthlessness, 'you should go to bed and I am going *out.*'

'I'm glad you said that. I was just beginning to feel sorry for you.'

'On the contrary, it is *I* who should feel sorry for you. What's the point of living if you can no longer fuck?'

The sexual imperative was the dominant force in Conrad's life. He would cancel any appointment, no matter how important, if there was the possibility of making love instead – especially if the woman concerned were a new conquest. The *emotion* of love hardly entered into it, although he preferred women who were fun and amusing as well as pretty.

It had not taken Laura long to understand this, although she found it sordid. She had always assumed that people who had affairs were in love with each other, but Conrad never told her he loved her and she gave up hoping he would say it. He seduced her by the authority of his age – she was used to doing what older men told her – and she began to understand that novelty and secrecy, rather than love, goaded his desire. She had never slept with a married man before and found that she too was excited by the illicit. In due course, mesmerized and flattered by their clandestine meetings and the pleasure he took in her body, she fell in love.

They met a couple more times at the Regent's Park flat. Once, in the middle of love-making, the telephone rang, making them both jump and freeze. After that Conrad said, 'A bit risky, coming here. If this is going to be a regular event – as I very much hope it is – couldn't we use yours?'

Laura thought of her low-ceilinged attic flat and the narrow room in which she slept, one wall lined with bookshelves made out of bricks and planks. She tidied it once a week, if that. There were posters on the walls of the living-room she shared with her flatmates and a screen in one corner with an ever-changing collage of newspaper cuttings and fashion pictures, postcards, recipes and scraps of material, anything that caught their eye. Coloured felt hats and long Indian scarves hung on the hall coatstand and, underneath it, psychedelic carrier bags stuffed with dirty clothes waited to be taken to the launderette at weekends. Letting Conrad see where she lived was one more invasion of her privacy. It would tighten his hold over her life – as her boss, her lover – if he were to become a secret visitor to her flat.

'I don't know,' she said. 'I'd have to ask the others. They might not like it. Judy disapproves of me having an affair with a married man.'

'Does she, indeed? What a little puritan! I am glad you take no notice. Are they ever there at lunchtime?'

'Hardly ever. Not unless one of us is ill or something.'

'Well, then . . . they needn't know.'

'I couldn't go behind their *backs*!' she had said, shocked, and he laughed.

'Do you all know everything about one another's lives?'

Of course we do, Laura reflected. Now that Constance was so preoccupied with her husband and babies, Laura was closer to her flatmates than anyone. In the evenings they all came home and swapped stories of what had happened to one another during the day. They offered advice and sympathy, shared their clothes and make-up, learning and teaching the difficult business of becoming women, finding a man, passing for grown-ups at work and in restaurants. They bickered about whose turn it was to wash the kitchen floor or the stairs and sulked if a favourite shirt had been borrowed and not put back clean. They complained about their parents, borrowed money from each other, had the curse at the same time. We're so close, she thought: I *do* know everything about their lives. Yet Conrad persuaded her, against her will, and she agreed to meet him at the flat in future.

This meant she had to keep her room tidy and make her bed each morning before going to work, in case Conrad wanted them to use the flat at lunchtime. On those days he would ring her on the internal phone and murmur, 'You free?' She always was. They would leave the office separately. He would be waiting round the corner in a taxi. She would jump in and they would speed up to Hampstead. They no longer bothered to have lunch or go for a walk. He would follow her up the stairs to the top-floor flat, stroking the backs of her thighs or her bottom, and balance her breasts in his hands as she fiddled with the front-door key. Once inside they would embrace, and she would say for the sake of form and hospitality, 'Coffee?'

He would take her hand and lead her to the bedroom – a housemaid's room it must have been once, long and narrow with a dormer window set into the roof. A numdah rug that her mother had bought from John Lewis to celebrate Laura's new independence lay beside the bed and a couple of posters from the National Gallery were pinned to her walls. Her clothes hung on a rail behind a curtain.

'Student life,' he said, the first time he saw it.

'I'm not a student!' she flashed back. 'I *earn* my living!'

'How could I forget?' he soothed. 'Come here, career girl . . .'

His caution in public made her realize that he did care what people thought, because people might tell his wife. She had always known that Conrad was married, but had not been much concerned with the unknown, never-mentioned third party, his wife. Most men had wives: stolid, domesticated, middle-aged women, providers of shirts and socks and square meals. They were what men *did* in the evenings: they went home to their wives. Laura could never imagine being a wife. Paul was heaven, of course, but she had seen too much of her sister's domestic drudgery to fall for that.

After she had been in Amalfi for a week, Laura asked over dinner, 'Conrad, what happened to your wife? Is she still alive? Has she ever been out here?'

'I would like her to see this place, but she won't come without Maurice and I won't have Maurice. Yes, surprising, isn't it? She did divorce me in the end. She waited until our daughters were grown up; then she moved out and after two years petitioned for divorce.'

'There must have been some reason.'

'Over the years she'd had plenty of reasons. What wife does not? But I had assumed by the time we reached our mid-fifties that we were stuck with each other for the rest of our lives . . . Not, in my case, unwillingly. People aren't in it for love, you know. Marriage is about habit, inertia, rows and, because of inertia, forgiveness. And also, I suppose, the handing-down of the genes.'

69

'Do you have grandchildren?'

'Is it so unlikely? Of course I have grandchildren. Two boys.'

'Was it a shock when she went?'

'Not exactly. What I *minded* was when she married again.'

'Maurice?'

'Maurice. The sort of self-important, pink-cheeked, stout little man that Goya painted, or Stubbs. A minor grandee without culture. I mind Maurice seeing my daughters and grandchildren, when I do not. I *mind* him being their surrogate grandfather and handing on his Maurice-isms. I *mind* her marrying a boring buffoon.'

After they had begun to meet in her flat, new possibilities opened up. Once, Conrad made her put on, over her nakedness, a full-length purple crêpe dress from Biba. She, Ruth and Judy, all three of them, had clubbed together to buy it. At five pounds each it had cost half their disposable income for the week. The dress had long sleeves and a high neck and beneath its clinging folds her nakedness was more exciting than if she had worn nothing. He stroked her and slipped his hand high up under her skirt. Laura shivered and closed her eyes. Conrad reached behind him to the chest of drawers for her hairbrush. He tapped her bottom through the material of the dress and brushed her nipples with the stiff bristles, then immediately stroked her with gentle fingertips.

'I would like to watch you learn the pleasure – the, oh, *unusual* pleasure – of sex alternating with pain,' he said. 'If you will give me the one, I promise you the other . . .'

She flinched from the sharp bristles and her skin grew cold and shivered at the threat. 'No,' she said. 'Please don't. I'm an awful coward. I just don't like pain.'

'Not simple pain,' he urged. 'Quite a delicate, erotic pain. Followed by great pleasure. Then a bit of pain again. Then more pleasure. Let me show you.'

'No . . .' she begged, hearing the pleading submission in her own voice.

He made her lie face down on the bed and tapped her quite lightly with the hairbrush. Then he stroked her through the long folds of the dress. Then tapped her a bit harder. Laura was worried that the brush might snag the delicate material. It wasn't just her dress – it belonged to them all. It was too long for Judy, too tight across the front for Ruth; it really only fitted her perfectly, so it had been very generous of the others. Conrad hit her a good deal harder.

'Take the dress off,' she said.

He peeled it off, rolling the skirt up along her back, pausing to tap her naked bottom with the hairbrush, then pulling the dress over her head and along her arms and outstretched hands. Laura was so relieved that the dress would not be damaged that she let him hit her bottom quite hard. As soon as she cried out – a childish 'Ouch!' that she could not suppress – he stopped and stroked her bottom and her long, arched back. Then he hit her again, with his hand this time – a sound slap across the buttocks that took her by surprise.

'It's no good,' she said robustly. 'I really don't like it.'

'My sweet child,' he said. 'I have scarcely *begun*.'

He stood up and took his own clothes off, pausing to let Laura admire him.

Laura submitted because it pleased and excited Conrad, and she loved Conrad. She never learned to enjoy the pain but she endured it for his sake, and because she was afraid of seeming frigid. He would hit her with the hairbrush or sometimes the cold silver mirror and occasionally even the granular sole of his shoe, or flick her with her bra – a sharp, momentary flick, always followed by a subtle caress. His fingers or tongue would swoop across her mouth, her breasts, but as soon as she relaxed and abandoned herself to pleasure his other hand would administer a stinging rebuke. As she drew in her breath to protest, the touch of pleasure would resume. He was attentive and delicate, responsive to her sensations, and meanwhile his own excitement would mount, especially when he lashed her breasts one after the other with the sharp side of the brush. He assured her that she would, in time, learn to enjoy the alternating sensations of small pain . . . great pleasure . . . greater pain . . . higher pleasure.

'If you enjoy it so much, why can't *I* hurt *you*?' she asked.

'Ah,' Conrad said, smiling, 'that's not the point.'

'What *is* the point?'

'Your submission.'

These episodes hardly ever culminated in an orgasm for Laura, though she always pretended they did. Loving Conrad, she wanted to gratify him, and she knew that not until he thought she had reached orgasm would he surrender to his own. Finally they would wash and dress. Conrad would go down into the street to hail a taxi while she grabbed an apple or a piece of bread and munched it while she watched him out of her bedroom window. Locking the door to the flat, she would hurry back to the office. Five minutes later he might pass her in the corridor with a smile and a nod. Sometimes he would glance meaningfully at his watch. 'Good lunch, I see?'

She would blush. 'Oh yes, lovely,' adding, 'Sorry I'm late.'

She used to wonder if the other girls speculated about her, or if Cameron, head of reference books and her immediate boss, could detect the recent, pungent smell of sex. Sometimes she deliberately invited his complicity by not washing. All afternoon she would feel Conrad's semen viscous between her thighs and inhale its gluey smell.

She was entirely dependent on Conrad's whim. He had been careful to ensure that she started taking the Pill, although their affair proceeded by random fits and starts. Several days might pass with not a glance or word, and her love would drive her to a frenzy of uncertainty. She would reproach herself for having been so stupid, so cowardly about the pain. It wasn't *that* bad, and if it pleased him . . . She worried that he would find someone else who liked to be hurt and would be more satisfactory in bed. Just as she began to droop into depression, his voice would murmur, 'You free? How about today? Have you missed me?'

'Oh, yes!' she would say gratefully.

In Amalfi, after they had been together for two weeks, she inquired about his solitary life. 'I'm surprised you never remarried.'

'So is my ex-wife. I never felt less than affectionate towards her but fidelity was too much to expect. I couldn't get used to another woman now. If Sally hadn't taken on that pompous ass Maurice, we would probably have got together again.'

So! she thought. He *is* lonely. That was why he had come to her dinner and paid for her to visit him for a month.

'You are still a highly desirable woman,' he prompted. 'What about *you*, Laura? Have you never felt inclined to marry?'

'Sometimes I felt I would have liked to marry a man and sometimes a man felt he would have liked to marry me, but on the one occasion when the two coincided it was impossible.'

'Ah! Love frustrated! Love denied! How tragic!' he purred. 'And now? Are you sorry? Women are supposed to want children.'

She bridled.

'Women nowadays can *have* children, husband or no husband, if that's what they want. But I hardly ever did. Sometimes when I was besotted with a man, I wondered what his child would be like, but . . . no, I don't have many regrets. Apart from dying young, of course.'

'Dying old is probably worse.'

The following day they went to Pompeii. Overlooked by Vesuvius, the ruins of the former city sprawled across a wide, flat plain. Its streets and pavements were deeply indented by the ruts of chariot wheels. Columns were truncated, statues restored, unnaturally white. Grass sprouted between the paving stones and tall cypresses edged the squares.

Tourists were wandering about, heads buried deep in their

73

guidebooks, looking up for a moment to check that they were seeing what they had been promised – Temple of Apollo, yup; Temple of Jupiter, yup, OK – and down again. Video cameras whirred and swung, pausing to focus on grinning, T-shirted figures. Look everyone, I'm alive and this lot are dead! Only the here and now matters; the rest is ruined buildings and forgetfulness.

Laura's sandals were dusty. The sunglasses slid down her nose.

'Were there any survivors?' she asked.

'None,' answered Conrad, 'except those who fled before the eruption. Most people stayed put. From inertia, I suppose – nobody wants to be the first to panic. It was August. Must have been very hot; people get lethargic and move slowly in August. They went indoors and waited for the tremors to stop and everything to return to normal. Then down it came. I'll show you how sudden it was.'

Near the entrance to the site there was a small museum. The preserved bodies of a couple of people and a petrified dog were in glass cases. The dog was arched into a rictus of agony, its teeth bared. Perhaps it had been tied up. So that was what death looked like. No wonder the dog had snarled in terror, cowering before the man in black with the scythe. Thousands must have died like that: men, women, children. Babies, fat brown babies, engulfed in scalding molten gouts of cinders and lava.

They left the cool interior and moved out into white sunlight. The day was heating up, more coaches were arriving.

'Shall we go?' Conrad said.

Once, naked together in Laura's room, they had heard the sound of a key turning in the front door and someone entering. Conrad stood up and swiftly propped a chair under the door-handle. They sat side by side in silence, listening to footsteps going into the kitchen, the slamming of cupboards. Laura's heart thundered so hard that, looking down, she could see it beating.

She took Conrad's hand and placed it against her heart. He cupped her breast and lowered his head. After a while the doorknob turned. The chair held. Moments later the front door slammed, and Laura heard footsteps retreating down the street.

Her orgasm was overwhelming.

'Now do you begin to understand the pleasure of the clandestine?' Conrad asked. '*That* is why happily married men have affairs.'

A year or two later, Laura found a smaller, more central flat – in a basement this time, but with a flowering patio at the back. She could sit out in the summer and watch the London sky by day or night. She was adopted by a stray cat. Yet even after she had left Lively and Parsons and the attic office, even after she had started a new affair, the telephone on her desk would sometimes ring and Conrad's voice would murmur in her ear, 'You free?' She hardly ever said no.

Why did she allow him to take possession of her body for so long, in ways she never learned to enjoy? Because in the end she became his confidante; because he needed her, and Laura's need to be needed was greater than her desire not to be hurt. What became important to her were the times *after* they had made love, when they would talk like old, intimate friends. He would tell her about the hitch-hikers he had picked up, young girls in long grubby skirts who would sit in the front seat of his car rolling a joint and then offer him a smoke. Sometimes he would say, 'I'd rather make love to you,' and sometimes they would answer, 'That's cool. Stop the car. I could use a fuck.'

Laura believed these stories. Sex was in the air; people looked at one another in open sexual invitation. 'If you dig me, let's fuck,' a stranger might say to Laura at a party. 'But I don't,' she might answer, and he would wander off peaceably in search of someone who did. They were like children gorging on Smarties, with no grown-ups to say, 'That'll *do* now – you've had enough. You'll make yourself sick.'

She herself, after the first two years of her affair with Conrad, began to have other lovers. He did not require her to be faithful – quite the opposite – and she was on the Pill: why not sleep with as many men as she fancied?

Conrad liked to hear Laura talk about these other sexual encounters, confident that he was her best lover. She never told him that it was not true. She preferred love to be liquid and murmuring, but Conrad watched her like a scientist in a vivisection laboratory. How does the animal react to this stimulus or that? His eyes would rest fixedly upon her face as he flicked and slapped, and when she turned her head from side to side to escape his gaze and the stinging pain, he would pause and caress her. She waited for the sex to be over so that they could talk.

Something bound her to him. Was it because he was the only man she had fallen in love with since Mick? She had an affair with a student called Joe, and when that went wrong she began to sleep with Edouard, but she didn't love him; then she started going out with Nicholas, who loved her; and when that ended, with Kit Mallinson who also loved her. Still she could not turn Conrad away. Brought up in a male hierarchy, taught never to challenge male authority, in the end Laura only stopped when another man told her to stop. By that time Conrad had been her lover for ten years.

This relationship did her a lot of harm. It made her undervalue marriage, ignore wives, and cultivate secrecy. It denied her close female friends and intimacy with other women . . . except, of course, her sister, Constance. Conrad did his utmost to convince Laura that perverse sex was better than loving sex, and he almost succeeded.

Conrad was reminiscing drowsily. 'We should have gone on making love all our lives.'

They had lunched at a small restaurant in the hills. Afterwards, Laura sat baking in the heat reflected from the hot tiles of the terrace, her face tipped back under the sunhat. The tablecloth flickered in the breeze. She leaned forward and folded her elbows on the table. His eyes were closed; he was almost asleep.

'No, we shouldn't,' she answered, and at the harsh note in her voice he half opened his eyes. 'We went on too long. You tried to corrupt me, Conrad, and you made a pretty good job of it.'

'Corrupt you! What an extraordinary thing to say!'

'You tried to make me ignore the responses of my own body and subdue them to yours. You like hurting women, Conrad, not pleasing them. You hurt *me*, and then justified your cruelty by telling me I liked it. I never liked it. You must have known that. Why should I like being hit? *You* never allowed me to hit you with my shoe or my hairbrush. You never went home at night with purple marks on your legs and arms and body where I'd hurt you. You said your wife might notice, but that wasn't the real reason.'

He sat upright, dozing no longer. 'It wasn't my role to be passive. I was your teacher; I was initiating you into the much more subtle pleasures of delayed release. An orgasm that has been earned is infinitely more satisfying than one reached directly. This is why men learn to delay their own orgasm while they apply themselves first to a woman's pleasure.'

'You're wrong,' Laura said. 'Why should I have to earn my orgasm? Why can't I be *given* it? Men please women by giving them pleasure, not pain – not to reward themselves with a bigger and better bang. It also helps if they love the woman they are fucking. You never once used that word to me.'

The waitress, hearing a raised voice, emerged from the dark interior wiping her hands on a tea towel. '*I signori vorrebbero ancora caffè?*' she inquired. '*Grazie, no,*' replied Laura, smiling to reassure her. '*Il conto, per favore.*' She turned back to Conrad.

'I haven't finished. You did corrupt me. Thanks to you, the worst time of my life was made worse still by a relationship with a refined sadist. Oh, he could have taught even *you* a few things!'

'And was *he* at your dinner, too?'

'Do you remember Rafe? The American? A connoisseur of antiquarian books, eighteenth-century furniture, and possessor of a curious little case of sexual toys. He liked to titillate himself by using those on me.'

77

'Why did you submit?'

'I told you – because you left your mark on me, Conrad, all too effectively. I had thought I was strong enough, after my experience with you, to choose my own pleasures. I discovered that the more vulnerable I felt, the more cravenly I submitted.'

'I should like to hear about this Rafe,' he murmured, but Laura could see that he was angry.

'No doubt you would, but I am no longer prepared to titillate you. I have made another discovery: being near death makes one feel strong.'

'Never mind. I doubt if you could have given me any new ideas. I have paid the bill. Shall we go?'

She left Amalfi and his glass and steel house a few days later. Conrad had not pursued their conversation but had risen from the table that evening as soon as he had eaten and, without explanation, roared off in his car. Laura had been asleep by the time he returned.

She did not regret having told him the truth. There were reparations to be made and scores to be settled if she were to unravel her life before meeting whatever it was that the petrified dog had so abruptly confronted. After a month of sunshine and ease, the fear and panic uppermost in her mind when she arrived had receded. She was grateful for that.

After breakfast on her last morning, while the maid packed and before the taxi arrived to take her to Naples airport, Conrad said, 'You know, my dear, we have this in common: neither of us comes *first* with anyone. For that, as well as a number of other reasons, I find myself sorry that you are dying and I shall not see you again.'

He can be generous after all, she thought, and honest. It is a sort of reconciliation.

'I am glad we met again, too. You have been good to me this month, Conrad. You have given me four weeks out of your life.'

'I wish it could have been more,' he said.

5

Joe Watson

One week – not a typical week – in the winter of 1971 Laura slept with five different men, four of whom she had never met before. Two were people she went to bed with after Christmas parties and never saw again; one, whom she encountered at a dinner given by newly married friends to show off their wedding presents, drove her home afterwards and came in 'for a coffee'. He never got in touch again, either. The fourth, of course, was Conrad and the fifth was called Joe Watson.

Sex without love was a skill, and Laura was getting better at it. Improvement brought her more pleasure and control, but passion – whatever that was – evaded her. Surely these upside-down coilings and wrigglings with heavy-limbed, hairy male bodies were not *passion*? Sometimes she got quite carried away and she often had orgasms, though not as often as she pretended. Perhaps faithful, contented Constance was right, and only mutual love could elevate the strenuous sex act into something more than a race to finish first.

The main reason for Laura's promiscuity was neither lust nor loneliness but opportunity. Yet in the aftermath of that particular week, just before she was due to go home for the usual family Christmas, a sense of unease lingered. She hardly knew whether to feel proud or ashamed of herself.

Laura had been born in July 1947 and was thus, unlike Constance, a postwar baby, a privileged baby, one of the fortunate generation whose childhood had not been marked by evacuation to the country or soldiers in uniform or even sweet rationing. The accident of that birth date brought her to adulthood in the heyday of sexual freedom. She could, in theory, fuck without risk of censure or pregnancy (though plenty of women were criticized and many babies were born). Yet she had been indoctrinated during the Fifties, and Fifties morality was still Thirties morality, the morality of her parents and teachers. Love and marriage. White for virginity. It's different for men. Nice girls don't. Second-hand goods. This long shadow darkened, but did not prohibit, her freedom.

Laura did not discuss her sex life with her parents, and not much with her sister either. She fielded her mother's anxious, roundabout questions by saying she wasn't ready for commitment. Occasionally she would bring some suitable male friend home for Sunday lunch – never, of course, Conrad – to reassure her parents. Her father would expect to be called 'Sir'; her mother liked to be discreetly flattered and flirted with. Afterwards the man would be described as 'a nice boy' or 'not, let us hope, a permanent fixture'.

Aside from these ambiguities, Laura's bachelor-girl life (as her parents cautiously referred to it) was fun. She had left university with the blithe assumption that once she got the hang of London geographically the rest would follow. In the last three years she had mapped out her territory. First Hampstead, the shops and launderettes, tube and bus routes near the flat; then Soho, which she explored in her lunch hours. She used to go to Speakers' Corner at weekends until she discovered that better debates could be overheard in the cafeteria of the new ICA in the Mall, or the milling foyers of the Academy or Paris Pullman cinemas.

Huge and indifferent as the city had seemed at first, it was never threatening. In summer it was a place of bells and chanting, musty bazaar smells and the clinging emanations of hash and pot and grass, smoked, inhaled, or eaten. This was the favourite recreation of the dreamy, dusky, grubby, heedless, undulating, careless, trusting young. In their shabby, half-transparent dresses, barefoot or in tightly laced boots, they drifted through the streets and parks in a benevolent haze, the accidental children of free love trailing at their heels.

Laura had never been drawn to hippiedom, but she was an early convert to feminism, which only its detractors called 'Women's Lib'. She was inspired by all the caryatids of the new movement. She read their books, watched them on television, and thought, They're talking about *me*! It was an exhilarating time. Conrad and Joe Watson, in their different ways, demonstrated how hard it was going to be to live up to the tenets of feminism.

Her obsession with Conrad and the need to be available at short notice – at his beck and call, in fact, though she never expressed it like that – precluded any other commitment for the first two years of their relationship.

Then one rainy afternoon she met Joe in a West End art gallery. Laura had just been treated to lunch by her brother-in-law Paul and was strolling along Bond Street, idly window-shopping, when the heavens opened. She ducked into an art gallery to avoid getting wet and found herself in a white space hung with large, vivid canvases. Picking up a price list, she wandered past them one by one. Although abstract, they had representational titles. She was trying to work out the connection when she realized that she herself was being scrutinized by a young man in a long, fringed Afghan coat and a Paisley-print shirt who was sitting on a leather bench in the middle of the gallery. When she turned round and met his eyes, he grinned and said, 'Hi!' Laura, embarrassed, muttered a faint answering 'Hi . . .' and turned back to the pictures, but she could no longer concentrate.

As she left the gallery he followed her out and said, 'You through?'

'Well, yes, but . . .'

'Good. Then we can go for a coffee. I know a place round the corner.' Glancing down to give herself a moment to frame a refusal, Laura's eye was caught by a pair of gleaming Chelsea boots.

'You dig them? Just bought them this morning. Christmas present to myself. I made the shop put my old pair in the bag so I could walk out in these.'

He swung the bag at her to prove it. Laura smiled, both at his boots and because his Northern-inflected voice reminded her sharply of Mick, her first love.

'I can't have coffee with you,' she said. 'I'm late back for work.'

'You *work*?' he said, as though this were an eccentric thing to do.

'For a publisher in Soho. And I'm already late from my lunch hour because of the rain. It's stopped now. I ought to be heading back.'

'Who'd you have lunch with?'

Laura bit back the schoolgirlish, obvious answer, Mind your own business. 'My brother-in-law.'

'Why? You fancy him, then?'

At that moment she should have been warned, right there at the very beginning. Instead, never for a moment thinking that a man she had only just met could be jealous, she said, 'Course not. Don't be daft. He's married to my *sister*.'

'I'd never have guessed!' He checked his watch. 'It's half past two already. Twenty minutes won't make a difference. Here. This is the place. I'm Joseph Watson but you can call me Joe.'

Joe was not handsome, hardly even attractive, but he was compelling. His intense gaze, his fierce, unguarded expressions and spontaneous moods made him a powerful and dramatic presence. He was impulsive and contradictory in a way that Conrad was not. Above all he was *young*, two years younger than Laura. Conrad's maturity often made her feel gauche, but Joe seemed even more confused and insecure than she was. Living on a drama student's grant, he was also much poorer. The real reason for his poverty was that he took drugs, but it was a long time before Laura realized this.

Joe lived in a bedsitter in a dreary north London terraced house lit by sixty-watt bulbs and smelling of old cat and old fish. His room was full of books and scripts; a typewriter stood on his desk with a sheet of paper rolled into it. This he covered ostentatiously when she visited him, and Laura never sneaked a look at what lay beneath. Under the basin in one corner stood a row of unwashed, sour-smelling milk bottles. A whistling kettle shared a plug with the electric fire. His single bedstead creaked. She only spent one night there, and from then on insisted that they made love at her flat. Joe pretended to sulk about this – 'So the way *I* live isn't good enough for you?' – but in fact he too preferred to avoid his landlady's prurient, disapproving stare when they left together in the morning.

Once Joe had inveigled himself into her life he became jealous, demanding and neurotic. No woman would have stood this after the first scene, the first yelling, weeping accusations, the final crumbling into melodramatic remorse, had he not possessed another skill. Joe was – no doubt about it – a marvellous and tireless lover.

Hitherto Laura had been passive while making love, letting the man take the lead, going at his pace and hoping they culminated at about the same time. Joe would ask her blatantly to do what *he* wanted, instructing her in the speed and rhythm, the touch, the grip. She had never met anyone with so few inhibitions. Joe surprised her by talking while they made love. He even laughed at her ineptitude.

'If you go *that* slowly I'll be asleep before I get there! No, ouch, give me a chance. Not that fast, either! Look . . .' and he pushed her hand away and showed her. Laura was excited by watching him and by the fact that she was licensed to touch and tease him until he was gasping, arched, and finally helpless.

'Don't wash,' he would urge, as she prepared to come to bed. 'I like the way you smell.'

Sex with Joe was not like dancing – something graceful and beautiful. The reality was dirty, full of grunts and rooting, clumsy, sticky, smelly. Laura was surprised and ashamed at first, but she soon accepted Joe's demands because with him, for the first time in her life, she made love on equal terms. From then on, instead of passively accepting pleasure, Laura became active in giving it back. Sometimes she got it wrong.

'That hurts! If you want to do that, you'll have to keep your fingernails shorter!' Joe complained. Laura filed her nails and from then on she often glanced at other women's hands to judge their readiness to do the secret and appalling things that aroused a man.

When Laura invited Joe to her dinner in February, she was well aware that unless he had changed out of all recognition, he would feel thoroughly ill at ease. She asked him all the same because it was neither Hugo (who took her virginity when she was twenty) nor Conrad but *Joe* who had turned her into a sexual being.

She traced him through an actors' directory. Against his name was that of an obscure agent. She rang the number.

'Joe Watson? Works under the stage name of Joseph Fountain. *When* he works. Haven't had a booking for him in – friend, did you say you were? – not in years. Don't see why you shouldn't have his number, gel. Here you are. All the best. Get him to give us a call sometime.'

Joe had arrived for the dinner wearing black jeans, a black shirt, and a modish black tie decorated with a yellow bird from the Royal Academy shop. To her momentary astonishment, he was bald. Then she thought, why not? He had always had thinning hair which used to worry him a good deal in his twenties. He would massage olive oil into his scalp, having heard somewhere that this prevented hair loss. Well, it hadn't worked.

'Look,' Joe said, to forestall comment, as he entered her drawing-room, 'black tie.'

'So I see,' answered Laura. 'Craigie Aitchison's canary, hm?'

'Yeah. My daughter's at the RA. Gave it me for Christmas.'

She laughed. 'Oh, Joe! You've got a *daughter*? Old enough to be an art student?'

'Yeah. I'm forty-two now, believe it or not. How about you? What's this dinner all about? You getting hitched in your old age?'

Just then the butler ushered in another guest and Laura was able only to shake her head and smile before turning to greet Hugo.

Joe had evidently held his own that evening. He was always the centre of an argumentative group. Some of the others had become pompous or wizened, but Joe had kept himself in good shape and his eyes were bright. Either he had changed entirely from the man she had known or, Laura surmised, he had found a devoted woman to take care of him.

Her guess was right, as Laura discovered several weeks later when she visited Joe in south London at the beginning of May. His partner's name was Dorothy Greaves, and she looked a few years older than Joe.

'Call me Dot,' she said. 'I never felt I was a Dorothy. Or a Doll. Joe sometimes calls me "Dorthy" like Marilyn Monroe in – you know the one . . .'

'*Gentlemen Prefer Blondes . . .*'

'Yeah, right! He calls me "Dorthy" when he's feeling randy, don't you, love?'

Laura thought, I could have waited a bit longer for that piece of information. 'Good for him,' she said noncommittally.

'Joe will make us a cup of tea while I show you where you can dump your stuff,' said Dot. 'Rosehip, camomile or orange pekoe?'

'Have you got plain ordinary housemaid's?' Laura asked.

'Have we got *what*?'

'You know – Typhoo, PG Tips, Lyons, anything? Just tea?'

Dot sighed. Joe said, 'I'll have a rummage.'

'Thanks.'

Joe and Dot had been together for several years. He had moved into her council flat in Camberwell the day after they had met on a 'Support the Miners, Coal not Dole' march in the bitter winter of 1984. Her late-teenage daughters had left home shortly afterwards, one to a nearby squat and the other to travel the hippie trail.

'Where's *your* daughter?' Laura asked Joe.

'Never lived with me. Her mother and I never married. Saffron's a brilliant girl, though. Dead creative. Stunning looker.'

'A real free spirit.' Dot chipped in. 'Once she can get away from the Academy and stop drawing plaster casts of Greek statues she'll spread her wings. Talent like hers will find its way to the real source. The roots.'

'Oh?' said Laura. 'And what are they?'

'The spirit and myth of landscape; the sacred places; the ancient myths and sites blessed by the goddess mother,' said Dot. Her eyes shone and she spoke without a trace of self-consciousness.

Laura nodded. 'Uh-huh . . . ?'

'In time I believe she will rekindle her deep female sense of caring for the sacredness of the land, for she is the spirit of the land, and the land manifests itself through her, and through all women.'

'Where was she born, then?' Laura inquired.

'Ealing,' Joe admitted, and stared fiercely into his mug.

Joe worked for the council's housing department. Dot taught art at the local comprehensive. It was part of her job to organize the painting of backcloths for the school plays. Joe, thanks to his former career as an actor, came in to give the producer a hand. They were both engrossed in the school's end of year production. On Laura's first evening Joe prepared a meal of couscous and salad with rough red wine, followed by a shared joint – Laura declined the wine and the dope – but after that she was left to her own devices during the day, and often in the evenings as well. This was a relief, since her condition had already worsened since being diagnosed four months earlier. Although she had not suffered another haemorrhage, she frequently had heavy nose bleeds. Her liver was now rigid, her abdomen bloated, and her appetite diminished. She slept for hours during the day, fitfully at night.

Dot was keen that Laura should investigate alternative therapies. She had no time for what she called 'straight' medicine.

'It's a vicious circle – the doctors are bribed by the multinational drug companies, who test their products on animals and have to sell the stuff at inflated prices, whether it works or not, to keep the shareholders happy. It's all corrupt.'

Anti-religion, anti-art, anti-establishment, anti-government; pro-Joe and the earth goddess, Laura thought: I am never going to last a month here. Yet she was interested, despite her scepticism, in alternative therapy.

'What would you recommend?' she asked.

'You ever been to a homeopathic doctor?'

'No.'

Joe joined them at the kitchen table and rolled a cigarette. Same green Rizla paper as all those years ago, Laura noticed. He joined in with gusto, eager to convince her by relating his own experiences. 'When they take your history, it's not like some overworked GP; they really *listen* to where you're coming from and where you're at.'

Dot put a hand on Laura's wrist and looked earnestly into her eyes. 'Ever tried acupuncture?' she asked.

'No.'

Joe went on. 'Then they, like, lay their hands on you. Magic. Blows your mind. You feel nobody's ever listened to your *body* before.'

Dot focused on Laura. 'Imaging? Aromatherapy?'

'Nope. Nothing like that.'

'After they've got you, like, separated out,' Joe continued, 'so you're a real individual, a really unique person, *then* they begin the therapy.'

Dot drew a pad and Biro towards her and wrote ALTERNA-
TIVE THERAPIES at the top of a sheet of paper. She underlined
the words firmly and Laura thought, yes, behind all that wavy,
wafty stuff there is a good teacher. Dot made separate headings
for two central London therapy centres and copied out some
names and numbers from her address book. Beside them she
added comments like 'very wise woman' or 'trained in China –
really good'.

'Do you use this sort of healing a lot?' Laura asked Dot
another time when they were alone.

'Used to,' said Dot. 'Mainly for Joe. How else do you think I
got him off all that shit he was into?'

'But the other night . . .'

'That's *quite* different. Dope's watered-down wine next to the
stuff he'd been doing. He'd never have managed to stay off
without a) the acupuncture – we did that first – and then b) a
homeopathic guy and c) the aromatherapy, as his treat. He'd be
well fucked by now, if it weren't for them. And me,' she added.
'As it is, *I'm* the one that's well fucked.' She laughed a raucous
laugh and her flesh shook.

'But how can they help *me*? Look' – and Laura smoothed down
her loose shirt to emphasize the great swelling mound of her
abdomen. 'I am actually, physically, affected. It's not something
that can be . . .' she paused to recall the word – '*imaged* away.'

Dot was unperturbed. 'How do you know? I've seen some of
these guys do miracles. You on any pills?'

Laura dug into her handbag and produced three small packets,
each with a computer-printed label giving the dosage.

'What makes you believe in those? I could just as well say to
you why should a little round pill make you better?'

'It won't,' Laura said. 'It can only modify the symptoms. This
thing' – she pointed to the right-hand side of her abdomen –
'this thing in here, in my liver, is going to kill me.'

'*Fight* it!' urged Dot.

*

'Fight it, Joe,' Laura used to say when he sat on her bed, head in his hands, muttering incoherently that he was hopeless, a burden to her, useless in class, couldn't act, didn't belong in London. '*Fight* it! You mustn't be so negative! Honestly, you've got so much creativity and you're so original. I've never known anyone like you before. It's terrible to talk of dropping out!'

After hours of praise and encouragement Joe would allow himself to be coaxed back into good humour. Laura would cook him something to eat while he play-acted around the kitchen, mimicking her, making her and Ruth laugh; showing off, happy to be in the limelight. Finally in the small hours of the morning they would make love. She would get up at seven-thirty next day and go to work, leaving him sleeping peacefully. Sometimes when she got home that evening, the whole performance would have to be repeated.

It was hard now to credit the urgency with which she had responded to Joe's sinewy white body, yet she had a clear memory of going to bed in a fury with him after a row. She had pulled the sheet tightly round herself and turned away into a foetal position, the image of angry rejection. Joe had stroked her back, silently, patiently, on and on. First she let the sheet slacken, as though by accident – eyes closed, breathing held steady. Then she relaxed as though into sleep, but Joe's soft circular stroking continued. Finally – he must have persisted for an hour at least – she had turned and clung to him.

'Fuck me, oh, fuck me, Joe!'

He had made her say sorry first.

Joe would roll a Rizla cigarette, packing it with a mixture of tobacco from his pouch and the dark grains of marijuana, licking the edges of the paper delicately and twisting off the tip. He would light it and inhale deeply, deeply, to draw the sweet fumes far down into his lungs, exhaling with a sigh of satisfaction and a diaphanous smile. Once more, and he would pass the joint to Laura. The first couple of times, nothing happened and Joe giggled.

'Relax, baby!' he said lazily. 'Let yourself go with it . . .'

'What if the police . . . ?' Laura asked.

'Forget the fuzz. They can't find us . . . Hey, that rhymes!'

One evening she felt under her extended fingertips the infinitely complicated texture of the corduroy material covering the sofa. It rippled under her wandering fingers, hill and valley, ridge and furrow, up and down. She drew her nails across it.

'Joe, this is really nice!' she said. 'Feel how nice it is.'

He smiled. 'See what I mean? Here, have another little smoke.'

Ruth, Laura's only flatmate now that Judy was married, tried to tell her that Joe was a burden and a parasite, a dreary, self-pitying, chip-on-the-shoulder Northerner.

'You're the most *appalling* snob!' Laura would say, side-stepping the truth of the other accusations. Then one day she flashed back, 'Maybe, but he fucks like a rattlesnake.' Ruth kept quiet after that.

Sometimes after rehearsals or acting classes, Joe would strut triumphantly. 'I know I'm good!' he'd say. 'Better than good, marvellous. I'm going to be a bloody *marvellous* actor. I'll send you a ticket to all my first nights, Laura. I've got what it takes, I know I have. Timing, movement, and the gaze. Do you know about the gaze?'

She would say no, although he had explained it many times before and sometimes would turn 'the gaze' upon her. His eyes blazed, and she would avert her own.

'Joe, that's incredible.'

'You either have it or you don't. Olivier's got it. Alan Bates has got it. Nicol Williamson has got it. You can mesmerize an audience just by looking into the darkness beyond the footlights. Every single person in the audience thinks you're looking at him.'

She loved it when he was confident. She listened while he learned his part in the drama school productions. She knew by heart great chunks of *The Duchess of Malfi* or *Saint Joan* and works by modern playwrights. They went to the Royal Court together, Joe on his drama student's pass, to see new plays. On the tube going home he would rail against the incompetence of the actors. If he got depressed afterwards, Laura knew that he had been bluffing, that he despaired of ever standing on a real stage before a real audience. He would leave her bed and go out into the night to walk home. He often telephoned at dawn from a call-box (reversing the charges) on the pretext of saying sorry, waking her up for yet more reassurances.

Joe's moods could be ugly as well. He was fiercely jealous. She never told him about Conrad, but Ruth let the name slip one evening when the three of them were sharing a casserole. Joe's glance at Laura was that of a flame-thrower. He followed her into the kitchen when she got up to make coffee and said savagely, 'Who's *Conrad*?'

'A chap at work. My boss. Sod off, Joe, he's at least fifty.'

'Why did you invite him in, then?'

'He gave me a lift home after I'd worked late one evening.'

'Why? Where does he live?'

'I don't *know*. Joe what is this? You've no right to cross-examine me!'

'Of course I have! You're my girlfriend! I have every right!'

'Conrad is my boss, OK? Finis.'

He raised his hand, and for an instant Laura thought in astonishment, he's going to *hit* me! Instead, he stormed out of the kitchen and she heard him questioning Ruth in the next room. How often had Conrad been here? What was he like? How long ago was this? Was he attractive? As Laura came in carrying three mugs of Nescafé, Ruth rolled her eyes in mock despair.

'Joe, either shut up or go home. You're just being pathetic,' Laura said. Instantly Joe rushed out of the door and ran down the stairs. Laura, leaning out of her bedroom window, saw him on the pavement. He looked up, raised his arms and howled at her before running off.

At four in the morning the telephone rang. His voice was leaden with tiredness. 'Laura? I'm such a bastard. Of course I trust you. I should never have doubted you. Do you love me? Say you love me, Laura.'

Laura doubted very much whether she loved Joe but he had coiled his dependency round her, trapping her with his need.

Dot was a big woman. She covered her lumbering body in pale, smock-like garments worn over baggy jeans, tracksuit trousers or flowing cheesecloth skirts. She wore no make-up. Her hair was wound into a loose bun on top of her head, from which tendrils endlessly escaped and were endlessly tucked back. She was ample and generous in every sense, the perfect person to look after Joe, and they seemed happy together. They agreed about everything, especially politics, both local and national. Their convictions underpinned their work. Joe was dedicated to the council tenants, whose housing needs caused him daily problems; Dot to the local children. She often brought their drawings or collages home to show Joe. Laura thought these pictures crude and talentless but Dot and Joe pored over them, finding images and symbols which inspired and thrilled them.

'Look at this,' Dot would say wonderingly, her eyes puckered to see through the smoke drifting up from a spliff or a roll-up cigarette. 'Here's a kid who's got into ancient sites entirely on his own, no pushing from me. These images surpass anything I could do. Doesn't a painting like this one *prove* that the ancient, mythic spirit of the White Horse still flies?'

Not a question I can answer, thought Laura. She looked at Joe.

'Dot took a party to see the White Horse in Uffington for the summer solstice last year,' he explained, 'and it made a real impression. This summer we'll take them on a coach tour round the chalk horses of southern England, to honour their wild and ancient spirit. We'll get the kids to draw and document what they find and get together with their history teacher to link those chalk horses with the horses of their grandparents' time, dray horses and hansom cab horses of a century ago. Their grandparents can still remember when the milk floats were horse-drawn – as late as the Fifties, you know.'

'Really?' said Laura.

'It's only by offering an alternative to their own culture – not that it isn't valid, don't think I'm knocking it – but they need to know that there are other forms, too.'

'Yesss ... right ...' breathed Dot, looking at him with shining eyes.

He handed her the joint that Laura had declined.

She really loves him, Laura thought, just as Beth loves Mick. What is wrong with me? Why could I never hold on to love beyond the first attraction? How do women manage to sustain this lasting, everyday, practical love? Now I'm left on the fringes of life, a loner, without ever having wanted to become one.

'I am lonely,' she said aloud, surprising herself.

Dot stood up immediately, came across and put her arms around her, enveloping her in a hot, not unpleasant smell of flesh and cotton. Her body was huge and soft. Joe smiled at them both.

Dot's flat was shabbily furnished. Posters and children's art brightened the walls. She and Joe shared the housework in a desultory way and the flat never looked really clean. Compared with the state of the communal stairs and walkways outside, however, it was pristine. The concrete block in which they lived was defaced with graffiti and littered with rubbish. Huge metal bins at the bottom of the stairwells overflowed with burst black plastic bags. Children clattered round the asphalt below on scooters, skateboards or bicycles. Laura leaned over the concrete balcony that bounded the walkway at each floor level and watched them, admiring their physical energy and wondering why they were not in school.

Her bedroom, formerly shared by Dot's daughters, was long

and narrow, and it was a tight squeeze between bunk-beds and the walls were covered with pop-group posters. Dot had filled a vase with spring flowers, added a small lacy pillow stuffed with aromatic herbs and put a scented night light on the floor beside the bed. Laura, dozing the afternoons away while Dot and Joe were at work, found the racket from the children on the estate pervading her dreams. She dreamed about children and small animals. They were often trapped or lost, and it was her responsibility to rescue them. Baby rabbits stared at her with round stupid eyes or kittens mewed for help. Laura knew better than to interpret these dreams as pining for her unborn children. She knew that the trapped helpless creatures were herself and the looming figure that she often sensed was her stealthy, ever-present illness.

The newly discovered pleasure of getting stoned had kept them together for a bit longer. Joe was Laura's only source of marijuana and she had no idea where he got it. When Ruth was out, Laura and Joe sprawled together, wandering from a marijuana high into a sexual high. The phone rang once when she was about to reach orgasm, and its double rhythm propelled her to climax. Laura stayed calm although Joe gripped her shoulders painfully while he interrogated her as to who the caller might have been. Somehow she kept Joe and Conrad separate.

One evening in spring she got back from work to find Joe spreadeagled on her bed in slack-eyed despair. His shoes, the Chelsea boots that had first caught her attention, lay like two wrecked boats on the floor, their once-taut elasticated black sides sagging. There was an odd, sweet smell in the room. When he saw her, he began to weep, a frightening, panicky weeping.

'What is it? Joe, darling, you look awful. What's the matter?'

'Talk to me, Laura,' he gasped. 'Read to me. Anything.'

'Are you stoned, Joe? What have you *done*?'

'I think I've OD'd. Laura, I'm scared. Hold me, Laura. Don't call a doctor. I've been waiting for you to come back. Why have you been so long? Hold me, hold me.'

'What do you mean, OD'd? You're having a bad trip? Let me get a jug of water.'

'This isn't dope. Don't go. Stay with me.'

She was terrified of his strange face, his shaking limbs, his evident terror, and of his strange lassitude, which deepened towards unconsciousness.

'Shall I make coffee? Why can't I ring a doctor?' she asked, thinking, He's going to *die*, here on my bed.

'Talk to me,' Joe mumbled. 'Prop me up. Don't let me sleep. I mustn't sleep. Don't ring a doctor. *Don't*.' His teeth were chattering.

She sat with him for more than three hours, trying to keep him awake by talking him through her old photograph albums, which she pulled out from a suitcase under the bed. She told him about her babyhood, her christening photos ('I know. Isn't it funny? I was actually christened Stella, but when my sister got engaged, I . . .'), babbling on about anything that might prevent him from drifting into a coma. She showed him deckle-edged black-and-white holiday snaps of Constance as a girl, her parents when young. Every time his head drooped forwards she would raise her voice and say, 'Look, Joe, look at *this* one!' His glazed eyes would refocus on Laura aged nine flanked by two grinning kitchen boys, the youngest of their black servants in Kenya; Laura winning the under-thirteens' high jump, Laura skiing, riding, collecting a school prize, or with her hair blowing in the breeze on a boat crossing Hong Kong harbour.

He would not let her leave the room, not even to spend a penny. With bursting bladder she showed him the pictures of her life. She tried to prop him on her shoulder and make him walk, but he was too heavy for her, a dead weight. Feebly, he kept whispering, 'Talk to me, Laura. Don't let me die!' In the end she urinated into the bedclothes rather than leave him. The hot, sour smell contaminated her bedroom. It was the worst night of her life.

A day or two later Joe admitted that his overdose had been

due, not to the usual dope, but heroin. It was not his fault, he said; heroin in its pure form was not dangerous. He must have been sold adulterated stuff. From then on she knew he was an addict. Hopelessness weighed them down. Laura despaired of freeing herself from Joe's dependence; Joe despaired of coming off the sweet, necessary addiction. She said nothing to Conrad or Ruth.

After she had been with Lively and Parsons for three years and had graduated from proof-reading dictionaries to responsibility for all foreign reference books, Conrad promoted her again. Summoning her and Cameron to his office, he said they both felt she had outgrown her present position. Starting in May 1972 she was to take over the foreign fiction department, reading and selecting books for translation. She would get a rise to reflect her new responsibilities.

Laura worked ferociously, spending almost every evening at home reading novels or synopses of foreign novels, commissioning translations of the best ones. When he was with her, Joe resented her preoccupation. He would distract her by making her listen to his lines for the drama school's forthcoming and final end-of-term production. 'All the big agents will be there – producers, directors – talent-spotting. You've got to help me, Laura. It's up to you to make sure that I perform at the top of my bent. Your bloody books can wait. Don't you see this is my once-in-a-lifetime chance?'

She dared not tell Joe that his future was *his* responsibility, not hers, in case he OD'd again. During the long summer evenings they worked on his role in *King Lear* until he was word-perfect and Laura knew the play by heart. 'After this I'll be able to recite it when I'm ninety!' she said.

In retrospect she felt a fool for not having seen the signs. Even when Joe told her not to come to the end of term performance, she put it down to shyness or superstition. Without letting him know, she went anyway, sitting as far back in the small theatre as she could. One or two of the student actors were obviously outstanding. Joe remembered his lines, moved confidently and had a good sense of timing, but he looked insignificant on stage beside those with real talent. The 'gaze' was not much in evidence.

Afterwards the cast took three or four curtain calls, their parents and girlfriends applauding with hands held high and wide smiles. During the last two curtains Joe put his arms round the actress who had played Goneril. She stood beside him in the line-up, and as the final curtain fell Laura just caught sight of them turning towards one another. She continued to gaze at the heavy velvet folds and, as though she were a clairvoyant, she could see – not imagine, *see* – Joe and the girl kissing passionately.

He did not telephone her that night, although she hurried back to her flat. She told herself he would ring in the small hours, as he so often did, when the euphoria had subsided. She lay on her bed without undressing and fell asleep at last, make-up prickling against her skin, her mouth sour with the old taste of Nescafé.

Next day Joe rang her at work. 'It was brilliant, Laura! I was great! God, I'm glad it's all over!'

'And how was your friend. Who played Goneril? The one you were worried about, you know?'

She heard the instant tension in his voice, the momentary shocked gasp, and knew her flash of intuition had not been wrong.

He recovered quickly. 'Yeah, she was pretty good too. Listen, Laur', you free tonight?' His voice cajoled down the phone, 'Cook me a steak, we'll smoke a little joint, go to bed 'n' celebrate?'

Laura had steeled herself to say no, but his brazenness enraged her. Her own voice dropped to a promising murmur.

'Right on, babes! Eight o'clock? We'll have ourselves a good time?'

He heard no mockery. 'Sounds good to Joe!'

*

97

He turned up brandishing a bottle of wine. Laura had learned enough about wine from Conrad to know that Mateus Rosé was revolting.

'No expense spared!' he crowed.

'How much?' asked Laura briskly.

Joe was hurt. 'Seventy pence – that's 13s 11d!' he said.

'Cheap at the price, for all those hours of coaching and listening to your bloody lines.'

She cooked the steaks, searing them first under a red-hot grill. Joe complained that his was practically raw inside; she ought to know by now that he preferred it well-cooked.

'Not any more you don't,' she said. 'When those agents I saw in the audience last night start taking you to the Ivy . . .'

'Hang on a mo',' he said. 'You *what*, last night?'

'Did you *really* think, after all these weeks, I wasn't going to be there?' she said. 'You'd better get to know human nature a bit better than that if you're going to be a great actor. You'd better use your eyes and ears, my friend, and not just your greedy little COCK.'

'Laura, baby, slow down, hey, hey, hey, hang *on* . . . Joe's getting left behind here,' he said, but his eyes were wide with fright.

'Of course I was bloody there. Couldn't keep your mitts off her, could you? Arms round her in every curtain call. You could hardly let it drop before you had her pinned against you, and "such a tongue that I am glad I have not" . . .'

'Steady on, Laura. Don't get so worked up. OK, I got a bit carried away in all the excitement, but it was just the adrenalin. I was on a high. We all were. Actors are like that. Doesn't mean anything. Let's you and I get high together, and I'll show you who's my old lady . . .'

'Forget it, Joe. It was a fine romance, but now it's over.'

A look of panic crossed his face, and in that look Laura suddenly understood how much he had taken for granted, had come to depend on her to supply the discipline he lacked, the food he could not afford, the attention he craved.

'What's her name?' she asked.

'Whose name?'

'Don't mess with me, Joe. What's her name?'

'Jude.'

'Oh how *very* suitable! Well, you go tell your little Judas that from now on *she* can supply your needs. Because all your money goes on drugs, doesn't it? You're an addict! Christ, I've been slow on the uptake!'

He was mutinously silent.

'Answer me, Joe! Doesn't it? Doesn't it?'

He began to cry.

'You're a bloody addict, aren't you, Joe, and I'm a fool for not having realized it. What about this Jude? Is she an addict, too?'

'She started me on it,' he muttered. 'Before I met you. Honest.'

'Well if *she* made your bed, *she* can fucking lie on it.'

Even then, misted with self-pity, he pricked up his ears at the word. 'Come to bed, Laur',' he whined. 'Come to bed, baby, and it'll all be like it was before, I promise.'

Remembering the night when he had stroked her until her treacherous body succumbed to his caresses, Laura stood up. 'Out!' she said. 'Get out of my room, out of my flat. *Get yourself out of my fucking life!*'

Dot's homeopath had unexpectedly fashionable premises near Regent's Park. Two female receptionists were studying *Hello!* magazine as she entered.

'Name?' said one of them without looking up. Laura stood in silence. The other raised her head.

'Your *name*?' she said. '*Name? Nome? Nom?*'

'*Thank* you,' said Laura. 'My name is Laura King. I have been recommended by Ms Greaves. I have an appointment with Mr Fremantle at ten-thirty. That is, in five minutes' time.'

'Downstairs. Room B. He'll buzz when he's ready.'

'Thank you,' said Laura distinctly. Both women were staring at her.

'Better mention that you're pregnant, in case he doesn't notice,' the first one said.

'I'm not,' answered Laura.

She waited downstairs beside a table scattered with leaflets describing the techniques offered at the practice and some health and healing magazines. When the buzzer went, she walked into Room B.

'Good morning, Mr Fremantle. I had better tell you that I am not pregnant.'

Afterwards she knew from the dead weight of disappointment how high her hopes had been. *Trained in Mexico and Sweden . . . Years of history and practice . . . Worked miracles . . .* Dot's phrases had made an impression, despite Laura's scepticism. But from the moment he smiled an over-sympathetic smile she knew Mr Fremantle was not the miracle-worker she had been hoping for. Nearly twenty years as an interpreter had trained Laura to decipher body language, facial expression and gesture, and she saw at once that, however well intentioned, he was a quack. He took her 'history', murmured reassuringly, laid his soft cold hands against her temples and her abdomen, palpated her swollen liver and told her to come back the following week. His fee for the first session was fifty pounds, and thirty-five pounds for each succeeding one. He asked her to bring a diet sheet next time, listing everything she had eaten over the previous seven days.

'Thank you,' said Laura, 'but I prefer not to.'

'You don't *have* to complete the diet sheet, if you would rather not, but it's a great help in diagnosis . . .' he began.

'No, I mean I would prefer not to have another consultation. I should not have come. I am terminally ill, you see, dying. I let myself be persuaded that there might be hope . . .'

'There is always hope,' he replied earnestly.

'Not in my case.'

She smiled at him as she left, but not at the receptionists.

That evening, Dot and Joe waited with shining eyes for her verdict. Laura had meant to modify her story, perhaps even pretend that she had made a second appointment, but exasperation at their credulity overcame her.

'Sorry, but I just couldn't take him seriously. He's probably fine for people who just need a friendly pair of hands. But I'm not in that category. I hate to let you both down. I'm beyond homeopathy, far beyond alternative therapy, beyond hope, beyond pretence, beyond everything.'

Dot was distressed. Tears welled into her blue eyes, smudging their black kohl outline. She came round to Laura's side of the table and stroked her hair. Joe took her hand.

'Even if you don't believe in it, just talking does you good. Human contact. You know . . .'

'Maybe. I just feel very tired and rather ill. You both have to go to a rehearsal now. I understand. Don't worry. Hope it goes well.'

Laura knew, as the front door closed behind them, that she would not be there when they got back. She began to compose her farewell note.

6

Nicholas Hope

LATE MAY

Laura King celebrated her twenty-fifth birthday by breaking up with Joe Watson and moving to a new flat. Since her promotion she could afford to live alone, and she looked forward to that independence. When Ruth left to go and work abroad, Laura chose this moment also to leave the Hampstead eyrie they had shared for four years and found a two-roomed basement flat with a tiny back garden in Fulham for which she paid £12 a week.

It was an immense relief to be free from the burden of Joe. Of all the men she had known over the past seven years, he had been the most demanding, yet from Joe she had learned her own capacity for sexual pleasure as well as the skill to give it. No one had yet given her what she most longed for: love.

Conrad was implacably honest about the prospects for their relationship. 'There's a lot to be said for being a mistress, and I can teach you several useful lessons. First, of course, varied, original and inexhaustible sex. Food and drink: the choice and consumption thereof. Dress sense. I'll give you presents from time to time ... not jewellery, it makes women greedy, but shoes perhaps. Shoes can be very erotic. We might even manage a weekend in Paris. But don't cherish any bourgeois illusions about marriage because that is not on the cards, *least* of all if you get pregnant. Take precautions and be warned.'

Laura tried to persuade herself that this was all she wanted, but still she longed for love. She never saw Conrad at weekends, for he spent those with his family at their country house in

Leicestershire. She sometimes gazed bleakly at the telephone, wrung with self-pity. London was full of *couples*. On Saturday mornings the Fulham Road was thronged with couples doing their shopping, sharing a machine at the launderette, choosing between pork and lamb for Sunday lunch. People visited art galleries in pairs; the cinema in pairs – everyone seemed to be paired except herself. It was in this vulnerable state that Laura met Nicholas Hope, who looked as though he might fulfil all her needs – above all, the need for love. And in retrospect there was no doubt that Nicholas *had* loved her – madly, passionately.

Nicholas's wife, Nell, swung Laura's suitcase vigorously into the boot of the car. She had always been a hefty girl, big-boned and mad about horses. On her wedding day, the full-skirted bridal dress had swished noisily between her thighs and she had marched up and down the aisle as though collecting a rosette at a gymkhana. Now Nell wore a cream Viyella shirt, Nick's by the look of it, sleeves rolled up to reveal freckled forearms. Laura, in a linen safari suit with matching silk scarf, felt overdressed beside her.

'Oompf!' grunted Nell, plopping into the driving seat. She grinned briskly at Laura and swung the car boldly out of the station car park on to the road.

'It's awfully sweet of you to collect me,' Laura said, trying to strike the right tone of voice.

'Taxis cost a fortune round here. Half of them couldn't find us, anyway. We don't often have people to stay. Nick works seven days a week.'

Thanks for the welcome! thought Laura. Still, why *should* she like me? His mother will have poured the old resentments into her ears – all the old, self-justifying lies, and Nicholas can hardly be expected to tell his wife that he married her on the rebound from his grand passion for me, let alone that I couldn't bear him to touch me.

'Pretty countryside,' she commented.

'You're lucky with the weather,' said Nell. 'It poured last week.'

'I was in Camberwell. It was quite dry.'

'Really? Another of your old flames, I suppose?'

Laura wanted to reply, yes, handy in a crisis, aren't they? Of course *you* wouldn't know. Nicholas was your first love. A virgin wife, keeping thee only unto him, forsaking all others, till death . . . Ever-present death. The blood courses ruddily into your country cheeks, you are vigorous with life, ardent with good health, unlike me.

Instead, she said, 'I'm not clear what exactly Nick *does*.'

'He's a fine arts and crafts co-ordinator,' answered Nell. 'The only one in the country.'

'Uh-huh?'

'He has a card index – well, it used to be; now it's all done by computer – of people like picture restorers or gilders or specialist fabric repairers all over Britain, and when an art collector or even one of the big galleries wants some work done, Nick tells them the best and nearest person for the job. He advertises in *Burlington* magazine, *Country Life* . . .'

Nell held forth on Nick's computer skills, the uses and versatility of the fax machine, the wonders of the modem, as though Laura were more familiar with the quill pen. Apart from murmuring, 'Does he *really*?' and '*Goodness*, how clever!' Laura was silent. Nell's petulance would turn to good humour without any more blandishments from her.

Laura looked out of the car window across flat Suffolk fields, their wide views broken by church steeples and huge barns. After a while the narrow road became a gorge between steep hedges and banks. Trees arched across it and sunlight dappled the tarmac. Nell turned to face her, still talking, and as she gestured with one hand and swung the steering wheel round with the other, Laura saw a couple of riders in the road ahead.

'Hey!' she shouted. 'Look out!'

Nell stamped on the brakes and the car squealed and slewed

across the road. The horses shied and the smaller one reared. A girl clung to the reins, veered sideways and slipped off, landing a few yards from the car.

'Oh *no*,' said Nell. 'Oh crikey. All my fault.' She turned to Laura with an expression of desperate entreaty. '*Please* don't tell him!' she implored before hauling open the car door. '*Don't* tell Nick!'

The horses stood trembling beside the road. Gathering their reins in one hand, the adult rider bent over the girl. She looked up as Nell approached. 'Oh it's you! Well, we're in luck. No broken bones, I don't think, just a bit shaken. Come on, ducky, let's see if you can stand up.'

'Daphne! How can I *ever* apologize? *Utterly* our fault.' Nell turned and indicated Laura, who had lowered the window to check on the fallen girl. 'We're on our way home from the station. This is Laura King, a friend of Nicky's who's come to convalesce with us. I'm afraid she must have distracted me just as I came round the corner.'

The other woman glared at Laura. 'Could have been a very nasty accident,' she said, so accusingly that Laura felt compelled to apologize.

'Well,' said Nell, as if to smooth things over, 'we won't spoil your arrival by telling Nick. At least, *I* won't and I'm sure Daphne'll be a sport?'

'Is your daughter all right?' Laura asked.

'I'm fine,' said the girl stoically. Deathly pale, she had dusted herself down and was stroking the horse's long flat cheek. 'So's Melody, aren't you, darling? *Brave* girl.'

Nell got back into the car and drove on. Laura thought, I'm not going to apologize to her as well.

After a long silence, Nell said, 'This is where we turn off.'

The road skirted a red-brick farm and turned into a narrow lane at the end of which Laura saw a meadow and a long, low cottage which seemed to grow out of the ground like the willows around it.

'Rest and peace is all we offer . . .' said Nick later that evening after dinner. Nell giggled, her colour heightened by the wine Laura had brought.

'. . . not glamour or sophistication.'

'Who wants *glamour*?' interrupted Nell.

'You can do whatever you want, get up late, go to bed early, lie around spending gentle afternoons in a deckchair – all that.'

'All that,' echoed Nell. 'Peace and quiet. Left to yourself. Far from the madding crowd. Though I don't suppose they madden *you* . . .'

'Just help yourself,' Nick interrupted. 'Books. Records and tapes. Read. Sleep. Relax.'

'Any time you feel like making yourself useful you could always help me,' Nell chipped in. 'We do all our own preserves here, you know. Bake our own bread, cakes, all those quaint old-fashioned skills . . .' She did not bother to conceal her hostility.

Eventually Nell leaned back and spread her arms wide in a huge yawn so that her broad soft bosom thrust against her shirt. I get the message, Laura thought. The lawful pleasures of the marriage bed beckon. She mimed a more discreet yawn.

'Can I give you a hand with the plates? Let me stack the dishwasher.'

'Not on your first night. Nick'll do it, won't you, darling?'

Laura awoke next morning in a low-ceilinged attic bedroom. Sunlight sharpened the pattern on the curtains and when she drew them back the same light vibrated through every blade of grass. The lawn was punctuated by a row of molehills, their soft exposed earth a rich black against the green. She opened her bedroom door and nearly fell over a tea tray on the floor and a vase of fresh flowers. *Pax*, then. She heard a car starting up and watched the big Volvo bump cautiously along the lane. She couldn't see who was driving. When it turned right on to the road, Nicholas called her name.

'Hello!' she replied.

'Good . . . you're awake.'

'Gorgeous morning. I've wasted half of it. Look at the time!'

'Ready for breakfast?'

'Give me quarter of an hour and I'll be down.'

'New-laid eggs, toast and marmalade do you? Tea? Coffee?'

'Four and a half minutes for the eggs; two pieces of toast, brown if poss; and coffee sounds wonderful.'

For the first time in weeks Laura felt hungry. After Dot and Joe's austere vegetarian fare, she relished the thought of real food.

When she walked into the kitchen, she and Nicholas both spoke at once.

'How long is Nell likely to . . . ?' began Laura.

'I'm sorry about last night . . .' began Nicholas.

They stopped.

'Come here. Let me give you a hug,' said Nicholas.

Even after twenty years, Laura felt a shiver of recoil. Luckily Nick misinterpreted it. 'Just an *innocent* hug. I'd do the same if Nell were here.'

'Oh no you wouldn't! Nick, listen, is she always that touchy?'

'We'll talk about all that in due course. Not on your first day. But you're doing nothing wrong and, yes, she *is* on the defensive. She's got you down as the great love of my life. Which you were,' he added.

'Dear Nick. I'm surprised she let me come in that case.'

'I didn't give her any choice. No, that's not fair: she is immensely generous. Nell genuinely can't bear to see anyone in trouble. I told her you needed a rest in the country and although she's intimidated by anybody she thinks of as a "career woman" she insisted you came.'

As he busied himself at the stove, Laura stood gazing out of the window. The lawn sloped towards a stream and ducks fussed around.

'Ducks!' she exclaimed.

'They come up twice a day to be fed, bringing their babies to show us.'

'Pretty creatures. But you've got lots of molehills.'

'I *caught* a mole once. Its forequarters were as powerful as a buffalo's. I couldn't bear to kill it, so I chucked it as far as I could into the next field. Now as you see, it's back.'

'Mole one, Nicholas nil.' observed Laura.

As she sat down at the table, the dog ambled towards her, wagging its tail.

'You hate dogs,' Nicholas said.

'Well remembered! I do, but this one seems harmless.'

'Entirely. Just an amiable old fool, aren't you, Christine?'

'Christine?' exclaimed Laura. 'What kind of a name is *that* for a black Labrador?'

'It's my mother-in-law's name. Or was.'

'And was *she* an amiable old fool?' Laura asked.

'Anything but . . .' replied Nick. He caught her eye, and they both began to laugh. 'She was a black-hearted old bitch.'

They giggled together like children trying out rude words.

When they had calmed down, he said, 'Actually, it was *sad*. She longed for us to have a daughter named after her. In the end, when she got ill, Nell bought a dog instead. Hence Christine.'

'And her mother died happy in the knowledge that her blood-line was secure?' Laura asked. Again they collapsed into guilty laughter.

'*Breakfast*,' he said sternly. 'Your toast has gone cold and Nell will be home soon. Here's the *Guardian*. I must get back to work.'

She had met Nicholas in 1972, when her affair with Conrad was still in full swing and the one with Joe had just ended. Nick had been a contemporary at university; she had seen him around at parties but barely knew his name. Four years later, coming home from work one rainy autumn evening, they had met at a London bus stop and greeted each other like old friends. Laura invited him back to her new flat in Fulham for coffee.

From that first accidental meeting a gentle and undemanding friendship developed – a relief after the trials with Joe. One evening, over a candlelit dinner at a more than usually expensive restaurant, Nicholas had clasped her hands (his were hot and sweaty, an ill omen for their first contact) and confessed his love.

Laura had been astonished and flattered. Nick's declaration was well timed, for she was beginning to shade her eyes and look for marriage on the horizon. Even after ten years Constance's example seemed proof that an attractive young husband and entrancing children could be a source of happiness and fulfilment for an intelligent woman. Several of Laura's contemporaries now had one or more babies to whom they gave curt, newly fashionable names like Jake or Kate. She was beginning to envy rather than pity their rumpled domesticity. Occasionally a young wife, bored with chores and fenced in by toddlers and lack of money, would claim to envy Laura, whose free-wheeling life seemed wonderfully bohemian. But at the age of twenty-five, Laura sometimes wondered if her mother hadn't been right after all.

Nicholas's sudden declaration made a lot of sense. He was a dear man, they had a lot in common and plenty to talk about. He was good-looking – at any rate, not *bad*-looking. The moment for telling him about Conrad passed. Nicholas assumed she was not seeing another man and their relationship moved into a new phase – unmistakably, that of courtship. He sent her flowers, escorted her to the theatre and afterwards to dinner, insisting that he paid. They were no longer equals, friends 'going Dutch'. He did not hurry her into bed but Laura began to feel guilty about her secret trysts with Conrad.

One stolen afternoon, curled in a nest of blankets after making love, she said, 'Conrad, you know I've got someone else, don't you?'

'I know what you choose to tell me. *Why* are you telling me? Are you engaged? On your way to the altar?'

'We haven't been to bed together yet.'

'My poor child, what *can* be the matter with him?'

'He says he's in love with me and he doesn't want to rush it.'

'A bad sign. Trouble looms. What do you feel?'

'I don't much care for him kissing me and I'm in no hurry to go to bed with him. Could it be because of you?'

'Compulsive fidelity?' he said sardonically. 'I wouldn't recommend that.'

'But he's so perfectly *suitable*. My mother would roll over and wave her paws in the air. I'm going to have to do it soon.'

'You sound flatteringly unenthusiastic. Come here: I want to sink my teeth into your delectable little bottom while it's still *all mine*.'

'Wait. Listen. Would you be jealous, Conrad?'

'I don't know the meaning of the word.'

'It means, would you mind?'

'Not if you shared your favours. Yes, if you only slept with him.'

'He says he loves me and it seems to be true, but I don't love *him*. I don't even know if I fancy him.'

'Let me tell you. You don't. Time you found that out for yourself.'

'Do you think so?'

'I don't think anything. Do what you want. But I'm going to punish you for confessing.'

He pulled the sheet back and she flinched from the sudden cold, and from the threat.

'Roll over. *Laura* . . .' He grasped her ankles and pulled on them to straighten her legs. 'Hand or hairbrush?'

Sex with Nicholas would surely be preferable to Conrad's treatment. Gentleness would be manna from heaven after that dry cynicism, those strange pleasures followed by long silences. Nicholas wanted her at the centre of his life, while Conrad kept her on the very edge of his. Laura made up her mind that next time she and Nicholas met she would get drunk and go to bed with him in the hope that alcohol would help to overcome her inexplicable reluctance.

In the event, the reluctance proved to be well-founded. Not even when acquiescing to Conrad's tart and hissing whims had Laura clenched her eyes and locked her jaw to prevent herself crying out in revulsion. Her flesh shrank from Nicholas's touch; her body arched away from contact with his hands or mouth.

'Light *off*, Nick! Dear Nick. Please!' were almost her first words.

'I'd love to watch you . . .' he murmured tenderly, 'but I understand. Plenty of time for that.'

Despite his efforts to prolong the event, impatience made Nick brief. Laura's simulated moans speeded him to climax. He collapsed across her, inarticulate with gratitude.

'Oh, darling – I'm sorry – so clumsy – I'll be better next time – I promise – oh, Laura, my *darling*!'

His skin was smooth, his breath sweet. His body was young and healthy, yet her flesh had flinched from his exploring hands and soft wet mouth. Nicholas apparently noticed nothing. Humbly, almost reverently, he tried to please her. Oh God, she thought, has Conrad programmed me? Is this revulsion *his* fault? Other women must have accepted Nick with pleasure. Is my love for Conrad making me frigid? Not with Joe, she remembered grimly.

After their very first love-making Laura knew she could never marry Nicholas. Each time she submitted, silent insults rose like foetid bubbles to the surface of her mind . . . Penis as wrinkled as an old pig's trotter, she found herself thinking foully. While Nicholas tried patiently, tenderly to coax her towards pleasure, she wanted to say coarsely, 'For God's sake, just put it in and get it over with!'

Yet despite these fiascos – of which he remained unaware, assuming that, while obviously no virgin, she was sexually innocent – Laura still enjoyed his company. At weekends they would visit museums. Together they stayed with his mother in the country, in a house unchanged since the wartime death of his father. Mrs Hope kept it as a shrine to her widowhood – partly because an ever-shrinking pension and a tiny trust fund compelled her to be abstemious, but also because time had stopped for her when her husband was killed. She despised women who married again, betraying the memory of the dead.

Even Laura's parents were more liberal than Betty Hope. Prim, thin, dry, correct, she was trapped in the amber of 1944, the year of her son's birth and his father's death. Nicholas surrendered to her jealous love, fastened now solely and exclusively on him. Her only son, he was 'the spit and image of his father', as she never failed to point out. Laura wanted to say, 'Don't worry, Mrs Hope, I'll *never* marry Nicholas!' but that would have elicited even more hostility, so she tried not to seem a threat. But however polite, deferential or mousey she contrived to be, it made no difference. Their mutual antipathy was palpable.

Laura cleared and washed up her breakfast things. Nicholas's study was at the far end of the house, and she walked through to offer him a coffee. His desk stood beside a window overlooking the rolling green expanse of lawn.

'Do you have a gardener?' Laura inquired.

'No. Mowing is my fetish, specially in the summer, but it helps me think. And – sounds silly, but I love to feel the contours of my land beneath its rollers. *My land!*'

'Coffee?' she asked.

'No, thanks. Sit with me for a while, Laura. Pull out a book. Nell won't arrive suddenly; I'll hear the car coming along the drive.' After a silence he remarked, 'You've changed your hair.'

'Oh Nicholas! Not just my hair. I'm twenty years older. What do you expect?'

'It used to be longer, and sort of puffed up at the back and curled under at the sides.'

'I remember. It took a lot of effort with horrible hot things called Carmen rollers.'

'I thought it just grew that way. Oh Laura, you were so touchingly pretty!'

'Unlike now.'

'Don't be defensive. I think you're beautiful now, but it's an older and more intimidating beauty. I wouldn't dare pick you up at a bus stop any more.'

'I wouldn't *be* at a bus stop. Taxis everywhere. And *very* expensive hairdressers.'

All that was on the surface – the so-important surface, now changed and decaying. But underneath we don't change much, she told herself. I feel the same visceral flinching as before. He does not attempt to disguise his love for me. Still, after all these years. If I were Nicholas's wife, I'd be anxious, too. Meanwhile the illness, this silent and invisible worm, gnaws away at me.

From that end of the house Laura could look down its entire length. Three rooms stretched before her, each leading into the next. On home leave in London, her parents had dutifully taken her and Constance as children to the National Gallery. She used to peer through the eyehole of a perspective box at the illusory vistas of diminishing Dutch rooms painted on its flat interior sides: an orderly domestic world of windows, chandeliers, furniture and doorways. That's what I thought I would be when I grew up: one of those full-skirted women seated at a desk writing a letter while in the next room a maidservant minded the child or plucked a hen. That calm, civilized life had been a *trompe l'œil*, too – though evidently not for Nell. This cottage possesses all four dimensions. Time makes the old beams creak at night, the walls expand and the worn floorboards strain. Time has flowed on for twenty years, changing and yet not changing us.

Nick interrupted her thoughts. 'The car!' he exclaimed. 'Laura – sorry – could you go, I don't know, upstairs, anywhere . . . ? I don't want to upset Nell, and she will be if she finds us together.'

She hurried guiltily from the calm room.

*

Guilt was the main emotion Laura associated with Nicholas Hope. It curdled even ordinary affection, turning it rancid, taking away all spontaneity. She felt guilty when she slept with him, guilty when she didn't, guilty about Conrad, guilty that she concealed his existence with denial and, in the end – when Nicholas's suspicions grew – outright lies. She felt guilty when she managed to deceive him into believing that she was happy and might come to love him, guilty when she could not simulate pleasure and he turned away from her with bitter disappointment. He was such a decent man; it was not his fault.

This unstable affair lasted for more than a year. The more uncertain Laura became, the more passionately Nicholas loved her. His voice acquired a despairing note, robbed of self-respect or pride. As his confidence ebbed, Laura was forced to pretend more. She had no desire to hurt him and she knew that her looks, words, movements, choices all delighted Nicholas for no other reason than that they were *hers*. She was the centre of his world. He thought about ways of pleasing her and often succeeded. He would say, 'There's an exhibition at the Tate I'm sure you'll love . . .' and he was right: she did love it. He would recommend books that she would enjoy, and enjoy them she did.

She told Conrad they must stop sleeping together in case *he* was the obstacle to happiness with Nicholas.

'I won't stand in your way,' he said at once. 'Only, you *will* ask me to your wedding, my dear? Promise?'

'Conrad, you are *vile*. It's so easy to be sardonic at his expense. I'm trying to give him a chance, in case it might work.'

'Of course you are. And so you shall. I shall leave without a trace.'

She hated Conrad's confidence, his certainty that he would be back. Conrad knew little about Nicholas, yet he never doubted his own priority in her life, and Laura realized that he was right. But now she wanted to find out whether, without Conrad, her response would change. She hoped that if she made love with *only* Nick, she might begin to desire him.

She also decided to change her job, to move away from Conrad's influence and power. He made no attempt to dissuade her and wrote an excellent reference. Laura found that her skills as a linguist were much in demand. She joined a translation agency in the Strand and spent days attending dreary domestic disputes at the Law Courts, where she might interpret for a sullen Russian and his cowed, bewildered wife, both unable to explain themselves in English or, as often as not, in Russian either. She acted as a mouthpiece for Chinese people accused of fraud by the Soho police, knowing that the Chinese despised her and the police mistrusted her. But she was paid by the hour and the money was good. She learned to translate in a manner accurate both as to the words and the voice of the speaker. It was seedy work, she saw into seedy worlds, but her knowledge of human nature grew.

Nothing could transform her relationship with Nick, which in the end was destroyed not by Conrad, but by one of his own friends. Laura and Nicholas, copying the domesticity that flourished among their married friends, had arranged a dinner party together at his flat: a move towards social acceptance as a couple.

Nicholas laid the table and put out the drinks while Laura melted chicken livers in butter for the pâté and browned caramel under the grill for *crème brulée*. She was just brushing her hair when she heard him greet the first guest.

'Darling, *you* remember Harkness?' Nicholas said as she entered.

'The name, of course!' she smiled.

'The story of my life!' he mourned as he shook her hand.

Harkness was American, very cool, very hip, very 'Hey, how you doing?', very Sixties and flip. He called Laura 'chick', 'babe' or 'honey-chile' with an openly mocking and untrustworthy smile.

The day after the dinner party, Harkness telephoned her at work. '*You* remember Harkness?' were his opening words. They met for a drink that evening and within less than two hours they were in bed and Laura was gasping like a woman parched with thirst.

Laura discovered that she could find a man physically irresistible without loving or even liking him. It was a sordid discovery. Like every woman of her generation she knew it was possible to enjoy sex without marriage. She had learned from her relationship with Nick that love and intellectual compatibility did not guarantee good sex. But not until she betrayed him with Harkness had she known that love need no connection with sex whatsoever: sex could be simply sex, body upon body, orgasm upon orgasm. It was months since she had slept with Conrad and a year since she had broken up with Joe. A year of sexual drought. For weeks she and Harkness fucked at every opportunity, sometimes two or three times a day.

Harkness did not ask questions about her relationship with Nick and Laura continued to see them both. One day Nicholas rang her while she and Harkness were in bed together. Harkness turned coolly aside and began to read the book on her bedside table. As soon as she had put the telephone down he resumed, coaxing her with his cunning fingers and artful tongue towards a treacherous and greedy orgasm.

Harkness was not decadent or perverse like Conrad, but he was amoral. He took it for granted that if their bodies pleased each other they should be indulged. Loyalty, jealousy, fidelity – these were qualities he seemed incapable of experiencing. Yet he gave Laura overwhelming pleasure. Nicholas and Laura were clumsy and inexpert children; Conrad was a stern adult and she a submissive child; Joe had been a delinquent and she his mother; but Harkness and she fucked like grown-ups, like equals who both knew what they wanted.

In the end it was Harkness who told Nicholas. For a while Nicholas said nothing to her. He wanted to see – she thought afterwards – if she would lie to him and, having found that she would, if he could stand it. Perhaps he hoped she would tire of Harkness, or Harkness of her. When neither of these things

116

happened, Nick told Laura without reproach that his misery with her had become greater than his misery without her.

'In the unlikely event that you should miss me, please don't ring,' Nicholas asked with harrowing dignity. 'I know that losing you and staying away from you will take all my strength. Do me this last favour, and promise not to contact me. Because if you do, I shall not be able to resist.'

His mother telephoned her shortly afterwards and unleashed her long pent-up ferocity. 'Why *my son*?' she asked. 'What did Nicko ever offer you but love and tenderness, generosity, protection? How could you be so *wicked* as to betray him? I hope one day you will suffer as he is suffering now! I hope I know of your suffering. I should like to know. It will make me *laugh*.'

Laura had no answer to this melodramatic outburst. She could not explain, nor did she feel she owed Betty Hope an apology. Instead, she rang Harkness and told him she didn't want to see him again.

'Pity,' he said lightly. 'Listen, you're a great lay. Remember that.'

She lasted on her own for two weeks before telephoning Conrad. She had dreaded his arid, sinewy voice but he was unexpectedly gentle.

'Poor *battered* baby,' he murmured down the telephone. 'You sound worn out. Let me spoil you – since it's nearly Christmas. What shall it be? Paris? The Ritz?'

'Oh, Conrad,' she said, 'couldn't we just be *ordinary*? Could you come to my flat for dinner, and listen while I talk to you?'

'Of course. I'll bring some wine. You cook. Nothing elaborate.'

'I wouldn't know *how* to cook something elaborate,' she said. 'Let alone be able to eat it. Oh, *Conrad* . . .'

Dependence is based on this: when the person who causes pain is also the only one who can offer comfort. The affair with Conrad resumed.

*

Nell staggered in holding a cardboard box, the dog dancing round her excitedly. She put the box down and stood with her hands on her hips. 'Done an hour's remedial reading at Framlingham Primary, an hour buying and arranging the church flowers for the Mitchell girl's wedding tomorrow, and a quick spin round Tesco's!' she announced as she unloaded the box into the fridge. Her movements were brisk and economical. Everything had its allotted place. Nothing was wasted.

She embodies, Laura thought, the ideal of a good woman: the only kind of daughter-in-law Betty Hope could have tolerated. The absence of children is a pity; but being childless enables her to pour out her surplus energy for the benefit of others – whereas I have lived almost entirely for my own benefit. Why else am I making this lugubrious tour of my past? Apart from Constance and her children and a handful of women friends, hardly anyone will even notice my absence. A few conference organizers, slow to pick up the news that I've died, may try to book me for a few months; perhaps some ageing men will pass through London and try my number, but other than that . . .

'Give me something to do,' she asked. 'It will stop me thinking morbid thoughts.'

Nell glanced at the draining-board and called to her husband, 'Nicky! Did you remember to cut some asparagus?'

Nick hurried through from his study. 'Christ! I forgot! Sorry, darling – I'll do it now.'

'There's nothing for you to do,' Nell said, smiling at Laura. 'Simple lunch. Fresh asparagus, apple tart and cheese to follow.'

'Can I at least peel the apples?'

'The tart's made. Just needs popping into the oven.'

'How efficient you are.'

'Life in the country's not quite as dozy as people think.'

'No, I'm sure . . .' said Laura and, as the phone rang, 'Shall I get that?'

'I will. Might be a client.'

Nell picked up the telephone.

Behind her hockey captain façade Nell tried to fulfil the injunctions she taught at Sunday school by being kind and thoughtful and telling the truth, though she knew she did not always succeed. She thought herself clumsy and ignorant because she had not been to university, and selfish because living alongside Nick was all she had ever wanted. She was overawed by Laura, who moved among the great men who made the world turn, but she envied her not for this but for having known Nick before she herself had. This envy made Nell resentful and guilty, the more so because it should have seemed trivial in the face of Laura's illness. She composed a quick prayer to salve her conscience and passed Laura a handful of cutlery.

Laura felt queasy after her large breakfast, and she could only pick at her food. When the meal was over, Nell beckoned Nicholas to follow her upstairs. After several glasses of wine she had become flushed and garrulous. Laura, opening and shutting drawers in the kitchen, wondered whether she wanted him for sex or a row. From their bedroom came a series of grunts and exclamations that could have been either. She heard Nell's voice, high and strained, on a rising crescendo: 'Nick! Please, no, Nick, *please* . . . no, no, *no!*'

Unwilling to go to her own bedroom, which meant passing theirs, or the drawing-room, which was underneath it, Laura took a book and went to sit on a bench beside the river, shivering a little in the brisk May sunshine. Bobbing and diving through the fast-flowing reeds, their feathers shot with iridescent colours like coal, the ducks busied themselves in the water's shiny depths. Laura dozed.

She kept her promise to Nick after their relationship had ended and had not contacted him. Within less than a year she received an embossed invitation. 'Lieutenant-Colonel and Mrs R. J. Armstrong request the pleasure of your company at the wedding of their beloved daughter Eleanora (Lora) Christine on 22 September 1974, at the church of . . .' Lora! she thought. Poor Nicholas!

He must have told her about me and she has forgiven him, but I've been invited to the wedding because she is curious to set eyes on me.

In the reception line after the service Nick met her eyes steadily. 'Laura!' he said. 'How lovely you look. I *am* glad you could make it. Nell, darling, *this* is Laura . . .'

'Hello!' said Nell, bright-eyed and shimmering with happiness on her big day. 'I was made to change my *name* 'cos of you! I've been *fright*fully curious to meet you! Gosh what a smart hat! Look, Nicky.'

Nicholas touched her elbow. 'Nell – sweetheart – I'd like you to meet my aunt . . .'

Laura moved on, smiled and shook hands with the bride's parents, and then Nicholas's mother, but afterwards she and Betty Hope stayed on opposite sides of the room. Mrs Hope wore an Ascot cartwheel and flashed a triumphant glance at Laura. The new Mrs Hope did not speak to her again, either. Laura caught Nicholas watching her a number of times, but he did not come up to her. She looked around for Harkness in vain.

Laura did not envy Nicholas his wife or Nell her husband, but she found herself envying their newly married state. Wedding presents were displayed on three long trestle tables at the far end of the marquee: non-stick frying pans, towels, Harrods sheets, finicky bits of silver, a Kenwood mixer – the trappings of a lifetime of shared domesticity. She envied this prospect of permanence.

She woke to the sound of Nicholas clomping across the lawn and turned with a smile. 'Whatever happened to Harkness?' she asked.

'Harkness! Good Lord, I've no idea. Last *I* heard of him he was living on a sex commune in Denmark.'

'He would!' she said, and paused. 'I don't suppose you ever forgave me for Harkness?'

'Laura. I forgave you for everything. Not that there was really anything to forgive. You couldn't love me. I understood that even then, and my *God* I understand it now! Are you up to a walk?'

'Nell . . .'

'She's all right.'

Laura grinned. 'Doesn't she *exhaust* you, Nicholas? All that healthy female vigour?'

'It's not quite what it seems.' He sat down on the bench beside her. 'Laura, let me tell you this and then try to explain. You can't stay. You're going to have to go. Today, I mean. This afternoon. Nell thought she could cope with having you here, but she can't.'

'Of course. I'll go and pack.'

'Not this minute. There's a train at five-forty-seven; I'll make sure you catch it. Let me talk to you first – please, Laura. I know I shall never see you again.'

They walked for over an hour through spring woods. Nicholas helped her over stiles and when she became breathless he made her sit down, spreading his jacket to protect her from the damp earth. He stroked her hair and told her she looked tired. He offered to pay for her to stay at a hotel in the country and for a nurse to go with her. No, Laura said.

As they walked he talked about his marriage. 'It isn't how it looks. That's a charade to save Nell's pride – and mine, I suppose. Nell is a virgin, Laura. *That*'s why we haven't got children. She was a virgin when I met her, and when she said she wanted to keep it for the wedding night, I agreed. I hadn't got over you; I was in no hurry to sleep with her.

'We went to Madeira for the honeymoon. The first night we were exhausted after the flight. The second night she got tipsy and fell asleep after dinner. The third night we were both sunburned and sore, so we just stroked each other a bit and said there was plenty of time. I didn't get an erection. By the end of our first week she said she was ready and we tried, but I still couldn't get an erection. I shall never forget her saying, "Why won't it go *in*, Nicky?" By the end of the fortnight I knew I had married a woman I didn't and *couldn't* desire. I can't tell you how many times in the last eighteen years I've wondered if it was like that for you, with me?'

There was pain in his voice but he was appealing for the truth.

'Darling Nick,' Laura began. 'There's no fault or reason on either side, except biology or genes or hormones. Who one desires must be programmed into the body at birth. Is it inherited? I don't know.'

Nick had blundered into the darkest recesses of her life as well as his own, but Laura's experience had been the opposite of his: she knew that sexual passion could be a tidal wave, a cyclone, a hurricane crushing everything in its path. Sex creates life but also destroys it. She was silent for a moment until her heartbeat had slowed down and she felt able to speak with a steady voice.

'Don't blame yourself Nick, poor Nick. Sex and lust don't work to order. If you don't fancy someone, nothing can change that: not romantic settings or sexy underwear, and *certainly* not therapy or counselling. Sexual response is not rational. Lust is simple, primitive and uncontrollable, even if you *know* it will have terrible and tragic consequences. From what you say, the consequences can be equally tragic and terrible if you cannot feel lust.'

'I feel no desire for Nell,' he said bleakly. 'I did and still do for you, but with Nell I never have.'

They walked on. Laura's stomach was hurting but she said nothing.

'Oddly enough,' Nicholas resumed after a while, 'it's got easier to bear. The first two or three years were the worst because it still seemed as though it might be all right eventually. We would talk about it, and Nell would offer various solutions. Perhaps she should dress up in sexy underwear, or like a schoolgirl? No good, of course. Perhaps we should go away somewhere completely different? We tried the south of France, romantic weekends all over the place. Useless. We were both medically examined. Everything in full working order. I leap to attention at the sight of a centrefold. But not for my wife.

'No point in going for marriage guidance – they'd tell me briskly that Nell is still *virgo intacta* and explain the mechanics. I don't need sexual techniques or penile implants. I just need to desire my wife. Anyhow, we gradually stopped discussing it. The longer a silence lasts, the harder it becomes to break. Now, by a sort of unspoken agreement, Nell puts on a terrific show for friends and visitors – when we have them, which is not often – to prove that all's well in the bedroom. When no one's around, we live like brother and sister. We hardly ever quarrel. But her body leaves me totally cold. I even find it quite hard to hug her and we never kiss.'

'Divorce?'

'I am, as you were to me, her grand passion: all the more so because it is unconsummated. What a heavy burden *that* must be to bear. The least I can do is not divorce her.'

'An affair?'

'She'd get pregnant with the first act. Well, maybe not any longer, but she doesn't want an affair. As for me, I have accepted her need to keep me under her supervision. She has more or less imprisoned me here. I work by phone and fax; I have no excuse to visit people without her and an affair would be impossible. Anyway, everyone believes we're this rampant, lusty couple, still doing it twice a day. Lucky us!'

Laura thought, Dare I ask the obvious question? She despised amateur psychology, its easy inferences and crude assumptions, yet . . .

'Nick,' she began cautiously, 'is your *mother* still alive?'

He turned to her, his face clouding. 'Yes, she is. Believe me, I know what you're saying. Will her death change anything? I doubt it. And in any case, Nell is thirty-eight and it's becoming less and less likely that she'll conceive. Obviously I've wondered what effect my mother's obsessive love has had. Not that she was ever unkind to Nell or jealous of her, the way she was of you. Perhaps she senses that we don't make love, though I have never told her. But it *is* odd that she has never asked when we planned to start a family.

'At the age of ten or twelve I became a substitute for my father, practically my mother's husband. She used to call me her "little man". Looking so much like him didn't help, either. When I married Nell, I was thirty: the same age as my father was when *they* married. I've compared the wedding photographs. Take away his RAF uniform and we look identical. Is it over-simplifying it to say I'm afraid that if I sleep with Nell it would mean being unfaithful to my mother? I don't know, Laura. *I don't know*. It didn't stop me sleeping with you, did it?'

Laura's stomach was distended and painful, but she knew this was her last chance to talk to Nick. 'Can I do anything *at all*? Talk to Nell? Recommend a shrink?'

'No. But you must leave. You saw for yourself: she cannot bear your presence. She is consumed with jealousy. She knows I don't look at her as I look at you. She knows I never loved her as I loved you, which is the way she loves me. She knows above all that I have made love to you and *not to her*.

'Yet she's cooked a larder full of things for your visit to show what a good wife she is. She's arranged dinner parties for you to meet our friends, to prove we're not country bumpkins. All this in spite of the fact that she was terrified of you.'

'No, Nicholas. Not me. It's *you* who frighten her.'

'What makes you think that?'

Laura told him about the accident on the way back from the station.

Nicholas groaned. 'Oh God, oh God ... Had she been drinking?'

'Not that I noticed. She smelled of cologne and mouthwash, not alcohol.'

'She probably had. I suspect she drinks a lot, mostly behind my back. Partly to avoid facing the facts, and partly out of sheer frustration. Rage, disappointment, the strain of keeping a secret: all the usual reasons. I have avoided admitting it, but I must tackle her before it gets worse.'

He turned to her. 'But Laura, tell me about you. We have a bit of time left. Have *you* had a happy life – until this bloody thing hit you?'

Happiness? she thought. How do you measure it? I know how the world turns. I have had lovers and friends, probably too many of the one and not enough of the other. I love my sister, and her children go some way to make up for not having had any of my own. In a dark corner I harbour a shaming secret, not one I could confess to you as you have just confessed yours to me. But have I been *happy*? I'd rather not investigate that.

'It's been wonderful,' she said.

'Thank *God* for that,' Nicholas said fervently.

7

Edouard de Trifort

Laura kept her private and precious letters in a dusty old Gladstone bag on top of her wardrobe. One evening, soon after her return from Suffolk, she climbed shakily on to a chair and took it down. Edouard's letters were held together in a bundle by an elastic band. It snapped as she unwound it. She settled in the wing chair in a corner of the drawing-room.

Edouard's letters, arranged more or less in date order, began in 1974 and petered out a couple of years later. She pulled out one taken at random from near the top of the pile and addressed to the Fulham flat.

Ma très chère petite Laure,

Here I sit, urbane chairman of a significant meeting, making conscientious notes on each speaker's main points. Only I am not. I am utterly flooded with thoughts of you. Since you may not remember, such was your agreeable stupor when we parted last night, let me repeat that I love you. I love your face, the tip of your nose, and even the corners of your mouth when you turn them down. I love what you are. You worry me when you call me clever because – although, make no mistake, I am – I suspect you mean *rusé*, insincere. I don't believe I have ever said anything to you, about you, that was not the unvarnished truth. Do not believe my love to be a thing of manipulation and cunning, nor am I *exigeant*. I can bed (forgive me) even prettier girls than you on the production of a fistful of notes, but ... Ah! Now I must concentrate! It will not stop me thinking of you.

From another letter six months later (there had been at least twenty in between), she read:

The office is a holiday compared with being at home. But unhappiness is part of the scenery for the matrimonial ballet, as every young bride should be reminded before she processes up the aisle.

Laura had first met Edouard de Trifort in the late autumn of 1974, soon after Nick's wedding. In the wake of President Nixon's ignominious resignation the world banking community had chosen to demonstrate its solidarity by holding an international conference in Washington. Edouard was there to represent the French. It was Laura's first major professional trip abroad.

Laura was only twenty-seven, but her pride in her talent as an interpreter was offset by the insecurity that Conrad encouraged, a volatile combination. Although the money going into her bank each month rewarded her linguistic skills, her need for love had not been satisfied since she and Nicholas had parted a year earlier. Edouard de Trifort had noticed both the confidence and the insecurity and, during his first-class flight back to Paris, had speculated about their cause, and about Laura herself.

He got her number from the agency and telephoned her when he came to London a week later. He took her to dinner at the restaurant which, he said, had been General de Gaulle's favourite during his wartime exile. The place was shabby, intimate and relaxed. Edouard had deliberately not set out to impress. He was curious to find out what sort of person she was, this clever, dark-haired young woman who had the translator's essential ability to concentrate for hours on end.

To humour her, he asked about Women's Lib, since they had both seen many of its placards and demonstrations while in Washington. 'Why do so many foolish, hysterical women want to burn their *soutien-gorges*?'

Laura was acerbic. 'Not *burn* their bras,' she said. 'Men try to belittle the women's movement by ridiculing it. Women want to take their bras *off*, just as men took off their codpieces three centuries ago. Why do I wear a bra? Is it for my benefit, or for yours?'

Conrad would have made some patronizing remark, a polished flick to remind her of the punishment in store for her effrontery. Nick would have blushed and lowered his eyes. Harkness would already have known that she did not wear a bra. Edouard said, 'I shall speculate, with no hope of verification.' He smiled at her and changed the subject.

His conversation was utterly civilized. He had an eclectic breadth of learning and talked about his enthusiasms in a beguiling bilingual voice. Laura, who had agreed to dinner as a favour to an important client, was surprised and enthralled. After the meal he paid the bill, hailed a taxi, climbed in after her, held her hand lightly, coolly, while it bore them to her front door, saw her safely inside, gave her hand a token brush with his lips and got back into the taxi. Laura, braced to resist his advances, felt a small sense of anti-climax.

She might never have gone to bed with him had she not been lonely that autumn and winter. She had telephoned Conrad after breaking up with Nicholas; he had welcomed her back without questions and treated her as his established mistress. He evidently saw no reason why their affair – six years old, as his wife must surely know by now – should not continue indefinitely, dwindling to a comfortable familiarity. Had Laura been less successful in her own right, her future might have been that of an unacknowledged second wife without rights or claims, yet wedded to Conrad by hope, habit and inertia.

It was not an entirely passive choice on Laura's part. She still loved him. He was the only consistent male presence in her life apart from her father and brother-in-law, and his dependence upon her, as both his erotic accomplice and trusted confidante, had increased. She often thought she must know him better than his wife. It is the common misapprehension of mistresses.

Loneliness delivered her, one Saturday in December, into

Edouard's bed. There were Christmas trees in other people's front windows and invitations on their mantelpieces. Laura had been asked to several parties, but not on that particular Saturday. It was a week before she was due to go home for the usual festivities and she had spent the afternoon shopping. As she settled on the rug in front of the fire to wrap her presents she was swept by a dampening wave of self-pity. I am twenty-seven, she thought. Clever, well-paid, with an interesting job. I am not bad-looking or boring, so *why am I all on my own?* She reached for another sheet of wrapping paper and twisted it into a cracker to enclose two crocheted ties that she had chosen for Paul. She had just got up to put a record on the gramophone when the telephone rang.

'Edouard!' she cried. Her voice rang with such welcome that he knew at once she was his for the taking. He had set his traps, baited them and smeared them with honey. It had taken two months, exactly as he had reckoned.

More than seventeen years later Laura and Edouard sat opposite each other sipping coffee from tiny jewel-coloured cups. She looked at him across the elegant Paris drawing-room and thought, you have grown old! He had always been dapper in the past, his hair combed back, eyes sharp and lively, sporting a bow tie and crisp handkerchief, his small feet encased in hand-made shoes. Now at seventy-four he was as wizened as an old turtle. His jowls drooped into lugubrious folds and his hands trembled as he lifted the scalding coffee to his lips. His eyes were hooded. His thin feet were shod in leather slippers and his voice quavered. *Old!* Was it better to come to this, or die young? A year ago, vanity might have misled her into opting to die young; now she knew she would rather have been given the chance to grow old.

Laura had never been in Edouard's apartment before. The room was dominated by an oil painting of a woman in evening dress.

'When was that painted?' Laura asked.

'It was done for my wife's thirtieth birthday, in 1956. I wanted to capture her *en grand beauté*.'

'She *is* beautiful.'

'She *was* beautiful.'

'Who painted it?'

'She wanted Bernard Buffet . . . Young then, beginning to be fashionable . . . but I didn't care to see her reduced to a stick-insect. I persuaded her to let me choose a more suitable artist for her, and she agreed on condition that Buffet painted me instead. I hated the picture. My son has it now. I daresay he hates it too, poor fellow.'

'How is he . . . Frédérique, wasn't it, your eldest?'

'Frédérique, yes. Waiting for me to die, but with good grace. Better grace than I myself.'

'Edouard! You aren't going to die for a long time! You look very well.'

'I am glad to hear it. But each day is spent in the same way. Café au lait with *Le Monde*; I dress; I take my small constitutional; I come back for lunch; I take a little nap . . .'

'Not while *I'm* here.'

'It is my hope that you will cheer me up, if you can bear to be seen accompanying such an old man.'

Oh God, she thought: are we to have this stream of self-pity for a month? I shall have to make another early escape. Edouard may have seen her expression change, for he said: 'Tonight I thought we might dine at Maxim's. We went there once before. Do you remember?'

Laura remembered vividly. It had been one more milestone along the road of her sexual sophistication. Edouard rarely met her when she was working in Paris; he preferred their meetings to take place further from home. They had both been present at a conference about Far Eastern economies in the aftermath of the war in Vietnam, hosted by the World Bank. Edouard had personal experience of Vietnam and his contribution had been the talking-point of the day. Gratified by his success, he had insisted on taking her to Maxim's.

Laura had looked her best that evening. She had put on, assessed, and discarded her jewellery, aware that nakedness emphasized her shoulders. Her legs were tanned so she needed no stockings, and her slim bare feet were cat's-cradled in finely strapped sandals.

She first became aware that she had good legs when she was about fourteen. In the communal changing room of her boarding school after gym or tennis, the girls would compare figures. Flat-chested Laura had looked with shy curiosity at other people's bosoms, some full and floppy with big dark nipples, others pertly separated with little pointed tips. She had always been slender, with a long, narrow rib-cage, long legs in proportion to her body, oval knees and fine ankles. 'Lucky old *you*. It's not *fair*!' Fiona had moaned. 'You've got *wizard* legs. Look at *mine*! Yuk!' Laura knew she had to make some modest disclaimer, but she also knew it was true: her legs *were* lovely.

When Laura left school in 1965, she put sensible brown shoes and sandals behind her for ever, graduating to the curvy little heels and pointed toes that were the fashionable footwear of the mid-Sixties.

When she left university three years later, she climbed on to thick platform-soled shoes, but not for long. That evening in Maxim's — it must have been the summer of 1975 — she wore sandals whose intricate strapwork was a miracle of lightness and balance. Her toe-nails were a shiny crimson, her feet arched and alluring.

'You are the most beautiful woman in the room,' Edouard told her. 'And the only one who cannot be bought!'

'How do you know?' she asked.

'I *look* at them. Women who hold your eyes for a fraction too long and do not then smile or blush are signalling a transaction. They are weighing up your wallet and you are weighing up their price, among other things.'

'But that one – over there,' Laura said, indicating a charming *ingénue* in white whom she took to be a grand-daughter being given a treat. 'She doesn't look as though she's even passed her *bac* yet!'

'You are mistaken, my dear, I assure you. They will go back to a discreet hotel where she will take off the Dior and dress up like a schoolgirl. That innocence is her stock-in-trade.'

'Try her,' Laura said.

A few moments later, as the waiter arrived with the laden cheese trolley, Edouard did so. Laura saw the beautiful child drag her shining eyes from the face of the gnarled old man and direct her gaze for a moment towards Edouard. Steadily, she held his look, and then fixed hers upon the old man again. She did not smile or blush. 'She must be only about sixteen,' Laura said.

'Twenty, I would judge, at least. She is reaching the end of this particular role. Soon she will have to find a new one, or lower her price.'

When the waiter presented the bill at the end of the meal, Edouard showed Laura the card hidden discreetly beneath one corner of the folder. 'Claudine,' it said, with a telephone number in the *seizième*. Laura wondered if he had ever used it.

On the afternoon of her arrival, after their coffee had been replenished by the Vietnamese housekeeper, Edouard excused himself and retired to his bedroom. Before going, he embraced her formally.

'*Fais comme chez toi,* Laura, for the next month. I am very happy to have you here. You must feel at liberty to investigate anything. I have no secrets – or none that will not die with me.'

Edouard's apartment, which was in a side street behind the Musée d'Orsay, was grander than its modest entrance at street level suggested. An elaborate cast-iron lift lumbered slowly up to the first floor. From the landing his front door opened on to a spacious hallway, whose apricot silk walls were almost completely obscured by portraits, most dating from the first decades of the century. Judging by the similarities between the faces, they were all members of his family.

Several concealed doorways lined each side of the hall. On the left, a set of mirrored double doors opened on to a large parquet-floored room. There were deep, low sofas at one end and a round dining table at the other. Two sets of french windows led out on to a balcony running the entire length of the salon, on which plants and greenery flourished. At the dining end of the room, another hidden door revealed Edouard's study, which contained a large desk, a swivelling chair, a green-shaded light and several thousand books.

Laura looked along the shelves. Some books were bound in red calf; others had plain paper spines still awaiting their embossed and gilded leather bindings. Edouard's desk, piled with correspondence, was neatly arranged. He had always been an orderly man, as fastidious in his working habits as in his dress. In this hushed and serious room she felt like an intruder.

She went back to the hall. There was a small bathroom and lavatory at the far end and three doors in the wall opposite the drawing-room. One, which Edouard had indicated earlier, led to her bedroom. It was lavender-blue throughout, from its moiré-covered walls to the thick carpet underfoot. Her bed was a curving Napoleonic *bateau-lit*, draped with a heavy dark blue bedspread over which was thrown a lace cover. A connecting bathroom was lined with mirrors. Not even Conrad had offered such all-enveloping luxury.

Laura unpacked and put away her clothes. When she had finished, she too lay down and rested briefly. Then, afraid she might sleep for hours, she got up and made her way to the kitchen, where she found the Vietnamese housekeeper in a white overall ironing shirts. Laura asked if she would mind adding to them some silk shirts of her own.

Edouard had not introduced Laura to his housekeeper. Now they shook hands, and she learned that the woman's surname was Chet Do and that she was of French colonial origin. Madame Chet and her husband lived behind the kitchen in two rooms overlooking the central courtyard. 'He is taking Monsieur de Trifort's car to the garage,' she said. '*Vous avez travaillé chez Monsieur depuis plusieurs d'années?*' Laura asked.

Madame Chet had first met her employer in the heat of the fighting between French forces and the Viet Minh in 1953, when Edouard was a rising young career officer in the French army. She was a little girl then, fleeing with her mother and two smaller children from their burned-out village. Edouard found them crouched beside the road, her mother clasping a blood-soaked infant in her arms. Edouard tried to staunch the child's wounds, but it was already dead. His section was forced to move on and he had to leave the terrified family huddling in a ditch. He could do nothing except give the children a bar of chocolate and, although it was of no obvious use, tell the woman his address in Paris. The six-year-old girl, whose name was Than Yeu, remembered it, chanted it and wove it into a fairy story, a promise of magic lands.

Twenty years later, when she and her young husband escaped from the next war, the American war, that name and that address had been their passport to safety. They had repeated it stubbornly – she told Laura in her high-pitched, staccato French – wherever they encountered officialdom. Edouard de Trifort was by then head of the family bank, a powerful man. Direct access to him was impossible, but his office confirmed that the address was correct and he had been in the war just as she described. Her obstinate insistence had tracked him down, and ever since then she and her husband had lived in the two gloomy back rooms in Edouard's flat and devoted their lives to him. 'I cheated death,' she said unemotionally to Laura. 'Twice.'

Madame Chet worried about Edouard. '*Il pense toujours à la mort.*' She glanced sidelong at Laura as though wondering whether her presence could lighten his mood.

'*Moi aussi!*' riposted Laura. '*Moi-même, je reflechis trop à la mort!*'

'*Donc,*' the woman said in her fluting voice, '*Vous serez contentes ensembles, Madame, vous deux.*' She made no attempt to deter Laura, or to pretend that Edouard could be 'cheered up'. She had learned very young that life was no joke.

Edouard had given Laura, at a raw stage in her life, more than money, more even than affection: he had given her the certainty of being completely loved, whatever she said or did.

'Completely?' her mother would have asked. '*Completely?* When he has a wife and children? How can he?' And Laura would have answered, 'Yes. Completely. He also loves opera, racing, his dogs, his children and his wife. I accept that. But he loves *me* completely.' After Conrad's cool, circumstantial love and Nicholas's pleading love, she cherished Edouard's all-embracing, headlong acceptance.

'*Nothing* is as beautiful as young flesh,' he told her the first time he took her to bed.

Laura had remonstrated, 'Any woman under thirty can offer that, and a girl of fifteen twice as well!'

'I embrace your flesh,' he told her, 'but without your *mind* it would be just flesh, which, as you say, any woman under thirty can offer. Do not, however, underrate the value of good legs.'

She laughed and stretched them languorously, watching him worship them, and her.

Edouard's letters fell, white and welcome as manna, on to her doormat twice a week. He was dangerously mellifluous on the page, so much so that in the flesh he was almost a disappointment. His physical love-making was never as good as the verbal seduction which preceded it. His letters coaxed and cajoled, reminisced and promised future delights. Above all, they assured her of his continuing love.

The temptation is to bombard you with odes and passion and declamation, confident that at any rate I can persuade you to read to the end of the page before you stretch out a hand for your waste-paper basket.

Tomorrow I go to Longchamp, because to leave the bank on Friday afternoon to bet on horses is like all the forbidden pleasures rolled into one. Only your image will be with me because you are in Washington or Rome or any other damned city but this one. When I know you are near at hand, I think of your voice. When I know you are miles away, I think of the lock of hair that curls round your left ear and your face in profile from the left. *Je te baise les mains*. The rest will follow.

Laura had never pretended to love him, believing that her love was still in thrall to Conrad. So as not to mislead Edouard she never confessed how much pleasure she derived from his letters. She surprised herself by the eagerness with which she awaited his visits to London, their expeditions to the opera, their dinners, his tuition in the subtleties of wine. 'I shall teach you about Burgundy,' he once said, 'and spoil you for all lesser wines!'

He took her to restaurants seldom penetrated by knowing girls with roving eyes and instructed her delicately in the art of eating. 'Not "oysters, ugh!" my dear,' he said. 'The oyster is a great aphrodisiac. One overcomes one's aesthetic recoil just as one does in the act of love. I assure you that what seems repellent now will come to seem quite ravishing, if you will allow your tongue to linger, caress and learn ... It is no accident that the oyster so resembles *le con*.'

During Laura's month in Paris, Edouard would appear in the drawing-room at seven o'clock each evening, having changed into an old-fashioned suit, a little too narrow at the waist, a little too wide in the lapels, and shoes as sleek as gloves. Behind him, carrying a tray, would be Madame Chet. He tired easily, he explained, and apart from their one visit to Maxim's he preferred to dine at home.

'Red wine is a little heavy for my liver these days,' he said, 'but there are exquisite white Burgundies too.' It was as if the eighteen intervening years had been no time at all. He turned to the tray, on which stood a bottle of wine and two glasses.

'This one is a Puligny-Montrachet 1978. The vineyard covers less than two acres. The wine is rare, and very fine.'

'Edouard!' she sighed with real regret, 'I have told you. I cannot drink at all. Not one drop.'

'This wine is nectar. It will bypass your liver, if I tell it.'

She laughed – it was so good to hear him joke – and relented. 'One glass.'

The wine that flowed over her palate was subtle and ravishing. Laura had drunk no alcohol since her dinner in February. Edouard watched her with pleasure.

'I had forgotten how very much I enjoy instructing you! I never had such a responsive pupil.'

She stood up, and the loose silk shirt rustled as she crossed the salon to sit beside him. 'Dear Edouard . . . and I had forgotten how generous you are!'

He took her hand and raised it to his lips. 'Why do you wear trousers?' he asked. 'Not that your figure cannot carry them, but I prefer to see your pretty legs.'

'I am, you know, altered by this . . . illness. I am misshapen. I hate to wear anything tight around my waist.'

'Very good. Tomorrow we will go to the Faubourg Saint Honoré and choose some dresses, *loose* at the waist.'

'I assure you, I can buy my own clothes.'

'Psst, *minou*, permit me the pleasure. I do not imagine I shall ever buy dresses for a woman again. Do me the honour of being the last.'

She smiled, cradling her cool glass, looking forward to the choice.

After a while she said, 'I never realized you had spent so much time as a professional soldier. Madame Chet told me how she met you, when she was a child.'

'Had it not been for my father's death, and my mother's insistence that I return and join the family bank, I could have been a soldier all my life.'

'It seems an unlikely choice for you, with your . . . fastidiousness.'

'It suited the nature of my marriage, to be apart from my wife yet not separated from her. It suited my need to escape the family.'

'Edouard. About Madame Chet – did *you* remember *her*?'

'Do you know that I was born here, Laura? Conceived here too, I believe, in the room in which I now sleep, and I shall undoubtedly die here.'

'What made you take pity, with so many wounded in Vietnam, on that particular family?'

'Indo-China, Laura. *L'Indochine*. There was the problem of my mother. My obligations, my position.'

'When Madame Chet turned up in Paris with her husband, could you recall the incident, or her as a child?'

'Her mother was a *pietà*, the weight of grief draped over her heart like the body of that dead baby. I *could not* forget. Whatever horrors you witness, some stay to haunt you. Tiny as it was, barely weeks old, it had drenched the other children with its blood. The little girl had such intelligent eyes: I *knew* she would remember. Just as I had not forgotten *her* name . . . Than Yeu.'

'She was lucky you were at the same address twenty years later.'

'These pictures, this furniture have surrounded me ever since I could crawl. My mother the widow was even more of a tyrant than my mother the mother. Isabelle and I lived under the shadow of her formal grief for ten years: a grief that was less for my father than for my brothers, who died before I was born.'

'You never told me any of this before, when we last knew each other.'

'Why, *ma chérie*, did I contrive to spend so many weekends with you in London? My mother was one reason. My wife another. Your youth and enthusiasm were a greater one. Why burden you with my *histoire*?'

'It's a most extraordinary story. You gave them shelter – a refuge.'

'The journey they took to get here. What a simple, impossible target! An address spoken to a child. And it suits me, to have them looking after me. The perfect couple: efficient and dedicated to my comfort.'

They waited on Laura too, making her bed, setting her room in order. Her clothes were not only washed but starched and mended. Fresh flowers appeared in great bowls every three days throughout the flat and beside her bed. The bathroom taps winked with polishing.

Edouard kept his promise. He took Laura to buy clothes, treating her with perfect discretion, not following her into the changing room but sitting outside while a young *vendeuse* served him coffee or a glass of champagne.

Edouard had given her presents in the past, bestowing luxury with ease, dismissing monetary value in search of the perfect gift – gold watch, silk scarf, Turkish rug, mother-of-pearl paper-knife. At first she stood upon her new-found principles and refused these offerings. He had been insulted by the implication that he was trying to buy her. By the spring of 1976, when he proffered the first gift, they had already been sleeping together for months. He did not argue but put the watch in its box and back into his pocket, never to reappear. Laura was mortified to find how much she minded.

When she rejected his second gift, a silk scarf – though with feebler protestations – he put that away too, leaving behind the flat orange box and brown ribbon to remind her of its beauty. Again she was shocked by her own disappointment. She had hoped he would urge it upon her, beseech her to overcome her scruples.

Instead he wrote her a letter, elliptical as Proust.

How clever you are to compose such a tortuous and interesting ideology for your life. How novel and original – and how demanding! Easier, I should think, to be a nun. The clichés of Fulham and the

New Feminism are just as narrow and ungenerous as those of Philistia, and, surely, even rich people can be likeable?

After that he had held her at arm's length for a month, telephoning once to say that he was in London, but – alas! – too busy to meet her. Again, Laura found herself surprised by disappointment. Letters arrived in March with London postmarks:

I wonder what you are doing and what I can do to see or speak to you without seeming intrusive or importunate. I think over our last meeting. I go into contortions of anxiety lest you should decide – not on grounds I could understand, like boredom or distaste, but grounds I cannot, of ideology or your much-vaunted autonomy – that we should stop meeting. I want to embrace you in public as well as in private, to flaunt and display you, and above all, to show that I love you dearly, for all the things I know about you, carnally and otherwise, as well as those I don't understand. I know above all that I love you, and everything else is a midwinter London fog.

When he telephoned to ask her to have dinner with him the following evening, Laura cancelled a meeting with her sister and saw Edouard instead. She did not refuse his presents again.

Conrad never knew about Edouard because he had stopped asking if she had other lovers, and Laura – fearful of making him jealous, and thus angry and inclined to punish her with real fervour – had stopped telling him.

He raised an eyebrow when he saw her first present from Edouard – an ox-blood red Afghan rug – but all he said was, 'An improvement on Casa Pupo.' He noticed, too, when she changed her scent for a subtler one, also from Edouard. These observations may have prompted the first – almost the only – letter she received from him until the one inviting her to Naples seventeen years later.

The following should be unnecessary, but I want to make it clear that I have no pretensions to your heart or your 'hand'. Three factors more than suffice: 1) I am eternally married 2) I am too old for you and 3) my feeling for children is such that I could never again undertake such a burden.

What I want from you is fun, fun, fun ... and some wickedness involving what my daughter's current beau, during our man-to-man chats, humorously refers to as 'the purple-headed bedsnake'.

Let me give you one hint (as an older man) for the benefit of your future lovers. Having made them notice you – which in your case, fortunate creature, presents no problem – you must say you cannot possibly see them tonight, even though you have nothing else to do; adding 'perhaps two weeks from Tuesday'. Postponement, my dear, is the bellows on the fire of love. But do not apply this advice to me.

I think of you – thanks to the invaluable Roget – lewdly, lasciviously, lecherously and lustfully, libidinously and licentiously.

I am yours, pretty Laura, although I can be everything to you except that.

Conrad

'Lovingly' also begins with 'l', Laura thought.

After two weeks in Paris with Edouard, Laura realized that for the first time the progress of her illness seemed to have halted. She felt no weaker or more lethargic than when she arrived, nor was her skin more sensitive, her breath shorter, her sleep at night more disturbed. On the contrary, Edouard had somehow made her feel better. Or perhaps it was Madame Chet, who woke her at nine with a cup of sharply scented herbal tea and prepared a bath billowing with steam, from which Laura emerged to find her clothes waiting in the open garde-robe.

Entering the drawing-room, where early June sunshine cast patterned stripes across the golden parquet floor, Laura would sit down in front of a tray of coffee and fresh croissants to read Le Monde and an English newspaper collected by Monsieur Chet from the corner news-stand. Edouard would emerge later to discuss the day ahead. Were it not for his weakness – for which he kept tediously apologizing – and a thin stream of complaints uttered under his breath, of which he seemed unaware, she could have stayed for ever. His slowness was no problem; indeed, it suited her own tempo.

After their relationship had continued for more than a year, neither Edouard's love nor his generosity were diminished but Laura had begun to prefer his absences. His sinewy body and lizard skin could not arouse her, however skilled his caresses. She liked his letters – elegant and restrained, amorous without being explicit, ardent without sentimentality – but was no longer impressed by perfectly presented dinners served by deferential waiters, who, she was sure, sneered at her out of sight in the kitchen. She knew she looked like an old man's darling, and would rather have been a young man's equal.

There were times when she envied her sister, Constance. For although all was evidently not well with the marriage, the intimacy which she and Paul shared was real, not intermittent, reinforced by their house and possessions, children, friends and family. Constance complained that Paul worked too hard at the agency and came home too late (but at least she had him with her every night, thought Laura wistfully). Laura could see for herself that Paul was becoming insensitive to her sister's needs and moods. He no longer behaved tenderly towards her, hardly even affectionately, but as if she were there merely to service his home and children.

'We hardly *ever* make love these days . . .' Constance sighed once.

Laura watched her sister spoon-feeding supper into the reluctant mouth of Kate, her youngest. Constance, as usual, wore no make-up and her hair could have done with a wash. Her shirt was spotted with food stains; her jeans wrinkled and baggy. Laura reflected that her sister was not exactly an object of desire, while – as Paul never failed to point out – being modishly dressed was a vital part of his job.

'I *am* the agency, as far as the client's concerned. Image is everything,' he would argue, justifying the purchase of another £150 Carnaby Street suit or a black cashmere polo-necked sweater.

Paul was now one of the top three men in his advertising agency, with the title 'Creative Director'. His success benefited Constance too. Indifferent to clothes herself, she spent money on decking out the children and the house. The children blossomed like flowers. Constance was at the centre of more than a dozen people, from whom radiated the interlocking forces — need, love, obligation, family, habit, routine, care — that governed her life. Laura did not discuss with her sister whether her charming and attractive brother-in-law was faithful; she knew too much about married men. What mattered was that Constance still really loved Paul and was happy with him despite their ups and downs.

Laura herself was on the edge of many lives but central to none. She was important to Edouard and Conrad, but they could be away for days, sometimes weeks, and it was increasingly hard to convince herself that being a mistress was worth the secrecy and the absences.

One evening over dinner she told Edouard about Conrad. The vehemence with which he responded took her aback.

'How old is this man?'

'Over fifty now.'

'And you are soon twenty-nine. Is he married?'

'Yes.'

'With children?'

'Yes.'

'Sons?'

'No. Two daughters.'

'How long have you been his mistress?'

'Nearly seven years.'

'So his wife knows and is *complaisante*. This man, Laura, will take your youth and your touching beauty, your love and gaiety, and give you *nothing* in return. He will drain you until you are a bitter old spinster. By then it is too late for marriage or children, and the love left between you will be like the ash in that ashtray. I *despise* men like this. They are thieves and liars.

'When he dies, what will happen? Will he have thought of you? No! You will lay eyes upon his wife and daughters for the first time at his funeral, but from a distance. You cannot present yourself. I have seen those women – twenty, thirty years younger than the wife, the same age as the children – who stand at the back of the church and stay behind at the cemetery. *No one talks to them.* They have no status, no support in their grief. A mistress thinks she knows about loneliness, but if he dies – or finds a younger woman – then *real* loneliness begins.'

Laura was stung to retort, 'And you, Edouard? In what way are *you* different?'

He slid a hand past his glass and across the damask tablecloth to hold her wrist. Her pulse under his fingers was rapid with agitation. 'I am different, *ma trésor*, because if I were free I would *beg* you to marry me; and if I could get free, I would. But my wife is ill. She is younger than this . . . *gentleman* of yours . . . but she has cancer.'

Laura said, 'I'm sorry. I didn't know.'

'Of course not. I did not tell you.'

When she met his eyes again, Laura said, '*Conrad* would marry me if anything happened to his wife.'

'What makes you believe that?'

She was silent, because she had no reason to offer.

'He is bad for you, *ma belle Laure*. He pretends that you and he are sophisticated people, that it is banal, *bourgeois*, to live according to the narrow scruples of society. He says that with him you enjoy pleasures more rarefied than those of the common herd. He says this, does he not? He says that women such as you should not be confined in a vulgar, suburban marriage – *does he not?*'

Laura looked steadily back at Edouard. 'Yes. He does.'

'You think I am jealous. *Bien sûr*, I am jealous. I love you, I adore you, you fill my heart. I am ashamed that your presence crowds out the suffering of my wife. But this man, Laura, has stolen *seven years* from you. Do you make love joyously with him? Laugh? Are you happy? You can tell me. Why don't you answer? What does that silence mean?'

A few months after this conversation, Edouard's wife died. He told Laura the news in a letter and withdrew for a while. The following year he asked her to marry him. Laura was depressed and frightened by what she thought was the imminent end of her youth, her thirtieth birthday, but she refused him. He gave her a glorious gold bracelet to mark the occasion and asked her again. But once more, albeit after a good deal of thought this time, she refused.

Edouard was sixty, exactly thirty years older than Laura; *but* he was immensely rich. He adored her, *but* she did not love him, and no longer enjoyed going to bed with him. She argued to and fro with herself for months. She could live in luxury, *but* it would have to be in Paris. She would have to leave her friends and family behind, her troubled sister, *but* they could always come and visit her. She revelled in her work and did not want to give it up. *But*, no one else had wanted to marry her, except Nicholas. Was Edouard better than Nick? Was any husband good enough? But she was only just thirty. Thirty wasn't old. Sixty was.

When Edouard proposed a third time, and she again refused, he told her very gently that he would not see her any more. A month later came his final letter:

Since I am already breaking my private vow not to write again, I will leave out much that ought to be said and more that wants to be said and just thank you for many kindnesses and hours of happiness. You have given me – a grizzled old soldier or formal old banker, the head of a venerable family, a dignified father and widower (for I am all of these things when you are not with me) – new dimensions of thinking and feeling. You have been more fair, sensible and compassionate than I had any right to expect. I invoke all the happiness and triumphs you want upon yourself. I even (do not underestimate the difficulty) invoke a happy marriage upon your deserving head.

I take back nothing I have ever said or written to you. I promised myself from the outset that if ever I feared my company was becoming tedious to you, I would withdraw. This I now do.

The Jardins du Luxembourg are full of sunshine and butterflies. My flat is full of dust and antiquity. Oh, Laura!

Yours, most truly and sincerely,

Edouard

It was about this time, just as she had entered her thirties, that Laura began to notice that although her women friends and colleagues referred casually to their 'bloke' or 'fella', as if liberated young women such as themselves no longer fell in love; although they pretended to lead easy-going bachelor lives in which males were no longer essential – nevertheless, as they too entered their thirties, many of them suddenly announced that they were getting married, often after unaccountably forgetting to take the Pill.

At the same time Laura became aware that she had been corrupted by Conrad and Edouard. She had become impatient with the modest offerings of men her own age. Accustomed to the polished splendour of Boulestin, Prunier or Rules, it was hard to be thrilled by an invitation to eat at a Greek taverna or French bistro, while any suggestion that she might go Dutch for 'a pie and a pint' or 'bangers and mash' was smilingly refused. Laura was no longer a free spirit. She was a mistress, but now, for the first time, a reluctant one.

Brilliant June sunshine fell across the portrait of Edouard's wife, Isabelle, bringing its rose and apricot shades to life. The face in the picture was soft and kittenish. Her boneless white hands were much in evidence, the one in her lap holding a half-open rose, the other on the arm of her chair displaying magnificent diamonds. A dress of eau-de-Nil satin swathed her pliant body. Only her hair, set in the artful waves of the mid-Fifties, looked curiously formal and outmoded.

The month with Edouard was nearly at an end. Luxury dragged at Laura's resolve, slowing her steps. The exhibitions she had meant to attend remained unvisited; the films she had urged upon Edouard remained unseen. Comfort wrapped her like an invalid's blanket. Already they had developed habits of life together, times at which they met and talked, times when they left one another alone. 'You have things to do,' he would say, and they would separate – Edouard to sleep, Laura to write letters or read. But soon she, too, would decide to take a nap. Late in the afternoon they would both wake. Tea would have been placed silently on the bedside table, a biscuit or two, a fragment of patisserie. Time to change her clothes before they came together again for a drink at seven.

The distension that had plagued Laura when she stayed with Joe and Nell seemed to have abated a little. Her arms and neck were no longer red from scratching and the long marks from her fingernails had subsided. The ominous tracery of lilac veins still bulged prominently against her rust-coloured skin and she thought herself hideously deformed. Yet such was the artistry of French cut and seaming that in the new dresses Edouard had bought for her she appeared normal, with hardly more than a womanly swelling to mark where her illness festered.

During her final week Edouard took her to one of the oldest restaurants in the neighbourhood. The wine waiter, his deference modified by long acquaintance, recommended various wines and Edouard settled on a 1947 Beaune Marconnets. Laura put a hand over her glass.

'You will insult the *sommelier* and, more to the point, me,' Edouard said.

'You still won't really accept that I am ill,' she replied.

'I know you are ill. But wine is the soul of France, and look at the date of this bottle: 1947, the year of your birth! *Écoutes, chérie*, what difference will it make to deny yourself this pleasure? Will it subtract a day from your life if you drink a glass or two?'

Laura was angered by the seductiveness of his persuasion. 'Edouard! I am ill. *I am dying.*'

'So am I.'

'Yes, yes, I know – so are you, and so are we all.'

'I learned my news at about the same time as you were told yours.'

'Everybody's dying – that's not the point. I am dying young and so *yes*, every day counts . . .' She stopped suddenly. '*Edouard?*'

'Not that illness makes a great deal of difference. I am seventy-four, and before you came I thought life had no more surprises left for me.'

'Edouard, I am sorry I have been selfish. Pour the wine and tell me.'

She sipped the rich, almost caramelized wine while Edouard told her that he had cancer. Already the relatives were circling, appraising his pictures and furniture, rumbling and cooing solicitously while at the same time glancing round the room to estimate the value of his possessions. 'Ah, Edouard, I've always loved that . . .' somebody would say, as though simply applauding his taste. When they had gone, Edouard might adjust his will accordingly. Or not.

They took a taxi home. Edouard kissed her drily beneath the portrait of his wife, and she retired to her room. Fifteen minutes later, Laura heard him call her name. She wrapped a red silk dressing-gown around her distended abdomen and opened the door on to the hall.

His voice came from the drawing-room. 'Laura! Will you sit with me, while I drink a glass of cognac?'

She sat in the opposite armchair. The sounds from the street outside had subsided. Only an occasional car passed. On the table between them was an oval tray with a bottle of brandy and the tiny jewel-coloured cups from which she had drunk on arrival. Books and magazines were arranged in heaps and at one end of the table stood a Michael Ayrton sculpture: man and minotaur confronting each other through a pane of smoked glass.

'Darling . . .' he said finally, and Laura lifted heavy eyelids to look across at him. 'Show me your legs.'

'Oh, Edouard!' She took the silken hem of her dressing-gown and draped it modestly across the tops of her knees.

'No. *Really* show me. I always loved your elegant young legs.'

'They are not young any more.'

'You are playing games with me. Please . . . Lift your skirt.'

Laura raised the edge of her dressing-gown and tucked it into her lap. Enlarged varicose veins showed up clearly. She placed her legs at an angle, one across the other, demure as a schoolgirl in the front row of the group photograph.

'We could get married,' Edouard said, not looking directly into her eyes. 'You could stay here, with me. I would take care of you. Madame Chet will look after us both.'

He offers marriage, she thought. An end to the packing and unpacking, to all further visits and plans and thank-you letters. Marriage, dependence, comfort. A meaningless marriage, brief and unconsummated, but a peaceful end to my life. He still loves me.

Edouard let the silence run for a minute, more, still more. Then he said, almost more to himself than to her, 'If you knew how many many times I fantasized about being able to make you my wife. My young, cherished, indulged, beloved wife. The family could have closed ranks against us both, but I would have been content if you had been my wife.'

Laura thought, I refused you three times when I was young. Now I am tempted to accept. The *relief* of handing over all responsibility, of staying and letting the Chets take care of us both, of dying in comfort. Yet there was still unfinished business to transact and she could not die until it was completed.

She lifted the hem of her dressing-gown and let it fall over her legs. 'Edouard. You are, and always were, generous to a fault. But now it is too late.'

'I know,' he said, his voice weighted like an anchor. '*Crois-moi*, Laura, *I know*.'

Interlude

'You've done very well,' said Mrs Ripa, Laura's senior consultant. 'It's six months since I first saw you. How are you feeling?'

'Tired,' answered Laura. 'For the first time I understand the meaning of the word "fatigue". Deep, slow-dropping. Total inertia. Sometimes I glide through my days in a trance. I have to nap every afternoon. I get breathless after climbing more than two flights of stairs.'

'All quite normal, but not much fun, I agree. I'll write you up some iron pills. Do you want anything stronger, to jump-start you?'

'No. I want to keep my head as clear as possible – it's bad enough as it is, these days. I feel so depressed. I have to fight against that and irritability all the time. I'm rude, nervous, impatient and intolerant. I do try not to snap at people, but it isn't easy.'

'Any other changes? How's your weight?'

'I have no appetite at all. I could cheerfully never eat another meal. Only common-sense and will-power keep me forcing food down. I've lost a few pounds, I think.'

Mrs Ripa checked Laura's patient file. 'Few kilos, actually. Nearly five. Too much. It's important that you continue to eat. Try several tiny meals a day, since you can't face large ones. You're staying off alcohol?'

'It's amazing how people seem to *want* me to drink. They keep offering me champagne and fine wines, and their generosity makes me feel guilty about refusing. But it's not worth the pain in my gut afterwards, or the nausea.'

The consultant stood up and came round to the other side of her desk. She tipped Laura's face to the light and pulled down her lower eyelids.

'Your colour's darkened a lot. Were you sallow before?'

'Sallow?' said Laura, stung. 'I'm normally palish in winter and a nice honey colour in the summer. I wouldn't have called it *sallow.*'

'Mm-hmm. And your eyes are rather yellow. All, I'm afraid, to be expected in the normal course of hep C.'

When Mrs Ripa had returned to her seat Laura took the black Chanel compact from her shoulderbag. She peered at her eyes, moving the compact from side to side to inspect first one and then the other. It was true. The whites of her eyes were a cloudy yellow.

'Can I have drops for that?'

'I'd try to resist the temptation to put drops into your eyes. They only stain them blue, it doesn't do you any good. Next . . . show me your hands. Palms down. Now up. Do they look redder than usual?'

'I don't *know*,' said Laura. 'I've never studied them before.'

She gazed down at the palms of her hands in the old, childish gesture. 'Have you washed your hands, darling? Show Mummy.' Her mother's voice rang a distant bell, its intonations quite clear. Laura looked across at Mrs Ripa. 'I don't *know*,' she repeated. 'I don't know what's happening to me. I don't know how long I've got to live. I don't know what dying will be like. All I know is that I hate it! Oh, Christ . . . Sorry. I'm OK. I'm not going to cry. I don't need a tissue. Just rouge.'

Mrs Ripa smiled. 'I sympathize. Believe me, I do. Now, I want you to listen carefully. You are a grown-up woman and clearly accustomed to making your own decisions. You told me early on that you did not want a liver transplant. I accepted that. You are not on the waiting list for a suitable liver – and in any case, there's no guarantee that one would become available. But for my own peace of mind, can I ask you to think again? You can see that your illness is taking its course fairly . . . rapidly. I am not trying to persuade you. I just want to be quite certain that you won't reconsider at a stage when the time for a transplant may have passed. No, you don't have to answer now.'

'But I can,' Laura said. 'I am quite sure. I *do not* want a transplant. I want the itching to stop. I want the foul taste in my mouth to go away. I want to be normal again, not to think about my health every hour of every day. But I do not want a transplant.'

Mrs Ripa did not ask why. The deep pain in Laura's clouded eyes was not for her to investigate. 'Very well,' she said. 'We won't discuss it again.'

She wrote out two prescription forms and passed them to Laura. 'Take the top one to the pharmacy. But the bottom one is important too. Here' – she filled in several different-coloured order forms – 'are some blood requisitions. I'm afraid you'll probably have to queue to get them done.'

Laura glanced at the prescription forms. The lower one said: 'Morale-boosters. Harvey Nichols or Browns. Not NHS payable.' She grinned at Mrs Ripa, who said, 'I mean it. You were beautifully dressed the first couple of times I saw you. Now . . . That jacket's too loose on you for a start. And are you growing your hair? If you can afford a bit of self-indulgence, now's your chance. It's good for morale. Depression drags you down.'

The Harvey Nichols sale was coming to a close and, like flowers in a midsummer garden, the clothes looked overblown and bruised. Red sale notices swung gently above them, twisting in the breeze of customers marching past. Laura threaded through the familiar brand-names, each with its carefully designed logo, in search of her favourite clothes – those soft and beautiful garments, tailored and yet luxurious to the touch, that had struck the perfect balance between efficiency and flattery in her working life. Their subtle colours – never beige but gold threaded with fine blue stripes, never grey but taupe, never navy but slate-blue or inky purple – and fine fabrics had given her pleasure each time she had worn them.

A notice announced: TODAY ONLY: 50% OFF MARKED SALE PRICE. Laura began to sift through the coats, suits and silken shirts, searching for her size. She had had the same figure ever since her twenties – French 40, English 12. She selected and found a suit her size in a lightweight mixture of silk and tweed.

Alone in a brightly lit fitting-room, Laura stared at herself aghast. She had avoided looking at her body, but now it confronted her – bulging, misshapen, with huge gnarled veins winding like a caul, covering her abdomen from her breastbone across her grossly distended belly. Yet her legs and arms seemed to have shrunk, and the flesh was loose on her upper arms. Her skin had lost its usual gleam and looked dull and bruised. There were red 'spider' spots all over her body – small rings with radiating lines, like a money spider seen under a magnifying glass. I am hideous, she thought. *Hideous*.

There was a knock on the door.

'Excuse me, Madam,' came the saleswoman's bright, ingratiating voice. 'Do you mind sharing the cubicle with another lady?'

'Just a moment,' Laura said, improvising an excuse. 'I've had an operation recently. Just let me cover up.'

'Never mind,' she heard the other customer whisper. 'I'll go somewhere else.'

Laura stepped into the skirt of the suit. There was a four-inch gap between the button and the loop, yet the jacket hung slackly across her shoulders. Even when she tried to pull her stomach in, the waistband refused to meet. Laura could not bear to look at her own eyes in the mirror. She stumbled out of the skirt and pulled on her own loosely elasticated jersey trousers. A notice fixed to the wall above the mirror caught her eye. It read: FOR REASONS OF HYGIENE, BODIES CANNOT BE EXCHANGED OR CREDITED.

Hanging the suit back on the rail, she found a matte-silk shirt the colour of putty. It was a size 42. Without bothering to try it on – for she would not risk another glimpse of herself – Laura bought it with the grey and gold Harvey Nichols credit card that had financed so many beautiful garments. The salesgirl wrapped the shirt in tissue paper, placed it in a carrier bag and handed it to her.

Laura saw, as though reflected in an endless succession of mirrors, a corridor of sober-suited men, their pupils distended and dark with anticipatory desire. Sometimes they had scarcely noticed the food and wine they ordered, so intently were their senses focused on the end of the evening back at the hotel, the hoped-for consummation. Laura in turn had presented herself to that predatory gaze, delectably wrapped and scented. Bodies would be exchanged, credit cards would be debited. Pleasure is never free. Now, Laura mourned, that cocoon of luxury and ancitipation would never again enfold her.

She made her way towards the Italian couture section, remembering an especially beautiful evening suit of fine black crêpe pin-striped with gold thread. Amid neglected rows she found a grey silk dress, so artfully draped that it might conceal her disfigured figure. Laura took it to an empty changing room. A year ago, the dress would have been a miracle of curves, coiling sinuously around her body, outlining it only when she moved. Now, it strained harshly across her belly. She began to pull it off and, muffled in the soft fabric, heard a saleswoman enter. The words 'How are you getting on?' died on her lips. Laura extricated herself from the dress and turned her back to the woman. In the mirror she glimpsed her shocked face. 'Had you thought of trying maternity-wear?' the saleswoman asked, before gathering up the dress and leaving.

Outside again in the mêlée, Laura saw on the other side of the floor a tall woman in her mid-forties. She wore a tobacco-brown linen suit over an orange silk shirt, with a soft brown handbag slung over her shoulder. Laura recognized her own 'look' at once: her kind of clothes, her colour scheme. She watched as the woman moved between the rails fingering the fabrics, checking the finish on seams and hems. That was me! Laura thought. She stood still, watching, charting the woman's progress. She was slimmer than Laura had been, her hair longer, but otherwise they were two of a kind.

As the woman approached, she sensed Laura's gaze and caught her eye. 'Are you all right?' she asked. 'Can I get you anything? A chair?'

'No . . . I . . . why?'

'Sorry. You don't look very well. You actually don't look very well at all.'

'That's frightfully kind of you,' said Laura, switching on the automatic, impersonal courtesy which she usually kept for hotel receptionists and head waiters. 'Honestly, I'm fine.'

The woman sensed a rebuff and smiled glacially. 'Just a hard night out, then?' she said, and moved on.

Laura remained stock-still. She must think I'm an alcoholic with a hangover, or perhaps an overworked tart! What else could she have meant?

The saleswoman came up behind her. 'I shouldn't really be saying this,' she whispered, 'but since we haven't got a maternity department, I see no harm in it. There's a very good one at Harrods, you know. Lovely clothes, very figure-concealing. Why don't you try there?'

Laura smiled gratefully. 'How kind of you,' she said. 'That's an excellent idea. I'll go and have a look. Thank you.'

She made her way towards the escalator, past the shoe department where she had once indulged herself in pliant, finely grained leather shoes, and let the escalator carry her down to the ground floor.

She walked through the perfumery department, its pampered hot-house scents swirling through her nostrils, sickly sweet, and made a detour to look at the silk scarves and bright ostentatious costume jewellery. Here the crowd was thickest, women scrabbling through baskets of gilt baubles in search of the perfect accessory.

Beyond, at the far end of the ground floor, young girls tall as giraffes were trying on hats. Their soft, vapid faces laughed at each other beneath over-sophisticated creations. Their legs, taut and slender, were emphasized by short skirts or black tights. Their voices were staccato and confident. From time to time a mother would attempt to restrain her daughter, and the girl would toss her head and turn away from the anxious older face. Youth was everything! Youth and health, thought Laura bitterly. *Those* are the only things that matter! But bodies cannot be exchanged ... Except, perhaps, in bed, and who would want mine now?

She pushed open the heavy glass door and emerged on to Sloane Street. She knew she would never return to Harvey Nichols. She hailed a taxi and, as she settled back into its black leather privacy, scene of so many clandestine kisses, she remembered that she had left the beautiful, putty-coloured shirt behind in the changing cubicle. She closed her eyes and let the taxi carry her home.

8

Bruno Linoli

Bruno's invitation to come and stay 'for as long as you want' had been sitting in her desk since February, but before leaving for Monte Carlo Laura lingered for a couple of weeks in London – resting, shopping, seeing some of her friends and family. She almost regretted having turned down Edouard's offer. The peace and luxury of his establishment had begun to seep into her veins; London seemed hectic by comparison.

Yet the streets of Chelsea were full of parking places, the queues at Waitrose and Safeway were short, and the voices on the King's Road were those of tourists, mainly Japanese or American. They did not seem happy but dutiful. People like them, Laura realized, doing the jobs they do, travel to Europe. They focus their cameras, not on Europe's scenic or artistic sights, but on themselves: look! we too have been there!

Uncountable billions of photographs must be processed every year in Japan, she reflected. I too have seen billions of images in my life. What will flash before my eyes as I die? Does that really happen, or is it a myth? Shall I enter a long, dark tunnel and see light shining at the end? Will my father, miraculously reconstructed – not the mangled body they pulled from the wreckage but the dear strong Daddy of my childhood – will *he* stand waiting, arms outstretched, to welcome me? Or is there nothing, nothing, nothing?

She arranged to see her sister's children and a few friends who had not yet gone on holiday. Everyone knew of her illness, if only because of the physical changes it had brought about in her. Now that they felt able to talk about her condition, even people much more firmly grounded in reality than Dot and Joe urged herbalists or faith-healers upon her, or asserted that magical healing powers lay untapped within her own body. It was as unexpected as if she had discovered them to be secret Jehovah's Witnesses.

Laura's tough, rational mind revolted against credulity just as it did against the far more pressing need to believe in an after-life. Yet everyone seemed to know of someone who had made an astonishing recovery, been granted five years' remission or a new lease of life. They urged her to find another consultant, another hospital, another opinion, another treatment. She could not resist asking: do you honestly think there's any hope? Occasionally someone counselled the reverse: confront death rather than flee from it. It was a relief when one woman said, 'Laura, you *know* there isn't any hope. By refusing a transplant, you've made sure there isn't.'

This was Madeleine, an old college friend. Madeleine had never been anything except a wife to the first man she fell in love with and mother to their five children. These priorities had given her a simplicity that others who had made more materialistic choices lacked. Madeleine occupied herself with her husband, her first grandchild, and her elderly parents; nothing else. Yet she alone of Laura's circle had the courage to say, 'If you hope when you know there is really no hope, it gives you a false perspective. Anything you want to do must be done now, Laura. *Now.* Face up to it: you'll get so much more out of the time left.'

Laura felt able to be perfectly truthful in return. 'I am already on the other side, Madeleine, and receding. There's a terrific amount of truth in the old myths about death. I feel as though Charon the boatman were rowing me gently away from the shore. Everyone I know is standing on the edge. Some people are waving, some calling me back, and some are trying to rig up ropes or cables to *pull* me back. But I have to go.'

Madeleine wore a long pale pleated skirt with a soft cream shirt and an embroidered, ivory-coloured waistcoat. She had made Laura comfortable by propping her on a yielding pile of cushions on the sofa. She moved gently, tranquilly round the room. Those are the skills I never learned, Laura thought, that *womanliness*.

Madeleine said, 'It's my impression that it gets easier the further away you go. My father is an old man now, nearly ninety. He'll die soon, and he is quite calm about it. He isn't afraid of death, he doesn't dread it. Death is so close, it's become the next stage in his life.'

'Yes,' Laura said, 'but I'm half his age. I shall be forty-five *next week*!'

One morning Constance telephoned with a request that was impossible to ignore or refuse. 'Laura!' she began, 'I gather you went to see Max and Dani! Did you have a nice time? You saw Kaspie, didn't you? Isn't he *heaven*?'

Laura remembered how Kaspar, the two-year-old son of her nephew Max, had stumped across the grass shouting happily, but on seeing her had stopped, turned, howled and buried his face in his mother's skirts.

'Yes, I saw all three of them,' she answered. 'Kaspar's gorgeous.'

'Have you written to Mother?'

'PPP,' said Laura. It meant 'postcards from posh places': an old family joke. Her parents used to complain that was all they ever had from her. 'I don't *want* to go and stay in ghastly geriatric Miami, and even *less* do I want her flying over here to stay with me.'

'She *is* coming over, in fact,' said Constance. 'She'll be here in a few weeks' time, so don't say I didn't warn you. I told her she hadn't seen Kaspar since his christening and it was high time she did. She asked about you, of course, and I said you were OK.'

'Coco, don't bully me. *Why* must I see her?'

'Will you come and see *me* before you hurl yourself on the mercies of the next ex? This coming weekend, for instance?'

'Not a *whole* weekend, darling. Could I just come for the day?'

'Laura, anything you like. I'd love to see you, and so would Gordon.'

Ah yes, Gordon. Gordon the Possleque. As detailed and dull as a computer manual, a human encyclopedia of software and development, printer capacity and Microsoft DOS 6.1 with special bonus give-away: a program for preparing your own tax return. Laura sighed.

'Gordon has to work on Saturday,' said her sister quickly. 'Why don't you come then? Just a simple lunch. No wine. Please?'

Laura, staunching the habitual flow of regret that welled up when she contemplated her once-brilliant sister's colourless life, agreed that Saturday would be fine.

Laura loved her sister, but she preferred the company of her women friends. Blood was supposed to be, and *was*, thicker than water, but she would infinitely prefer to spend a day with Jenny, who would be at her side the moment she telephoned, her low, resonant voice calling a greeting as she got out of the taxi, her ardent soul reaching out to comfort Laura.

Sisters were for memories and home truths; men were for sex and secrets; but *women* were the best bet in the end for love and friendship. She recalled how her mother used to meet women friends ('the Girlies') in London after visiting the sales or the hairdresser ('Might as well make a day of it'), and together they would all go to a musical or a play. These treats were foolish extravagances that husbands had to put up with, even though it meant coming home from the office that evening to detailed instructions for scrambling eggs – that is, if supper were not already cooked, only needing the oven to be turned on.

Laura was luckier than that. Had she been born thirty years earlier, she would no doubt have grown up to a life like her mother's. Six years earlier, and she might have been Constance, and then *she* would have been married to Paul, and Kaspar would have been her grandchild.

She lay on her bed, listless but unsleeping in the muggy summer afternoons – not quite able to read, too exhausted to write letters or go through paperwork. She had hours in which to reflect. Her strength was draining away, the last grains of sand slipping rapidly towards the neck of the hourglass.

A week later Laura packed the summer dresses and sandals she had worn to visit Conrad in Amalfi, chose a couple of luxuries from Hermes for Bruno and his wife, and booked herself a first-class return to Nice.

The only person who had behaved badly on the evening of Laura's dinner party five months ago had been Bruno. What did 'badly' mean? Bruno had not been suave and restrained, had not murmured his shock or sympathy into her ear. Bruno had become maudlin, lachrymose and, by the end, extremely drunk. He had pulled out a huge handkerchief, buried his nose in it and hooted violently. As he left, he had enveloped her in a large embrace, sobbing into her hair, his whole frame shaking in disbelief at her news. Was *that*, Laura wondered, bad form, bad manners, bad taste? Or was it honest and spontaneous?

It was the same animal spontaneity that had first attracted her to him. There was something feral about Bruno. His eyes were the shining black eyes of a fox; his complexion was swarthy, his body hairy; he had an animal's small feet and his head bristled with abundant curly hair. As though sensing his own dangerous, compelling carnality, Bruno was immaculately groomed and faintly perfumed. He was like the wolf in 'Little Red Riding Hood'. After the intense suffering from which Laura, in her mid-thirties, had only just begun to emerge, his frank sensuality was irresistible.

'I would come and pick you up at Nice,' Bruno said on the telephone when she announced her imminent arrival in Monte Carlo, 'but it's much easier for you and *beaucoup plus amusante* to take the helicopter from Nice airport to Monaco. Look out for Heli Air Monaco – there's one every few minutes – and make sure you sit on the left for the view.'

She was helped into the seat next to the pilot, who assumed, as most people did these days, that she was pregnant and thus deserved every consideration.

Bruno was waiting inside the helicopter terminal. When he caught sight of her, he burst into tears again. Laura suppressed a moment of irritation and was enveloped in a richly scented embrace.

Laura had met Bruno in 1982, at the lowest ebb of her life. Conrad was by then a thing of the past, she had not seen Edouard for five years, and she had broken up with her lover after aborting his child, just after the death of her father.

Laura took two years to mourn these losses, two celibate years during which she bought the Markham Street house and prepared to set up as a freelance interpreter. She doubted whether she still needed to pay 10 per cent or more of her fees to an agency, as she was now well known. For two years she had almost no private life, which enabled her to work longer and more gruelling hours than ever before.

One day she received a call from an Italian whose name was unfamiliar. He said that he had rather an unusual assignment, which called for a Russian/German/Italian speaker of impeccable reputation, with absolute discretion. Laura was both flattered and curious.

'My German isn't up to much,' she pointed out.

'German is the least necessary. If need be, they can call in a local German-speaker,' she was told. 'The money is good – very good indeed. A hundred pounds a day. And the job is in Rome.'

'A *day*?' Laura gasped.

'Plus another fifty pounds a day expenses. *And* we cover your hotel bill.'

She was being offered more than three times her usual rate. 'How long is it for?' she asked.

'Hard to say. A week; ten days. Could be as much as two weeks. We'll pay you a minimum of seven days whatever happens.'

Laura stifled a *frisson* of anxiety. The terms were too good. But she would be in Rome, not some dubious *mittel*-European or Far Eastern location. She could always get away if the job turned out to be dodgy. She had become tougher of late, learned to look after herself – and the money was irresistible.

'I'll do it.'

She demanded a down-payment of five hundred pounds. When it arrived in her bank account, she boarded a plane for Rome.

Her unknown client had booked her into a hotel at the top of the Spanish Steps. Her room overlooked a courtyard scattered with tables and huge earthenware pots brimming with tropical flowers. The first night she ate dinner alone, determined not to be seduced out into the humid Roman evening. Motor-scooters buzzed through the streets until the small hours and the city sounded like a giant coffee-grinder. Next day at eight-thirty she took a taxi to the address she had been given.

It was a small office block in a modest street. She did not notice that she was photographed as she entered the building. She took the lift to the fifth floor and knocked on a door that said Worldwide Exports. It was opened by a man with thick hair and a wide smile.

'*Sono Bruno Linoli!*' he greeted her.

Had she been attracted by him at that very first instant? Undoubtedly. Her nerves, her unfamiliarity with Rome, her uncertainty about the exact nature of the assignment, would all have made her vulnerable, but even at her most assured it would have been difficult to resist the appeal of Bruno's thickset body and black eyes.

He led her into a room where four men sat round an inlaid marble table. A blind was drawn against the intense light and heat. A fan buzzed. Bruno introduced Laura. The men glanced up, muttered '*Buon giorno, Signora,*' and scowled at her cursorily. After a few minutes a fifth man arrived and they got down to business.

It was clear at once that 'business' was arms-dealing. At first Laura did not fully grasp the details, but of the nature of the transaction there could be no doubt. Bruno's boss was arranging to sell a large consignment of arms to the two Russians, presumably acting as intermediaries, to be transported by a boat chartered in Hamburg and sent to Libya. Its final destination was not specified though she suspected Northern Ireland. Payment was to be made in Deutschmarks.

From time to time Bruno would disappear into another room, returning with maps, marine charts or detailed catalogues of weaponry. Laura lacked the specialized vocabulary which the deal required and said so, hoping to be released from this ugly transaction. That was no problem, said Bruno cheerfully, it was only to be expected, and he disappeared again to find a technical dictionary.

The machinery of death was carefully itemized; its velocity and speed calculated and accuracy of aim guaranteed. Armoured vehicles would be shattered, glass – even toughened glass – splintered on impact. The effects upon the human body were fastidiously avoided.

Laura strained to concentrate, but her mind projected a recurring picture of herself as a child, picking at a scab, tearing off the dry brown crust and watching bright blood fill the tiny crater. Within an hour she had a thundering headache, but she dared not request a break. They stopped at one for lunch and the older Italian ordered Bruno to take Laura to a nearby trattoria.

The two of them were shown to a table under a trellis of vines. Laura said at once, 'I can't go ahead with this. I had no idea this job was about selling weapons. I can't possibly translate for an arms deal.'

He reached across the table. The back of his hand and wrist

were covered in fine black hairs all growing in one direction. They looked soft and desirable, not coarse at all. He lifted her hand, and she trembled at the contact.

'You have such beautiful long fingers!' he murmured. 'The sign of a musician, you know. I am sure you are musical?'

'No,' she answered abruptly. 'I do not much care for music. I prefer poetry. Words are my medium. Signor Linoli, will you please tell your employer that I wish to be released from this assignment?'

'Bruno. My name is Bruno. I will tell him, of course, if that is your wish. But first, let us have lunch together. You will tell me something about your life and why a lovely young English-woman should look so sad.'

He ordered tender roast veal, goat's cheese and a basket of figs, with which they drank a bottle of Barolo, treacherously strong. He forgot to order the mineral water she requested. Thirst drove her to drink two glasses of the wine. Her head swam.

'Are you married?' he asked. 'I myself am married, but it is not easy to be a husband. There are so many beautiful and inviting women. It is a man's duty to pay homage to beautiful women.'

Laura was aware that this was preposterous, a banal attempt at seduction. If she responded she would also have to continue interpreting between the parties making this obscene deal. She was muddled by the heat and the wine, edgy with the strain of the morning, the difficulty of going from Italian into Russian and having to translate German documents as well. Bruno's eyes burned. He took her hand again.

'I have renounced love affairs,' she told him.

Her table napkin had fallen to the floor. Bruno bent and picked it up. He slid it into her lap. 'I accept the challenge,' he said.

The deal was completed in three days. The Italian and the dour Russians wound up their business with nervous haste.

Laura was left with four days booked and paid for in a luxury hotel; indeed, she could take another ten days, if she wished.

That evening, Bruno drove her to a restaurant on the outskirts of the city, almost in the countryside. On the way back he stopped the car beside a field to show her the distant, illuminated panorama of Rome by night. They lay down under an indigo, glittering sky and he made love to her. He drove her back to the hotel and made love to her again. And again, next morning. Laura had been celibate for two years.

Sexual pleasure was, to Bruno, entirely natural and he enjoyed it, in consequence, entirely without guilt.

'You might as well feel guilty about hunger!' he protested, as though stating the obvious.

'But your wife?' Laura asked.

'If she objected, it would only give her pointless unhappiness. If she were jealous and made scenes, we would have to part.'

'And if *she* had a lover?'

'Why should she? I make love to her as often as she desires. I know her body and her tastes. Why should she need another man?'

'Why do *you* need other women?'

'Because I am a man, and men are different.'

She stayed in Rome for the full fortnight.

'I will make sure that you are paid for working fourteen days,' Bruno said.

'But I only worked for three!'

'But so well, my treasure, my clever, quick-witted, multi-lingual little English girl, that we achieved in three days what would have taken fourteen with another interpreter. And, thanks to your command of three languages, we only needed one interpreter. Normally we would double the risk by having to work with two. Believe me, you have earned your remuneration.'

'I will accept the seven days I was contracted for, but I can't allow myself to be paid for making love with you.'

'You are not.'

Laura knew better than to expose all her actions to the
searchlight of conscience, yet she felt that she was prostituting
something. Not her body – she made love to Bruno of her own
ravenous choice – but her sense of probity, of truthfulness and
honour: all the decent, old-fashioned qualities associated with
her father that were slipping away now that he was dead. She
did not discuss this notion with Bruno but he must have sensed
her unease, for he tried to explain himself.

'A woman you have never had is like a rare steak,' he said.
'Tender, delicious, simple and satisfying. But after a few con-
sumptions – you notice, it is the same word as consummation? –
the steak needs to be cooked more elaborately to provide the
same pleasure. When you have satisfied your appetite a few
more times, it has become like minced meat: ordinary, boring
food for every day.'

Laura was outraged at the comparison. 'But *I* am not a piece
of *meat*!'

'My rosy little woman, that is exactly what you are!'

Parked outside Monaco heliport was an open-topped Italian car.
Bruno put Laura's suitcase in the boot and handed her carefully
into the front seat, bending over her to fasten her seat-belt. He
had to loosen it from the right-hand side and as he manoeuvred
the buckle, she smelled again the dark feral smell lurking beneath
his eau-de-Cologne and hair pomade. A flicker of desire and
nostalgia curled for an instant. Bruno leaned across, clicked the
belt in place and, in passing, kissed her slowly on the lips. No
one had kissed her like that in the last six months and she
thought, I can't look *that* bad, then! Maybe there is a chance, a
mere vestige of hope after all.

'My shy Englishwoman!' he murmured. 'How sad you look!
We will try to make you happy, Marie-Dido and I!'

'Dido?' she asked.

'Her name is Dominique, but I call her Dido and so must

you. First we shall have a drink on our own at the Beach Plaza Hotel and then I shall take you to the apartment, to meet Marie-Dido and have lunch.'

The air-conditioned hotel foyer was cool after the clinging heat of the streets. Brilliantly lit glass cases displayed jewels, watches, pens: the paraphernalia of international wealth. Sliding double doors at the end of the foyer opened on to the terrace, where tables sheltered from the sun under huge parasols. Beyond the terrace, down a wide flight of steps, was a swimming pool, and beyond the pool the blinding sea.

Laura put on her sunglasses. A waiter hovered at their side.

'A bottle of Krug!' ordered Bruno.

She put her hand on his arm. 'Bruno, you are very generous, but I am not allowed, absolutely forbidden, to drink alcohol.'

He did not argue. 'A bottle of Krug *and* a bottle of mineral water, and three freshly squeezed oranges.'

When the waiter had gone Laura said, 'Tell me about your wife.'

Bruno explained that his first wife had died. He had met his second five years ago in Paris, a young woman of excellent family. 'BCBG: you understand?' She was a good Catholic, although she did not desire children. 'A relief, since I have four adult children and would not wish to start that merry-go-round again. She enjoys living in Monaco which is also fortunate, since, for me, it is a necessity.'

I bet it is, Laura thought. Bruno's business was not one that invited scrutiny.

'Do you still . . . are you, these days, still *un homme d'affaires?*' she inquired.

'Only when I cannot avoid it. Officially, I am retired. It was, as you no doubt realized, a world in which even the most cautious rarely got the chance to grow old. And you, Laura? Is your health really so grave?'

'Shall I just say *yes*?'

Predictably, his eyes filled with tears. He lifted his glass and drank to her.

Bruno's flat was smaller than Laura had expected, but it looked directly over the sea. The walls and curtains were white, the floors were pale marble veined with grey. Bruno introduced her to a slender, dark-haired Frenchwoman in her late twenties. She wore a white linen shift with Roman sandals whose straps criss-crossed her tanned legs. She held Laura's hand in her own small bony one and murmured a welcome.

'I 'ope you will call me Dido . . . ?' she said, pronouncing it Dee-do.

Would this have been my fate, Laura wondered, if I had married Edouard? I was a bit older than Dido is now but Bruno is not quite sixty yet, so the age difference would be the same. She must have done something wrong or why should a good Catholic family have let her marry him? For money alone? Here she is fossilized in luxury and driven insane by futility. A heavy punishment for drugs or a teenage pregnancy. Perhaps she loved her father too much. Poor Marie-Dido!

The dining-room seemed to emphasize the emptiness of their married life. Pale net curtains trembled at the windows. The furniture was modern, made of glass and steel, but the cutlery was silver and the dishes white porcelain. Laura was surprised that Bruno, with his ebullient sensuality, could feel at home in such a setting – modish, yes, but drained of all colour and appetite, a room for anorexics.

An elegant lunch was served, accompanied by a bottle of Krug.

'Do you *always* drink Krug?' Laura asked Bruno smilingly, trying to lighten the atmosphere.

'It is usually counted the superior champagne,' said his wife. 'And we prefer it.'

Laura explained, yet again, about her liver and Marie-Dido requested a bottle of mineral water. Conversation was made . . . How was the flight? Oh, very comfortable. Was it on time? Yes, most punctual. Is the weather too warm for you? Well, it is quite hot. For Monaco it is normal at this time of year. We shall rest after lunch.

The french windows in Laura's bedroom opened on to a small balcony hung with bougainvillaea. A table and two cast-iron chairs faced the sea. Inside the room, beside the bed, were a vase of hothouse flowers, a stack of glossy magazines and the *Herald Tribune*. She splashed her face and neck with cold water and ran the tap over her wrists to cool them, then lifted the mosquito net and lay down.

She was too exhausted to fall asleep straight away. The journey had tired her; the conversation at lunch almost more so. Bruno must crave respectability at last. Laura was drifting towards sleep when she was disturbed by the sound of raised voices from the next-door bedroom. She did not want to make it obvious, by closing the windows, that they could be overheard and in any case she was curious. The voices grew louder.

'Bruno, this woman is half-*dead*!' she heard Marie-Dido say. 'She looks like a cadaver! I understood she was taking a convalescence. Had I known she was so ill, I would never have let her come.'

'This woman – who is, let me remind you, *my friend* – honoured me by requesting shelter,' Bruno said, his voice cold. It dropped to a murmur and Laura could not distinguish the words.

'You should never have accepted!' his wife objected again. 'I will inform my doctor. He should be on hand in case of a crisis. You must find out exactly what she suffers from. She might at any moment . . .' The sharp, spoiled voice trailed away and Laura heard the sound of a slap and a stifled cry.

So: she looked mortally ill. Until that moment she had been able to disguise the fact from herself, and assumed it was not obvious to others. Bruno's wife had done her a favour by revealing the truth.

Laura got out of bed. In the bathroom she pulled off her slip and pants and stood naked in front of a full-length mirror. Her face and eyeballs were a rusty, sallow shade – that she knew – but now the whole of her body was covered with dark purple blotches like bruises and bright red spots with radiating veins that might ooze blood at any moment. She gazed at herself, thinking, The Black Death must have looked like this. Why is death black? Why not red? Or purple or yellow or green. No, not green. Green is the colour of life, just as white is the colour of innocence.

As she returned to the bedroom, from the open balcony windows came the sounds of Bruno and his wife making love. They had clearly reached some agreement and were now enjoying the progress towards climax. 'Daddy, Daddy, no!' Marie-Dido protested, and then, in ascending squeals, 'Bad Daddy! Mustn't do that! Marie-Dido isn't *allowed* . . .' Finally she screamed, 'Daddy please! Daddy please! Now, Daddy . . . Go on, please.' Bruno's sexual inventiveness was evidently undiminished. Laura closed the balcony window as quietly as possible and picked up *Vogue*.

Ten years ago the hotel room in Rome had been tiled in marble, its windows shielded from the scorching Roman heat by blistered wooden shutters. In this room she and Bruno had spent ardent and exhausting days. They ate and drank and washed and slept only in order to have enough energy to make love again. The first time Laura closed the bathroom door because she needed to go to the lavatory, Bruno called out in dismay, '*Ma' Laura? Cosa fai?*'

'I want to spend a penny,' she said primly.

'Leave the door open! Let me hear! If it's part of *you*, I love it!'

It was not true, she reflected. He didn't *love* her in the least; in fact she doubted if Bruno were capable of love, unless it was for his mother and his sons, the genes paying homage to their own. But she happened, for the moment, to be the object of his desire. The affair with Bruno carried no responsibility, no questions, no aftermath and, above all, no guilt. And, while Bruno never pretended to love her, he was loyal, kind, generous and demonstrative. Their relationship was not in the least cold or mechanical, but full of affection and warmth.

And in fact *she* did not love Bruno in the least, either. She deplored his profession and found his egotism infuriating and childish. But Laura was in her mid-thirties, the age of her greatest sexual capacity, and that capacity had lain dormant for too long. Bruno offered her pleasure and satiety. For ten days they indulged every physical appetite until Laura was sore and even Bruno would sometimes glance down at himself and say fondly, '*Poverino cazzo! Come stanco!*' Her mouth hurt, her flesh was bruised, the skin on her face had been abraded, her body smelled sour; but the memory of her last unsatisfactory love affair and its bitter, harsh and painful ending had finally been cauterized.

Laura would wake late, like the rest of the household, and wander into the drawing-room, where Marie-Dido sat, usually talking in French on the telephone. She would hold up an imperious little paw, at which Laura would shake her head and smile, indicating that she was not about to interrupt. The first few times she left the flat, Bruno accompanied her, helping Laura to orientate herself in Monte Carlo's higgledy-piggledy pile of expensive building blocks.

She quickly realized that she loathed Monaco. The streets were filled with boutiques selling flowers, jewellery, watches, handbags, shoes and designer clothes, but there was not a butcher or baker to be seen. The steep shopping streets and arcades were connected by lifts so as to spare the rich the effort of climbing stairs, and the white-uniformed police force, invisible in their headquarters, monitored the television cameras installed in every lift.

Bruno took Laura to the coffee shop at the Café de Paris next to the casino, where they sat on the terrace beside a table of heavy-eyed Greeks and languid young women. Bruno stood up and shook hands with two of the men. He gestured towards

Laura — 'a very old friend'. The Greek gestured indifferently at one of the girls — 'a very new one'. When the waitress had brought coffee and an array of patisseries, Laura stretched her hand over the now-greying hair clustered across the back of his. 'Bruno, why are you doing so much for me?'

'My sweet Laura, ten years ago in Rome you gave me several days of pure pleasure. That, in a man's life, is rarer than wordly success and *much* rarer than money. You asked nothing, made no reproaches, you simply surrendered yourself to enjoyment. It was one of the greatest gifts I have ever had. I am glad of this opportunity to thank you.'

'I, too, remember great pleasure.'

'Of course! I would have been very much at fault if you had not! You were a golden interlude in my life. Do you suppose those girls' — he gestured at the long-limbed creatures sprawling and yawning at the neighbouring table — 'are doing for my Greek friends what you did for me? They cannot conceal their boredom. But you gave and took with equal gusto until — you remember? — we were both so exhausted that we couldn't fuck any more.' He smiled and gave her a surprising, boyish wink.

Laura said, 'I do not think I shall ever fuck again.'

'My treasure, if you want to be fucked, we shall go inside this minute and inquire about a room!'

'Bruno, I mean I *cannot*. My body is a sad sack that lumbers me. It has no energy, no desire and, God knows, no attraction. It is almost extinguished by my illness. *Look* at me, Bruno. Look!'

Tears rose again to his eyes, and he said, 'Little Laura, I long to take you in my arms, to hold you, even if we cannot make love. Let my naked body comfort you.'

She felt a gust of gratitude, even desire, but it was not enough. She could not expose her body to his eyes or to even the gentlest love-making. Pride and weakness prevented her. She shook her head and turned away.

A day later Marie-Dido questioned her.

'Your illness – is it contagious?'

'No. I assure you it's not.'

She thinks I have Aids, Laura realized, and wants to know if they should both be tested for HIV.

'Forgive me, there is much in my husband's past that I do not inquire about. Did you know him well? Why have you come to us?'

'Ten years ago I had a relationship with Bruno, yes. After that, when he came to London on business, he would take me out for dinner. We stayed in touch. Your husband has been a good friend to me. When my illness was diagnosed – and it is a liver disease; not anything sexual, I do assure you – I turned to my friends to look after me. I have never been married. I have no children.'

'*Donc*, you are making a tour around those who owe you obligations?'

'I did not intend it to be like that. I wanted to see those who loved me and whom I loved for the last time.'

'And my husband: did he love you?'

'No,' Laura assured her, 'but he was always generous.'

'Has anybody said no?' Marie-Dido asked curiously.

Laura laughed. 'Yes! And some *said* they would look after me and when I arrived found they could not. Usually' – she added deliberately – 'because of their *wives*.'

She thought this conversation would put Marie-Dido's mind at rest, but a day or two later, during which time, Laura noticed, she had heard no love-making, Bruno took her to the Beach Plaza Hotel again. They sat on the terrace and she sipped orange juice.

'How do you like this hotel?' he asked.

'It seems . . . very comfortable, very expensive, very efficient . . .'

'Perhaps it would be easier if you were to stay here?'

At once Laura understood.

'Bruno! Please! You have been so good to me, but I am not

entirely at ease here in Monte Carlo. I find the heat very tiring. I did not want to hurt your feelings or I would have said so earlier. I have been here nearly a week ... We have seen each other and talked ... *That* was my real purpose. I would hate to cause trouble between you and your wife. Let me move my return flight to an earlier day. Tomorrow?'

He clenched his teeth and curled his fingers inwards and she heard his heels drumming on the tiles beneath the table. She could not help thinking maliciously, Daddy's little girl is in for a hard time!

He extended his hand and stroked her cheek gently, looking into her eyes. He said, 'If I were alone, you know I would take care of you until . . .'

'I know, Bruno. You are the most generous of men. No, for God's sake don't cry *again*! Stop it! Smile at me! Order a glass of champagne!'

He clapped a giant handkerchief to his face, wiped his eyes and blew his nose. He then summoned a waiter.

'The Krug here is the most expensive in the world because they won't let you buy it by the glass. You have to pay for a whole bottle! So, won't you share just *one* glass with me?'

Fuck the illness, Laura thought, lifting the sunglasses so that he could see her eyes.

'Yes!' she said.

When they had toasted each other with real affection, he said again, 'Laura? Can I take you upstairs? They know me here. I have a nice, discreet room . . . ?'

She laughed aloud. 'Oh, Bruno! You are wonderful and marvellous and totally incorrigible! "They know me here." I bet they do! *How* old are you?'

He bridled. 'I am sixty next year. What has that to do with it?'

'Nothing,' said Laura. 'It will make no difference when you are seventy or even eighty. Here's to life!'

'Here's to *sex*!' he replied. 'Which is the same thing.'

'Let us go and change my ticket together,' she said, 'I am sure they can do it at the desk. After lunch I shall go *out* for the afternoon, and leave you and Marie-Dido in peace.'

As Laura walked out of the apartment block after lunch she was enveloped in a blanket of heat. From the beach came shrieks of laughter and the sound of speed-boats whizzing across the bay. There were roadworks everywhere. Tall cranes splintered the blue sky and the noise of pneumatic drills roared in her ears. She had intended to find a food shop, perhaps even a market, but the noise drove her off the streets. She saw a signpost to the Musée des Automates and decided to visit that.

It was almost deserted and blessedly cool. Laura found herself in a series of silent rooms containing glass display cases. Inside them were hundreds of old dolls, formal courtly figures in frayed and faded costumes whose colours had dulled to powdery beige or silver-grey. Only their glass eyes were still bright, bulging through stiff rows of black eyelashes with an alert and penetrating gaze. The puppets' eerie immobility was disconcerting. Hell could easily be like this, she thought. Not busy black devils poking pitchforks into bonfires at all, but silent ranks of modishly dressed people paralysed in attitudes of frivolity. Death as a parody of life. I am being morbid, she told herself, pointlessly, self-pityingly morbid. She hurried out into the bustling human activity of the white-hot afternoon.

'You cannot come to Monte Carlo and not visit the Casino!' Bruno said when she returned to the flat. He made her lie with her feet up on the sofa while his wife organized lemon tea. Marie-Dido, having got her way, was now in an amiable mood.

'The Casino! Bruno is right! In spite of the horrible old American ladies with their notebooks and black jewelled handbags, and all the pretty young girls with fat old men looking down their *décolletages*, it still has some glamour. We will make ourselves chic! You will rest, Laura, and if you have nothing to wear I will lend you . . . Yes! I have a caftan that I bought in a street market in Morocco. You shall wear that! I will *give* it to you!'

She swept off to her bedroom, returning with an exotic swathe of patchouli-scented fabric which she thrust at Laura. 'Here it is! This you must have for tonight!'

Laura knew that if she were to stay awake in the evening, she needed at least two hours' sleep. She closed the shutters, lay down on the bed and drew a single sheet over her body. The climb up the hilly streets had tired her and she fell asleep at once.

It was nearly eight when she woke. She showered and made up her face before lifting the caftan over her head. Its folds enveloped her with their dark foreign smell. It was heavy but not clinging, obscuring her shape with its complicated pattern. Stripes of colour were separated by ropes of gold threads; jewelled butterflies frolicked between the stripes. It was lined with silk on the inside so that the fabric's slubbed texture would not irritate the skin. Laura had brought two amber necklaces, one a present from her mother, the other from a lover, and she hung these round her neck before confronting the long mirror. For the first time in many weeks Laura saw that she looked wonderful.

Bruno and Marie-Dido were waiting. Bruno, wearing a white dinner jacket, clasped her thumbs, spat on his hands and performed various other peasant rituals invoking luck. He checked his wallet.

'I have plenty of money,' Laura protested.

'Nothing is ever "plenty" in a casino,' he said. 'Do you want to hit a winning streak and run out of money? Of course not! Here: we'll take fifty thousand francs and lose that and then we leave. Good?'

They drove along the Avenue de la Costa. The street lights were just coming on and the evening air was balmy. In front of the casino was a circle of lawn, brilliantly coloured flowers and a number of large modern statues in bronze. Behind it there was a panoramic view across the harbour. Against the darkly lapping sea were strung, and strung again upside-down in reflection, the lights of yachts parked in berths like taxis on a cab-rank.

'First we shall have a drink at the Hotel de Paris,' said Bruno. 'We shall display ourselves, sniff the air, get a sense of the mood. Is it a lucky night? I feel it is. Laura?'

She was filled with exuberant delight, a feeling she had not had for months. '*Undoubtedly* lucky!'

Attendants in white gloves and Ruritanian uniforms greeted them as they mounted the wide central steps leading to the casino. They entered the foyer. On the left was a bank of fruit machines and a handful of roulette tables at which tourists were playing. Straight ahead was the baccarat room, the very heart of the casino, glamorous, seductive and vibrating with concentration and the magnetic lure of money.

At each table sat old women with feverishly glittering eyes, rouged and lipsticked like puppets, marking every turn and drop of the cards. The croupiers were swift and lithe, rakes flashing as they pushed piles of tokens to and fro: mostly towards the bank.

'I will change some money,' Bruno said.

Laura passed him five thousand francs. 'Can you change this for me?' she asked.

When he returned, Bruno handed Laura a large number of brightly coloured counters. Carefully, she memorized their denominations, and they went in to the main *salle de jeu*.

Laura had often played roulette in the past – it was a favourite way of ending a successful conference abroad – and had devised a simple system which, while it had never yet brought her a big win, usually prevented her from losing too much. She bet on each of the dozens in turn and also selected three numbers at random from within the same dozen. This gave her a one in three chance of winning each time and a further one in four if her dozen came up. If it did not, she lost everything. Whether she won or lost, she moved her counter after every spin of the wheel to the next dozen.

Bruno was betting on single numbers, apparently according to whim. Marie-Dido sat at the table placing the counters and he stood behind giving her instructions. They seemed to lose consistently. Laura wandered away to sit at a different table.

After a while her system began to accumulate a pile of counters. 'Her' dozens kept coming up and after a couple of hours she also won on a single number. She was beginning to attract attention. Bruno left his wife and came to stand protectively beside Laura.

'Do you want to go now?' he murmured. 'You must have made a thousand pounds.'

Laura opened her handbag so that he could see the jostling mass of counters inside. 'Three,' she said evenly. 'Perhaps more.'

Marie-Dido joined them. 'Do you want to go?' she asked casually, but her voice was thrumming with tension.

'In a minute,' replied Laura. 'It's not yet midnight. The witching hour.'

The croupier was looking at her from under his eyelashes. Laura offered Marie-Dido two high-denomination counters. 'Here!' she said. 'Just for the spin and the fun of it . . . You lose these and I'll lose a few and then we'll go.'

Bruno and Marie-Dido strolled away, realizing that Laura did not want to be watched. She let two turns of the wheel go by without betting, then on an impulse placed her largest counters on the zero. A *frisson* ran through her and she felt it pass like an electric charge through the observers around the table, one or two of whom rapidly added a counter of their own to lie on zero. Every nerve-end shivered. The ball spun, trembled, paused, dropped. Zero.

The croupier's rake wound with serpentine speed across the green baize, curling round every stake but three. He dragged the rattling piles of counters towards him, then pushed a huge stack in Laura's direction. She passed him a five-thousand-franc token, nodded towards the least impassive of the faces round the table and stood up. She was aware that the eyes of the casino staff followed her as she threaded past the other tables towards Bruno. She smiled at him.

'Shall we change our money back?' she asked. 'I am ready to leave, if you are.'

She knew she should feel jubilant and incredulous; she had won a huge sum of money. But although her hands shook slightly, her chief reaction was one of heavy sadness. Money was not the sort of luck she needed; a big win could only be an ironic twist upon her fate. She would give all her winnings for a month, a *week* of her former self.

Next day, as Laura waited at Nice airport for the flight back to London, she was detained and questioned by security staff with impeccable courtesy but, she felt, unnecessary thoroughness. Her luggage held only the few clothes she had brought with her, and Marie-Dido's gift of the caftan. Her winnings, Bruno had explained, would arrive in her English bank in a couple of weeks' time, by some trustworthy but untraceable route. Laura realized, with a wry smile, that a woman who is dying has no reason to fear police, customs, the taxman or anyone else.

9

Rafe Freeman

Constance laid a hand on her sister's arm, glanced at her and said, 'Laura, listen, you will go a bit *easy* on Mother, won't you?'

'Oh, Christ. Here we go already. Constance Liddell, mother and martyr.'

'Laura, she hasn't *seen* you for a while. Just give her *time*.'

'Time,' said Laura savagely, 'is the one thing I haven't got to give.'

Constance blushed, apologized and turned her attention to manoeuvring through the Saturday morning shopping traffic of Tunbridge Wells.

It was a cool, overcast August day. Rain swept intermittently in soft sheets across the garden. Too much of a risk to eat lunch outside, Constance said brightly, shepherding Laura through the front door. 'I'll make us all some coffee while you say hello to Mother,' she murmured, and then, loudly, '*Mummy!* Here's *Laura!*'

Laura drew a deep breath and turned to enter Constance's tidy drawing-room.

The small figure of her mother rose to greet her. 'Darling!' she said, on a swoop of momentary joy.

'Oh, Mummy!'

Laura was encircled in a soft, alien-smelling embrace. They hummed wordlessly into each other's ear. 'Mmmf!' her mother exhaled firmly, as though an audible gust of love had escaped from her heart. They stepped back and laughed at each other.

Laura's mother touched her daughter's arm and patted her shoulder. She turned round, looked for her handbag, and re-assured, sat down in an armchair opposite Laura.

'Well! Here we are! Goodness! Let me have a look at you!' her mother said, with a bright smile.

'What's that new scent you're wearing? It's different,' said Laura. 'You always used to wear Blue Grass when I was little.'

'People in Miami *love* this one. Leonard treated me. It's called Giorgio by Giorgio of Beverly Hills.'

I might have known it, Laura thought crossly, a real petrol-swamper.

'Laura darling, that's a lovely dress, it must have cost a fortune, but the new foundation doesn't really suit you. I'd better tell you, in case no one else dares. It's too dark.'

'It isn't *foundation*, Mother: it's *jaundice*. The dress is from Paris.'

'Oh, I see. All right. Was I tactless, then? I'm sorry.'

In the pause that followed, Laura searched for some safe topic. She was about to say 'How *is* Uncle Leonard?' when her mother asked coquettishly, 'How do you like my *hair*?'

Six years of living in Florida had been long enough for Laura's mother to take on the protective colouring of a Miami retiree. Her hair was dyed a soft pinkish blonde; she had a deep, kipper-coloured tan, highlighted with pink lipstick and lilac eye-shadow, and she wore youthful clothes in soft, sunny colours.

'It's very pretty.'

Her mother patted her coiffure proudly. 'It costs a *fortune*,' she confided, 'but Leonard says it's *worth* it for morale. Talking of morale, darling, how's yours?'

Constance entered with a tray of coffee, three of her best mugs and a plate of mixed chocolate biscuits.

'Oh, darling, *biscuits*! I *shouldn't*!' said her mother. 'Well, just *one*.' With a naughty giggle she leaned over, took a biscuit and popped it into her pale pink mouth.

'Laura says she's that colour because of *jaundice*,' she said to Constance after taking a sip of coffee.

'Yes, I know. Look, do we have to discuss it straight away? Can't we have a nice lunch first, and later on perhaps . . . ?'

'What do you mean?' said their mother uneasily. She looked from one to the other, knowing and not wanting to know. 'Is it really awfully *serious*? Worse than I thought?'

Laura said, '*Do* you want to discuss my health now, or later?'

'Mother's simply thrilled about seeing Kaspar . . .'

'*Now*,' said Mrs Elphinstone.

'All right,' Laura answered.

Laura sat in the kitchen watching Constance efficiently boil, blanch and season the vegetables and toss together a fresh salad. Their mother was in the drawing-room weeping down the telephone line to Florida.

'She seems happy with him,' Laura observed.

'Oh, blissfully, I should say. Mother was always "a man's woman".'

'As she never tired of telling us.'

'You must admit, she looks marvellous for her age.'

'I think she looks grotesque. Tight *white* trousers – and that blouse is practically transparent. How old does she think she is?'

'Don't be so bitter, Laura. She's travelled thousands of miles to see you. Why do you have to make it so hard for her?'

'She's come to see *us*, not just me. How can I deal with a mother who looks like a superannuated bobbysoxer?'

Constance turned round, frowning in exasperation. 'Don't you *ever* see beyond how people *look*? How they're *dressed*? Read the signs, Laura: *you're* the interpreter. It should be easy for you. Mother is enjoying a new lease of life with a husband who makes her very happy, in a community where old age is normal . . . not something to be ashamed of, to hide behind drab, dowdy, colourless clothes and old grey hair. Yes, she's dressed young by your standards, but she doesn't look grotesque, or ridiculous or pathetic: she looks *normal*. Is she supposed to wear beige Jaeger for ever, just to fit in with your expectations? She showed a lot of courage in embarking on a new life at her age, and now she's come over here to face you.'

'Is that so hard?'

'Yes it *is* – and you're making it *worse*. Stop being so bloody selfish. Here: take these things in to the dining-room. You're not with one of your millionaire boyfriends now.'

'Oh, very sarky!'

'Laura, don't be *childish*.'

'*I'm* not the one that's being childish . . .' They looked at each other and laughed.

'We both are,' said Constance. 'It's the effect of Mother, I'm afraid.'

Mrs Elphinstone had dried her eyes and freshened up her make-up by the time they sat down to lunch. She smiled brightly at Laura and said, 'I went to see *Phantom of the Opera* last night. Have you seen it, dear?'

'No. Was it good?'

'Very good, but why do they have the music so *loud*?'

'You should have turned your hearing-aid down.'

'Acutally I had turned it *off*, and I was still deafened. The Princess of Wales has seen it *three times*, apparently.'

They talked safely about the Princess of Wales, a topic her mother found enthralling. Was she still in love with Charles? Had they read that awful book – such a load of rubbish! Would the marriage last? What about those men she was photographed with? Well, when all's said and done she dresses *beautifully*. She's got *perfect* taste. Even Princess Margaret (now *she* was a beauty) was never . . .

After lunch her mother and sister urged Laura to have a little nap. She would have preferred to lie in the drawing-room and watch, with the closest she could manage to filial love, while they gossiped about family and friends, but they insisted she went up to Constance's bedroom for a proper sleep. Sensing that they wanted to discuss her alone, Laura submitted.

Her sister's bedroom had all the signs of being shared with a man for the first time since Paul had left fourteen years ago. Now Gordon's hairbrush stood on Constance's dressing-table. A pair of his huge shoes was discarded beside the chest of drawers and the rank, dry smell of his hair was discernible from the next pillow. On 'his' bedside table were a recent thriller, a sci-fi fantasy and, to Laura's surprise, the Bible. A spare pair of spectacles lay neatly folded beside them. Laura was tempted to see if the drawer held a packet of condoms, since she felt certain that her post-menopausal sister and the Possleque would only practise safe responsible post-Aids sex, but she couldn't be bothered to lever herself up from the pillow and check.

Her emotions towards her sister had always been complex, and never more so than now. They had got on best when Constance was a young wife and mother, content in her marriage and children. Laura had suffered for her through the appalling pain of the divorce and the problems of three angry teenagers. She had approved of Constance's decision to leave north London: selling the big family house when the property market was at its peak and buying a smaller house in Tunbridge Wells, thereby releasing enough capital to preclude any financial problems later on. All this Laura had supported. She had watched with wry amusement as Constance stumbled into her first awkward relationships as a single woman again: the odd, solitary chaps whom she met through her job as a librarian, the decent former boyfriends who reappeared to assess her; the impossible ones who turned up out of nowhere – there had been a Polish refugee, Laura recalled, of *singular* unsuitability . . .

But with the arrival of Gordon, the Possleque, as the first real replacement for Paul, Laura was torn between resentment and jealousy. After years of comparing herself to Constance and feeling she came out of it rather well, she was now ill (no, corrected the inner voice, *dying*) and alone, while her sister flourished with a partner, whom, however improbably, she loved. Laura clenched her fists, tightened her lips, and picked up a book from Constance's bedside table. Henry James: *The Wings of the Dove*. Typical! she thought. After the first few pages she drifted into sleep.

When Laura came downstairs, lunch had been cleared and her mother and sister had, they informed her, been for a nice little walk between showers.

'Mummy,' she asked, as she had determined she would, 'do I really look *that* bad?'

Her mother threw a panic-stricken glance at Constance and took a deep breath.

'Laura, my darling, my littlest girl, what do you want me to say? You *do* look very ill. You must know that I – we both – are very worried about you. With all this crazy flying about visiting people, you can't be attending the hospital regularly.'

'Oh, I do.'

'What do *they* say?'

'They say . . .' Laura paused, thinking, Will I still blush when I tell a fib? 'They say I don't qualify for a liver transplant.'

Her mother leaned forward eagerly. Here at last was something positive she could do. She spoke in soft, fervent sentences. 'Laura, American doctors are *marvellous*. They're far more advanced than the ones you have here. The NHS is finished. Why don't you come over to Florida and let them examine you? Of course, you'd have to *pay* for treatment but *I'll* pay your fare, and I know Uncle Leonard would help out, and you must have *quite* a bit of money of your own?'

Laura thought of her winnings at the casino less than a week ago. It would be more than enough to cover the flight and medical investigations. Her heart jumped at the prospect of a reprieve. She could feel it pumping, thrusting forcefully, as though it were signalling 'Live! Live! Live!'

'I've been through all that long ago,' she said. 'First of all the prospects of a transplant succeeding aren't good. All those immuno-suppressant drugs you have to take – the side-effects are horrible. Secondly, I'd hate to be stuck in some American hospital –'

'*I'd* visit you, darling: every single day, without fail! Guides' honour!'

'And thirdly, why? What for? We all think we can cheat death nowadays, that it's just a question of having enough *money*. But maybe we can't. Maybe my time has come and I have to die, aged forty-five.'

Tears sprang to her mother's eyes. '*Don't* talk like that,' she implored. 'Laura – darling – *please* don't. I can't *bear* it! My little Stella!'

Looking at her, Laura saw that it was literally true. Her mother could not bear to contemplate her death. None of the men she had spent the last six months visiting had reacted with the same pain, the pain of blood and bone, as her mother. They had taken on the burden of her care, yes, but none had railed against her death. They accepted its inevitability. Their chief thought was, At least it isn't *me*. They would grieve, no doubt, if they happened to see the announcement in the Deaths column. Bruno would cry. Nick would be very quiet for a few days. Edouard would mourn her. But none like her mother, whose whole being revolted against the injustice, the world-turned-upside-down, of her daughter dying before she did.

'Mummy, you are generous and good and loving and it is wonderful that you care so much. And Coco,' she added, glancing across at her sister, whose face was clenched and twisted. 'But no. I have really thought this through and decided. No.'

'Why not?' asked Constance.

Heavily, finally, Laura replied, 'Because my time has come and *I deserve to die.*'

She cried, eventually, and her mother embraced her and wiped her hot face of its tears. Constance sat on the other side holding her hand. In the warmth of emotion Laura rediscovered her mother's unchanging smell of sweat and skin and clean hands. She felt terribly tired, as though vital energy had seeped out with her sobs.

After a few minutes Constance said, 'I'm sorry everyone, but the Possleque'll be back in about an hour. Shall I make tea now?'

'Tea, a nice cup of tea!' said their mother, turning gratefully to the comfort of the banal. 'What a brilliant idea! Yes, *tea*.'

They sat round the dining table, as they had done when they were children, eating little cucumber sandwiches and biscuits. Constance passed the plates and they helped themselves politely. They chatted about Max and Dani. Wasn't it nice that they were so happy together? Wasn't Kaspar gorgeous? 'Just you wait, Mummy, till you see him! He's good enough to *eat*!' And married life really *suited* Max.

But these banalities could not be sustained for long. 'None of this would have happened if *you'd* got married,' Mrs Elphinstone said, turning accusingly to Laura.

'Oh, Mummy, don't talk such rubbish! In any case, *you're* the one who was forever telling me not to throw myself away on the first man who came along.'

'Like I did, I suppose?' said Constance.

'You *know* I didn't mean that, Connie. Anyway, Paul was fine, until . . . until . . . well, never mind that. I approved of Paul from the beginning. And he's been a very good Daddy to the children.'

'Well, what *did* you mean?' Laura asked.

'I meant you should *wait* till you were sure you'd found the right man.'

'And how was that great enlightenment supposed to manifest itself?'

'Laura means how could she tell?'

Their mother was silent. They way *she* had known was very simple. Her husband had been the first man for whom she had felt the stirrings of what she assumed must be sexual desire. There had been a tingling in her bosom and between her legs when he kissed her, and she knew she wanted to go to bed with him. No other man's kisses had produced this feeling – though not many others had kissed her. *She* had never been fast, not even in the exciting cocktail party world of Kenya. Not *really* fast. Just a bit . . . naughty, flirtatious, with a taste for a little innocent fun, teasing the men.

'When you love a man because he's a good, honourable, decent chap, and yet you feel sort of . . . *naughty* about him – you feel he's got S A – *that* means he's the right one,' she said bravely. Both her daughters laughed.

'Mother, you're a *hoot*, you really are,' said Constance. 'I haven't heard anyone use that expression for *years*. S A! Sex appeal?'

Laura said, 'You're describing how I've felt about a whole lot of men, Mother, in my time. What am I supposed to do about that?'

'You should have married the first one.'

Laura felt very weak and the tea made her nauseous. She stretched out on the sofa, hoping the feeling would pass. She thought back over the men who might have married her: Mick Charles? S A, yes; good honourable decent, etc, no. Hugo? S A, yes – that's why she had let him have her virginity – but not the sort of man she could proudly present to her parents, even if he had become suitably pompous and important since then. Conrad? Hardly. Joe Watson? Heaven forbid! Nicholas Hope? Decent and truthful, yes, but fatally lacking in S A. She cantered through the list with gathering speed. Edouard de Trifort? A married Frenchman twice her age. Jürgen? German: enough said. Kit Mallinson? No good on the S A front. Bruno? Dear heavens, no, not Bruno!

'There's been a curious shortage of men in my life whom I fancied *and* of whom you and Daddy would have approved,' she said finally.

'You must have been far too fussy. You should have settled for a nice ordinary man like your father, a *good* man, instead of looking for some Gregory Peck.'

'But Mother, you told me not to settle for second best!' said

Laura. 'I was only doing what you had drummed into me throughout my adolescence. "Don't throw yourself away on any old chap, Laura. There are plenty of fish in the sea!"'

Mrs Elphinstone tightened her lips and glanced upwards in exasperation. It was true; she could hear her own tones in Laura's accurate imitation. But their younger daughter – so talented, so pretty, such a good girl, and with her amazing gift for languages – they thought she'd make a wonderful catch. She remembered saying to Daddy, 'Just you wait, dear, Laura'll be an ambassador's wife one day!' And Daddy had said, 'Don't jump the gun, Paula!'

Her eyes swam with sorrow as she beheld her daughter lying on the sofa emaciated and ill. 'Darling, we only wanted what was *best* for you. We only had your interests at heart!'

Constance stood up. 'Mummy, darling, don't get upset. Laura knows, don't you, Laur'?'

'Yes, OK, I know. I do, honestly. You meant well. And, anyway, even if I *had* married, I'd probably still've got this. Happily married people die like anybody else, only in their case it's sadder.'

Mother and daughter had one last embrace before Constance drove Laura to the station. Mrs Elphinstone asked if she could come round for a little drink one evening, and wouldn't it be fun if she brought one or two of the Girlies along too? Laura, astonished that the Girlies were still *alive*, let alone still Girlies, said yes, of course. She suspected that her mother could not face the fact that this, now, might be their last meeting. It enabled them to part without melodrama or tears.

The following day Laura was back at the liver unit, which she visited twice a month nowadays for the progress of her disease to be tested, charted and recorded. The tiny red spots on her face and body sometimes bled spontaneously, she reported to Mrs Ripa, a new development.

'My bones ache and they feel heavy,' she went on. 'Everything is an effort. My muscles ache; my mouth feels dry; I have no appetite. Even my mind is clouded – thank God, not all the time.'

'Do you *really* have to do so much travelling?' Mrs Ripa asked.

'Why not?' said Laura. 'Is it dangerous?'

'No. But it *is* tiring and unsettling, and, besides, there is a risk that you might have a crisis when you are far from any hospital. Now, listen. I want to propose a drug that may help, or *may* make you feel much worse. It's new and experimental. Little is known about its side-effects. In trials it has been found to benefit 65 per cent of patients, but unfortunately the other 35 per cent develop further unpleasant symptoms. Will you think about it?'

Laura refused the drug – instinctively, almost without a moment's reflection. It was another cable flung from the shore towards Charon's boat. She knew it would fall short.

'The choice is yours,' her consultant said. 'I can give you antibiotics which may reduce the ascites somewhat, although they are contra-indicated by the state of your liver.'

'Is there nothing else that will bring down this swelling?' Laura indicated the great mound in her lap. 'It itches. It's rock-hard. And it hurts more and more.'

'We may be able to draw off the fluid through a needle. The procedure carries a small risk of infection. We try to avoid doing it if we possibly can. Does lying down ease it?'

'A bit. Temporarily.'

'Lie down more often, then.'

I lie down all the time! Laura thought resentfully. And anyway, that doesn't stop my liver from growing like a malign pregnancy, gestating death. But aloud she promised that from then on she would carry a note stating her condition and the department's emergency telephone number.

When she had gone, Mrs Ripa wrote up her confidential file:

Patient displays normal psychological reaction to terminal illness, and after 33/52 from diagnosis has progressed from shock and denial towards angry but passive acceptance. Prognosis: max. 6/12?

The following week Laura flew to New York at Rafe's expense, knowing that Mrs Ripa had been right. Exhausted by the long cramped flight, she promised herself upon landing at JFK airport that it would be the last time she left England.

It was typical of Raphael Freeman that he had changed his surname from Friedmann to Friedman to Freedman to Freeman in the course of his first fifty years, only to revert, when he was almost sixty, to the original version. The death of his father had filled him with remorse and he decided to honour the family's original immigrant surname. Fortunately he did not have to alter the single classically lettered initial 'R' above his premises in New York, Nantucket and London. He preferred his European customers and business acquaintances to think that Rafe stood for Ralph. Only among his few personal friends did he resume his original name of Raphael.

Rafe himself looked anonymous yet distinguished, with smooth skin and soft silky hair. German by origin and mother tongue, Rafe had left Hamburg as an infant in the early Thirties. His father, Josef Friedmann, was a successful diamond merchant and jeweller, but he was also a serious scholar, who could have become a rabbi with little further study had he chosen to do so. Raphael, an only son, grew up in New York City, playing on its streets, dropping dimes on the tram tracks and watching the passing iron wheels flatten them.

He had been too young to fight in the Second World War, but not too young for Korea, where he acquired a life-long loathing of Orientals and a closer acquaintance with death and cruelty than is healthy for a sensitive and impressionable nineteen-year-old. Witnessing his comrades being killed taught him to kill in turn, and he learnt the dangerous lesson, that it could be done with pleasure.

Raphael Friedmann came out of that war an all-American boy with Ivy League pretensions and a European mind. Since childhood he had imbibed the requirements and ethics of business practice but had disdained to join his father's jewellery business, strung on the tight internal threads of the Jewish community.

Instead, he travelled to Europe and took one diploma in fine art at the Courtauld Institute and another at Sotheby's. Then he went back to America and set up as a dealer in antique furniture, with – for the two often went together – a sideline in antiquarian books. By putting into practice the taste and expertise Europe had given him, during the years before Europeans had grasped the value of their own possessions, he rapidly became rich. It was at this point that he dropped the last 'n' in his surname.

At thirty Raphael married, but to the deep sorrow of his parents his wife gave him neither sons nor daughters. Eventually he divorced her and two years later, now forty years old, he married again, a gentile this time, in whose honour he dropped the 'i', becoming Freedman. But his genes seemed destined to remain within his loins, for the beautiful Jennifer, despite fine breasts and wide hips, was apparently as barren as her predecessor, and Rafe, watching with some distaste the antics of his contemporaries' teenage offspring, decided that he would prefer to stay childless. For this reason he did not divorce Jennifer, lest he be tempted into a third marriage. When his mother died, bewailing the fact that life had deprived her of grand-children, Rafe marked her passing by dropping the 'd'. His father had developed Alzheimer's disease, so he would never know, and who else cared?

Soon afterwards Rafe Freeman met Laura. By now he had a docile wife who ran their exquisitely decorated homes in mid-town New York and downstate Sag Harbor to his entire satisfaction, and left him in peace. He travelled the world in search of beautiful objects for his thriving business. In Laura, Rafe knew he had found the one thing that had been missing: the perfect partner for his very private fetishes.

While her father was alive, Laura had never ceased to court his approval. She felt sure he did not know about her sexual experiences but dreaded his finding out. He, not God, was the voice of her conscience. After his death in the car crash in Greece something gave way, some final solid counterweight collapsed. Scruples were a thing of the past. Angry, bitter and hurt, Laura looked for solace in pleasure: above all sexual pleasure.

With that restraint gone, Laura fucked anyone she fancied. A good-looking woman in her late thirties may initiate younger men or yield to older ones – and the older ones were particularly rewarding. Men over the age of fifty found their sexual self-confidence beginning to wane. Laura knew how to boost it, and as a result had plenty of sexual encounters and a couple of affairs but no emotional anchor.

With her father dead, her sister divorced, and her mother preoccupied first with widowhood and then a new marriage, Laura was very much alone. She abandoned all thought of becoming a wife and planned her future as a single woman. She began to cultivate and value her women friends: some of whom were divorced now, others approaching the menopause in the knowledge that they would definitely not have children. These single women formed a mutually protective group that, along with money and success, was some compensation for being unmarried.

Laura had met Rafe by chance one afternoon in 1987 a few weeks after her fortieth birthday. They had been standing side by side examining antiquarian books before an auction at Sotheby's. Laura had been acting as assistant and interpreter to a wealthy private collector and was familiarizing herself with lot numbers and guide-prices. Rafe was buying for American clients who specialized in erotica.

'This engraving is particularly fine . . .' he murmured.

Laura looked, then turned the page with a white-gloved hand

to find the real object of his interest overleaf: a tiny engraving of a girl tumbled on a bed, haunches up-thrust. 'And so,' she met his eyes without smiling, 'is this.'

Rafe had become rich by understanding and satisfying the collector's obsession. He knew that people would pay quite unreasonable sums to acquire the *last* of something, or the only one, or to complete a set of first editions. Occasionally he came across these desirable objects by chance, more often after assiduous searching. Collectors paid dearly for his expertise.

He became Laura's lover at a time when people were realizing that Aids did not restrict itself to gay men. It meant the end of sex without responsibility. The days of careless promiscuity, which had lasted for twenty years, were over. Aids was all-embracing. Before going to bed with Laura for the first time, Rafe had produced a condom. 'I have made it an invariable rule,' he assured her silkily.

'Does that include your wife?' she had asked.

'I do many things that exclude my wife. Especially in bed.'

Rafe prized unusual sexual experiences. It was in the nature of this hobby that he often needed a partner. Laura possessed the necessary worldliness as well as beauty, and appeared to be unencumbered by other relationships that might prove tiresome. Rafe set about finding out whether she was willing to share his pursuit.

First, however, he tried to fascinate her. He combined a fastidious physical presence with a powerful intellect, expressed with original and heartless wit. The effect might have been unpleasant, were it not for his natural good manners. These secured him admission everywhere.

Rafe knew a rich, Parisian woman who organized erotic ceremonies for small groups. A ritual was enacted whose object was to give the most extreme pleasure to the participants. Yes, he said, it had elements of cruelty, pain, even danger. But it was theatrical – everything was controlled and everyone took part voluntarily. 'We all know one another and we have certain tastes in common. All the same, the build-up beforehand, the tension and, above all, the *release* is quite extraordinary. I promise you a very special experience.'

Laura, at first alarmed, soon became intrigued. Men were invariably the 'victims', Rafe told her; women inflicted certain 'punishments' which the men could interrupt by their skill in caressing their tormentors. As soon as a woman achieved orgasm, she stopped punishing. Since, however, the men enjoyed the punishment . . . 'You see?' he said. 'The rhythm becomes exquisitely complicated.'

At other times these scenarios might take the form of a rape – apparently genuine, except that all concerned were willing and all desired one another. A fantasy was played out, in every respect as though it were real – there were elements of surprise, even terror – yet by offering to take part, the woman had implicitly consented.

'It is sexuality staged like drama,' Rafe explained. 'Complete with timing, role-playing and, above all, a climax. Remember, the women are always dominant and the men submit to their control and do whatever they demand. You need not be anxious. I believe it will give you great pleasure.' Laura, duly fascinated, went along as Rafe's companion the next time he was summoned. Her pleasure, as he had promised, was intense, and so was the self-disgust she felt afterwards. She attended these orgies for three years.

At her February dinner party Laura had told the assembled company that her illness was liver disease and not Aids, but if anyone wished to check, the hospital letter vouching for this was in the downstairs lavatory. Rafe had been the only man to check.

Rafe's chauffeur, a sleek, sullen Hispanic, collected Laura from JFK airport. He wore a uniform and cap that made him look like some dubious dictator. He did not speak to Laura nor did she attempt conversation. These days she avoided all unnecessary effort. He drove her to Sutton Place and carried her bag into the lobby of a handsome red-brick apartment block overlooking the river. A doorman ushered her into the lift. On the fourteenth floor he placed her bag outside a door marked 'F', rang the bell and glided away.

Rafe held Laura at arm's length while he pretended to examine the state of her health. He could not have met her at the airport, he said, because nowadays he avoided going outside unless absolutely necessary. The humidity of New York's late summer made it a breeding-ground for germs. She saw that his preoccupation with hygiene, always a mild idiosyncrasy, had matured into a full-blown obsession. He also announced that he had reverted to his original name and wished her to call him by it: Raphael.

The drawing-room was a treasure trove of beautiful objects whose value only increased his paranoia. Scattered across the floor were gorgeous rugs. She pointed at one and inquired where it came from.

'No, no – I can show you some much more interesting things. I hope I shall not disappoint. I have a few ideas with which to distract you. Refined, yet, I hope, novel – if you feel strong enough . . .'

'I'm well past playing games,' she replied. 'Surely that's obvious.'

Rafe's former promise of sophisticated sexuality had given way to a beady wariness. He now seemed corrupt – worse than corrupt: morbid, rotten, a foul creature festering under the fastidious surface cleanliness. I am too close to death, Laura thought, for this black comedy.

But Rafe persisted. He had some extremely rare and interesting books she might enjoy – eighteenth-century, never displayed in public, recently acquired from a Frenchman's *cabinet secret* . . . No, she said, she didn't want to look at any more pictures.

'Well then, poor Laura, beguile me with some of your adventures.'

'No,' she answered abruptly. 'It's too late. You tell me – since I am concerned with dying now, and not any longer with sex –

how do Jews approach death? What are your secrets, your rituals, how do you prepare? Your father, for example: what did *he* do in his final months?'

He flinched and swiftly counter-attacked. 'You ask the question because *your* father – as I seem to recall – was not granted time to prepare?'

'And yours,' she said equally quickly, 'if I remember rightly, was granted too much.'

They were expert at hurting each other, but in the past it had been a calculated pain reached by an excruciatingly well-timed series of steps that halted just before they became unendurable. Rafe had been the only man she knew – aside from Conrad and the hairbrush – to specialize in sexual gadgets. He had tiny implements with which to excite her, beautiful objects made from leather or steel, encased in velvet-lined boxes, and larger implements with which to immobilize her. To this array of *joujoux* he added the tale-telling skills of a Baron Münchhausen, creating fantasy worlds in which Laura starred as heroine or victim, *ingénue* or brothel-keeper.

What kind of moral coma, she wondered during the next thirty-six hours, had allowed her to involve herself with someone whose humanity had so curdled and soured? Raphael was ashen-faced and expressionless, impervious to her pain, yet morbidly fascinated by her imminent death and its effect. He wanted to know when, and how much, her sexual appetite had faded and whether fantasy could stimulate it. Had she, he asked, considered paying for the services of a vigorous younger man, or would she prefer pornography or voyeurism? Laura knew that Rafe felt no concern for her but was anticipating his own decline. He wanted a glimpse of the future. Raphael had exposed her to the ugliest truth about herself. Her present decay was physical, but now she understood for the first time that their so diverting, so unusual and *recherché* relationship had been morally corrupt. For five years she had been Rafe's mistress and played Rafe's games. With him she had wanted only to be stimulated, entertained and gratified. Affection or kindness – even the kindness of a Bruno – had not entered into it.

After less than two days in New York, just long enough to gather her strength for the return flight, Laura said she would like to leave as soon as possible. He did not demur or ask for a reason.

'Let me book you on Concorde,' he suggested.

'Certainly,' Laura said. 'I apologize. I have disappointed you.'

She felt like a leper as she was driven away the following morning, picturing him already under a scalding shower, wondering whether he would have the whole apartment, or only her bedroom, fumigated.

The small, slender aircraft offered every luxury except the chance to sleep. Not only was it jarringly noisy in flight, but Laura found that she was expected to consume ceaselessly: caviar, champagne, smoked salmon, wild strawberries – all the favourite indulgences of the rich.

'I really don't want anything,' she protested. 'I'm afraid I am not very well. I should just like to sleep.'

'May we radio ahead for a doctor to meet you?' the stewardess asked, smiling glassily. 'Do you have a number for your personal physician?'

'No. Or rather, yes, but she's a very busy NHS consultant. Isn't there a corner of the aircraft that might be curtained off to let me sleep?'

'I'm afraid our flight is so short that most passengers prefer to work or relax rather than sleep. But if you like, Miss King, I would be happy to bring you a blanket and a sleep mask. Would you care for a glass of water? Do you carry a supply of sedatives?'

Laura was enveloped in a navy blue blanket and made herself as comfortable as possible in a cocoon of sound. She was thinking too fiercely to be able to sleep. *Why* had she acquiesced in the repellent sexual games of that repellent man? Why, for that matter, had she acquiesced in Conrad's rituals, the forerunner to Rafe's?

As she sank into self-pity and reproach, she had the illusion that below the aircraft's mechanical whine she could hear her father's bass voice saying, as he said so often in her childhood, 'Come along, Laura, buck up! Pull yourself together! Shoulders back – chin up – smile! *There*'s Daddy's happy girl! Better now?'

It is our fathers who shape us, she thought: their expectations, their presence or absence, whether they cherish or punish. Fathers wield stern, adamant, grown-up power over our soft childhood selves. Do they realize it at the time, and if they did, could they behave as they do? Why could he never approve of what I *was* instead of trying to shape me into what he thought I ought to be? I have spent my life rebelling against, and yet searching for, a man like my father; I have refused to be the kind of woman he thought women should be. I tried to rebel against the great paternal monolith and have ended up lost and weeping at its feet.

10

Kit Mallinson

It is so easy to dismiss unrequited love. We watch coolly, wondering at the poor victim's inability to see that there isn't a hope. But in fact hope is all he does possess. In the name of hope the unrequited lover sacrifices real life for fantasy, not knowing, or not caring, how ludicrous a figure he cuts. Hope blinds him to the indifference of the beloved.

Laura met Kit Mallinson in 1977. This was before her affairs with Bruno and Rafe but *after* she'd refused Edouard's proposal – a critical, vulnerable time. She'd just had her thirtieth birthday. If she were to meet a husband it had better be soon, and Edouard had made her realize how much the thought of marriage appealed to her.

Kit Mallinson ducked automatically as he preceded Laura through his front door. He put her suitcase down in the tiny hallway and turned left into a cluttered drawing-room papered with fading cabbage roses.

'It was cheap because when I bought it Porton Down was still going. *You* know – biological warfare research establishment. All closed now, but in those days, late Seventies, it was still very hush-hush. Estate agent in Salisbury asked a lot of questions. Didn't make any difference to me. I never got caught up in CND and all that. Too late for National Service and Cyprus, too early for the Falklands . . . the eternal ducker-outer, me . . .'

He always used to talk a lot when he was nervous, Laura remembered. 'Kit, you're not apologizing?'

'Wait till you see your bedroom. It's *minute*. Other than young Max – who's my godson, remember – and that nice Polish wife of his I don't often have people to stay. And *they* haven't been for ages. I used to take him fishing along the Bourne. Great fun. Good lad. Hey' – he stopped and looked at her – 'You all right to climb stairs?'

Do I look *that* bad? Laura thought, and then remembered the mirror in Bruno's bathroom: yes, she did. 'Fine,' she reassured him.

She looked around the low-ceilinged drawing-room. The furniture had collapsed into comfortable shapes that held the impression of Kit's long, sprawling body. Low tables were buried under old newspapers, envelopes, books, sheet music and bills. On the mantelpiece stood a studio portrait from the war years of his parents, his father's Sam Browne belt gleaming. Beside it were a couple of snapshots of Max and Cordelia, Constance's older children; a bust of Beethoven and some other composer; two coffee mugs and a stained teaspoon, a jug of roses; a stopped clock; and a black-and-white photograph of herself. She crossed the room to examine it.

'I'll take your case upstairs,' Kit said.

The picture dated from a summer long before she'd even known Kit. It had been taken by her sister and showed Laura lying on her stomach on a lawn laughing up at the camera. She remembered the scratchiness and smell of the newly mown grass. Her face was rounded and the neckline of her dress showed more of her breasts than she had probably realized at the time. Her hair shone with health. Her eyes were hidden behind dark glasses.

She turned as Kit came back into the room. 'Don't I look *young*?'

Kit did not try to deny it – he was a man without artifice – but merely said, 'It's the only picture of you I've got. I begged it from Constance. I would have preferred one that showed your eyes. I always liked your grape-green eyes.'

'The last time we met, apart from my dinner – was that Max's wedding to Dani?' she asked.

'They very sweetly invited me to play the organ. Great compliment. But I must have seen you since then, surely?'

'I don't think so,' said Laura. 'Though we've been *assiduous* with the Christmas cards. Did they invite you to the christening as well?'

'They did, but I couldn't go. I was filling in that weekend – must have been organing somewhere else. If it were just the choir, I could have got out of it. Did it go well?'

'I wasn't there, either.'

She had avoided big family occasions for years, except when it would cause real pain. It had not been difficult to convince the family that celebrations coincided with urgent professional commitments.

'Their child Kaspar is gorgeous,' she added.

'I'm not much good with small children.'

'*This* child is amazingly good with large adults.'

Laura followed him into the narrow kitchen behind the drawing-room. On the hatch connecting the two stood a neatly laid tea tray with two porcelain teacups and a scalloped plate of biscuits.

'Positively my one attempt at daintiness!' Kit said. 'I've been given tea by enough clergy wives to know how it ought to be done.'

'You must be a permanent challenge. I'm surprised they let you play the organ in the cathedral.'

'Call it constructive forgetfulness. So long as I believe in God they are prepared to overlook my being a Catholic. There aren't that many decent organists about any more, and a lot of those were trained in Catholic public schools. Can I show you my garden when we've drunk our tea? September is rather a good month for it.'

In the garden he pointed out the different varieties of delphinium ('Bit of a speciality of mine') and old roses, stooping to

204

dead-head a bloom or tweak out a weed. In contrast to the chaos indoors, Kit's garden was a miracle of controlled shape and colour, texture and pattern.

'Proves that one never forgets anything,' he said. 'I hadn't realized how much influence my mother had on my gardening until my sister came to visit me for the first time.'

'Miranda?' asked Laura. After fifteen years the name swam into focus from some recess of memory, like a shrimp into a rock pool.

'Mim, yes. She lives in Toronto now. Her job's something to do with medical research at the university. Hates to leave her laboratory. The white mice all die or something. She took one look at all this and said, "It's *exactly* like Mother's private bit." As soon as she said it, I remembered Mother's patch: the one area the gardeners weren't allowed to interfere with. That was bursting with delphiniums and old roses. We left that house soon after the war; I can't have been more than five or six. I planted delphiniums at this end because they like the evening sun. Then roses, here – Mrs Coombes put some in your bedroom, by the way.'

'You mean you have a *cleaner*?' Laura asked, and she began to laugh.

Kit looked at her, baffled. 'What's so funny about that? She does me and the church on alternate weeks.'

'Both as an act of charity?'

'I probably subsidize the church. I pay her three pounds an hour. It's more than I earn for teaching the organ.'

Laura sat down on a wrought-iron garden seat that still held the warmth of the afternoon.

'Oh Kit, you're going to do me an immense amount of good.'

He looked at her, weeds trailing from his clasped hands. 'I'm glad.'

Kit Mallinson was seven years older than Laura. He had been a friend and contemporary of Paul, Laura's brother-in-law. The two had been taught by Jesuits at the same public school, gone up in the same year to the same Oxford college to read the same subject: English. Laura used to wonder why Paul, rather than Kit, had fallen in love with her serious, bookish sister. Now she realized that they probably both had, but that Constance was more attracted to the charming, irresponsible, confident Paul than the gawky, cerebral Kit. He still didn't look entirely comfortable in his body. His arms dangled awkwardly in front of him and his corduroy trousers were too short.

'I've known you for more than twenty years,' Laura mused, and smiled at him. 'It's extraordinary to think you must be over *fifty*.'

He grimaced. 'Don't remind me. There was a brief flurry of activity around my half-century: several young women – young-*ish* – were produced for my benefit, but that's stopped again. I'm now a confirmed bachelor, though not the sort usually meant by that euphemism. I was quite glad when the flurry died down. They all seemed to expect to be taken out for *dinner* and my salary doesn't run to luxuries, much.'

Laura wondered what he earned. Kit lectured in medieval English at a minor university and he wasn't going to rise much further up the academic ladder now. He had that shabby, run-down look common among intellectuals whom television and the media have failed to colonize. Laura doubted if Kit had got as far as acquiring a word-processor. A hundred years ago he would have been a familiar and respected figure in both the academic and this village community. Today, he was an anachronism, practically obsolete, his courtesy outdated, his kindness unfocused, bewildered at the speed with which modern life raced away from him.

The following morning Kit brought her a cup of tea in bed at eight-thirty. 'I'm off now,' he said. 'Mrs Coombes is coming in this morning, if there's anything you need. I've left my number by the telephone. There's lunch in the fridge. I've arranged to make it a short day: I'll be back by three-thirty.'

'Term hasn't started yet?'

'Not yet. I'm winding up various curriculum committees, discussing the new intake, wrestling with last-minute UCCA forms, and fielding letters from importunate Heads of English whose prize blooms failed to get the required grades . . .'

'Sounds horrendous. Time you were off.'

He bent over the faded eiderdown to kiss her and she caught the sharp smell of shaving cream. He straightened up. 'Gosh, it is nice having you here!' he said. 'I wish you hadn't got to leave . . .'

'I'm here for a *month*, if you can cope with me that long.'

'The longer the better for me. Now, Laura, is there anything special you need? I've put the number of my GP beside the phone.'

'I've got everything with me. All I need is TLC. Tender loving care.'

'Tender loving care is what I yearn to give.'

As the days went by, the solitary nature of Kit's bachelorhood became more obvious. His bathroom held many clues. He possessed half a dozen unopened brands of aftershave – Christmas presents, she supposed – but no shampoo. He presumably used soap or even washing-up liquid. His medicine cupboard held Beecham's powders and aspirin and Scholl's corn cushions. There was foot powder in a tin so old that it was priced in shillings and pence and rust had fused the lid. He had an embrocation rub (her heart contracted at the thought of Kit with his stick-insect limbs twisting as he tried to rub Deep Heat into his own aching shoulder) but no sticking plasters or bandages, no ointments or antiseptic, no mouthwash or deodorant, and no thermometer.

'What happens when you're ill?' she asked.

'I'm never ill.'

'You must be. Everyone gets flu occasionally, or a heavy cold.'

'I keep going. Or I drink a bottle of whisky and go to bed and sweat it out.'

The kitchen on the other hand was well supplied with modern gadgets and Kit evidently patronized a good Oriental food shop. Inside one of his cupboards, neatly arranged in alphabetical order, was an array of spice jars, several packets of exotic dried ingredients and bottles of soy and other sauces.

'Do you cook properly for yourself?'

'I do if it's my birthday or if I'm celebrating something . . .'

'Like what?'

'Oh, if one of my students got a First, I'd celebrate that. But mostly these are for when people come to supper. Or to stay, which isn't often. That's why *you're* such a treat.'

'What do you usually do during vacations?'

'I can sometimes get a bit of tourist guiding, or even dress up as a cleric for one of those medieval banquet events. Pretty phony, but I spout Chaucer at them and they love it.'

'Oh Kit! You must *hate* it.'

'Anything that introduces people to Chaucer has to be a good thing. You never know when a spark will catch.'

'"A clerk there was, Of Oxenford also . . ."'

'Come on, Laura! You can do better than that!'

'No, I can't. I read French and Russian, not English, remember. With supplementary Chinese. The only time I did Chaucer was at A level.'

'There's lots of great stuff before Chaucer, perfectly comprehensible by someone with your facility with words. Do you know the *Harley Lyrics*?'

'Not at all.'

'Wonderful stuff! The bit where the king banishes himself because his wife has been spirited away by magic: "Once grey and varied furs he wore / Had purple linen on his bed." That's a rough translation. "Now he lies on the rugged moor / With leaves and grass upon him spread." Full of telling detail, too: "All black and shaggy his beard had grown / And to his girdle-place hung down."

'You see how that shows you a) that he was still a young

man, not a grey-beard and b) exactly how long the beard was? Marvellous stuff. *Marvellous!* And then he sees his wife in a vision – how does it go?'

'Kit!' Laura said, and stretched a hand across the table. 'Kit! You're lecturing me.'

He stopped, hurt. 'But it *is* marvellous stuff?'

'Yes, I know. But I'd rather talk about *you*.'

He withdrew from her fractionally, and she saw she had struck at what mattered to him most. 'Just tell me how it ends. Does the king get her back?'

He brightened, unable to resist. 'He finds her, in this astonishing passage, in a hall full of people, alive but paralysed: "As if asleep at height of day / Like that they had been snatched away / And taken there by fairy riders." Anyway, the king – he's Orpheus really, and his queen is Eurydice – plays his harp to the king of the Underworld and tricks him into letting his wife go.'

'The old stories are best,' said Laura.

'There *are* no new stories,' replied Kit.

'*Your* life is one of courtly love,' she said. 'Like the poem.'

He flashed a look. 'Don't mock me. I'm not some dusty old don.'

'I'm not mocking. I mean it. You would rather love a lady from afar than marry one of fallible flesh and blood.'

'I would have married you, if you'd have had me. I would marry you still.'

'Kit, dear impractical over-sensitive Kit, I am *dying*. I am already, in a sense, on the other side. I look at the vigorous lives of you, my friends, of people in the shops and on the streets, as though already from the far side of life. I feel closer to death.'

Tears sprang to her eyes.

'I'm sorry. They're not tears of self-pity – I just cry much more easily these days. Emotion is closer to the surface. I was never sentimental but now the most absurd things move me instantly to tears. Television. Children. Bloody puppies and kittens!'

'Don't apologize to me for your tears.'

209

She looked at him with swimming eyes. 'Oh, Kit, why do such dear men stay single, and such bastards marry?'

'I ask myself that sometimes.'

She thought, He *would* marry me, even now. And I could leave him the little house in Markham Street, or the use of it during his lifetime, and he could hand it on to Max . . . oh, stop fantasizing, Laura!

Kit prepared her tempting tiny meals, and seemed not to mind if she ate only minute quantities. Her stomach was less and less able to tolerate food.

'It seemed simple to me in those days,' Laura said to Kit over supper a week later. '*Feminism* was the answer to every woman's problems.'

'The females in my department would drum me out for saying this,' Kit said, 'but beauty is wasted on feminists. You *were* lovely, Laura, and in such a different way from Constance (who was also lovely). But you had *such* beautiful eyes. I've never seen eyes as green as yours. Wide, open eyes.'

She shut them, conscious of how yellow and jaundiced they had become.

Kit continued, 'You were right when you said the other day that the only sort of love I'm really capable of is courtly love. I fall in love with my students. In my own defence, all I can say is that I hardly ever do anything about it, unless they seem to be pursuing me – which *does* occasionally happen. I brood about some long-limbed, clever girl not yet out of her teens, clumping around in those dreadful black orthopaedic shoes they all wear. I direct my lectures at her, and probably give her higher marks than she deserves.'

'Always women?'

'Give me *that* much credit – always women. For a year or two, this creature, blessed with youth and good looks, fills my fantasies. She moves on, inevitably, and I mourn for a bit – but there's always another one.'

'Do you get jealous of their boyfriends?'

'I don't, really. I regret it when I see these magical unicorn ladies turned so quickly into staid housewives, without even the blessing of a wedding ring. They think they're liberated, but in no time at all they've moved in with some youth and are washing his T-shirts and jeans and taking responsibility for cooking his meals. The soft powdery patina, the sweet-and-twenty bloom, disappears. The youth looks cleaner and better fed, the maiden looks downtrodden and hands in her essays late.'

'Maybe they'd be just as happy looking after you. Have you ever thought of that?'

'Laura! I am twice, almost *three times* their age! These are scarcely more than children. Eighteen, nineteen. I am fifty-two. Older men don't marry young girls unless they are exceedingly rich or exceedingly stupid, and I am neither.'

'Can I ask a very personal question?'

'There are only two very personal questions. Which one is it?'

'What do you do for sex? Or are you celibate?'

'I'd rather that question than the other one . . . You would be aghast if you knew my salary. You probably earn five times as much as me.'

Yes, thought Laura. You think you are exaggerating, but in fact I probably do. No: I *did*.

'Are you going to answer?'

'Aren't you afraid I may disappoint or shock you?'

That, she thought, would be difficult. Compared with what she had seen, Kit's confession could hold few surprises. 'You don't have to tell me,' she said.

'I am not quite celibate. I do not go to prostitutes. I seldom make love to the girls I yearn for – though very occasionally one will surprise me by interposing her young body between me and my scruples. But being that rare creature, an unattached male, I do get a regular supply of invitations to dinners and other university functions. I am wheeled out for predatory visiting female academics, some of whom – the American ones, usually – make it quite plain that they expect me to take them to bed, and the hell with political correctness. So . . .' – he spread his hands before her in a self-mockingly helpless gesture – 'unless they're absolutely hideous, I do.'

'But nothing ever comes of it?'

'I have sometimes wondered whether any of them get pregnant. One is at risk, I believe, as an intelligent and more or less physically normal male, of serving as a sperm bank unawares. But if this is the case, I have never been informed.'

'I meant, you're never tempted to fall in love, or even embark on a civilized and compatible relationship?'

'Laura, you know me – courtly lover out of his time. I'm perpetually wedded to the Belle Dame Sans Merci.'

He was trying so hard to keep the tone light, yet he looked so bleak that Laura stood up from the armchair beside the fireplace, smoothed her skirt and bent down to cradle his head in her arms. As she did so, her body brushed against his shoulder.

'Laura, forgive me, this is crass but – why do you look pregnant?'

'It's the illness, Kit. I said at my dinner: it's called ascites, this huge swelling stomach. Used to be known as dropsy. I was only ever pregnant once, and then I was made to have an abortion.'

'Bastard!' he said. 'The *bastard*!'

'You speak as a good Catholic. You don't know the circumstances.'

'Did you want the baby?'

'Deep waters, Kit . . . Very deep waters. I'd rather not.'

In the mornings after Kit had driven off Laura would lie in bed till noon. She read, she dozed, and tried not to scratch her itching, aching body, knowing that it only made the condition worse. Her skin felt thinner than usual, as though it were tissue paper stretched finely across the yellowing bulk of her intestines. Her mind was febrile but her body was ageing fast, and with its disintegration her tiredness grew worse. If she made no physical effort during the day, she could be attentive to Kit in the evenings, but if she went for a walk or even had too animated a conversation on the telephone, her energy was used up by the time he returned. At first she took the iron pills Mrs Ripa had prescribed, but they seemed to increase her tiredness and she discontinued them.

Her days slipped gently past. She would get out of bed when the sun set, dust motes swarming in her little plastered bedroom. After a warm bath she would slip a loose cotton dress over her head and lie on a faded deckchair in the garden listening to birdsong and the buzzing of bees.

She had little appetite and rarely bothered with lunch. She spent most of her time deep in her thoughts. She tried to write a diary, but it became an apologia for her life which was not what she had intended, and so she stopped after a few days. She took the French exercise book labelled LAURA KING, SEPTEMBER 1992, wrapped inside two plastic bags from Tesco, tying each one at the neck, and dropped them into Kit's rubbish bin under the sink.

Instead, whenever the sky clouded over, she went indoors to write letters on the marquetry desk that had belonged to Kit's mother. For Joe and Dorothy she ordered, on impulse, a pair of elephant-embroidered cushions and a matching bedspread from an Oxfam catalogue that fell out of a Sunday colour supplement. She wrote to Nell, praising her cooking and her well-stocked larder. She resisted the temptation to urge counselling. She knew a separate letter to Nick would never pass Nell's Cerberus-like vigilance, so she signed off with 'Fondest love to you both'.

She found a copy of the *Harley Lyrics* on Kit's bookshelf and amused herself by translating its archaic, rustic language into modern English. This she sent to Edouard in Paris, attaching a note which said, 'My last labour of love for you, *cher* Edouard . . . I wish I did not have to go; I would even settle for half the year in the Underworld.'

After two weeks she had written all her farewells, and sorted out a will in her mind. Making it legal would have to wait. The next time Mrs Coombes came, Laura asked tactfully whether she could help her to spring-clean Kit's bathroom. The lino under the claw feet of the old free-standing bath was torn and ragged, and the wrinkled wallpaper behind it harboured grey balls of dust.

'I would, Miss, but I don't have the right materials,' Mrs Coombes complained. 'Mr Mallinson's that absent-minded, he never looks at my lists and if I bought them myself he'd not remember to pay me back.'

Laura proffered a twenty-pound note from her purse. 'Here!' she said. 'That should be enough. If you can find something to take the rust stain off the inside of the bath as well, that would be marvellous. *I'll* have a go at that.'

Mrs Coombes looked at her. 'You couldn't wash out a china thimble, Miss, never mind scrub at those stains. They've been there twenty years. They'll not shift.'

'You can buy special stuff now,' Laura said firmly. 'From any good ironmongery. I think it's a sort of paste.' She extended the note, knowing that if Mrs Coombes took it, this would signify assent.

The telephone rang. Mrs Coombes took the money and Laura went into the drawing-room and picked up the receiver. The caller was Paul Liddell.

Laura felt caught out, but they hadn't spoken in years – he might not recognize her voice.

'Can I speak to Kit Mallinson?' he asked.

'I'm sorry but he's out,' replied Laura.

'Do you know what time he'll be back? Would you tell him I called? My name is Paul Liddell. Tell him I'm only over for a short time.'

Laura looked around. Mrs Coombes was watching her. She beckoned her over to the phone and gestured into it. Mrs Coombes picked up the receiver and began laboriously to write down a name and telephone number. The twenty-pound note lay on the dining table. Abstractedly, Laura picked it up and put it back in her purse.

'The gentleman asked who you was,' Mrs Coombes said sullenly, 'but I couldn't remember your name.'

'Laura King. It doesn't matter. He was calling for Mr Mallinson.'

Laura went upstairs to the tiny bedroom and dug out a book at random. She tried to concentrate on it but its weight was greater than the pleasure justified and she laid it down on the folded sheet. She thought about Kit, remembering their brief and unsuccessful affair.

She had been amazed and more than amazed – filled with pity and horror – to find that he was still a virgin at thirty-seven. Long afterwards Kit told her some of the reasons: his love for her sister Constance, his striving to be a 'good' Catholic, the controlling power of his mother. 'But in the end,' he said, 'after the age of about twenty-five, you're a virgin because you're a virgin. It simply becomes too paralysing to let any woman know. There was I, in the midst of the randy, free-loving Sixties, a virgin! I cringed at the thought of discovery.'

Kit and Laura might never have gone to bed were it not that she had just had her thirtieth birthday. Edouard had departed after she had refused his third offer of marriage and, although she didn't regret the decision, she missed *him*. She was on her own – apart, of course, from Conrad – but that relationship was now quite without love or joy. Kit was a suitable potential husband. Her mother would approve. Nature and nurture tugged deep in Laura's reproductive system.

Paul and Constance had often talked about Kit Mallinson and she'd seen him at their parties, a lofty presence, towering above most of the other guests, anxious to please. One day, when Laura visited Paul and Constance for Sunday lunch, Kit was there too – relaxed, funny and endearing. His hawkish nose and the flat planes of his cheeks and chin seemed attractive for the first time. He was very solicitous towards Constance; he leapt to his feet to clear away the plates and insisted on washing up while she made coffee and the children dried. Laura and Paul, lingering at the table, could hear them discussing medieval English in the kitchen.

'She ought to have married Kit, not me,' Paul had said.

'Nonsense,' Laura answered. 'She's very happy with you.'

'You think so? What about me?'

'I don't want to know. Don't tell me. I don't want anything to do with your rows. She's my sister and I love you both.'

'Love, love,' Paul said. 'Such an over-used word. You love me. I love you. What does it mean? It's all advertising: an unconscious trigger word, like "new" and "young".'

'Nothing. Desire. Intimacy. Family. Security. Everything.'

'Take young Christopher. I wonder if any woman's bedded him yet? He really *is* unloved, poor old Kits. Not that I'm suggesting *you* should be the one to start him off. Heaven forbid.'

The first time Laura and Kit went to bed together had been a humiliating disaster, giving neither pleasure or satisfaction. Despite her guidance, Kit had been clumsy, hasty and ignorant. His first aim had misfired, to their intense mutual embarrassment. In the bathroom she caught sight of her face, reddened and blotched by the friction of his unfamiliar skin. When she returned to the bedroom, washed and lubricated, he had fallen asleep.

At dawn he had woken her with pleading kisses. 'Can we try again? By the morning I shall be so mortified I'll creep away otherwise.'

'Slowly, Kit, *slowly*,' she said. 'Why don't you let *me* lead?'

She had nothing but pity to guide her: pity for his long, ungainly limbs, his laboured expression, his eyes clenched tightly shut, his inexpert fingers, fiddling and twiddling. She didn't love Kit in the least, but she felt bound to free him from this hell of ignorance. 'Don't feel you have to *do* anything,' she murmured, trying to coax him into passivity. 'Lie back and listen to your own sensations. Don't worry about mine.'

So he lay still, and under the white tent of the sheets she guided him towards a successful climax.

After their first coition Kit had been desperate to make up for lost time. He could not stop touching her, stroking her. He wanted to court her gradually, take her out to dinner and the cinema, but his hands were always on her thigh or slyly brushing against her breast when he thought no one was looking. He tried to conceal his impatience, but Laura knew he longed for the end of the evening when he could take her home – never to his flat, which he shared with two other men – and to bed. It was as though the river of his pent-up sexuality were breaking its banks and flooding into her. Had she been able match his ardour, it would have been wonderful – arranged marriages must start like this, she once thought, with this mutually explosive discovery. Instead his clumsiness irritated her and because she did not love him, she soon lost patience.

Had he been more experienced, Laura would have told Kit straight away that they were sexually incompatible, but the fear of debarring him from sex for the rest of his life prevented her. She could not tell him how crass he was, and he had no way of knowing. It was wonderful for him: a glory, a revelation. How could it not be good for her? She told herself she would give him another month or two, let him down gently, and then introduce him to one of her women friends.

On another occasion when Paul and Constance invited them both to dinner, Laura realized at once, from their conspiratorial smiles, that Kit must have told them. He winked at Paul, and she wanted to say, 'Oh, for Christ's *sake*, Kit, don't be such a *schoolboy!*' He exuded glee. Laura made an excuse and left the room. Constance followed and found her reading to Katie.

'Laura! What is it? Why are you so jumpy?' she asked.

They settled the child to sleep and withdrew into Constance's bedroom. Laura sat down at the dressing table and began to brush her hair vigorously. She picked up Constance's scent and sniffed it; then Paul's cologne. He used Givenchy Gentleman. Kit used Old Spice. The difference seemed absurdly significant.

'Are you going to talk to me, or not?' Constance asked.

'Not,' said Laura, like a sulky child.

'Well then, I will. It's perfectly obvious that Kit has fallen madly in love with you. He can't take his eyes off you. I think that's terrific. He's a darling man, an absolute sweetie. Paul's known him for ever and he's one of our best friends. He's exactly what you need, and I can't think why it didn't occur to me long ago.'

'I don't need *you* to match-make for me, thank you very much!' Laura snapped.

'Oh, no? Well you haven't had a lot of luck doing it for yourself. You're over thirty now. Time you got married.'

'Just because you're a cosy wife and mother doesn't mean I have to be. Not that your marriage looks particularly *cosy* just now.'

'That was a cheap gibe,' said Constance.

'I'm sorry. It was. I'm sorry. How are things? Paul seems OK.'

'Paul's OK. I'm OK. The children are OK. But it used to be so much *better* than OK.'

'Isn't that what always happens? The first fine frenzy ends and you settle down together. You've been married for years, after all. How many is it?'

'Thirteen. Ominous. A bad number. I'm glad it'll soon be fourteen. Yet *I* still love him. I really do. I don't fancy anyone else, not even Steve McQueen! Oh, it'll blow over. We'll be all right. Paul's working desperately hard; there's some sort of takeover plan in the air. If it comes off, he'll be rich and we can buy a big house and send the children to private schools and it'll all be plain sailing. Meanwhile he works all hours and comes home at midnight.'

'You see?'

'But Laura, about you and Kit . . . why *not*? Mummy would be thrilled. She worries about you.'

'I am *not* going to get married to please my *mother* and my *sister*.'

'No of *course* you're not. I know that. But think about it, will you? Laura? Sweetheart? Little sister? Hmm?'

They hugged each other and returned to the dining-room. Kit stood up as they entered. Paul was sprawled languorously, smoking, cradling a glass of wine.

'*I* know,' he said. 'Girl talk.'

'And you've been doing men's talk,' said Constance. She stooped to kiss him. Kit extended a hand to pull Laura towards him and she thought savagely, What a deceptively touching little scene!

As they left at the end of the evening, Laura insisted on catching a taxi home, but Kit looked at her with such wounded eyes that she relented. This is the last time, she thought to herself as she got into Kit's car. So he took her home and climbed into her bed and her person and brought her coffee and the Sunday papers next morning and had no idea of the farewell letter she was composing in her head. But relationships seldom end as tidily as planned. Arrangements are made in advance that cannot be cancelled; tickets are bought, invitations accepted. Rather than go on her own, Laura allowed things to trail on.

This was no basis for a marriage, Laura realized. She tried to warn Kit, but he was impervious to the hints; or perhaps he deliberately ignored them. One evening over supper together she said, 'The problem is, it's not *really* me you want, Kit. It's Constance you're in love with.'

Yes, he admitted, he had been in love with her sister, and before that with Paul.

'With Paul! At school?'

'Laura, *every*one was in love with Paul at school: including some of the priests. Not merely because he was good at games and good at sport and head of house but because he had that wonderful lazy, heavy-lidded charm.'

'Did you and Paul ever . . . ?'

'Go to bed together? Mutual wanking. The kind of things adolescent boys do.'

'But you're still bowled over by the famous charm?'

'It was better when it was quite, or *almost*, unconscious.'

'Bit more calculated now!'

'I dare say, although at sixteen or seventeen he was totally unaware of it. He just had to look, and smile, and he conquered. But I knew I wasn't gay, so when we got to Oxford and he and Constance got together, I fell in love with her too. I loved what Paul *was*, so I loved what and whoever he loved. Loving Constance began as part of loving him. I don't love either of them in that romantic sense any more. Nowadays I love you – you don't doubt that?'

'I think through Paul you fell in love with Constance, and, through Constance, me, rather than me for my own sake.'

She was being unfair to Kit in an attempt to extricate herself. He did love her too, but she had not been able to love him back.

Kit was the husband her parents and sister would have approved of. Had Laura been able to settle for intellectual conversation and domestic shabbiness; holidays staying with friends and family rather than abroad; wine only once a week and on birthdays; books from the library; clothes from better-off friends and second-hand shops; a lifetime of good manners and a clear conscience – then Kit would have made her happy.

If Kit had been a more practised lover or less *gauche* at parties, he might have succeeded in transforming the deep affection and ease she felt in his company into romantic love – although she suspected that, after a few years, this would have worn off to leave merely deep affection and ease once again. It would have been a decent, *Guardian*-reading sort of marriage, as good a buffer as any in a disordered world. Yet Kit never even began to take a hold upon her heart.

Laura was no longer prepared to settle for plain, ordinary contentment. It was 1977 and, like many other women of that time, Laura had the intoxicating realization that the choice was no longer between being a Girlie or a spinster; she could be *grown-up*. She was beginning to flex the wings of her power and to realize that she could go to places her mother's generation had only visited as the appendage of some man. That year Laura stopped paying rent and bought her own flat — three rooms on the first floor of a pretty, leafy street in Brook Green. She had a huge mortgage (or so it had seemed at the time), but the flat was hers.

Kit rang Laura one day soon after Christmas. It was obvious by this time, after less than six months, that their relationship had no future, though he had not yet admitted it. The letters Laura composed in her head had not been put on to paper; or if written, hadn't been sent. Her first thought, when he said he needed to talk to her, had been that he was going to end the relationship himself, but she was wrong. Being Max's spiritual mentor, he felt obliged to intervene, however clumsily, to try to shore up the crumbling marriage of his godson's parents. That was what he wanted to talk about.

'Constance and *Paul*?' she asked in surprise.

'You know about it? I feel that, as Max's godfather, perhaps I ought to beard Paul.'

'Does he confide in you?'

'No.'

'Why don't you try Constance, then?'

'I have, a bit; that's how I know. Has she discussed it with you?'

'She probably finds it easier talking to you. I think it's quite hard for her to discuss her husband's infidelity with me.'

Laura thought Constance naïve about Paul's infidelities. If she felt so badly betrayed she would be better off divorced. This was no comfort to Constance who, after fourteen years inside the hermetically sealed glass dome, the Wardian case of family life, feared for her children if their father left and was terrified of being single again.

The two sisters had never been further apart than during the critical months when Constance needed her most. Laura salved her guilt by sending morale-boosting presents – clothes, scent, luxurious underwear – all of which Constance immediately sold or gave away, preferring the camouflage of shapeless boiler suits, the uniform of Women's Lib clothes that hid her good figure and transmitted the clear message that she was *hors de combat*.

But the telephone call galvanized Laura into action, perhaps by demonstrating that even a marriage based on mutual love offered no guarantee of happiness. She wrote, tore up, rewrote and finally sent a letter to Kit. After receiving it, he rang her just once. His voice was cracked like a broken bone.

'Do one thing for me,' he said. 'Don't try and be my *friend*. Leave me alone. I can't go back to where we were and I don't want to. All right?'

'All right,' she had promised.

Long afterwards, Constance told her Kit had got drunk and stayed drunk for a week. Yet later on a solid friendship *did* take the place of fractured love. The decency of their relationship, in which neither had ever tried to hurt the other, and their mutual concern for Constance and her children, enabled affection to survive the pain of that distant winter.

On the third Saturday of her stay Kit and Laura drove into Salisbury, left the car in a supermarket car park and pushed a trolley round in search of suitable treats for Max and his family. They had planned the menu that morning as she sat up in bed balancing a tray while Kit on the end of her bed cradled a cup of tea.

'Classic English Sunday lunch, don't you think?' he said.

'I'll make a summer pudding,' she suggested. 'Tonight, so the juice has time to seep through. Do we want a starter? Will you let me contribute smoked salmon?'

'Leave all that to me,' he said, scribbling a list. Under his breath he muttered 'Cod, limes, spinach . . . Check coriander . . .'

'Then let me buy the wine. I'm not bad on wine.'

Laura leaned on the trolley for support, hoping Kit did not

notice her great weakness. He helped to steer it round corners and down the aisles as they both scanned the shelves. She would have liked to buy luxury ingredients for him – really good olive oil, really good coffee – but she suspected that he would refuse them. Instead she bought a clear pale green Chablis to go with the fish first course, a wildly extravagant 1986 Burgundy for the lamb, and a half-bottle of Muscat to accompany the pudding. She went ahead at the till so that he should not see how much her purchases cost.

Later that afternoon they worked for a couple of hours in his kitchen. The wireless was tuned to Radio Three, and from time to time Kit would drop everything to conduct or sing in a strong bass voice. They argued with *Kaleidoscope* and left the radio on while they ate a salad supper so that they could hear the end of a programme.

'After only three weeks I feel utterly relaxed with you,' Kit said.

'You want to do the same things as I do; I never have to defer or humour you.'

'It wouldn't last long,' she said. 'The illness has made me pliable. I'm usually much bossier. I *am* enjoying this, though . . .'

'How old is this child of theirs?'

'Kaspar. I forget exactly . . . Eighteen months? No, must be two by now. A gorgeous age. It's the brief interlude between rag doll and Sherman tank.'

'I can't really cope with children until they can converse,' he said.

'I quite agree – and then the first thing you want to do is ask them how they used to *think* before they could speak?'

He turned to her, delighted. 'You're absolutely right! I've always wondered that! Just as I look at my parents today, both so old, both afflicted with Alzheimer's, and wonder if they still make perfect sense in their dreams.'

That night, brought close to Kit by their companionable time together, Laura dreamed about him. They were undressing in a bath house or sauna, then naked together, and she was washing his back. His shoulder blades protruded and the knobs of his backbone stuck out like raw potatoes. She had a foaming face-cloth with which she was trying to scrub him, but there were bruises or mud stains on his skin that she could not remove.

Kit was saying, 'Don't hurt me, Laura. You're hurting. Be careful. Stop it!'

'Keep still,' she replied, 'and then it won't.' She took a nailbrush to rub more vigorously but his skin first reddened and then began to peel off as though he were being flayed.

He bent over his knees sobbing into the bath water. 'Laura, must you do that?'

'Don't be such a *baby*!' she replied.

She woke up, her heart thudding, with the guilty realization that she had been trying to hurt him in her dream. As it receded from her, rolling backwards into her unconscious as though steam from the bath house were obscuring the images, she reached for the book on her bedside table. She could see clearly in the moonlight. It was two o'clock. Through the thin, uneven wall she heard Kit snoring. She switched on her bedside light and tried to read but she could not concentrate, so she groped her way downstairs to the kitchen and began to make a cup of tea. She took it into the drawing-room and sat on the window seat looking out over Kit's still garden in the silvery moonlight. The roses – deep red, scarlet and orange by day – had paled to mauve, lilac and milky coffee, their leaves to pistachio and olive-green. The brilliant lawn was misted to a bluish lavender. The moon was high, obscured from time to time by wisps of white cloud. Laura opened the front door, thinking to walk between the flowers and smell their intense night perfume, but the chill air made her shiver. She took her tea upstairs and climbed back into bed.

Max and Dani rang from the station and Kit went off to

collect them. Laura laid the table, admiring the soft Georgian silver. The sound of happy shrieks from the garden drew her to the window. Remembering little Kaspar's innocent recoil last time he saw her, she put dark glasses over her jaundiced eyes and a cardigan over her thin and mottled arms. Bracing herself, she walked out into the sunlight.

I I

Constance Liddell

Often in the autumn mornings, when the sun shone through thinning trees and a white sky like a Chinese watercolour, Laura would wake with the childhood sense that another day of exciting possibilities had dawned. An unspecified memory would loom and she would be vaguely aware that something fearful had happened. Exactly what that was she had for the moment forgotten, and would try to go on forgetting, but within seconds she would remember – I am ill, mortally ill, I am dying! Nine months had passed since Mrs Ripa had broken the news, yet she continued to feel aghast, incredulous.

Like anyone condemned to death, she half-hoped for, even half-expected, a reprieve – a medical discovery, a breakthrough, a new drug, a liver that matched only hers. Or perhaps it was a false diagnosis all along. They had got her notes and tests mixed up with someone else's, and would write a deeply apologetic letter saying so – in which case, she thought, planning it all, I will be magnanimous and not sue, and even thank them, saying that the experience has taught me a lot, and I shall live differently in future. Her heart would lift and leap and begin to race, but then she would go into the bathroom and see her dull face, its orange skin and yellow eyes deeply underscored with grey, and the anchor of death would weigh her down again.

There were fewer and fewer people she wanted to see. It was a relief when Hugo Hammond anticipated her phone call to say that she was now too ill to travel with a letter (typed, of course, by his secretary, probably composed by her as well) regretting that due to a very heavy programme of official duties . . . blah blah – Laura skipped the details – he would not after all be able to offer the hospitality he had so looked forward to extending; meanwhile he and his wife both sent their warmest regards. Ah, the honeyed hypocrisy of the successful, she thought wryly.

Well, she would manage without Hugo. She had written to cancel Jürgen. Now there was only Desmond left, who had been her neighbour here in Markham Street for ten years. She planned to defer visiting him until the end of the year. They might spend Christmas together, a sort of parody Christmas, two single people round a stunted Christmas tree, but better than Christmas with her sister – if she lasted that long. She had always hated spending Christmas with Constance.

The only people she *must* see were her lawyer and her accountant; the only people she wanted to see were her women friends. Laura knew by now that she loved her sister with a deep, almost reluctant love, but she felt much more at ease with her friends. Constance, who gave love uncritically (like their mother) rather than as a reward for good behaviour (like their father) had always loved her younger sister and nowadays, judging by her solicitous telephone calls, she loved her more than ever. But did Constance *understand* her, know who she was? Could Constance begin to grasp the sort of life Laura had led, so different from her own? Could she accept everything and still forgive? If she could do *that*, Laura felt, then her sister's love would have proved itself. Before she died she craved that proof, and that forgiveness.

Laura lay on the yellow sofa overlooking the street, along which pedestrians were hurrying, heads down against a chilly wind. She had skipped lunch and was reading the paper, which carried appalling photographs of a plane crash in Amsterdam. An eyewitness recalled three or four seconds of screaming at the moment of impact as the plane hit a block of flats and dozens of people died simultaneously. After the sound of tearing metal and grinding wheels, according to the eyewitness, there was a deep, eerie silence.

Laura felt bile rise in her throat. She levered herself off the sofa and just managed to reach the bathroom before vomiting. She rinsed her acrid mouth and returned to the sofa.

In the foreign news pages, a survivor from the Serbian camps described men screaming all night as they were tortured to death. Laura imagined the moment when heart, brain and lungs, even with a young man's strength, could not function a second longer but must surrender, extinguished by cruelty. Why didn't *she* scream? Or did people scream only when they died suddenly or painfully? You couldn't scream for a year. She often wanted to scream at night, but you couldn't scream alone and screaming in company would be selfish, cowardly; it would alarm and embarrass people. Oh no, you couldn't *scream*.

The telephone rang. It was her sister. Constance had to come up to London on Wednesday: OK to drop in? She needed to do some shopping at John Lewis. Might just as well make it Peter Jones – same thing. She'd only be round the corner. No, not lunch – too much trouble. Just coffee would be super. Longing to see you. The brave, cheerful voice died away gradually, leaving Laura alone once again.

Laura thought, I was bridesmaid at her wedding: the only one. I was sixteen and she was twenty-two. I was glad she was marrying the man she loved and deserved: tall, dark and handsome, just right for my big sister, just what we'd predicted with daisies and prune-stones all those years ago. What an innocent I was – and Constance hardly less so!

She remembered one night in what was still known as the nursery, although Constance must have been twelve by that time. They had pooled their childish ignorance about sex and Constance had told Laura she was *pretty* sure the man didn't put his thing into your tummy button. *She* thought it went between your legs.

'What, where your penny comes out?' Laura – who was still called Stella in those days – had said, 'Yuk!'

They had examined each other's tender little parts to see if it were possible. Constance's looked like the inside of a walnut, divided into two wrinkly halves. Stella's was more like an apricot, with a soft fold. Neither seemed to offer a way in for a man's thing.

'Mummy calls Daddy's his dicky-bird!' Constance had whispered. Laura tittered and said, 'Does he peck a hole in her?' Then they both giggled, feeling warm and tingly.

She remembered urgent discussions later on in their shared bedroom in Kenya. Constance had explained how animals mated and little Stella had asked, 'But how do *people* get babies?'

Her sister answered – Laura remembered her heart thudding in excitement, horror and disbelief – 'Mummy and Daddy mated too. They had to mate to get us.'

'I don't believe you!' she scoffed, knowing all the time that it was true. She had watched the mangy dogs in the compound climb on to each other, the top one's back legs hopping along behind as the underneath dog tried to get away, then the top one holding tight while it bumped and shuddered. Then Mummy would come out and take her hand to show her something interesting in the house.

Laura had first realized that mating might not be disgusting after all when Constance brought Paul home for the first time – 'home' being the service flat off Sloane Square that her parents had taken between postings abroad. Even at the age of fifteen she saw straight away why her grown-up sister had fallen in love. Paul Liddell was tall and well-built, with a neck and shoulders like a young bull.

He was so clever that he had won a full scholarship to a public school, thanks to a personal recommendation from his parish priest. From the very beginning he had charmed her mother into overlooking the fact that socially he was NQOTD, as her parents would say, meaning 'Not quite our type, dear'. They had inquired casually where his parents lived and Paul said in a semi in Purley. Laura didn't know what a semi was and he explained – before her mother shushed her – that it was half a house.

'*We* haven't got a house at all,' Laura had told him. 'So you're half a one up on us anyhow! This poky old flat is rented and all *our* furniture's in store. Purley sounds lovely – like pearly gates.' Paul smiled his wide smile at her, and she glowed.

Hastily, her mother had offered Paul a sherry. Laura watched sidelong as he drank it and Constance sipped hers, with increasingly shiny eyes. Laura was full of pride in her clever sister, who not only passed exams and got into Oxford but could bring this glorious masculine creature home. Cold air emanated from his sports jacket into the stuffy, centrally heated atmosphere and his presence filled the room, as if some wild creature had been captured and was biding its time, reining in its natural untamed movements.

That first time, when Constance paraded him for the family's approval, he was asked only to stay for a drink before the two of them went off to the Royal Court to see some angry young man's play. Later he came for dinner, then supper, and then he and Constance would drop round casually for something to eat so that they could save money on a meal out. He turned up in jeans and chunky-knit sweaters and started to call her mother 'Paula' (at her flirtatious request), though he went on calling their father 'Mr King' or 'Sir'.

'Did you like Paul?' Constance had asked her sister after he had been round once or twice. Laura felt honoured at being consulted. 'I think he's terrific!' she said. '*Frightfully* good-looking. Is he absolutely potty about you? I bet he is. Go on. Own up. Has he kissed you yet? Oh tell me, Coco, do – what's it like?' Laura screwed up her face into a swoony expression and pursed her lips. 'Show me,' she persisted. 'Don't be a *spoil*sport. I want to *know*. Oh, you're so *lucky*. Nobody's ever kissed me except spotty Derek Phillips after the Lower Fifth's dance, and then I wouldn't let him open his mouth and things. Conce, I bet you and Paul do it *all the time*?'

'Stella!' Constance cried, amused by her younger sister's impatience. 'Take off that silly face, I'm not going to kiss you. All in good time. But yes' – she dropped her voice to a serious whisper – 'it's *lovely*, sweetie, absolute heavenly *bliss*.'

After that the Kings were posted abroad again, the service flat given up, and Laura seldom saw her sister except at the beginning and end of term, when Constance would sometimes collect her from the school train and take her to change out of the hated school uniform into her mufti before setting off to London airport to catch a flight to Hong Kong. In a Lyons corner house or the airport lounge they would have catching-up conversations about exams, and Paul.

One afternoon the sisters were alone together at Aunt Joyce's house in London, their aunt having gone to the hairdresser.

'Coco . . . Have you and Paul been to bed together yet?' Laura asked.

'I'm not answering – and it's jolly nosey of you to ask. It's a private matter between two people and nobody's business but their own.'

'Aha!' Laura exclaimed triumphantly. 'So you have! I promise – *promise* – not to tell Mummy. Was he the first?'

'Of *course*.' Constance answered, shocked. 'What do you think I am?'

'*Some* girls sleep with lots of people before they get married.'

'Well, not me. I'm not that type.'

'So you're engaged, then?'

'Actually, yes. But it's still unofficial, so *don't* tell Mummy and Daddy. Swear.'

'I swear. What's it *like*, Constance? Going all the way?'

Her sister considered carefully before replying. 'To tell you the absolute honest truth, it's not all *that* marvellous the first few times. You even wonder if you've actually done it – really finally *got* there. I was just as keen on, you know, snogging.'

'I *loved* snogging with Jamie Lockhart! He put his hand up my front at the last Christmas party and it felt simply gorgeous.'

'Heavens, don't tell Mummy! You're *far* too young for that.'

'No I'm not. I'm sixteen. Anyway it proves I know what you mean. Go on about being in bed with Paul.'

'I suppose it's something one does for the man. I don't mean it's not nice – it's actually beginning to be *very* nice – but Paul wants it much more than me. I worry a lot about getting pregnant but I couldn't tell lies and pretend we were married, so I can't get the cap and we have to do it with, you know, johnnies. The rubber things men use. They're pretty revolting, too.'

'What do you mean, *too*? I thought you said it was nice.'

'Listen, *you*, you ask too many questions. Now you have *promised* not to breathe a word, haven't you?'

'Solemnly, Guides' honour, on my oath, I swear.'

By the time Constance married, Laura had changed her name from Stella for good and bullied people till they accepted it. She had also been kissed a few times, manoeuvred behind the shrubbery at school dances by some damp-handed, sticky-haired boy who would beg her urgently, 'Please, just for a moment. God! You're so – oh, Laura, let me, let me . . .' There had been an embarrassing evening when a bachelor friend of her parents had taken her out to dinner and danced with her, stiff and clinging at the same time. He told her she was going to be a very beautiful young lady, if indeed she wasn't already, and she had had to lean back and giggle a lot to avoid being kissed by him.

Constance and Paul came down from Oxford the following summer: Constance with a First, Paul with a Third. They were married before the autumn so that they could live together in London where they were both starting their first jobs. Laura was bridesmaid, slim and starry-eyed in her short pink dress but completely outshone by Constance in full-length gauzy white.

Life quickly became serious and even drab for Constance. She conceived her first child almost at once – by accident, she told

Laura. So she gave up her job on a magazine and buckled down to young motherhood, which she described as nipples and nappies. She put on weight and the cheap skirts and slacks she had worn at university stretched and became sexless and shapeless. Paul meanwhile, because of his job in advertising, had to dress fashionably, which justified his buying sprigged Liberty lawn shirts worn under narrowly cut jackets, with tight trousers and high-sided Chelsea boots: polished, it turned out, by Constance. He looked far more attractive than his tired wife. When Laura commented on this, telling her sister to stand up for herself and insist that Paul buy her something new to wear, Constance laughed. 'In this family, I'm the peahen. But don't you think he looks gorgeous?'

I do, Laura thought, and by the time she was twenty she began to wonder who else thought so too. Paul flirted with a good many other women, and even *her* – out of sheer habit. But Constance was not unhappy. Far from it: she was deeply content with her home and her young children, and utterly happy with Paul. Laura assumed that her own ardent nature made her read too much into Paul's languid manner and his deep, dark-eyed glances. I'm sex-mad, she told herself. He smiles at everyone like that.

Paul had very white, straight teeth and a mannerism she had never seen in anyone else: he would smile while talking, in mid-sentence, which gave his words extra persuasiveness. She asked Constance if he knew he was doing it and Constance said, 'Of course! Everything Paul does is deliberate.'

'Does it ever worry you?' Laura inquired frankly.

Constance laughed. 'No, why should it? First of all, we're married and we love each other and Paul adores the babies, so if I spent my time being jealous he'd only think, "Might as well be hung for a sheep as for a lamb." Second, because it's to all our advantage. He's doing fabulously at the agency. They think he's the bee's knees. He got another rise this year – over 5 per cent – because he's so brilliant at his job. Crikey, I'm *delighted*. He can charm people as much as he likes, so long as he still charms me.'

'And does he?'

Constance leaned across from her dressing table to where Laura sat on the end of the big double bed. '*Yes!*' she said with great vehemence.

Laura thought, Well, that's all right then, and stopped wondering if anyone else basked in the glow of Paul's smile.

At university in the mid-Sixties she encountered very different sexual expectations from those which had governed Constance. The college doctor prescribed the Pill to anyone who asked for it. Within a few weeks of losing her virginity, Laura, pleading heavy periods, asked for it.

She slept with Hugo only a couple of times, but thereafter other men eyed her at parties as though aware of her changed status. A Hungarian refugee called Gabriel turned his liquid-black gaze in her direction and murmured seductively in bad English. She submitted to his melancholy caresses, and then to his very opposite, a pale young Englishman called Christopher Rumbold. Within a year of her first encounter she had been to bed with three different men and necked with several more. Constance would have been anxious, had she known, while her parents would have been incredulous and appalled.

A chasm opened up between Laura and her family. She became a stranger, full of secrets. Her carnal life was more various than her mother could have imagined 'in her wildest dreams' (as she would have said), while her father, had he known, would have been 'rocked to the core'. Constance was fortunate. She had only ever wanted to be Paul's wife. By the time Laura was in her twenties, falling in love and making love were crucial to her, and *passion* was the goal of her life. That central pursuit had never changed: the pursuit of passionate love and, much later, sex.

Love ruled her sister, too, but in her case it was love for her husband, her children, her parents and sister; and after them, love for humanity. Constance embodied the notion of a good woman, gentle, modest, self-effacing, and in addition to these qualities she possessed an intelligent heart. She was tender but never sentimental; conventional but never intolerant; imaginative but not in the least impressed by the new icons of the Sixties. Hippies and chanting gurus, the I-Ching and the Book of the Dead, psychedelic drugs – none held the slightest appeal for Constance. But if the PTA at her children's school needed a secretary, Constance would volunteer.

This very goodness proved to be the Achilles' heel of her marriage. Infidelity happened to other people, not to Constance, not by Paul. Sublimely she ignored the signs, even when they became so obvious that Laura was impelled to warn her sister that an affair rather than overwork might account for Paul's late nights.

Constance smiled effulgently and said, 'Sorry. You don't understand, Laura. I would *know* if Paul had been unfaithful. I'd know instinctively, at once. I know him so well.'

Laura was humiliated by such innocence. To the pure in heart, all things are pure.

When Laura embarked on her relationship with Kit, it had been enthusiastically promoted by her sister. Kit, Paul and Constance had been a threesome for several terms: the happy, loving couple accompanied by their envious, ambivalent friend. Constance retained a sisterly, almost proprietorial interest in Kit. She knew that he had been in love with her and never ceased to feel slightly sorry for him because she had rejected him. When Kit met Laura, Constance encouraged him to believe that her sister was keen to marry.

By the time Laura and Kit were invited to dinner as a couple, nothing could disguise the bleak indifference that Paul displayed towards Constance. He either ignored her or was irritated by her – though he was touchingly demonstrative towards their six-year-old, Katie, a gorgeous child with Paul's dark blue eyes and a round face illuminated most of the time by Paul's smile.

Some days after this dinner Paul telephoned Laura at work. This was not unusual: he had taken her out to lunch from time to time, showing off his expense account, inviting her to restaurants where the head waiter greeted him and the wine waiter deferred to his judgement. Laura was no longer tremendously impressed; tutored by Conrad and Edouard, she could have selected the Burgundy as knowledgeably as he. What made this invitation different was that for the first time he said, 'I'd rather you didn't mention it to Conce – this lunch, I mean.'

'All right, but why ever not?'

'Look, can I explain when we meet? Chez Solange do you? Just by Leicester Square tube station?'

'I know it. Cranborne Street exit.'

'That's the one.'

She knew then. She walked not blindly but knowingly to her fate. She willed it, welcomed it, ran into its arms. She had waited fifteen years for its embrace.

At lunchtime on Wednesday, the day on which Constance planned to visit Peter Jones and drop in on her sister, Laura's mother telephoned from Miami.

'Hello darling!' she cooed. 'It's a lovely morning here. Has Connie arrived yet? You're having lunch together, aren't you? I shall think of you both, my two girlies having a nice gossip.'

'Hello, Mother,' Laura answered wearily. 'You're up early.'

'I like the early mornings best. I walk along the beach before anyone else is up and watch the sea birds swoop over the waves catching fish. It's so quiet and beautiful at that time of day. I always liked mornings best. Do you remember, when we were in Kenya and Hong Kong, our breakfasts together on the verandah during your school holidays?'

'Yes, I do – oh, I *do* remember!' Laura said, and a ravenous nostalgia for her childhood engulfed her: for simplicity, innocence, certainty, health. Tears rose to her eyes. She tried to keep her words steady and casual. 'Are you playing bridge today?'

But across three and a half thousand miles, her mother detected the break in her voice. 'Oh my *baby*!' she cried, and they wept together, apart, on the telephone.

Constance arrived punctually at two o'clock. She scrutinized Laura. 'I think you're looking a bit *better*,' she said carefully, although in truth she was shocked by her sister's appearance. Laura was dying, there could no longer be any doubt of that.

'That's because I'm at home, I dare say. I've made up my mind: no more gallivanting. *Least* of all on Concorde.'

'What was New York like? I thought you were going to stay longer. Who was it this time? Anyone I've met?'

'Doubt it very much. Rafe Freeman. Raphael Friedmann.'

'Nope.'

'A snake. A polished snake. Coffee?'

'Let me do it.'

'It's already set up in the kitchen. Just needs boiling water.'

They sat in the plump comfort of Laura's deep armchairs and talked about Kaspar – the delight of Constance's life – until Laura asked about the Possleque. 'Are you going to marry him, Coco?'

'Laura, how unexpectedly conventional of you! Does it make any difference?'

'Yes. Funnily enough, at the end of my life . . .' Her sister winced, and so Laura amended her words. 'At my stage in life I rather think it does. The last few months have made me realize that I would give a lot to have a husband, even an *ex*-husband. Actually some of them have suggested it. Kit Mallinson for one.'

'*Kit?* What did you say?'

'Nothing, really. It wasn't a down-on-the-knees job, so I sort of let it pass.'

'Why *didn't* you marry Kit? I mean, originally.'

Laura thought, Because. Because he used Old Spice instead of Givenchy Gentleman. Because he was never more than a pale shadow of your husband, just as in his eyes I was never more than a pale shadow of you. Because his limbs were white sticks, and sea water ran in his veins, and I was *carnal*.

But all she said was, 'I don't know. Just because. Why don't you marry him now? He's still free, *and* he still hankers after you.'

'Because I've got the Possleque – and also, I suppose, for the same reasons that you didn't.'

'Do you call him the Possleque in bed? Do you say, "*There*, Possleque. Yes, go on, there, that's *lovely*!"'

'Good heavens, Laura, what an extraordinary thing to say!'

'No, but *do* you?'

'We don't in fact *talk* all that much in bed.'

'But you do, *do* it?'

'Oh yes, we do it all right.'

'I can say anything, you see, now that I'm dying. I'm licensed to do anything I like. Are you going to marry him?'

'Well, since you ask, I think probably not. No.'

'Why?'

'Because I still, deep down, feel as if Paul's my husband. In spite of the divorce, the decree absolute, his second wife, everything. He's the father of my children: that makes a tremendous difference.'

'Do you still love him?'

'In some ways yes, but it doesn't upset me any more. We were together all through Oxford and married for fifteen years. It's a huge chunk of my life. I still feel as though he is the man of my life. I think women only ever have one. Even you. You may have had a dozen lovers for all I know, but only one was the man of *your life*.'

'Mother rang before you came,' Laura said.

'I thought she might. How was she?'

'Fine. Chirpy. She cried. We both did. I cry frightfully easily these days. The tears just well and spill. I never used to be so weepy.'

They drank the tepid coffee. Laura heard about the children: their achievements, Constance's worries about their money problems.

'Coco, listen, *I* could help,' she said.

'Don't!' replied Constance. 'They'll manage. I shouldn't have mentioned it. They have to stand on their own feet.'

'Well, anyway, when I'm dead I want you to have my clothes. Might as well be decently dressed for the first time in your life, and it's either that or give them all to Oxfam!'

Constance winced.

Laura thought, When I'm dead the kids'll be all right money-wise. She wondered whether to tell her sister about the roulette win. She had arranged to have five thousand pounds paid into a trust fund for each of them. Constance might try to talk her out of it or suggest a different division of the spoils, and Laura no longer had the strength to argue.

When Constance inquired about her latest hospital appointment, Laura thought, Of course, she wants to know how long I have left. 'You can ask me, you know,' she said.

Constance looked startled. 'What?'

'How long they expect me to live.'

'Darling! I wouldn't dream of it.'

'Why not? Isn't it what you most want to know? *I* do.'

'They can't know exactly.'

'That's true. But I am – as you can see – going downhill quite fast. I lose over a kilo a week. They've given me a sort of revolting fattening liquid food, but what's the point?'

'Are you in pain?'

'Not all the time, thank God, apart from the infernal, eternal itching and a fairly dreadful ache in my gut – no, my *abdomen* I'm supposed to call it.'

'Does it keep you awake at night?'

'Used to. I've given in now. I knock myself out with sleeping pills.'

'Shouldn't you be in hospital?'

'Not yet. I'll stay at home as long as possible.'

'Do you want me to – oh, help, this is awful – do you want me to arrange a hospice?'

'I'd rather die on the ward, if they'll let me, among the people

I've got to know. My own consultant and so on.'

'I don't want you to die.'

'Big of you!'

'Laura.'

'I won't die just yet. Might make it to Christmas. That reminds me: what do you want for Christmas? I'd better order it now.'

'An exercise bike. I used to go to aerobics classes, but now I've got the Possleque there never seems to be time. You?'

'A pair of *very* high-heeled sandals with complicated straps. *Red*.'

Constance looked up in astonishment and then laughed. Laura laughed too and soon their laughter turned to hysterical giggles until they dared not catch one another's eye for fear of spluttering and shaking and giggling again, or weeping. Laura struggled for breath. Constance got up and changed the tape that was playing in the background.

'What do you want?'

'Anything. Mozart.'

'Laura. Sorry, but I must ask: should I summon Mother? When . . . ?'

'No. Only if you must. If *she* insists.'

'You're unfair to her. She'd never insist. Do you – oh, Christ, Laura – do you want *me* there?'

'*Yes*. Only you. *Yes*, Constance, please, I do.'

'Make sure the hospital knows . . .'

'Your number? They do already. You have to give next of kin and state your religion. I'm C of E and you're my next of kin.'

'Next of kin. Of course. Right, then. That's done. I must go soon. Trouble with men, they always want *supper*.'

'Coco . . . Just hold my hand for a minute. Nobody ever touches me any more, except the medics.'

Constance sat down on the arm of her chair. Laura held her sister's hand, warmer and rosier than hers. On the back of her own hand blue veins threaded through transparent skin and her fingernails had yellowed like her eyes. I have got so ugly, why should anyone want to touch me?

In the room Mozart played celestially. Beyond they could hear distant traffic streaming along the King's Road. Laura listened to the sound of her sister's breathing.

By the time Constance had left, Laura was exhausted, worn out by terror, apprehension and doubt, and by the effort of pretending not to feel any of these emotions. Slowly, she climbed the stairs up to her bedroom, noticing how hard she had to lean on the bannister. She drew the curtains against the early autumn dusk and slept. Twice the telephone rang and the answering machine in the hall recorded its messages. Her body, lacking any routine or discipline, rested whenever it could. When she woke, it was seven o'clock and nearly dark.

She rinsed her face and mouth in the bathroom. Peering in the mirror, she saw that she looked much older than her sister, although Constance was fifty-one and she herself, a year ago, could have passed for forty – or so she used to think. Dear God, such vanity! She dotted cologne round her throat and wrists, combed her hair and, switching on the lights, descended shakily to the basement kitchen. She was opening a tin of beef consommé when the front doorbell rang. A long pause, a long silence. She stood motionless. It rang again. Laura knew from experience that a caller standing at the top of the three steps to the front door would be invisible from the kitchen window. Could it be a special delivery parcel? Flowers? The bell rang again. Loud, urgent, insistent.

She went upstairs and peered through the spyhole in the front door. She could see a grey-haired man with bowed head. She switched on the outside light above the door and he swung his face up towards it. The man was Paul Liddell.

Speechlessly, Laura held the door open and he came in, shivering with cold. He slipped out of his overcoat and held up a plastic bag from which he produced a bottle of whisky.

'See?' he said. 'I brought my own booze.'

'I'm not allowed alcohol.'

'Conce told me. OK to hang my coat over the bannister? I rang and left two messages on your machine.'

'Oh?'

'Do you *want* to talk in the hall? We can, of course. Nice wallpaper.'

'Come in.'

'Cosy. Where are the glasses kept?'

'In the kitchen. I'll get one.'

'Let me.'

'*I'll go.*'

The drawing-room, bathed as always in apricot light, had never before contained Paul, though she had often imagined him there. She handed him a tumbler and placed a jug of iced water on the table beside him.

'You've aged,' she said mercilessly.

'That was you on the phone at Kit's, wasn't it? You said, "I'm sorry but he's out." Then you handed the phone to someone else.'

'I knew your voice at once, too.'

'Why didn't you say something?'

'We haven't spoken to each other for exactly thirteen years.'

'I know,' he said. 'Believe me, I fucking know *that*.'

He drank deeply from the tumbler of whisky. His face was haggard, his marvellous eyes hooded and wrinkled. He hunched in the chair. His shoes, she noticed, were scuffed, his trousers baggy and worn at the knees. He was thin.

'Of course I've bloody *aged*,' he said. 'Don't look at me like that. Mind if I have a fag?'

She thought, You are the man of my life.

She arrived at Chez Solange that wintry day in January 1978 to find him waiting for her. He stood up from the table, leaned across and kissed her fraternally on both cheeks. Givenchy Gentleman.

'*Love* the trouser suit,' he said. 'Jean Muir?'

'Oh, you clever thing.'

'Brand names. The account executive's great weakness. Used all Jean Muir on our last commercial. Now, then: a drink while you choose?'

'Is there a special reason for this lunch?'

'You know there is. Must I launch into my spiel straight away, or can you wait till pudding?'

The wide smile in mid-sentence. No: I am not going to be charmed. A waitress sashayed past and accidentally Paul's out-flung cigarette left a trace of ash on her rump.

'*Oh! Pardon!*' he said beautifully.

The waitress smiled and with a sideways inclination angled her hip towards him. He brushed the ash from her black wool haunch and she walked on, barely checking her stride.

Laura thought, You smoothie! She frowned and said, 'It must be about you and Constance.'

'Of course.'

'You've got a mistress.'

'*What* an old-fashioned term! But you're quite right. I *am* having an affair.'

'Not the first.'

'The first that makes me behave badly towards your sister.'

'Why?'

He offered her a cigarette, took one himself and lit both. 'Do you think Constance has changed?'

'Of *course* she's changed! She spends her life minding your children, doing your laundry, keeping your house in order – what do you expect? Intellectual fireworks? The Sensuous Woman? Linda Lovelace?'

'No. But it would be nice if when I came home in the evenings, she didn't *always* sit with her head buried in a book, or the latest batch of letters for Amnesty, or the PTA minutes. It would be nice if she didn't smell of washing-up liquid at best and old plimsolls at worst.'

'It might be nice if you bought her scent occasionally, or new clothes, or took her away for the weekend.'

'It would be nice if she made me want to.'

'So you take your mistress away instead.'

'Can't. She's married, too. Not all men have affairs with their secretaries.'

Yes, Laura thought, as the waiter slid a plate noiselessly in front of her, your mistress will be twice as sophisticated as my sister: highly paid, beautifully dressed, worldly, childless . . .

'Does she have children?'

'No, as a matter of fact.'

. . . childless, and she fancies you (as who would not?) and flatters you to death and does fascinating, dangerous things in bed.

'A wonder between the sheets?'

'That I decline to answer.'

'Why do you want to talk to me about her at all?'

In the pause that followed she watched him picking half-heartedly at his *escalope de veau*. She had little appetite herself. He laid down his knife and fork.

'Because I want you to talk to Conce. I do actually still love her, in a way, and I adore the children and I *don't* want our marriage to break up. But she must stop being so . . .'

'Devoted? Domesticated?'

'*No*. Drab. Depressed, defeated, down-trodden. For Christ's sake, we're not yet forty, either of us. I don't ask for glamour, but I don't see why my wife should look like a fifty-year-old! You're her sister: teach her how to use make-up, get her hair decently cut.'

'Is that all you want? A more acceptable spouse to show off at advertising award dinners?'

'Jesus, Laura, you've got a sharp tongue. I need some more wine. Will you have a glass too if I order a second bottle?'

By the time they left the restaurant, they were both fairly drunk. He had urged a final cognac, saying black coffee would neutralize its effect, which was a lie. Laura was high-coloured with the emotion evoked by her passionate defence of her sister, yet also by Paul's confession. The idea of him in bed with another woman disturbed her.

In the privacy of the taxi she leaned towards him and said blurrily, 'Why did you want to tell *me* about your affairs?'

He answered with sudden, teeth-clenching violence, 'Because I couldn't *stand* seeing you with that *wanker* Mallinson.'

She looked at him provocatively, fatally. 'Why not, Paul?'

'Because I want to *make love* to you *and I always have.*'

Impervious to the passengers peering down at them from a bus stuck beside their taxi in the traffic, Paul Liddell and his sister-in-law kissed as though no one had kissed before nor ever would again, as though the air-raid siren had gone off, the four-minute warning had sounded, the end of the world was nigh. He thrust one hand between her legs, the other held her breast; she clasped him, they groaned. When he left her in the taxi outside his office their faces were red and their mouths hot and wet, misshapen from kissing. They stared at one another wild-eyed and everything in their lives had changed.

'Conce told me you were dying,' he said. 'I couldn't believe it. I had to come and see for myself. But it is true.'

'Yes, as you see, it is true.'

They looked at each other from beneath their eyebrows, hardly wanting to look openly, such was the contrast between their present hollowed faces and the wanton young features of the past. Where Paul had once been extrovert and confident, his black hair springy with energy, he was now stooped and greying, his face drained, his expression one of bitter resignation. Laura's heart was liquid with pity for him. To stop herself breaking down she said briskly, 'I didn't know you and Constance kept so closely in touch.'

'Since my marriage to Lulu fucked up. You know she took the child and went back to her Mum in Leytonstone, leaving me on my own?'

'I heard about that. I'm sorry.'

'I was in a bad way. Times like that you find out who your real friends are. Good old Conce, stalwart to the last.'

'Are you still living in Holland? Amsterdam?'

'No choice. Post-Thatcherite Britain doesn't exactly welcome failed advertising execs. And Dutch social security's pretty good.'

He drained the tumbler of whisky and poured another.

'Do you always drink that much?'

'Yup. More, usually. I made a special effort to stay sober for you.'

'Since when?'

'Ooh, let's see now . . . started about thirteen years ago, I'd say. Slowed down when Lulu got pregnant and we married. Speeded up again after she fucked off. Now it's full-blown, like Aids.'

'You haven't . . .'

'I *haven't* got Aids, though God knows why not. Have you? Is that the real reason?'

'No. Go and have a look in the downstairs loo. I've got a letter from my consultant in there to prove it.'

Laura leaned her head against the back of the armchair and closed her eyes. She heard him light another cigarette.

'You'll have to go. I tire very quickly these days. I shall be asleep in a minute.'

'Let me watch you sleep. *Sleep, my baby, sleep so softly . . .*'

Hoarsely, he murmured the lullaby her mother used to sing to her, the one that she had heard Constance sing to their children. The simplest things conspired to remind her than he was her brother-in-law.

'Paul. Go away. Leave me alone. Please.'

'Can I come back? Tomorrow morning? I'll be sober.'

She could not refuse. 'Yes.'

She did not plan the words or frame them but her voice said, 'Hold me, Paul!'

He lurched from the chair, knelt at her feet, clutched her knees. She sat forward, laid her head on his shoulder, put her arms round him and they held each other.

He telephoned the evening after their lunch at Chez Solange.

'Laura.'

'Where are you?'

'At the office. Are you alone?'

'Yes.'

'Can I come round?'

'Yes.'

He arrived without flowers or excuses, he did not lay claim to guilt or prevarication, they did not mention Constance or the children. By the time he arrived, Laura had already taken the phone off the hook. She double-locked the door behind him and switched off the light in the hall. She led him to her bedroom, sat down on the bed and watched, dry-mouthed, while he took off his clothes.

That was six months after her thirtieth birthday. In the space of the next year, Laura learned all she would ever know about passion – among other things that neither Conrad nor Edouard nor any other man had begun to release it in her. She was astonished that her body continued to function in public as if nothing were happening. The bedroom became such a magnet, so much the centre of her life, that, going to put a bottle of milk away in the fridge, she would find herself carrying it into the bedroom instead, as though every impulse and every thought led there.

After a long, ardent night she could not imagine how other people underwent such powerful experiences, such physical up-heaval, such stretching of limbs and body, yet still behaved normally next day. She would watch people in the agency or the interpreters' rest room at a conference – some diligent, dowdy woman greedily devouring an éclair with her morning coffee or sucking a pencil while she listened to the phone – and think,

Does *she* do the things that I do to Paul, for Paul, with Paul; and does her lover do the things Paul does to me? Do her nipples burn between his lips, her breasts rise to meet him? Does she liquefy and gasp at his touch and his tongue? Does his body crush her, hard and heavy and rough against her smoothness, and does she make my strange guttural noises? If everyone does these things, all the thrashing and probing things, the searching into every orifice with lips, tongue and fingers, how do they appear so ordinary, how *can* they bicker about whose turn it is to make coffee or do the first session after lunch?

Yet like everyone else, Laura tamed her wildly branching night-time self into a quiet workaday creature. One thing she could not tame. However thoroughly she washed herself, whenever she went to the lavatory the faint but unmistakable smell of sex would reach her nostrils, the smell, sour and unique, of what she had had and would have again.

Nothing could have prepared her for such power. Conrad's love-making had been fastidious, scientific, dry, cool and detached. Only by hurting her, demonstrating his capacity to cause pain – since, as she now realized, he must always have known that he did not give her pleasure – could he excite himself. She told Paul about Conrad and he, outraged that she had allowed herself to be hurt for years, made her swear never to sleep with Conrad again. Laura in any case could not now allow anyone but Paul to make love to her. She wrote one letter to Conrad, who did not reply, and never went to bed with him again.

The things she did with Paul and let him do to her would have seemed disgusting except in the heat of passion, but they were never cruel. She never did anything against her will, and as liquid flowed from her, her mouth wet with saliva, her fingers sticky with juice, her body damp with sweat, her hair wringing, their bodies gluing and ungluing, she willed everything she did, following where he led and forging ahead of him, demanding this – and this – and that frenzied, unthinkable, unimaginable act. He brought visions to her mind, which sometimes made her say strange things. 'Oh, my silver-sticked, top-hatted lover!' she would cry, and then demand, 'Fuck me, oh fuck me, yes *fuck me*, my *Paul*!'

She knew that she was propelled by the primal sin of incest. What Paul had loved in Constance, what Constance had responded to in Paul, reached its perfection in Paul and Laura. It was in the genes that they should love each other. The same impulses programmed into both sisters, Constance and Laura – Laura even when Stella – were magnified by Paul. Actions that her conscience would have rejected – *had* rejected for fifteen years – in the temperate zone of family life were transformed and made possible by the tropical heat of sexual passion. Laura had spent her life searching for this, and for him.

Laura knew that what she was doing was wicked and still she did it, whenever and wherever she could. In her own bed, hotly or languorously; on the floor behind the locked door of Paul's office, hastily, so that her spine was rubbed raw by the coarse carpet underneath her; in taxis, incompletely; hotels, occasionally; car parks, desperately – they made love. Once, when Constance had taken the children home to her parents for a weekend (who were Laura's parents too), she and Paul even made love in the marital bed.

'A standing prick has no conscience,' he said.

Laura replied, 'That's such a cheap cliché! There is no excuse for what we're doing. Constance could never forgive us. It would destroy her, or she would murder us. And she would be justified.'

'I know.'

'You must never tell her – not in anger, revenge, weakness: you must never, never confess. Paul! Do you swear to me?'

'I promise. *Never.*'

'And nor will I. I swear to you. Nor will I ever tell anyone else.'

'She may still find out. Someone may see us lunching together, or me turning up at your flat.'

'So what?' Laura said. 'She knows you have always given me lunch from time to time. You could be mending something for me at the flat. It wouldn't cross her mind that there was anything suspicious about our being together.'

'My angel,' he said. 'You look so beautiful when you are concerned. You are my only, only love.'

Whatever happens for the rest of my life, Laura thought, I have experienced passion. I know the hollowness of its cinematic images – as though *Last Tango in Paris* or *Emmanuelle* could begin to depict what we have! – and the dishonesty of the romantic version, which is as feeble as chocolate-box kittens beside a tigress. When I die, I shall not regret this. I know perfectly well the enormity of my betrayal of Constance and her children and even my parents, but I cannot say I am sorry, for I never want it to stop. For fifteen years I have waited for Paul and for this rank and carnal ecstasy.

After some months Constance confided in Laura that she felt sure her husband was – she didn't say 'having an affair', Laura noticed with leaping heart – 'in love with another woman'.

'He's all moony and loony, mopes about distracted, doesn't listen, can't concentrate. I know he works desperately hard – the agency's planning some big takeover that involves him – but this is different. I don't know what to do.'

'Do nothing,' Laura counselled, unable to add, 'It'll pass' or 'I'm sure it's not important' or any other stock phrases of comfort.

A few weeks later her mother came up to London and asked if she could spend the night at the flat with Laura.

'I'm worried about Paul and Connie,' she confided over supper. 'Constance is so loyal, but I can tell she's terribly unhappy. She's lost her bloom. Paul's an attractive man, and men like him tend to stray . . . What do you think, darling? Are husbands faithful nowadays?'

'Not very often,' Laura said.

'There are so many divorces,' Mrs King bewailed. 'They

should never have changed the law. If you make it easy for men, of *course* they'll go off with some younger and prettier woman. Men are like that. In our day marriage was for ever. People might not always have been happy, but they stuck it out. What should I advise poor Connie?'

'To stick it out, if that's what you believe,' Laura said. Constance duly stuck it out - not because of her mother's advice, but because it was in her nature, and because she loved her children, and her husband.

They had been lovers for more than a year. It was midnight and Paul was dressing to drive back home when he suddenly said to Laura as she drowsed in the tangled bed, her face reddened with kisses, her eyes heavy with satiety, 'This is madness. My life has become a total fiction. I feel like a schizophrenic. I lie to everyone: Constance, the children, people at work, clients . . . You have become the only person I ever tell the truth to. At this rate I shall crack up. Do you know that I have to keep a false diary to remind me of the lies I've told? It's driving me crazy, it doesn't help Constance and it must be bad for the children. I've made up my mind to leave her.'

'Where will you go? You couldn't live here.'

'Anywhere. I'll rent a flat – buy one, – borrow one. I don't care. I've got to get out. We'll go away – abroad. You can work anywhere and so can I. I love you. I can't live without you. I'm going mad.'

'Yes. So am I.'

Two months later he left, having salved his conscience a little by completing the purchase of a house for Constance and the children, larger than any they'd had before or ever imagined owning. Paul left her in possession. He had scarcely spent ten nights under its roof.

The next morning at nine o'clock, when the children had gone to school, Constance rang her sister.

'Paul's left me,' she said, dry-eyed.

'I know,' Laura answered. Never lie unless you must.

'You *know*? How?'

'Paul told me.'

'How did he sound?'

'Distraught.'

'He's been like a madman for the last six months. Sometimes I've feared for his sanity. If I could get hold of this woman I'd kill her.'

'I know.'

'Oh Laur' . . . do you have to work today? Can you come round? The house is upside down and so am I. Mother's quite hysterical.'

'I'll be there as soon as I can. I'll get a taxi.'

The house was piled with tea-chests, heaps of books tottering unsorted in the dining-room, half the kitchen equipment still packed away. Only the children's bedrooms were more or less normal. Constance wore a white boiler suit of the kind painters and decorators use. She looked shapeless and neuter.

'Where's Paul?' Laura asked.

'Gone to work. He says he's going to look for a flat. Meanwhile if I want to talk to him I have to ring him at the office. For some reason he can't live with *her*. I suppose she's married too. Oh Laura, he's my husband – their father – and we love him so much! How can we live without him? What am I to do?'

Laura rocked her sister in her arms. Ours are the bodies that Paul has held, she thought, the rhythm pounding like a nursery rhyme in her head. *These* are the *bo*dies that *Paul* has *held*! Constance was weeping and her blotched face was hideous, swollen and sweaty with pain and tears. Her clenched hands were sticky. She looked a cruel parody of a woman after sex.

'Laura, oh Laura, what shall I *do*?'

The pointless, unanswerable question.

'Sshh . . .' Laura said. Her head swarmed with pictures of the punishments she deserved for her lust. I should be put in a ducking stool and humiliated before drowning; sat in the stocks and pelted; my forehead should be branded 'A' for Adulteress and my arm tattooed 'T' for Traitor and my breasts 'W' for Whore.

'Ssh, Coco, there there.'

'What shall I *do*? How shall I *live*?'

'You'll live,' Laura replied. 'You have to. For the children.'

'I haven't told them yet, though Max and Cordy must suspect. I've just said Daddy has to go away on business.'

'That'll do, for the time being.'

'How can I tell them?'

'Maybe *he* will.'

'He'd never do it. No, I'll have to.'

'Wait a bit. Oh, darling . . . Oh, Conce, I hate to see you suffer!'

They wept in each other's arms and Laura thought, I should cut off my breasts and gouge out my vagina for having brought her to this. Yet she knew she would not give up Paul.

He came back to the house in Markham Street next morning, as he had promised; sober but no less sunken-cheeked and hardly less unkempt. Laura had taken a sleeping pill the night before, and her movements were slow and heavy, her eyes dull.

'How did you catch this thing, this . . . liver disease?' he asked. 'Did you drink a lot? You never used to.'

'Probably abroad. In fact it may have started in Africa when I was a kid, and bided its time. After that . . . China, Soviet Union – anywhere the water's not clean. Who knows? And I got lazy about my hepatitis jabs. For quite a long time, you know, I didn't much want to live.'

'How long have you had it?'

'Who knows? The diagnosis was confirmed in January.'

'They do liver transplants these days.'

'Not on me they won't. I have low social priority.'

He looked around the room, taking in her pictures and ornaments, the expensive lighting and good furniture. 'I'd have thought you could afford to go private.'

'I could. I won't.'

'Why not?'

'*Because I deserve to die*. Why do you drink so much? Same reason.'

He hung his head, fumbled for a cigarette, inhaled deeply and blew out the smoke in a long, old-fashioned vee.

'Do you regret it?'

'I won't answer that,' she said.

'So you do?'

'I won't answer.'

'I lost my wife, my kids, my home, my job, my self-respect, my friends, and you won't tell me whether you regret having loved me?'

'Did Constance ever know?'

'Not from me. Kept my promise. No, I doubt if she knows. Nor do I think the children ever sussed. So now you regret it. I need a drink. Is there anything in the house?'

'What do you want?'

'Scotch.'

She stood up, and retched. She staggered to the downstairs lavatory and he heard her throw up violently, heaving and choking. He got up and walked downstairs, past the bathroom, to the kitchen and found the drinks cupboard. He gulped a draught of whisky straight from the bottle, then took a glass and a jug of water back upstairs.

Paul's agency, by the end of the Seventies, had done well. He and two others set up their own company, taking with them the best of the young lions by the simple expedient of offering to double their salaries – which few could resist. Once he had left his wife and children, Paul seemed to abandon all ethical constraints. He became ruthless and implacable, poaching accounts from former colleagues who had trusted him. In his late thirties, Paul's talent grew and became more original, at the very time when originality was most prized. If he thought the agency could win an account by making their pitch in the form of a song-and-dance routine, Paul would write it brilliantly and persuade others to perform it with him. His charm was now directed chiefly towards professional ends, and the shock of black hair and mid-sentence smile, along with a newly confident manner, were hard to resist. His passion for Laura protected him from sexual distraction.

He rented a flat in Chelsea not far from hers, to which the children sometimes came at weekends. What could be more natural than that he should bring them over to have lunch with Auntie Laura? They were children; why should they suspect? And if they told their mother – well, it mattered not in the least. She knew Paul couldn't cook.

Even so, it was a relief when Laura found herself working abroad more and more often. Her fluency in three languages plus her expertise in two more, combined with her availability and willingness to travel, made her highly sought-after and extremely well-paid. Paul could frequently justify flying to New York, Paris or Rome for the weekend on expenses – a client to visit, a new account to check out. They loved each other and only the fear of discovery dogged them. They were never safe. At any restaurant or café, no matter where, they might bump into a friend who would betray their secret. They perpetually feared disclosure. Paul suffered nightmares, and Laura's imagination was equal to anything his unconscious mind could project.

Once Paul had gone, Constance began gradually, half-heartedly, to adjust to her new single status. She found a job in the local library which helped to distract her. She was not happy, but she had ceased – Laura and her mother agreed – to be miserably unhappy.

'She'll marry again,' Mrs King began to predict. 'She's made to be some lucky man's wife. Then that bastard will realize what he's lost! Serve him right. Do *you* ever hear from him?'

'He brings the children round for lunch on Sundays quite often,' Laura replied.

'Has he got a new girlfriend?' her mother inquired conspiratorially. 'I'm sure he has. He's still very attractive, blast him!'

'I imagine so,' Laura answered.

'Well, she'll find out what he's like,' said her mother vengefully. 'What about you, Laura? *You* haven't brought any nice men home lately. Is there anyone on the horizon? You can't afford to waste any time, you know ... Make sure you don't leave it too long. Oh,' she sighed wistfully, 'Daddy and I would love another grandchild! A new baby to cuddle!'

'Yes, Mother.'

Laura realized that the nature of her relationship with Paul – dangerous, incestuous, taboo – prevented it from ever becoming dull. They were together, yet seemingly far apart. They could not do the most banal things together. They never stood in a cinema queue holding hands or shared a supermarket trolley; they could not go to parties together or arrive as a couple at dinner. It was rare for them to be able to spend more than two successive nights together. This fuelled their mutual desire, which after making love – how many? five hundred times? – was unchanged. Laura doubted if after this fragile balance of having him and not having him, the tension between the imperative need for secrecy and their sexual need for each other, she could ever settle down to an everyday, comfortable relationship, sanctioned by society, approved by her parents, an ordinary English marriage.

Paul found himself avidly pursued by female colleagues at the agency, clients, strangers he met at parties or in restaurants. Aware of his professional success, his flat, his car, they issued subtle or blatant invitations. They were liberated women who no longer waited for a man to make the first move. He never told Laura, knowing her sexual antennae to be far more highly tuned than Constance's. Then, at the age of thirty-two, Laura discovered she was pregnant.

When she had finished being sick, she rinsed her mouth and

came back to the drawing-room where Paul sat in a deep chair, a cigarette in one hand, a whisky in the other.

'You'll have to go in a minute. My cleaner's due soon.'

'She won't know me.'

'She might. You look very like Max, and she's met Max.'

'Does it matter any longer?'

'*Of course it matters!*'

'I haven't anywhere to go. I spent last night in a crummy b & b. I came to London to see you.'

'Before I die.'

'Yes.'

'What do you want?'

'This.'

'*What?*'

'This. I want you to leave me your house. I want to come back to England. I'm sick of Holland, sick of living abroad, sick of scraping along the bottom. I could make a new start here. I promise to hand it on to the children in due course.'

'Paul, are you mad? Why should I?'

'I lost everything, after you . . . Oh, Laura, I didn't come here to quarrel. I have no recriminations and no regrets. I don't blame you. I'm asking: let me have this house. I would be near my children. I could get a job.'

'If I left it to you, Constance would want to know why.'

'You can say something, make something up. It's only temporary.'

'You'll live another twenty years. Alcoholics always do. They *never* die.'

'Do you want me to die?'

'No!'

At the sound of a key turning in the front door Laura levered herself off the sofa and went into the hall.

'Morning, Carmen. I have a friend visiting me. Can you start with my bedroom, then the bathrooms?'

'OK, Laura. Is good. You want coffee, cakes?'

'Nothing, thank you.'

She came back into the drawing-room and he said bitterly, 'A *friend*? Is that what I am?'

Laura lay down on the sofa, while Paul poured another drink, lit another cigarette. She gazed at him, adapting, accepting everything.

'Paul. It's so long ago. A lot has happened since then. But you were my only love. You are the man of my life. We wrecked each other's lives, didn't we? I aborted my only child to keep our secret. I won't risk it now. I'll give you money, if you like – I had a big win at Monte Carlo a few weeks ago: I can give you nearly twenty thousand pounds. I don't know what you'll do with it and I don't really care. But I *can't* give you this house and you must go away now.'

'*Am* I the man of your life?'

'Oh, Paul, of course. How could I love like that twice? Did you?'

He looked across at her, his eyes burning. 'Do you still love me?'

'Is this a catechism?'

'Fifteen years we waited, Laura, for less than two years together. And now I've waited nearly as long again to see you. I want to make love to you.'

Who else, she thought, if not you?

'I'm hideous, Paul. Look at me. Swollen, bruised; I'm covered with huge, distended veins. I bleed at a touch.'

'I've seen cirrhosis before. To me you look the way you did when you were pregnant with my baby.'

'That's a cruel as well as a sentimental thing to say.'

'All right, I'm sorry. But let me come back. My darling. Let me stay with you tonight.'

'Yes. Eight o'clock. Now go away.'

She had missed a couple of periods and started being sick in the mornings. Her stomach became rigid and occasionally painful, as were her breasts. So certain was she of the Pill's prophylactic power that it did not occur to Laura that she might be pregnant. She assumed she had some sort of minor gynaecological problem and rather then waste time with a referral from her GP, she took herself straight to Casualty at the Soho Hospital for Women. It was the lunch hour. She was due to fly to New York in a few days' time for a fortnight's contract at the United Nations. Best clear it up before I leave, she thought. No point in paying American medical bills – cost a fortune.

She was seen by a briskly efficient young doctor, who listened to her symptoms and then examined her, first externally, then internally, and then both together, one hand palpating her abdomen, the other exploring gently inside. Laura lay back, sensible and passive. Abcess, she wondered. Cyst? Polyps? What female complaint have I developed, and will it mean Paul and I can't make love tonight?

The young doctor straightened up. 'OK, you can sit up now,' he told her. Laura swung her legs over the side of the couch.

'It's perfectly simple ... You're about twelve weeks pregnant.'

'Sorry. Say that again.'

'Twelve weeks gone in pregnancy, I'd say. Possibly thirteen. Hard to be precise. It's your first, isn't it? Not married? Is it such a surprise?'

'Surprise?' she said. 'It's a *miracle*! Pregnant? Halleluia!'

He grinned at her. 'Well, that makes a change. Not many of the women coming in here react like you.'

Laura repeated, 'Pregnant? Oh, golly!' Her face was split by a wide smile that she could not control.

'Got a steady boyfriend?'

'Oh, yes.'

'That's all right, then. Think he'll be pleased, too?'

'I don't know. I'll have to see what he says. *Pregnant!*'

'How old are you again?'

'Thirty-two. Yesterday, as it happens. When's the baby due?'

'About the end of January. Get yourself booked into a hospital . . .' She hardly heard what he said. She walked out into the sunshine of Soho Square buoyant, exultant, pregnant.

She rang Paul at the agency and spoke to his secretary. 'Please ask him to call his sister-in-law at home.' When Paul telephoned she said, 'Oh, my love, *good* news, but we need to discuss it. No, I can't tell you over the phone. Can you come round? Now? How soon?' She had told him about her appointment at the hospital but he had evidently forgotten.

He said in a business-like voice, 'I've got a client meeting at four. Last an hour or two. Then I ought to take them out for a drink. Eight o'clock too late?'

'Make it earlier if you can. I love you.'

'Me too.'

She had gone home, and cancelled her two weeks in New York. Then she undressed and looked at herself in the long mirror in her bedroom. Her breasts, she now saw, were fuller than usual, the nipples brown and prominent. Her belly was slightly more convex – surely – than before. She stood sideways and scrutinized her profile. An infinitely gentle curve swelled outwards from her rib-cage and declined inwards, disappearing into her pubic hair. She said aloud, 'Paul, darling, we're going to have a baby!'

She tried it another way. 'Mummy – brace yourself, sweetie – I'm expecting a baby!'

How about, 'Constance, what do you think of this? I'm expecting a baby in January. The father? Oh, darling – just someone. I'm not going to marry him. The main thing is . . .'

Or even, 'Hey, Cordy, guess what? Your Aunt Laura's got herself pregnant!'

Paul came to her flat soon after eight, bright-eyed and garrulous, brandishing a bottle of champagne.

'Clinched it! Great new deal! Bloke from Simon & Sinclair's a total wally . . . Sorry, sweetheart. Tell me the good news. What's happened?'

Her mouth went dry and she could not, for a moment, speak. He put his arms round her. 'What's wrong, love? My darling? Isn't it good news? Tell.'

'Paul, I'm pregnant. I didn't mean to, it was an accident, but I'm going to have a baby.'

'Oh, fuck,' he said involuntarily. 'Fuck me! Bloody hell. A baby.'

He wrenched the cork out of the champagne bottle. Laura held a glass towards him as the champagne spilled over, running in a bubbly trickle down its sparkling transparent sides. She cradled the glass, feeling the liquid moisten her fingers, and held it up.

'Cheers,' she said.

Two weeks later she went to Gatwick to see her parents off on their holiday to Greece. Her mother fussed about getting to the airport in good time: 'They like you to be there two hours before departure at least.' Laura, who never arrived more than forty minutes before take-off, controlled her exasperation. Her father, she noticed, was stooped and his sparse hair was nearly white. He had aged. She took the larger suitcase from him despite his protests, and found a trolley. When her parents had checked in their luggage, they went and sat in the café on the upper floor, watching people milling about below.

'It's not like you to drink tea!' her mother said. 'I thought you were a coffee addict!'

Her father craned to read the departures board. 'Don't *worry*, Daddy.' Laura said. 'I won't let you miss it.'

'You can't write to us,' her mother said, 'but we'll send you lots of postcards. PPPs.' They all smiled at the old family joke.

Laura embraced them and watched as they held out their boarding cards for inspection. Her mother turned again just before disappearing.

'Take care of yourself, darling!' she called.

Her father turned too. 'Stop *fussing*, Mummy!' he said, and winked at Laura. 'Bye, Laura.'

'Goodbye,' she said to their backs. Goodbye, goodbye, and baby says goodbye, too.

A week later Constance phoned, her voice clogged with tears. 'Oh, God, Laura, – prepare yourself – sit down – it's terrible, awful, they've been in a car crash and Daddy's not expected to live! The British consul from Thessalonika rang just now. Oh, Laura, *Daddy* . . .' she choked and groaned – 'is going to *die*.'

Laura sat down. Her face felt as though it had contracted stiffly inwards and her stomach fluttered oddly. The child leaped in her womb, she thought.

'And Mummy?' she said.

'Injured, but by a miracle not nearly so seriously. I'm ringing her at the hospital in five minutes. I booked a call. I wanted to tell you first. Oh, Laura, Laura!'

'He might not die.' Laura said.

'The consul – I can't remember his name – said we should be prepared. I think he was breaking the news gently.'

'Oh, Coco . . . Oh, Jesus, what else?'

Constance flew out to Greece, dealt with the hospital and organized the paperwork, booked a flight and, with her mother, escorted the coffin home. Laura watched from the observation area as the two figures dressed in black walked slowly across the tarmac. She would have liked a Union Jack to be draped over his coffin – her decent, dutiful, patriotic father, who had spent a lifetime in the colonial service – but they only did that for people killed in the course of duty. Not for a stupid car accident caused by two crazy Greek youths showing off, racing down a cliff road, not looking where they were going, careening into the slow, careful oncoming hired car. Again she felt her stomach contract, and did not know if it were sorrow or the baby.

At the funeral they all met for the first time since Paul and Constance had separated. Laura did not look at him. She and her sister flanked their mother, Paul following behind with the children. It was a month since she had discovered she was pregnant. Life ends, life starts. How sad that Daddy never knew about the baby. What would he have said? The singing faltered around her. She could hear Katie's young voice soaring confidently, and Max's half-broken adolescent mutter. She stood very straight in the front row so as to conceal the swelling bulge, gazing fixedly at her father's coffin, thinking, Don't cry, don't cry; if I cry, Mummy'll cry and she needs to be told she was brave and he would have been proud of her. Paul stood directly behind her. His child leaped, impervious, in her womb.

Paul had refused to discuss an abortion. 'It's entirely up to you,' he insisted. 'Your decision, your body. A woman's right to choose.'

'Do you *want* a child? With me?'

'I adore children, as you know. We can certainly afford it. But you must make up your own mind. I'll support you either way.' She fantasized about disappearing, like Lord Lucan. She and Paul could go and live in Kenya or Hong Kong; set up a new life, marry, have their baby, become normal human beings, a family. The word tolled like a leaden bell: family, family, the burden they could not put down.

After the funeral Constance suggested that she and Laura should take it in turns to spend weekends with their mother while she made up her mind whether to stay in the house in Somerset or sell it and move closer to her daughters. Constance and Katie went down for the first weekend and busied themselves sorting out his clothes while his widow told an anecdote to go with each garment. Memory was stuffed into plastic bags and taken to a charity shop.

'She keeps saying, "Three-score years and ten was Daddy's allotted span,"' Constance reported back. 'She's desperately stoical. I think she's fine while we do this kind of church fête stuff, she's used to all that and she goes through the motions, being beautifully mannered and not letting herself think. There's bound to be a delayed shock reaction soon. Do you want to take Max or Cordy down with you this weekend?'

'No,' Laura said. 'I'll cope on my own.'

The low red-brick house still smelled of her father's presence. Laura kept on hallucinating the bowed figure of her father rising courteously from his winged armchair to greet her as she entered the room, or his apologetic intrusions into the kitchen: 'Sorry to bother you, darling, but could I have a coffee?' She saw him everywhere: in the garden, astride the motor-mower; at the head of the table, carving; sitting in his favourite chair, reading or 'zizzing', as he called it, after lunch.

She felt a cavernous sense of loss, as though her heart or lungs had been ripped out leaving her rib-cage empty. Her balance, so precarious of late, depended on his steady gaze and predictable view of the world. His priorities had never changed from the simple Church of England morality inculcated in his childhood. She was certain that, had he known about her pregnancy, he would have said, 'A life must never be taken: least of all a new, innocent life.' On the strength of that conviction she made up her mind that whatever catastrophes lay ahead, she would keep her baby.

But after two days busying herself about the house, going through her father's papers (they were in apple-pie order, as befitted a civil servant) her mother suddenly said, 'Laura! Do that again! Turn round like that!'

Laura turned swiftly to see what her mother meant, and the loose overshirt wrapped itself treacherously round her belly.

'Darling! *Surely* – I can't be wrong – you're expecting a *baby*?'

Laura met her mother's eyes and could not hold back a great smile. 'Oh Mummy,' she said, her voice breaking like a wave with the relief of admitting it. 'Yes! I am!'

They hugged with tears on their faces and her mother said that Daddy would have been a bit shocked – 'You must forgive us, Laura, we're old-fashioned enough to believe in marriage' – but once he'd got used to the idea, of course he would have welcomed a new baby in the family.

'Are you going to get married? We never knew you had a boyfriend, Laura dear, though we often wondered.'

She could have lied. She might have invented a man who had left her when he heard the news, or a married man who refused to give up his wife. She could have devised any number of fictions to deflect her mother. Instead she said, 'I can't tell you that, Mummy. Believe me, I can't. Don't press me: I just can't. What matters is that the baby's due in January and I'm overjoyed.'

'Have you discussed this with Connie yet? You must have done. Why didn't she tell me? What does she say? Does *she* know who the man is?'

'No.'

'Not your *sister*?'

Laura was emotionally worn out, vulnerable, unguarded. She said, '*Least* of all her!'

Her mother was raw and unusually highly tuned or she would never have read between the lines, behind the words. She said, 'It must be Paul. *Laura* . . . the baby's father is *Paul*, isn't it?'

They looked at each other with stricken faces. Her mother saw that she had uttered the truth, named the one unthinkable man.

'*No*, Laura. Oh no. No, no.' She shook her head to and fro. 'No, no, *no*.'

Not in each other's arms this time, but separately, Laura wept with guilt and remorse, with longing for her baby, for Paul, for an end to secrecy. Her mother wept with shame and grief, for her loneliness in the first crisis without her husband, for his death and the imminent loss of her unknown, unborn, doomed grandchild. Her tears became rage and she turned on Laura savagely.

'*Pull* yourself together and stop that howling. You have committed a dreadful sin and your poor innocent little baby must suffer for it. Well, you should have thought of that. I will *not* let Constance, or Cordy and Max and Katie, be hurt. You must have been *mad* to think you could get away with this! Your child by Paul is practically their sister – or brother. It would look exactly like them! And you thought no one need know? You must be not only wicked but mad, Laura. Utterly crazy. Tomorrow, first thing, you book an appointment at the London Clinic. If you don't *I will*.'

Even when they had tidied themselves up, restored the appearance of order and control, made supper, and were sitting opposite each other in the big, Aga-warmed kitchen, her mother was still adamant. There could be no possible argument. Laura must abort.

'Thank God there's still time! How far gone did you say you are? Due in January . . .' She counted backwards on her fingers in the age-old reckoning of gestation: 'January, December, November, October, September – five months, about twenty weeks. Just in time.'

Laura would never have guessed that her mother could be so stubborn. She was ruthless, implacable, her face set like a rock.

Much later, Laura realized that, newly bereaved, her world scattered like a burgled house by the suddenness of her loss and sorrow, her mother was literally out of her mind; nor was she herself quite sane. At the time there seemed no alternative but to obey. She rang the London Clinic, booked a consultation, was assured by a mellifluous voice that 'if it turned out to be necessary' she could be dealt with and 'the problem solved' the same day.

A week later she was indeed in and out of the Clinic within a day. A great pain lay in wait behind her drugged numbness, as though some vital organ had been torn out of her tender body by gleaming steel jaws.

She told Paul what she had done only when it was done, and glimpsed the moment of sheer relief that he could not suppress. That apart, he behaved most tenderly. He clasped and comforted her, sent huge bunches of flowers for weeks afterwards. He took her out to dinner more publicly than ever before, booked them into a suite at the Cipriani in Venice for a weekend; he even accepted that she did not want to make love for the time being.

But he did not guess, although Laura had realized at once, that with the death of her father and the killing of her child, something had gone for good. Decency, probity, innocence, perhaps; the capacity for trust or simply the hope of ever being ordinarily happy. Laura knew she would never have a clear conscience again, or try to live according to her father's morality: the simple rules her mother and her sister had always stuck to, the rules Constance's children had been brought up to believe in.

She performed one final virtuous act. Decisively, without tears or melodrama or passion, she told Paul at the end of October, two months after her father had died, six weeks after the abortion, that their affair was over. 'I shall never see you again.'

She dozed the rest of the day away after he had gone. Carmen put clean sheets on her bed and Laura switched on the electric blanket and slipped between them. She had given Carmen money to buy food, thinking, he won't have eaten properly. She tried to sleep. Her mind was cloudy again. These days the boundary between dreams, imagination and wakefulness was not clear.

She dreamed vividly of going to a party and dancing like a Bacchante with a man who was Paul, though he didn't have Paul's face, just his matching gyrating body. Everyone said, 'Look at Laura dancing!'

After the party the man took her home and they made love and she thought, 'Oh, thank God, it was all a dream, the illness. I dreamed it!' He was still with her and they went for a walk on the Heath, not Hampstead Heath, some different heath with poplars, silver birches, silver bracken, wind and the sun in her eyes and blowing through her hair. From this she woke to her own bedroom and the realization that it was not a dream. She was dying.

She slept again and dreamed of making love with Paul for the last time, brutally, without subtlety, huge bodies like boulders grinding each other, like Soviet state art, vast monolithic trunks and limbs, heaving and grunting, caught up in a frenzy of compulsion that allowed no tenderness or skill or unselfishness. She thought in the midst of the dream, It is one of the oddest things about human beings that they should *want* this pounding, pounding, battering, hammering, this hard, ruthless crashing of body on body, that they should want it. Still in a dream, she admitted to herself, No, I am lying, that *I* should want it. I like it, like it, *like it*.

After this, Laura woke and knew that the dream had been her last walk, her last party, and her last fuck.

He came at eight o'clock, all tidied up and without a bottle this time. He was downcast and subdued, his voice low. Why did he speak so quietly, she asked.

'I feel so harsh if I talk loudly,' he replied. 'Your voice, my love, has dwindled to next to nothing. It's like a thread, a fine silver thread.'

She had put a couple of potatoes in the oven and made a salad. She took him down to the kitchen and grilled a steak for him while he drank her whisky. She showed him where the plates and cutlery were kept and he laid the table. Knowing he had to have wine, she had found a wonderful bottle of Burgundy and he drank that, trying to take it slowly. She ate next to nothing, but Paul was so hungry he didn't notice.

'I followed your progress,' he said. 'I used to ask Constance, casually, what you were up to. I knew when you bought this house. I came and had a look at it. The children would mention you from time to time. It was obvious they had no idea. I had masses of women. I was very ugly towards women for a while. When Lu decided to sod off, that was the end of everything. That was in '86, Christmas. It's been downhill ever since. Laura, is there another bottle?'

'Not of this. Will anything do?'

'Anything.'

She pointed to the cupboard under the stairs and he pulled out a bottle without glancing at the label.

'What about you?'

'I slept with an awful lot of men. Anyone I wanted, really. Once you stop looking for love or marriage, it leaves you amazingly free. I wanted nothing, only pleasure. That I *did* demand. Didn't much matter whether it was sex or food or money. Instead of you I settled for luxury, posh restaurants, five-star hotels – my standards got very high. Men are simple. They need sexual flattery, especially when they get to around sixty. Their powers are waning, and they like to talk about past triumphs and hear themselves praised. They want to be flirted with and made to feel potent, powerful, irresistible. Sometimes they'd rather have that than sex. If you can do that convincingly, they'll give you anything.'

'You clever girl,' he said. 'You always were *such* a clever girl.'

By ten o'clock he was relaxed, glowing, slurring his words. His gestures had become clumsy, his voice liquid. She watched him, knowing that he was pathetic, despicable, the man of her life.

'Do you want coffee?' she asked.

'Want to take you to bed. Want to make love to you. Bugger coffee.'

She put him to bed in the spare room eventually. He was maudlin and tried to embrace her, but even against her feeble strength he had no power. She unlaced his shoes and dragged them off his feet, pulled his trousers down – his legs were thin and sinewy, not the great tree-trunks of his youth – and urged him between the sheets of the spare bed. Grumbling, fumbling, he groped like a child towards comfort and sleep.

12

Desmond Osborne

Laura asked her lawyer, Neale Ward, to visit her at home to finalize her will. She had to parcel out her strength very carefully and knew that by now she could not dress, make up, travel (even by taxi) climb two flights of stairs, confront an alien receptionist *and* be clear-headed about the details of her legacies. Where hospital appointments were concerned, she was now classified as 'non-ambulatory' and thus entitled to an ambulance. How many people, she wondered, believed it meant just the opposite?

Ward sat in her Markham Street drawing-room, his pin-striped knees clenched together (he assumes I have Aids, she thought). Laura half-sat, half-lay on the sofa. The round table between them was covered with papers, insurance valuations, inventories, deeds.

'I want to make absolutely certain that the house is willed to my nephew, Max Liddell, and in no circumstances could anyone else, not even one or other of his parents, gain possession of it,' she said.

'In the case of his death, the house will pass to his son, Kaspar, except that you have granted the child's mother, Danuta Liddell, use of it until the boy reaches his majority, with the proviso that he continues to live with her,' Ward confirmed in his precise legal voice.

'Only the mother! No one else!'

'That is what the will specifies. May I raise a different point,

Miss King? The distribution of property between your nephew and nieces is unequal. That is your wish?'

'There is nothing I can do about that. Unfortunately I have not managed to amass a quarter of a million pounds' worth of jewellery, since it does not appreciate in value as rapidly as property. But all three will benefit quite considerably from these bequests.'

'Certainly. And finally . . . Forgive me – you desire a *non-*religious funeral followed by cremation; and you have requested no flowers, no memorial service, and only the simplest announcement.'

'Correct. In addition, in case they should miss that, I would be obliged if you would notify the people on this list of my death.' She held out the addresses of the twelve men whom she had invited to dinner in February. Edouard's name had been crossed out. Madame Chet had telephoned her three days previously, with the news that '*notre grand Monsieur, notre réfuge et notre abri*' had died. Her tinny voice had been precariously dignified.

'*Je l'ai aimé.*' Laura had said.

'*Nous aussi, Madame,*' came the laconic answer.

'No messages . . . ?'

'Nothing. Only the most straightforward notification. I leave the wording to you.'

'Very well, Miss King. And now, if I may . . .' He extended a sealed envelope bearing her name. He lowered his voice. 'My firm's account. I'm sure you will understand.'

Laura wanted to laugh at his effrontery: the haste, the naked anxiety lest she might die before they could get their money, thus obliging them to justify their charges to her heirs.

Keeping her expression formal, she said, 'If you would be good enough to pass me my handbag . . . ?' She gestured towards the desk. He had the grace to look discomfited.

'Oh, it isn't necessary . . . *immediately* . . . I assure you, Miss King. At your . . . um . . . leisure.'

'No, no, Mr Ward, let us be realistic. I might die any day

now. Does this bill include VAT? Who knows, I may, on the other hand, be granted long enough to reclaim it. One of us will benefit, whatever happens.'

He mumbled yes and she wrote out a cheque.

After he had left, she hauled herself up the stairs to her bedroom, lay down and slept. She was woken by the telephone. Her bedside clock said five past six.

A light-hearted voice in her ear said, '*I'm* sipping a glass of white wine. What are you sipping?'

'Desmond!' she said drowsily. 'Hello. How lovely. *I'm* not allowed to sip anything except water.'

'In that case, my dear, I shall lay in vast stocks of mineral water and we shall do comparative tastings. Now then. When am I coming to bear you away?'

'Oh, darling, I don't think I can be borne any more. I'm pretty far gone.'

'I have become used to that,' he said. 'Very well. I shall decide for you. Not tomorrow, to give you time to prepare yourself, but Sunday – that's October 11th. Can you be up and dressed by eleven?'

'Certainly,' she said with a trace of indignation.

'Excellent. Many cannot, you know, especially on a Sunday. I shall arrive at 11, you will direct me as to what needs packing, I shall rummage disgracefully in your underwear and then I will bear you away.'

She laughed. 'Where are we going?'

'To my flat, if that's acceptable to you. I should like to look after you myself.'

After her father had been killed, her child aborted and her lover banished, Laura fell into a depression that lasted for almost a year. When it was over she had a new, deep crease between her eyes and fine downward lines on either side of her mouth. Her sister (but never her mother) commented on this unexpectedly profound grief.

'I miss Daddy dreadfully, of *course*, but not half as badly as you. Even Mummy seems to have come to terms with it better. Poor love.'

Then Constance would change the subject, hoping to distract Laura. 'I saw Paul last weekend. He's got *another* new girlfriend!' she reported cheerfully. 'She came with him to collect Katie. *Nice* girl. Young, of course, they usually are. This one's only about twenty-five; Lulu, she's called. He's looking much better suddenly, thanks to her.'

Laura would think it was four years since her sister had lost Paul. If Constance could come to terms with it, surely she could too? But the picture of him with another woman lacerated her. She began to have periods that lasted for weeks on end and she thought, My womb weeps because my child has gone and my lover has taken another woman and no longer occupies himself with me.

It had taken Paul no more than a month to accept that Laura's mind was made up. Once the flowers, letters and pleas on the telephone had ceased, Laura experienced a week of relief followed by utter despair. It was a struggle to get up in the mornings, a struggle to dress and go outside her own front door; almost impossible to present herself positively. She donned interpreter's headphones, translated like a zombie, and escaped as soon as she could. Her movements became sluggish and she walked with her head down, watching her feet, the bloody fan of wing and feathers where a pigeon had been run over, the slimy mess of dead leaves in the gutter, the grey slush after London snow. She watched rain lashing the windows, black in the sky, slanting under the street lights. She avoided her friends and instructed her family to leave her alone.

The flat in Brook Green reminded her constantly of Paul, although she tried to eliminate every trace of him. She had torn up his letters and the few photographs which showed them together, and sold everything he had inadvertently left behind. In spite of this the place seemed imbued with his presence. He had planted roses in the tiny back garden, painted the kitchen yellow as a surprise for her one weekend, and together they had bought bits of furniture and pictures at auction, as well as a clock, an art nouveau jug, and a set of candlesticks that had caught their eye.

After six months she was no better. She could not concentrate on reading or listening to music. She had to take powerful pills to focus attention on her work, for otherwise her mind drifted within a sentence or two. As a result of these pills she could not sleep at night. When she did sleep, she dreamed vividly. Once she was in the Royal Opera House. The stalls were overgrown with grass in which small animals hid from people who were firing at them from the grand tier of seats above. She managed to rescue a large creature like a rabbit with whorled fur and carried it away distractedly in her arms. She awoke thinking, What was in danger? My child? My sanity?

She bumped into Nicholas Hope one February day as she sat in a café in the City, postponing the moment when she must go home and re-enter her haunted flat, filled with the ghost of Paul. Nick had missed a train from Liverpool Street and was whiling away time before the next. He suddenly appeared in front of her and said tentatively, 'Laura?'

She looked up, heavy-eyed. 'Yes? Oh, Nick. Goodness. Hello.'

'It *is* you. I wasn't sure for a minute. You look different. I read about your father's death,' he said without preamble. 'His obituary in *The Times*. I'm dreadfully sorry.'

She looked at him bleakly. 'Yes. It was awful. Poor Daddy.'

He bought her a cup of tea and an unasked-for bun, and was gentle and kind. She was tempted to confide in him, to let her sorrow and loss burst their banks and flood, but just as she was about to begin he said, 'It's impossible to talk in here. I can miss my train and catch the next. Come on, let's stroll across Tower Bridge.'

They walked in the mauve dusk of late afternoon, watching

the river swirl past, the commuters hurrying across the bridge, the street lights coming on. Having controlled her dangerous impulse to confess, Laura admitted only that she was deeply depressed, had been for months, but no, she definitely didn't want therapy.

'In that case you need activity. Move house. Go and live abroad, get another job — anything. Rattle the kaleidoscope. Shake up the pattern. If you *can* change things, *do*. You're lucky to have that much freedom.'

She saw him on to his train and he had hugged her — the first man to touch her, apart from a handshake, for several months. She went home and thought about what he had said. Her father had left her enough capital to pay off her mortgage while her mother, after selling the house in the country and buying a small flat in Kensington, had insisted that each of her daughters should have half the money that remained. With this and her own considerable earnings, Laura was now well off. She need not stay on in her melancholy flat any longer.

Laura was galvanized into action. The day after meeting Nick she rang two estate agents, put her flat on the market, and instructed them to find her a house in Chelsea. Three months later she moved, leaving behind the palpable, tangible, intractable figure of Paul that lurked in every corner of the flat in which they had made so much love.

When she moved into Markham Street in 1980, more than ten years ago, Desmond had been her next-door neighbour. He stood outside his front door as the removal van was unloaded, openly appraising her furniture. Half an hour later he turned up with a tray bearing two cups, a cafetière, a plate of biscuits, and his business card: DESMOND OSBORNE, FINE ANTIQUES.

'Welcome to Markham Street!' he said.

At first she found him amiable, witty but exceptionally secretive. Soon afterwards, having observed the youth and sex of his evening callers, she deduced correctly that Desmond was gay.

She asked him outright. Desmond said, 'Oompf, yes. Good, *that's* out of the way! One's never *quite* sure how people are going to react.' Laura understood perfectly that there were aspects of his life he preferred not to discuss.

Within a few years the spectre of Aids was beginning to evoke terror and suspicion. Nearly two decades of sexual openness had freed Desmond almost as dramatically as Laura herself. Now suddenly it behoved homosexuals to be wary again. Laura welcomed Desmond's sensitivity and restraint after the intrusions of her family and women friends, baffled by her five years of apparent celibacy.

Like her, Desmond had to present a brave face to the world. A middle-aged gay man cannot bewail his lost lovers or allow his concentration on his business activities to falter, or go into mourning for a faithless and, from time to time, fatally stricken beloved. Desmond understood better than anyone what it was to suffer in silence. He realized from her solitariness and the gap in her past that Laura had lost a great love about whom she too could not speak. With infinite tact and subtlety he consoled her. For the first time, in her mid-thirties, she learned the comfort of a gay friend.

They would go to see a film in the King's Road together if amorous escorts were lacking. He would advise on her dinner parties, cook half the menu if she had to work late, and fill in as 'spare man', sitting at the head of the table.

At Christmas time Laura and Desmond decorated their houses competitively, the golden windows blazing side by side for the admiration of the street and the pleasure of passers-by. She learned that his mother was still unable to accept the fact that her only son was gay. On alternate years – the years when Constance, their mother and the children went to Paul and his (hateful phrase!) 'current lady' – Laura would spend Christmas Day with Desmond and his elderly mother. The first time this happened Desmond, more apologetic than Laura had ever known him, said, 'Could you, do you think, try and remember to call her Mrs *Osmond*? Rather than Osborne?'

'All right,' she said.

'It's not that I'm snobbish about my origins. But even *my* parents could see that a working-class lad from the North trying to make his way selling posh furniture wasn't going to get very far in the late Sixties with a name like Donald Osmond. I changed it as little as possible.'

'Oh, Desmond, that's glorious!' Laura laughed with relief. 'OK. I'll do my best.'

She answered his mother's hopeful questions with a straight face. 'No, Mrs Osmond, I've never been married. No, I haven't closed my mind to the possibility. Yes I might even have a child. Who knows?'

Afterwards Desmond said, 'Now she can go back to Newcastle happy and tell all her friends what a *nice* new girlfriend I've got!'

They giggled together about conventional maternal expectations. 'Next year I'll subject you to *my* mother,' Laura threatened, and he warned, 'I'll charm her rotten. She'll give you no peace till you marry me!'

He taught her a great deal. She learned how to choose off-beat, subtle colours to decorate her house, not matching the furniture too obviously lest the rooms look like a provincial mayoress at a royal garden party. 'Turquoise hat, turquoise gloves, turquoise bag and turquoise peep-toe shoes,' he mocked, and Laura added, 'Just like the Queen Mum!' He told her always to introduce a note from the opposite end of the spectrum for emphasis, and to group objects in a huddle rather than scattering them.

He sold her good pieces of furniture cheaply. ('Don't think I haven't still made a profit; it's just a bit less outrageous than usual!') They both benefited from the affluent, prodigal Eighties, and if they were both emotionally poverty-stricken, they constantly reflected that at least they were miserable in comfort.

Desmond appraised her male friends. Bruno he approved of. '*What* a little cracker! No, don't tell me what he does. I don't care. One look at him and I can see he fucks like a fox!' Rafe he loathed, seeing straight through his pretensions. '*That's* no Ralph. What's more, he couldn't even tell my real Biedermeyer from my brilliant (it *is* brilliant, I grant him that) fake. Bring him here again and I'll let him think he can buy it. We'll see what he offers. *Not* for you, that one: though I bet he's a small pearl-handled pistol in bed, hmm? Oh, sweetie – I never knew you could blush! You shouldn't be embarrassed . . . Don't ever underestimate the value of sexual pleasure. It's as good as any of the other pleasures and just look what people are willing to pay for *those*! A Louis Quinze desk went for £374,000 at Sotheby's last week. Madness. All that ormolu. To say nothing of those ghastly overblown rubicund Renoirs. And then they're spiteful about *us*!'

'*I* don't pay Rafe!' Laura objected.

'Of course you don't, darling. *That's* a pretty ring . . . Have I seen it before?'

Five or six years later, as the property market shot upwards, Desmond took his profit on the house – a jewel of interior decoration that was now worth ten times what he had paid for it – and moved to a large, anonymous block in Holland Park.

It was here that he brought the dying Laura, carrying her tenderly from the bed he had improvised in the back of his furniture van and cradling her in his arms as the lift travelled up four floors. 'Desmond,' she whispered in her pale voice. 'You've done this before!'

'Yes,' he agreed, 'but never with a woman!'

'Does it feel different?' she whispered; and he said, 'By this stage, no.'

Desmond called Aids 'Death's Little Helper' with the gallows humour that he brought to bear on everything to do with sickness and dying.

'In the last ten years,' he told Laura, 'I've seen dozens of my friends die. Several of them I loved very much indeed, or could have done, if the Little Helper had allowed us time. Two or three I nursed here, in this room, in this bed – if that doesn't upset you? Believe me, I've seen it all. You may throw up, piss and shit with impunity. You can break out in bubbles and suppurate with sores. Nothing disgusts me and I can make you lovely and fresh again afterwards. Name your preference ... Roger & Gallet Extra Vieille? That was Michael. Dior, Eau Sauvage? That was beautiful, beautiful Guy's favourite. Givenchy Gentleman? Peter liked that one.'

'Anything,' she said quickly, 'except Givenchy Gentleman.'

He glanced at her quizzically, but of course – dear, sensitive Desmond – made no comment.

One dank afternoon he brought her into the drawing-room to sit in front of the fire and nibble at a crumpet. It was a real fire, not a gas imitation, and it reminded Laura of a weekend she and Paul had spent in a castle in Ireland. Huge stone rooms were warmed at the centre by Henry VIII log fires, while their corners remained damp and shadowy. There had been a fire in their bedroom, too, throwing dancing patterns across the beams in the ceiling. The light had flickered rosily over her body and carved new hollows in his. How beautiful they had been!

'Desmond,' she asked. 'You don't have to answer this, but what do you do these days about sex?'

'SNPS, if anything.'

'Meaning ... ?'

'Safe, non-penetrative sex.'

'Doesn't sound much fun. Is it worth it?'

He laughed. 'I sometimes ask myself that! I suppose I've had less sex in the last five years than I used to have in a single weekend in Brighton. In those days you could walk into half a dozen pubs in one evening and within ten minutes, someone would catch your eye and you'd be off and away, at it like dentist's drills. Later on there might be a party. After that you'd go home with someone else, and by lunchtime when the hangover had worn off, you could be starting all over again.'

'Was it *enjoyable*? I can't imagine having sex with a dozen different strangers in two days and finding it anything other than exhausting and, I suppose, horrible.'

'Other people's sex always seems horrible, don't you think? You must have heard camp gays talking about women? "*Imagine*, darling, all those great floppy *tits* lolling about!" Silly old queens. Driven by desire, the most appalling things become wonderful. I used to think it was like blood-lust and big-game hunting. At the beginning the idea of killing a living thing is unthinkable, but once people come to terms with it, they can't get enough.'

'Yes,' she said drily. 'I know what you mean. So you do miss it?'

'Of course I *miss* it. Two things help to make it bearable. One, I'm getting older, appetite's on the decline. I feel sorry for boys in their twenties. Two, I get a lot of satisfaction from nursing people; and I'm *needed*. This thing, this disease, has given gay men the chance to be tender, unselfish and loyal in a way that we seldom were before.'

'You're wonderful at it,' Laura said. 'Though a month with me sounds a pretty poor exchange for a weekend in Brighton.'

'If you'd put it like that ten years ago, I would probably have agreed!'

Another evening they talked at length, for the first time, about death: the one thing that couldn't be avoided and that no one could report back on.

'I've seen plenty of people die,' Desmond recalled, 'and in the end it came as a relief for most of them. Very few people die fighting. They get tireder and tireder . . .'

'I *am* tireder and tireder . . .'

'Most seem glad to let go. If they can.'

'What do you mean?'

'Well, sweetie, a lot of people have quite heavy unfinished business.'

'Such as what?'

'Love unspoken, sins unconfessed, promises unkept, parents or children abandoned – the usual human baggage. Some of them get round it by talking to a priest. Others think they can hang on and resolve it. Don't scratch at your nail varnish or I shall have to do it all again. The main thing is not to die alone. Not much chance of that in your case.'

'I am afraid of death,' she admitted.

Desmond slipped out of the room, returning with a balloon of brandy. He swirled the topaz-coloured liquid inside its bulbous curve. 'Have a sniff. Gorgeous, isn't it? Now, tell me how you see death?'

'A black skeleton with a scythe on a thin, jaded horse, like in all those Dürer etchings and medieval frescos. I'm culturally indoctrinated. He's coming to drag me away in a parody of the rape of the Sabines.'

'Cruel, then. Painful, murderous, final.'

Tears rose to Laura's eyes. 'Desmond, I know what you're trying to do and it's generous of you, and honest, but can we talk about something else? To you, on the side of life, all this is just speculation, a sort of psychological exercise. To me on the other side, Death is the next man in my life. The last man. I've been sleeping with him for nearly a year now.'

Desmond was both attentive and self-effacing. He was always there if she needed him, ready with a moist sponge for her dry lips, ointment for her itching skin, delicate baby-food meals if she had a spark of appetite. After two weeks, however, he said tentatively in the small hours of one morning, as he sat wakeful beside her sleepless shape, 'Had you thought, lovey, about entering a hospice?'

'No. I can't. I have to go to the hospital where they know me, and my condition.'

'No "have to" about it. You don't *have* to do anything any more, least of all take *my* advice. And I will look after you for as long as you want.'

'Desmond,' she breathed, in her wraith-like voice, 'you should have been a nurse!'

'I was. A bright lad with two A levels, one in Biology, one in Chemistry, from Heaton Grammar doesn't set out to become an antique-dealer, you know.'

She lay back on the pillow and turned her eyes towards his face, the magnet, now, of her nights and days. 'Tell me . . .'

'My dad was a butcher in Newcastle, so I wasn't squeamish about the insides of things, and I thought I was pretty well acquainted with death, which I wasn't, but never mind. Didn't stand a chance of being accepted for medical training as a doctor. Working-class lad like me: forget it! What did that leave? Nursing. So I started training at the Royal Victoria Infirmary. I was the only boy in a year of forty-six girls: better than any of 'em – *and* everyone knew it. I loved the work. Loved the hierarchy of the hospital, adored the young doctors, as you can imagine . . .' He grinned at Laura, but her eyes were closed. '*As* for those big, four-square, hoary old surgeons: whoof! Well, anyway, after three years I passed all my final examinations and there I was, Donny Osmond, SRN.'

The shadow of a smile passing over her face assured him she was still awake.

'I did a couple of years in the RVI because the hospital had trained me, I felt I owed them that, and then in 1968 I came down to London. I got a post in a private hospital: King Edward the blah blah's Hospital for Officers. However stoic and stuck-up they may be, they're all laid low by pain and illness. After a few months a lady I had been nursing after an operation – nice old bird; a dowager marchioness, as it happened – asked me to come and live with her as her private nurse. I was sick of having to lodge in the hospital and I imagined her surrounded by sturdy young grooms and gardeners straight out of D. H. Lawrence or E. M. Forster . . .'

He glanced again at Laura, but there was no answering flicker. Her breathing was slow and faint. Desmond went on, talking to himself.

'I stayed with her for over a year. Game old bird. Lasted a lot longer than any of them had thought. *How* they gathered round, the family, towards the end. Vultures-in-waiting. Anyway, that gave me my first introduction to good furniture. She used to make me wheel her round the house and she'd point out her favourite pieces. "Look at that, Donald," she'd say. "That workmanship! You won't find cabinet-makers like that today! Perfectly flat marquetry, after two hundred years. That's why I'll never permit central heating. It *ruins* furniture! They can do it when I'm dead – and they will."

'I learned straight from the horse's mouth. Got my eye in. When she died, she left me a bit of money. Not a lot, but I hadn't expected anything. It was enough to start picking up the odd piece here and there, repairing them, giving them a good patina with a few weeks' polishing, and then selling them on. That's how I started.'

Laura was asleep. Desmond stood up, put the chair noiselessly by the wall, checked her pulse and straightened the sheet, dimmed the light and tiptoed from the room.

Over the next few days Laura reflected on Desmond's words about unfinished business. She had said goodbye to her mother and her nephew, Max, and to Cordelia and Katie, her nieces, though they might not have realized it at the time. She would deter any further visits. She had also taken leave of her close friends and visited the men who had shaped her life. Her legal and business affairs were complete. Even Paul, by breaking his promise and their thirteen-year silence, had enabled her to say goodbye to him too, after a fashion. Only Constance remained.

She told Desmond that she had once wronged her sister

unforgivably, but had felt at the time that the harder path was *not* to confess.

'Have you forgiven her now?'

'Have *I* forgiven her?' Laura expostulated faintly. '*She's* the one who needs to forgive, did she but know it.'

'Perhaps she *has* known all along and is punishing you by pretending ignorance? Sisters are pretty intuitive. Maybe she's been stringing out your torment for years. Could you forgive her for never letting you get past your guilt, having to carry the burden all this time?'

'You're wrong,' Laura said. 'It's a clever theory, but it's wrong. Constance is incapable of deviousness.'

'I don't suggest she's doing it *deliberately*.'

'No, Desmond. What I did . . .' Laura hesitated. She had been about to say 'was the great unforgivable thing', but she had never told anyone and Desmond was not the person to receive her confession. No one, not a priest, not a doctor, not a friend, no one knew that she, Laura, had committed incest with her sister's husband. *Least* of all – she heard the echo – Constance.

'I'm talking about the person closest to me, the person I've known and loved for forty-five years. If she knew, I would *know*.'

'If she *doesn't* know,' he said, 'perhaps you need to tell her.'

Laura's face contracted. 'I couldn't,' she said, sounding agitated.

'It may be hard for you to die until you have. Listen to me, Laura. Few of our sins are as bad as we think. They usually arise from love or loneliness, jealousy, or fear. All the roots, the basics, everyone shares.' He broke unexpectedly into song: 'The fundamental things apply . . .' But she did not smile in response.

He resumed. 'In the last few years I've watched people suffering with Death's Little Helper who *swore* their parents never knew they were gay and it would kill them if they found out. The irony of it! These people sometimes prolonged their death for weeks – months, even; the final will is incredibly strong – with the most elaborate lies and medical explanations, meanwhile keeping their lovers away in case the two sets of visitors should ever meet, before realizing that they had to tell the truth before they could let go. So *finally*, they confess, and it turns out that the parent has known all along. Imagine the loneliness on both sides, loving and being separated by the great unspoken! I know others who held on to their secret. They died in the end, fighting, the truth trailing behind them like ectoplasm.'

'But being gay isn't *wicked*,' she said. 'What I did was.'

'It isn't, no, but it felt wicked to *them*.'

Laura turned her head peevishly away. 'What I did was *wicked*,' she insisted. 'Evil, by any standards.'

He looked at her with pity. 'How have you *lived* with it all this time, my poor sweet?'

'I always knew it would kill me, because I deserved to die. Oh, Desmond, I'm so tired, and so frightened.'

Laura could not compromise her lifelong belief that death stops us in our tracks, body, mind and spirit, much as it would have suited her to take on an eleventh-hour faith in the after-life; yet she could not deny that her father felt very close. During the day, the few times Desmond left her alone to attend to his shop, a client, or an unavoidable sale, her father appeared before her more vividly than at any time since his death. She would see him not exactly in a corporeal sense, not as a solid presence like Desmond, but none the less he would be entirely recognizable. He seemed as wise as he had when she was a little girl, the source – as then – of certainty and comfort, yet she still feared the last stage of the journey towards him.

Her other source of certainty was Desmond. He understood the slow, soft tides of her day, the way she slipped in and out of sleep. He would catch her when she was at her most awake and alert, making her smile with an observation from the world outside. When she was hounded by anxiety or pain he was a marvel of competence and calm. Even when her mouth filled with blood, terrifying her, he remained calm, staunched it, rinsed it, refreshed her.

'*How* you look after me!' she breathed gratefully.

'I can't do it for very much longer,' he told her reluctantly. 'You ought really to be in hospital now. They have access to drugs that I can't get, not even with my contacts. They could give you things to make you breathe more easily, help you keep your food down, even to lift your depression.'

'I'm not *depressed*, I'm *dying*,' she said, with as much emphasis as she could muster.

'Sweetie, I know, but the two things are separate. You are depressed *and* you're dying, I think, rather than depressed *because* you're dying. I can't take decisions for you. I will look after you here till the end, if that's what you want. But I'd like someone else to be involved. Your sister's the obvious person, only —'

'Don't ring Constance,' Laura said. 'Ring my consultant. Mrs Ripa. She'll organize an ambulance. You are right. It is time to go.'

Quietly, efficiently, Desmond packed the few remaining things she needed: her nightclothes, washing materials, pills, a photograph or two. Laura remembered travelling out to Conrad in Amalfi a mere eight months ago, laden with two suitcases. How unencumbered she was now by comparison. She had shed her baggage, bit by bit – all except for one thing.

Desmond wrapped her in a duvet and carried her downstairs, as he had carried her up nearly a month ago. He laid her tenderly in the back of the ambulance and just as the double doors were about to be closed he produced, seemingly from nowhere, a huge bunch of anemones.

'Oh, Desmond,' Laura said, tears flooding down her face. 'My *favourite* flowers!'

'Do me a favour!' he said. 'You think I don't know *that*, after all these years?'

She insisted on travelling to the hospital alone.

'I'll come and see you tonight,' he told her. 'Make sure you've got the best room; check out the houseman!'

'I love you,' she answered. 'Oh, heavens, Desmond, I do love you.'

13

Dr Todhunter

It was obvious that Desmond had left the NHS many years ago, Laura reflected as she was wheeled into the liver ward by a cheerful porter. There was no chance of having a room to herself, let alone the best one. The area was sub-divided into half a dozen side wards, each with four to six beds. She was decanted expertly from the stretcher into one of these. The starched hospital sheet and the rubber bed cover beneath were cold and uncomfortable. The woman opposite stared at her with hostile curiosity. In the next bed another woman slept, a large, pink teddy bear tucked in beside her.

Laura's details were taken by a first-year nurse and Laura, knowing that this routine was for the trainee's benefit rather than her own, submitted patiently to a litany of questions. Name? Next of kin? Name of partner, co-habitee, spouse or former husband? Any children? Any pregnancies? Reason for premature termination of pregnancy? Date? Was it followed by complications? Just the one? No spontaneous miscarriages? Dead-pan, in a voice that had become as silvery and fine as her hair now was, beneath Desmond's expert rinse, Laura gave the dates and details of her life to the placid, polite nineteen-year-old.

Supper came round on multi-storey trolleys at half past six and Laura endured the nauseous smell of her meal as it sat untouched on the table spanning the end of her bed. At seven, with the first wave of visitors, came Desmond.

'My *darling*!' he said, reverting to the mock camp voice he used in moments of stress. 'Do you mean I *forced* myself to be parted from you only to have you subjected to *this*?' He lifted one of the tin lids covering the food and turned away in exaggerated disgust from the miasma of tepid steam that rose sluggishly from its contents.

'As for your *pillow*! Foam rubber *croûtons*, I'll be bound! Never mind, at least they're not in the soup. Well, sweetie, tomorrow you shall repose on cotton lawn and finest goose down. Now then, let's cast an eye over your patient notes.'

The woman in the next bed stirred. 'You're not supposed to,' she quavered. 'Those are for the nurses.'

'I *am* a nurse!' said Desmond, in Lady Bracknell tones. He scanned the clipboard expertly. 'Looks all right to me, but lay off the Temgesic,' he advised. 'Not in pain, lovey, are you? No. Well then, no need to give you morphine. Not that I'm worrying about you getting addicted, but morphine will give you night-mares and we don't want *that*.'

He fussed over her anemones, thrust by a busy nurse into a standard-issue plastic vase. Lengthening a stem here and there and breaking others off short, he transformed them from a hasty bunch into a subtle sheaf of colour. Just before he left he said, 'Now, darling, own up. Have you talked to your sister?'

'No.'

'I'll have a hunt for the ward telephone *now*.' He went off and wheeled it back on its trolley. 'Where's the change I gave you?'

'Bedside drawer. No, don't you dial it, Desmond. I promise I will as soon as you've gone. I need to summon up courage first. And a bit of voice.'

She was tempted to put it off until the following morning, but who knew where the telephone might be by then? Propped up against the pillow, the end of the bed raked at a supportive angle, Laura fed the portable telephone with tenpenny coins and dialled her sister's number.

'Constance?'

'Laura! Oh, thank heavens you rang! Where are you? I had no

idea where you'd *been* for the past three weeks. I was getting frantic. The hospital swore you weren't there and –'

'I'm in hospital now.'

'Thank God! I was on the point of coming up to London and breaking your door down. I managed to get hold of Carmen once, but she just said, "Miss King, she go away. She no very good."'

'I'm sorry,' Laura said, genuinely remorseful. 'I've been with a friend in London. A former neighbour. Former nurse as well.'

'You might have told me – given me her address – I've been worried to . . .' her voice trailed away.

'. . . death,' Laura supplied mentally. 'I'm sorry.' she repeated. 'I'm here now for quite a while, I imagine.' She dictated the name of the ward and verified the telephone number. Already her voice was fading into nothingness.

'I'll come and see you as *soon* as possible,' Constance said. 'It can't be tomorrow as I'm helping out with a friend's surprise fiftieth birthday party so the next day – let's make it Friday.'

The energy in her sister's voice, the sweeping gust of a busy life, tired and irritated Laura. 'Come when you like,' she said. 'They want to put the lights out now. I'm not going anywhere. I'm here for good now. If good it is.'

As the lights were turned low and the ward darkened, Laura fell into a shifting, troubled doze. She was aware of the soft padding figures of nurses patrolling on crêpe-soled shoes. After a time a young doctor passed her bed and peered down at her.

'Why are you propped up?' she asked.

'I don't know,' Laura told her. 'My visitor winched the bed up, and nobody's wound it down.'

The doctor clucked almost inaudibly. 'Wouldn't you be more comfy lying flat?' she said, and at Laura's nod she turned the handle at the foot of the bed like an old-fashioned crank for starting a car. 'I'm Dr Todhunter, the houseman on this ward. If you need anything, want to ask anything, let me know. We're a bit understaffed on the nursing side at the moment. OK? Will you be able to sleep now?'

Laura smiled gratefully. 'Hope so,' she said. Then she added, 'Look, there's something I'd like you to know. It has no legal weight, and it could make things tricky for you, but I don't want any last-minute intervention. I don't ever want to lie here with tubes and drips, in a coma. I want to die *compos mentis*. I want to be *let go*. I am of sound mind, I have thought about it, I have wound up my affairs, I have no dependants. I mean it. I don't know who to tell, if not you.'

The young doctor held her wrist for a moment between her cool fingers, then smoothed the sheet across Laura's chest. 'Right. Now you have told me, and you can forget about it. Good. Night-night, then.'

The patient in the opposite bed talked in her sleep. Laura could only catch a few wandering words. 'Cupboard . . .' she heard and then 'blue and white' and 'useful . . .'. Such small-scale, domestic words, so banal a glimpse into a lifetime's homely preoccupations. Laura curled up in the narrow iron bed, tucked her hand in comfortably, and slept.

Next day a flotilla of doctors headed by Mrs Ripa gathered at her bedside. The now-familiar medical phrases drifted round her head like a flock of circling birds. Dr Todhunter murmured a summary of Laura's condition, medication and diet since admission to the ward. No, Laura confirmed, she had not eaten breakfast; no, she had no appetite; yes, she would try to drink more. No, she didn't feel sick, but she would if she ate.

'Do you mind if the students examine you?' Mrs Ripa inquired.

The curtains swished around her bed and one by one, fresh cool young hands were laid on her abdomen, palpating her liver; gentle fingers pulled down her lower eyelids. Obediently she extended her tongue and her fingers for examination. They turned her hands over to inspect her palms. The flock of birds turned; they were migrating now, a V of white shapes heading into the distance.

At lunch she was presented with a special soft-food meal

which a nurse patiently spooned into her mouth. An hour later Laura felt the bile rising in her throat. She began to retch. A nurse hurried to her side and pressed the emergency bell behind her bed. Dr Todhunter was there within moments.

'Try not to vomit, Laura,' she said, with calm insistence. 'If you can possibly hold it down, do.'

'Why?' Laura asked, turning desperate eyes towards the white-coated figure whose outline swam through a mist of nausea. Her stomach heaved in rejection of the food; her forehead felt clammy.

'Your oesophagus is very vulnerable. If you vomit, you could trigger a bleed, and we want to avoid that if possible. Here are a couple of pills to suppress the nausea. Good girl. Well done. That should help. Now, see if you can get a bit of sleep.'

They left the curtains drawn around her bed and Laura drowsed. Her childhood kept coming to mind. She remembered tiny details – trivial objects, forgotten for forty years: the insipid pictures that hung in her nursery, Margaret W. Tarrant illustrations of the Child Jesus surrounded by baby animals and flocks of birds in a perpetual soft spring; the alarm clock that stood on top of the chest of drawers, too high for her to reach, each hour marked by a luminous green blob; a book that had been in her father's schoolroom when he was a boy, called *Jock of the Bushveld*: an adventure story set in the South African bush at the turn of the century, peopled with simple or treacherous blacks whom gallant white settlers fought or tried to civilize.

My knowledge of the world stretches back decades before I was born, she reflected, composed of my parents' memories and the objects that filled their lives. Pictures, photograph albums, names of relatives unseen and long-dead, anecdotes repeated every Christmas and at every wedding. My memory will be prolonged by the people who have known me. Max and Dani, living in my house, will say, 'Aunt Laura left it to us. Aren't we lucky!' Katie, as she uses my furniture, hangs my pictures and reads my books, will continue to infuse life into the objects that were mine. My forty-five years are only the middle third of a span covering a century and a half, forwards and backwards. If I were to return during the next ten or twenty years, I would still have friends, recognize places, I could still fit in. Only when all that has gone will I be truly dead. Other people will think about me from time to time: Joe and Dot, Nick and Beth, Mikey and Nell. They'll say to each other, 'Do you remember that time Laura came to stay, after she'd been told she had only a year to live?' I won't be forgotten at once.

Her mind reduced everything to basics. If you're a woman, she thought, the world judges you by whether or not you have a man. These women in the next beds could tell that Desmond wasn't my husband. Even if they didn't spot that he was gay, they would have seen at once that he was too vivacious, too alive, to be my husband. Husbands stand stiffly beside the bed saying things like 'How soon are they going to let you come home?' They assert their rights over the woman lying there, prone and passive in an alien bed, by condescending to the junior doctors, who in turn assert their rights by using medical terms that these anxious, abandoned husbands don't understand.

Already these three women have marked me down as a creature of lesser status. Take the one who clutches a teddy, Pinky, to her breast like a child. She talks to her husband in a baby voice, saying, 'Pinky's vewwy *cwoss* wiv Daddy for leaving poor ickle him all on his *own!*' Even she thinks herself superior to me because she has a husband and they share a private language. I've had so many men, so many more than she, but where are they now?

Outside the picture windows that overlooked north London the sky was as dark as an El Greco, the clouds mustering for a storm. 'Pity,' Laura heard one of the nurses say. 'It'll wash out the fireworks.' She struggled to focus her concentration and then remembered: Remember, remember, the Fifth of November, gunpowder, treason and plot! Tonight must be Guy Fawkes night. Fireworks and bonfires. Potatoes baked black in the ashes, tasting smoky, burning your fingers, even through warm woolly gloves. 'Where's the salt? Anyone got the salt? Pass it here, greedy pig!'

They used to build the bonfire at the end of the games field, a great funeral pyre with a scarecrow on top. Why burn him to death? Poor Joan of Arc! She was a martyr to her voices and the English goddams. *She* believed in the after-life, opening her eyes confidently to heaven, but the flames burned her all the same. The agony, the agony, as the faggots heated and little flames began to crackle. It must have been nice at first, nice and warm. Did she extend her hands involuntarily in the childish gesture, splaying her fingers and letting the palms see the heat below? Did her limbs begin to sear and blister? Did the flesh darken? Did the goddams laugh or fall silent?

'Laura dear, what's the matter? You're crying!' It was Dr Todhunter.

'Nothing. Silly. Sorry.' How to tell a doctor of the terror of death? It is her stock-in-trade.

'Look, this'll cheer you up. I've brought you some very delicate, delicious food. Your friend Desmond rang to say he had arranged to have it delivered from a restaurant and it arrived just now. There's an asparagus terrine and some *crème brulée*. Could you eat that?' Laura turned her face aside so that the tears ran into her coarse, lumpy pillow. Dr Todhunter extended a fistful of tissues.

'Come on, let's wind up the bed. See if you can manage a bit.'

Laura levered herself weakly into a sitting position and attempted, out of pure good manners, to close her lips over the proffered teaspoon of food. Suddenly she tasted the green bile in her throat, thin and acid, rising in a vicious tide of bitterness. It dribbled down her chin and stained the clean white front of her nightgown. She retched again – a huge, heaving struggle this time.

'No, Laura! No! Lie down! You *must* resist the urge to vomit. Flat.'

The bed creaked as Dr Todhunter cranked the handle frantically and Laura pressed a hand over her clenched lips, her
mouth filling with the vile taste of nausea. With a tremendous
effort she controlled it, swallowed, and the heaving subsided.

'Good! *Good* girl. Well done,' sighed Dr Todhunter
gratefully.

The sky that night was lit up intermittently by fizzing showers,
arcs that lifted brilliantly, hung for an instant, and then plum-
meted, detonating small explosions like fountains in their wake.
The noise penetrated the thick plate-glass windows: whoosh,
swish, crackle-crackle-crackle, as the fireworks flared and died.
So brief, Laura thought. All that energy and drama for a split-
second display. A large rocket exploded high in the sky, a
whirling Catherine wheel of red and green, culminating in a
bang that made the glass vibrate and sing.

'Thou art a soul in bliss, but I am bound upon a wheel of
fire!' Paul used to quote as they made love. We were both in
bliss, she thought, yet I cannot recapture a flicker of those
physical sensations. They ruled my body for less than two years,
yet from then on my conscience was corrupted and the whole
course of my life diverted. Why, of all the men in the world, did
it have to be *Paul*? Did I ruin his life as well? Would he have
been forced to beg for money and alcohol if he had stayed with
Constance and their children? A last great firework soared and
died in a coronet of light, a splash and a sputtering.

The woman in the next bed said, 'Aren't the fireworks
pwetty, Pinky? Do us fink they're bootiful?'

The following day Constance came to see her. Under her service-
able fawn raincoat she was wearing black. Her face was swollen
as though after a beating, or tears. She took off the raincoat,
closed the curtains round Laura's bed and sat down.

Laura attempted a morale-boosting joke. 'Bit premature, all
this black. I'm not dead *yet.*'

Constance clutched her sister's hand in her own freezing one.

'Oh, Laura . . .' she said. 'Oh heavens, Christ, how can I do this? No, I've got to.'

'What's happened?' Laura wheezed. 'Is this for *my* benefit?'

'No,' Constance said in a voice clogged with emotion. 'It's Paul. He fell from a rooftop last night. Five floors to the ground. He's dead.'

There was a pause, the pause between a baby's pain and its cry, before a groan of anguish broke from Laura, as though Paul's very soul were escaping through her lips. It was the sound of the hare when the dogs rend it, the howl of a mother on the pavement seeing her child run into the road, to be crushed by a car. She called out his name: '*Paul? Not Paul!*'

Constance sat stone still, her face blanching to the colour of candle wax, the blood ebbing visibly from her rosy, pulsing throat. She stared with neon intensity into Laura's collapsed face. 'It was you, Laura! *You* were the woman he never named. Paul's secret. All that time it was *you*. Dear God!'

Their voices brought Dr Todhunter hurrying through the drawn curtains. After checking that Laura had not suffered a haemorrhage, she withdrew Constance to a chair at the other side of the ward and administered a tranquillizing injection to Laura. As the deadening liquid sped through her veins, Laura heard her sister's explanation.

'My husband – I mean, ex-husband – was at a Guy Fawkes party last night, on someone's rooftop. He stepped backwards and fell. He was killed. I told my sister, because I thought she'd hear it from someone else otherwise. His name was Paul.'

Someone must have brought Constance a cup of tea, for the last words Laura caught before oblivion closed in were, 'No sugar, thank you.'

Then she was in an aircraft as it penetrated the cloud cover, bumping and shuddering through misty whiteness, before emerging to fly evenly over the undulating surface of the clouds. She seemed to hear, above the throbbing of its engines, a child's reedy, piping voice: 'Oh dearly, dearly has he loved, / And we must love him too, / For we believe it was for us, / He hung and suffered there . . .'

When Laura awoke hours later the ward was in darkness. She lay still, conscious of a great horror. She thought, This is it. I am dreaming my death. I am taking leave of my senses. I am suffocating. I cannot hear, or see, or − she flexed her fingers − but I can still move.

She reached for the emergency bell beside her pillow and pressed it. Footsteps squeaked along the corridor.

'Hi there! I'm Judy Morton,' said a breezy Australian voice. 'I'm from the agency, just for the night. What can I do for you?'

'Is Dr Todhunter here?' Laura murmured.

'She's on duty but I think she's gone to try and get some sleep.'

'What time is it?'

The young nurse tipped the watch hanging from her breast-pocket towards the overhead nightlight. 'Half past two. Could it wait till morning?'

'Yes.'

'Anything else? Want me to turn your pillow?'

Laura raised her head from the hot pillow to receive the balm of its cool side. As she moved, she remembered: Paul is dead. Constance knows.

'Have I been written down for sleeping pills? If so, can I have one?' she asked.

The young woman went away to find the sedatives that would return Laura to oblivion.

Next morning, as the trolley came round with newspapers, magazines and garishly wrapped chocolate bars, Constance entered the ward.

'There's going to be an inquest,' she said without prevarication. 'They may suspect suicide. I need to know when you last saw Paul.'

Laura thought, I haven't the strength for this. There is so much to say, and it's too late.

Constance waited for her to speak, and when she didn't, went on, 'He phoned me a month or two ago, from Amsterdam. He often did. He liked to hear all our news. I told him then that you were very ill. He said he might come to London and if he did he'd look you up. I didn't think he really would. You hadn't met for years.'

Laura said, 'Not since soon after Daddy died.'

'But you saw him recently. He came to see you. Why?'

'He wanted me to leave him the house in my will. I said no.'

'What else?'

'He got drunk and spent the night in the spare room. He went next morning.'

'Was he depressed?'

'Defeated, hopeless, a shambles.'

'He's been like *that* for the last six years. Don't think it was you that broke his heart. It was Lulu. He really loved that girl.'

'Constance. Can't you forgive me?'

'Never. Don't think *you* are why he killed himself. It was an accident. His friend whose party it was, Andrew Lloyd-Simpson. *He* rang me. Late on Thursday. Midnight.'

'I've carried it for years: the burden of guilt.'

'He said Paul was laughing and talking. He stepped back to watch the fireworks and' – her voice stumbled – 'fell backwards over some low railings, off the edge of the roof.'

'Mother knows about him and me. She told me not to tell you.'

'Shut up. Paul was dead when the ambulance got there. You may have to make a statement to the police, for the inquest, though not if I can help it. The children never knew?'

'Never. Oh, Coco, I'm so *sorry*.'

Her sister looked at her tearlessly, her face set in granite. 'Don't call me that. I have to go now. I don't know if I'll be back.'

Exhausted, drugged, sorrowing for herself and her lover, Laura slept. Dr Todhunter looked at her, took her pulse, drew the curtains round her bed and told the nurses not to insist on feeding her. She scribbled on Laura's notes: 'Do not resuscitate – patient's request.'

Late that afternoon Desmond appeared, clutching a bunch of flowers and a bottle of champagne. '*Chilled!*' he said. 'Accept no compromises. There's this wonderful new silver-foil wrapper you put round. Cools it in ten minutes.'

He fished in his coat pockets and extracted a long glass from each. He placed them on the table spanning Laura's bed.

'*And* . . . here comes the *pop!*' The cork flew across the ward and he poured the foaming, silvery-gold liquid into a glass, which he held out to Laura.

'I'm not allowed to drink,' she said.

Desmond laughed. 'Not allowed to drink? Says who? *Who*, my dear Laura, has authority over you now? Will the renunciation of a glass of champagne prolong your life by ten minutes, do you think, or fifteen? Don't let me hear such *utter* rubbish.' He poured a glass for himself.

'Here, let me sit you up. Bet you never mastered the art of drinking while lying down. By far the most difficult of the bedtime skills.' He wound up the end of the bed, reached across and lifted her expertly into a sitting position, then placed her glass in her hand. 'Cheers!'

The alcohol made her drunk very quickly, so that her tongue ran away with her and she told Desmond about Constance's visit and its import.

'My poor sweet! *What* a heavy secret! No wonder you never told. But that reaction was shock. She'll come and see you again. You're her sister. She has to. Blood is thicker than anything, even husbands. Do you want me to send him flowers for you?'

Laura shook her head slowly from side to side, hearing it rustle against the pillow. 'What am I? Not his wife or the mother of his children, not one that lived, anyway. Nothing. How can I send flowers? I don't even know when they're burying him.'

Her eyes were glazed. She could not see clearly. 'Is it getting dark, Desmond?'

'Yes, darling, it's clouding over. There's going to be another storm. I'm going to put your poor flowers in water. I'll be back in a sec.'

Laura thought, I am taking leave of my senses. Words are slipping away – and I used to be so good at words. What is the French for death? Good, Laura. And now the Italian? Very good. And in Russian? Ah, that's harder, isn't it? Different root, you see. But how about *Chinese*? Eat up, dear, think of all the starving Chinese who'd love to eat your nice dinner. They can have it! Don't be rude to your mother, Stella. Apologize, or leave the table. Sorry Mummy. Speak clearly: don't mumble. I'm *sorry*, Mummy. What for? I'm sorry Mummy that I was rude. That's all right, darling, Mummy forgives you. Now eat your semolina. Look, Connie's eaten all hers! It's easier for her to be good than me. Don't talk nonsense, dear.

A great immensity stretched ahead, a wide plain across which she was walking alone. After a bit, at one side of the path, she saw a clump of flowers. She stopped to smell them.

'Aren't they gorgeous?' said Desmond. 'People say it's bad taste to bring lilies to a sick-bed, but they look beautiful and they smell divine. And they cost' – he lowered his voice roguishly – 'a *fortune*!'

Laura opened her eyes to see a man's face very close to hers. His eyes glittered and sparkled.

'Flogged that Biedermeyer sofa this morning! Well, if the customer doesn't ask to see its provenance, is the vendor obliged to offer it? Tidy little profit *that* made us! You think *you've* got lilies – my dear, the flat positively pulsates with lilies. And the *fragrance*, as the judge said of Mary Archer. Breath of cherubim and seraphim!'

Footsteps approached the bed and a familiar voice said, 'Good! She could do with a visitor to cheer her up. What glorious flowers. I'm Dr Todhunter, how do you do?'

'Desmond Osborne. Glass of champagne?'

'More than my life is worth, on duty. Just give me a sniff, though. Mmm, *very* reviving. Has Laura had one?'

'Yes,' said Laura emphatically.

Time passed and she wasn't in pain. She wasn't in anything. She felt sombre and immense. The figures of her father in a formal grey suit, and her sister in a long white dress like her wedding dress, swayed in and out of her consciousness. They seemed to be dancing, though not together, gliding round a huge polished space, ceremoniously circling to unheard rhythms. She waited for her father to extend his hands and swirl her on to the floor, but although he nodded and dipped as he passed he ignored her outstretched arms, and she was glad, really. She didn't know if she had the energy to dance. If only Paul had been there she could have danced with him, but there was no sign of Paul. Of course not. There'd be no more men in her life now. Just death, the messenger, the clerk, ticking her off his list – coldly, professionally. No, no mistake: you're down to go next.

Then she saw Constance approaching, wearing a white dress. She slowed to a walk. A man was with her.

'Laura, open your eyes,' said Constance clearly. 'Look at me. Do you know who I am?'

'My sister.'

'That's right. And do you know who this is?'

'Postlethwaite?'

'The Possleque, you mean. Yes. Gordon.'

'How are you?' Gordon asked.

'I'm fine,' answered Laura. She looked at her sister. 'Paul wasn't there or you could have danced with him. I wouldn't have done, honestly. I might have danced with Daddy, though.'

A third figure appeared beside the bed and voices murmured above her head.

'. . . not making perfect sense,' said Constance.

'. . . could give her a booster jab, but it won't last very long . . .'

'Will I rise again?' Laura asked clearly.

'Like Lazarus?' asked Gordon.

'Laura, you're no Lazarus,' Constance said.

'She's not even dead yet,' said Dr Todhunter. 'Are you, Laura? God, relatives! Who needs 'em!' She grinned. 'Back in a moment.'

They settled themselves in plastic chairs on either side of her bed.

'Nice flowers,' observed Gordon.

'Pretty morbid,' said Constance.

'Heavenly . . .' Laura whispered defensively, and exhaled hard to get the second word through her lips, '. . . smell.'

Something sharp shot into her arm. 'Ow! That hurt!'

'Give it a few minutes to take effect. But remember, not too long.'

'Gordon, I'm OK now. You can go, honestly,' Constance said.

'. . . think I ought to stay . . . moral support . . .'

'. . . no, really and truly . . .'

Laura opened her eyes. She felt clear-headed and positive.

'Go away, Possleque,' she said, 'I want to talk to Coco alone.'

When he had gone, Laura wiggled her fingers and after a moment Constance took her hand.

'How warm you are!' Laura said gratefully. 'I'm always cold nowadays. Are you happy with the Possleque? Because if you are you ought to marry him.'

'I think I probably will, now.'

'What day is it?' Laura asked. 'People keep coming up and asking me and I don't know.'

'It's Friday, November 13th.'

'Sounds about as unlucky as you can get. Have they had the funeral yet?'

'Yesterday. The inquest concluded accidental death and Paul's body was released straight away. He was cremated at Putney Crematorium after a Catholic funeral service. All the children

302

were there, and Lulu and her one. Mother didn't come. I told her not to. I thought it was best. You've done your goodbyes, you and her. She sends love.'

Laura tightened her grip on her sister's hand. 'Coco, I've got hardly any time.'

'Yes.'

'Please look at me. Please. I humbly beg your forgiveness for my sin. Will you give it to me?'

Constance dropped her head on to her chest, so that her face was hidden by her hair.

'Please,' Laura implored urgently. 'Say you forgive me.'

Constance's head shook from side to side in what might have been pain, indecision or denial. Heavily, she sighed. She raised her head up, looked towards the ceiling, and then into Laura's eyes.

'I forgive you,' she said. 'And I forgive Paul too.'

They sat in silence. Laura felt normal, as she had not done for weeks. Perhaps I'm not dying after all and it was an ordeal, a test of our love for each other. In that case, we have come through.

'"God in his mercy lend her grace, the Lady of Shalott",' Constance quoted. 'I keep thinking of those lines, I don't know why.'

'All sorts of things come into my head,' Laura agreed. 'Old hymns and nursery rhymes. My life is all jumbled up and only the simplest things matter now. I do love your children. I've given all my stuff to them. If there's anything *you* want . . .'

'"'Tirra lirra by the river,' sang Sir Lancelot",' Why *that*? Mad, isn't it?'

'"'A curse is come upon me!' cried the Lady of Shalott",' Laura said, and she smiled. 'Remember how we used to laugh at that, because of the curse? Menstruating was always called the curse. What do the girls call it?'

'They just say "my period".'

'Lucky them,' said Laura. 'All that must be much simpler for them.'

'Doubt it.'

They sat quietly for several minutes, holding hands and inhaling the heady scent of the overblown lilies.

'They could do with fresh water,' Constance said eventually.

'No, stay . . .'

'Do you want me to pass on any message to Mother?'

'I don't know. The usual. Tell her I love her and miss her. Give my love to Daddy, too.'

'Laura?'

'What?'

'Nothing.'

'I'm terribly tired. Would it be very rude if I had a bit of a doze?'

'You sleep.'

'Would you please undo this button here, on the front of my nightie? Thank you.'

Constance leaned across the bed and took Laura's hands, warming them both between her strong palms. Her sister's eyes were shut. As she had done forty years ago across the nightlight in the nursery, calling from her own bed into her sister's high-sided cot, she said, 'Night-night.'

Laura murmured, ' "I am half sick of shadows" ' . . . and they ended in unison, ' ". . . said the Lady of Shalott".'

Constance bent towards Laura's sunken pallor and kissed her on both cold cheeks. 'But I kissed her little sister and forgot my Clementine!' She left the ward and as her footsteps died away down the corridor, Laura whispered, 'Goodbye.'

She was walking along a beach, barefoot, beside a long curve of water. At the top the beach was pebbly, but as it sloped gently towards the sea the pebbles dwindled to small stones, like gravel, and then fine sand. The light was very clear and young; it must be dawn. Laura thought of her mother in Miami, walking on the beach in the early mornings, alone. But her mother wasn't there. No one was there. At least I am leaving my footprints behind me in the sand, she thought. Mummy can follow and catch me up. We ought to have a proper chat. I ought to say goodbye. Heaven knows when I'll see her again.

Someone moved above her head – she could feel the air stir around – but she couldn't be bothered to open her eyes and see who it was. She could hear quite clearly. People came and asked her questions. Day, food, bedpan, wash – what did it matter?

This can't be all. She waved away the thought that this was it and stepped back into memory. Which one? Long ago, one summer vacation, she'd been hitch-hiking with a friend. Friend's name? Forgotten. They had been in Germany somewhere. It was late one evening, a warm, balmy night. Stars. She'd gone dancing and two German boys she met had invited her to come boating on a lake. She had left her cautious friend behind and gone with them. Thunder hummed far away. The boys knew where a rowing boat was moored, and Laura stepped into it and sat facing the two of them while they rowed through soft splashes into the middle of the lake. Great warm drops of rain began to fall. One boy moved round the rocking boat to sit behind her. He opened a big umbrella and held it over her head. Black water, black sky. The other boy, the one who was rowing, sang a song, *Der Erlkönig*, in a beautiful, unselfconscious bass voice. They all got wet, drenched to the skin. The rain was as warm as the lake. How happy she had been.

She slipped back to reality and found herself drenched. She had peed in the bed. Her forehead was clammy. No more escaping. This was it. She twitched her hand convulsively on the rough counterpane. A warm hand enfolded it.

'Laura,' said the tired voice of Dr Todhunter. 'I'm here.'

'Oh, Dr Todhunter, I'm still afraid of Death . . . the man in black . . . with a scythe.' Her words emerged slowly, separately, one by one. Dr Todhunter held her hand more tightly.

'Death isn't a man in black. Think of a woman, a woman in

white. I won't leave you, Laura my dear. Death has been beside you all your life. Just as I am now.'

THE END

Acknowledgements

First and foremost I must thank Mr Henry Mitrani of Istanbul. The medical details in this book are based on his vivid description of the physical and emotional consequences of hepatitis C. In reponse to my request in *LiverLink* (a magazine for liver patients attached to the Royal Free Hospital, London NW3) he generously and courageously sent me an extremely full personal account of his experiences with the disease. Unlike my heroine, Mr Mitrani was offered, and accepted, a liver transplant in 1990. He has made a full and happy recovery.

I also owe fifteen years of gratitude to the consultants, doctors, nurses and all other medical staff at the same hospital's Hassall Ward, and in particular Professor Neil McIntyre. My research (not all of which was done for the purposes of this book) and their expertise and kindness gave me much insight into the problems for people with liver disease.

In addition, I would like to thank Shirley Conran for giving me a detailed description of the casino at Monte Carlo for Chapter Eight.

I am greatly indebted to the editor of the *Independent*, Andreas Whittam Smith, and to its Features editor, David Robson, as well as to all my colleagues in that department, for letting me take time off in order to write this book.

The fact that some elements in *The Constant Mistress* are based on research may mislead some readers into believing that its plot or characters are also factual. I should like to state, with even more vigour than is usual in such disclaimers, that the book is a novel and a work of pure fiction.

Angela Lambert
June 1992–June 1994